GADGETS

A DARCY McCLAIN AND BULLET THRILLER

PAT KRAPF

THUNDER GLASS PRESS

Copyright © 2015 Pat Krapf

All rights reserved. The use of any part of this publication reproduced, transmitted in any form or by any means, electronic, mechanical, photocopying, recording, or otherwise, or stored in a retrieval system, without the prior written consent of the publisher is an infringement of the copyright law.

ISBN 978-1-941300-02-2 (E-Book Edition)
ISBN 978-1-941300-03-9 (Print Edition)

Edited by Caroline Kaiser, Leslie Lutz, and Arlene Prunkl
Book design by Fiona Raven
Proofread by Zetta Brown

Printed and bound in USA
First Printing January 2015

Published by Thunder Glass Press
P.O. Box 93234
Southlake, TX, USA 76092

Visit **patkrapf.com**

Praise for *Brainwash*

The ending was fabulous, Pat Krapf! Can't wait for the next one!

—JEAN ERATH

Can't wait for book #2. I need another fix of Darcy. You are a wonderful mystery writer.

—AUDREY LAKE FOX

Pat kicks serious butt with her ending. Holy cow, Pat—awesome book!

—KATHRYN BULLON

Brainwash was a "don't-put-it-down-until-you-finish" read.

—PAT DAVIS

I just finished reading *Brainwash*. From page to page you don't know what is going to happen next. Pat has done a great job with describing the setting so that you feel a part of the never-ending action. Don't blink because you might miss something. I can't wait for the next book in the series.

—BRENDA CEJKA

Great first book from Pat Krapf. Looking forward to the next installment in the series. Darcy is a bold lead character and Bullet is a lovable and intelligent sidekick. It will be interesting to see the relationship between the two develop. Pat does a great job describing the beautiful New Mexico landscape and makes you want to visit.

—KELLY PRICE

A glowing recommendation for Pat Krapf's first thriller, *Brainwash*. A gifted writer who weaves an exciting tale. Her description of the geography of northern New Mexico really puts the reader in the surroundings. Using her journalism background, she explains medical and scientific concepts in terms that all people can understand yet all the while developing a plot that truly is a page-turner. Can hardly wait for the next book.

—TINA FIELDS

Just finished the first of a new series with Darcy McClain as supersleuth, a likable heroine with spunk and smarts who doesn't shy away from a challenge. The technical parts of the story sets it apart from an average thriller. Very enjoyable.

—GLORIA PETERSON

Excellent page-turner. Well written and very obviously well researched. I can't imagine the time it must have taken this talented author to discover the amazing detail she's put into this book. I missed a few nights of sleep for this one, and I'll do it again for her next offering!

—GEORGE BARTEL

To my parents for being parents.
You gave me life and faith.
I've needed little more to make my way
through this journey called life.

Prologue

My captors came at midnight. They yanked me from a warm bed and dragged my frail body down the black hallway to the dark place. The door slammed, and the leader threw the dead bolt. I pinched my eyes shut and prayed. *No, please God, not again. Save me.* My breath quickened and my pulse raced. Fear suffocated me. I begged silently for death, but even that haven deserted me.

As I lay prostrate and blindfolded with my wrists and ankles shackled to the bedposts, the cowards ravaged me—committing such unspeakable horrors that, nineteen years later, the nightmares still haunt me. At times I have found solace in prayer, but I've never known true peace until the day God showed me the way. Now my life has a purpose. Revenge.

1

"Osko?"

Darcy froze in midstretch, hardly believing her own ears. Seated beside her but facing in the opposite direction, Bullet growled, warning her that a stranger approached. She already knew who called out her nickname, so without looking, she reassured Bullet. "It's okay, boy."

She turned, surprised but happy to see Samantha Logan standing on the sidewalk outside Darcy's San Francisco home. Sam hadn't changed much: brown hair streaked blond, tanned, fit, but older looking than the last time Darcy had seen her some two years ago.

"Can't be you." Darcy hurried down the walkway.

The two women hugged. Bullet growled.

"Ah, come on, big guy." With her fingers Sam combed his

beard into place. In four seconds flat, he had already warmed up to the stranger. "Going for a run?"

"Later. I'd much rather visit with you. Come in. I can't believe you're here."

Over the years, Darcy had known her share of friends, but her relationship with Sam ran much deeper than most. The strong bond between them developed at the age of three, in Mexico, when Darcy's father hired Sam's father to run McClain Import Export. As only children, the two begged their parents for siblings but never received any, so they made a pact for life: *sisters till death do us part.*

In the kitchen Darcy put on a pot of coffee while Sam slid into her familiar spot at the window seat in the breakfast nook. "Still a crack shot, Osko?"

"Not sure," said Darcy. "I haven't had you to practice with."

One shot, one kill: Osok. When Sam dreamt up that dumb nickname they were ten, and it didn't take long for her to skew the letters into something more pleasant to the ear. "Your new nickname is Osko," she'd declared one day. Sam had always loved nicknames, for everything and everyone except herself— unless the name Sam qualified. "Besides, Sam is much more CIA-ish than Samantha, which is too girly girl," she'd informed Darcy. From the time they were in grade school, they'd both dreamed of being spies. But their parents dreamed of having attorneys in the family, so the two teens appeased them by enrolling in law school at Stanford. Besides, at nineteen they couldn't have cared less what they majored in as long as they could hang out together and have fun.

"You know, I must've called you a million times," said Darcy, "but always the same answer."

"'She's on assignment,' right?" Sam finished Darcy's thought.

"Right." As soon as the coffeepot quit chugging, Darcy

placed the carafe on the table along with some pastries and slid into the bench seat next to her best friend.

Sam poured herself a cup. "Won't happen again. I left the CIA."

Darcy jumped up. "You what? Are you insane?"

Bullet barked and ran to the window.

"Sorry, boy. It's nothing. Settle down."

He resumed his seat near the table, hoping for a handout.

Darcy sat down. "Why did you leave?"

"Hey, I know your dream was to work for the CIA, and I felt awful when I made the cut and you didn't."

"Move on. I have. So why did you leave?"

"Frankly, I'm tired. Tired of running, hiding, being hunted, being someone else." Sam sipped her coffee. "And tired of not being around for the people I love when they needed me the most. No one told me Dad was gravely ill. Why? Because I was undercover in Bosnia and unreachable. And I didn't know Benni and Ali had died until I surfaced in Budapest."

Darcy smiled at how Sam still used her childhood nicknames for Darcy's parents. "I understood. When did you leave the agency?"

"A year ago."

"A year ago, and you're only now getting in touch?" Darcy rested her hand on Sam's wrist. "Sorry, no guilt trips. What have you been doing? Where are you living?"

"Before you jump on me again," Sam said in a congenial tone, "let me give you the entire story."

Darcy eyed her friend's sheepish. "This better be good."

"Technically, I've been stateside for three years."

"Three years!"

Bullet raised his head and growled.

"Sorry, boy." Darcy lowered her voice. "Three years?"

"I said *technically*. Let me explain. I told the company I planned to quit. My boss promised me a desk job back in the States if I stayed on for another three years, so I agreed. I wasn't in Texas six months before he pleaded with me to sign up for one final op."

"Why did you agree?"

"Can't tell you. Not yet. When I came back two years later, a bit battered and bruised in more ways than one, I wanted to contact you as soon as I was stateside, but I've also been through a lot these past few years, and I needed time and space to sort things out." She took a deep breath and rubbed the back of her neck, something Sam did when she was trying to control her emotions. She forced a smile. "I wanted to be alone...with my dogs."

Darcy glanced under the table at Bullet. "I know the feeling."

Sam smiled. "I knew you'd understand. One day, when the wounds aren't so raw . . ." She stared off, as though in another world. "Do you remember Bondo?"

The comment caught Darcy by surprise. "As in Switzerland? Of course. Anything specific?"

"Yeah, Christmas."

Darcy chuckled. "When our parents bought us bows and arrows as gifts? I recall thinking, are they trying to tell us they wished we'd been boys?"

Sam burst into laughter. "Certainly made me wonder."

"Then they bought us crossbows."

Sam snickered. "How can I forget? A skill set I never mastered but one you were evidently born to."

Darcy shrugged off the compliment. "And that first summer, remember how bored we were when our parents left on that buying spree for the company, and we were stuck out in the middle of nowhere with nothing to do for three weeks?"

Sam leaned forward, placed her elbows on the table, and rested her chin on her folded hands. "So we bought a dozen watermelons at the market, lined them up against the back fence, and pretended we were practicing for some covert mission that required archers. Silent and deadly."

"We made a bet, didn't we?"

"We did," said Sam. "My bow and arrows against your crossbow and quarrels. And if I recall correctly, dead-eyed Darcy won."

"I don't remember."

"Sure you do. You won. Why can't you accept a compliment? Because you really hate being in the limelight, even in a small way, don't you?"

"Guilty as charged. Now can we change the subject?"

"Okay," said Sam, her gaze on Bullet. "I'm dying to know, how did you wind up with a giant schnauzer?"

Of all the topics she expected her friend to bring up next, this was not one of them. "What? Sorry, but your question caught me by surprise. I adopted him. I killed his owner—by accident. Are you familiar with the breed?"

"Should be. Bought my first giant while on assignment in Berlin. When I moved back to the US for that so-called desk job, I started breeding them."

"You're kidding."

Sam laughed. "No, really. I live in Kerrville, Texas, where I own Target Kennels and breed giant schnauzers."

Darcy grabbed Sam's hand. "No way."

Sam frowned. "What?"

"Back in a minute." Darcy ran up the steps to her office. She snatched a manila folder off her desk and rushed back to the kitchen. "Take a look. His AKC registration, health records, et cetera."

Sam leafed through the papers in the file. "This is really strange." She smiled at Bullet. "What are the odds?"

"I was told Target Kennels went out of business."

"I bought them in bankruptcy, which is one reason I agreed

to stay at the agency for another three years. I needed the money to buy the business, refurbish the grounds, and buy the giants I wanted."

"So who cared for your dogs for two years?"

"I estimated I'd be gone a year tops, but I didn't set foot on US soil for two. Before I left I hired a woman I'd met at an SPCA fundraiser, Claudette Ornate. Clo, as I call her. I don't think she expected me to be gone for two years, but she stuck with me, and the dogs."

"Must have been an important op for you to be gone so long."

Sam forced a smile. "The entire two years were tough, period. Your Bullet—his registered name is Target's Trajectory—was from my first of only two litters."

Darcy noticed the tears in Sam's eyes, so she scooted closer to her best friend and wrapped her arm around her shoulder. "What's wrong?"

"As any good breeder would, I've been worried about what happened to him. I can account for the other four puppies in his litter but lost contact with Bullet's owner when he moved from one location in New Mexico to another. He simply did not leave a forwarding address and never communicated with me again. I've never sold a puppy to anyone who hasn't owned a giant before because, as I'm sure you know, the breed can be a handful."

Darcy laughed. "An understatement."

"He'd owned one prior to Bullet, a female. Someone stole her out of his backyard. I had reservations about selling Bullet to him but let my emotions interfere. I felt sorry for him for losing his dog." She squeezed Darcy's arm. "I can't tell you how happy I am that he's safe and in the best of homes. Now I'm really interested in hearing how you rescued him."

"Long story and not a pretty one."

Undeterred, Sam said, "Think I can handle both—the length and any ugliness."

"Not sure how accurate I'll be, but most of the details should be right on the mark since Bullet's former owner kept a detailed log, some of the entries quite disturbing."

"Did Pa—"

Darcy held up her hand to silence Sam. "He still reacts to his former owner's name, so I never say it if I don't have to." She leaned over to look at Bullet, draped across her feet and sleeping peacefully.

"Sad," said Sam. She refilled Darcy's cup and drained the remainder of the coffeepot's contents into hers.

Darcy hesitated, reluctant to relive Bullet's story. Soft yellow light danced across the white-tiled floor as a brisk wind tossed the tree limbs outside her bay windows. "About your comment earlier . . . no, I'm not such a crack shot anymore, and my story will prove it."

Sam snickered. "Don't BS me. I know you. If you really want someone dead, you'll kill him on the first shot." She slid a pillow behind her back. "Now, let's hear Bullet's story."

2

A piercing cold wind skipped over the snowcapped Sandia Mountains, whistled through verdant canyons dusted in white, and sliced an icy path across the desert floor. Hours later, the arctic front drifted to the east, snow clouds and frigid gusts scudding along, leaving behind dead-calm skies—ideal conditions for the second day of the Albuquerque Hot Air Balloon Fiesta.

Paco's Ford labored up the ramp to the interstate, hampered by the weight of the laser bolted to its bed. He exited the freeway and traveled west toward the Rio Grande. Ahead loomed the Santa Clara Savings and Loan, the tallest building northwest of downtown. He pulled into the vacant lot, his sights set on the five-story parking structure at the rear of the bank.

He slid the stolen ID into the meter slot at the kiosk. The

reader whined and then spit out the badge. Paco slid it into his pocket just as the metal pole rose slowly into the air.

On the roof level, he edged the truck to the outer wall and climbed out. An icy breeze whispered over him. Trash swirled across the pavement and came to rest in dark corners. He flipped up his collar. Damn weather. What a nuisance. Still, no reason to cancel his plans. He collected his laptop off the seat and sprang Bullet from the warm cab.

The giant schnauzer jumped into the back of the pickup after his master and watched Paco fight with the sailor's knots on the worn tarp that shrouded Ronnie, an invention designed specifically for this occasion. He yanked off the canvas cover and paused to stare at his newest creation, a machine that worked with such precision his hands shook with excitement every time he deployed the device.

He lifted the Plexiglas shield that protected the Nd:YAG's control panel and key-coded coordinates into Ronnie's computer. The LED lit up. "Device activated" flashed on the face screen. He pressed Test.

An infrared beam shot from the laser. The detector ray located its mark, and Ronnie beeped: confirmation the rangefinder had locked onto the homing device. The distance to target pulsed on the digital display. Coordinates stored, he placed the laser in Fire mode and sank onto the tailgate to wait, Bullet at his side.

The cold seeped into his bones. He cinched the drawstring of his parka hood tight around his head and slid his gloved hands into his jacket pockets to warm them. A hard object jabbed his palm; the presence of his brother's ID badge comforted Paco.

Time dragged. He sipped black coffee and shot glances at Ronnie while he gently kneaded Bullet's nape. Machines and four-legged folks Paco loved. Mankind he tolerated, and not well.

He bent forward to check Ronnie's clock. Time was running out. He slid off the tailgate and walked to the outer wall. Binoculars cupped to his eyes, he surveyed the valley. The launch field hummed with activity, but still no sign of Randolph Colton or his convoy. Anxiety gripped him. What if there had been a change in plans and they didn't show?

He watched Larson and some woman, a stranger, mingle with the chase crew around Larson's truck. At least Paco could count on him to be punctual, which was why he'd chosen Larson's vehicle as a plant for one of the homing devices. And the test had gone off without a hitch, so he had every confidence the second device would perform equally as well.

A black trailer lumbered into view, then another. Randolph's convoy. Paco's spirits soared. He trained his binoculars on the caravan, his eyes fixed on the workers as they off-loaded their equipment. The crew set up in record time, Colton's hot air balloons billowing to life minutes before dawn patrol lit up the sky. Pink striations crisscrossed the heavens and ribboned to earth, the fuchsia trails dissolving to gray as the skydivers spiraled to earth seconds before the first shades of day broke over the fairgrounds.

Paco trembled, not from fear but excitement. The countdown to mass ascension had begun.

3

Darcy McClain stepped out of Zachary Larson's truck onto a dusty field splashed in moonlight. A shiver skittered down her back. She snuggled deep into her wool turtleneck and wrapped her arms around herself. A California native, she detested the cold. In fact, she wasn't even particularly fond of those chilly, foggy days that engulfed San Francisco, but she soon forgot the weather and focused on her reason for being up at this ungodly hour. An avid photographer, she'd jumped at Randolph's invitation to attend the balloon fiesta. After all, what could be more impressive than the mass liftoff of over nine hundred hot air balloons?

She unpacked her camera gear and then swept the area around her. Nothing but darkness and an occasional far-off light. Hot grease and burnt toast permeated the air. She yawned at the same time her stomach growled. As if on command, Zach sauntered to the rear of his pickup.

"Too early for the concession stands," he called out, "but I brought coffee." He dragged a huge thermos toward him.

She yawned again. "Coffee's all I need. Hardly slept a wink."

He filled a Styrofoam cup, set it aside, and poured another. "You came all the way down here just for the balloon fiesta?"

"Sure did," she said, the answer a half truth. Her primary reason for driving down centered on business, but she wasn't sure if Zach knew about Colton's cracker, so she didn't mention the security breach. And as owner of the aerospace firm, as well as Zach's boss, Randolph would want to know first.

"Here you go."

Darcy took the thirty-two ouncer Zach offered. "Wow, this should do the trick." She raised her head to the sky. "Don't be surprised if you see me flying up there."

He chuckled. "Bet I get farther on propane than you do on caffeine."

"I wouldn't be so sure."

"As soon as everything opens, someone will go for grub."

"Good, because Randolph promised me a fat breakfast burrito, but in the meantime"—she unzipped the side pocket of her camera case and removed a paper bag—"I brought my own energy booster."

"What are those?"

"Jelly donuts. Want one?" She held out the sack.

"No thanks." Zach wrinkled his nose. "Do you eat a lot of those?"

"My share." She bit a hole in the donut, exposing the raspberry filling. "I run off the calories."

He smiled. "One alone would require a marathon."

Darcy laughed. She'd liked Zach the minute they met. Unflappable, he seemed completely calm as he immediately outlined a plan to save her father's firm from bankruptcy; the import-export firm was her primary source of income since she had resigned from the bureau. It was expensive to live in San Francisco, run a detective agency, and afford her sister Charlene's tuition to Stanford, never mind finance her growing wardrobe and all the sporting events she thrived on. When Randolph learned of Darcy's financial dilemma, he'd sent Zach, Colton's CFO, to clean up the mess left behind by her father's accountant.

In the distance a motor whined, and the predawn peace that hung over Fiesta Park gave way to the low hum of vehicles zipping by on their way to their assigned stations. Included in the onslaught were two trailers, their bodies painted black with turquoise and coral interlocking Cs on the cabs.

"Randolph's here," said Zach, his excitement contagious. "And he brought the dragon lady."

"Who?"

Zach cocked his thumb at a woman with an air of authority about her who stood on the running board of a black SUV. After she scrutinized her surroundings, the woman marched across the grounds, her head held high. As she drew closer, Darcy recognized Ashley Lynn Colton, Randolph's third wife, from pictures Randolph had shown her. Behind Ashley trailed Randolph. He hadn't changed much since Darcy had last seen him—a bit plumper but still dapper. Ashley joined the chase crews, and Randolph's stride quickened as he approached.

He embraced her. "Glad you came, especially on such short notice."

"For you, anything." She kissed his cheek. The familiar scent of his aftershave brought back old memories. She and Randolph had always been close, but that bond had deepened after her parents' sudden deaths in a plane crash.

"How's Charlene? Wish she'd come with you."

Dealing with her sister was a constant struggle, but Darcy glossed over the question with "We're doing better." Randolph had more pressing matters on his mind, and she'd rather discuss them than her personal problems. She leaned closer. "Anything new on your cracker? I mean, hacker." Randolph didn't differentiate between the two labels.

He looked in the direction of his balloons. "Tell you what, I'll make time to discuss both Charlene and our unwanted visitor, but later, okay? Crews are running late."

A man waved to Randolph. "Gotta run. That's Buzz, my pilot, flagging me down. See you after we land. Come on, Zach. We'll need help," Randolph called out as he passed Zach's truck.

Darcy watched Randolph walk away, happy to spend time with him even though their visit involved mostly business. She dug in her jacket for the schedule of events and skimmed the listing. Five thirty, dawn patrol. An hour later, the pilot briefing. Then, opening ceremonies and the El Paso Marching Band. Finally, mass ascension. She checked the time, grabbed her camera gear from Zach's pickup, and hurried toward Colton's launch site.

Under Randolph's supervision Buzz and Zach lifted a gondola out of the trailer, dumped the envelope from its carrying case, and unrolled yards of red fabric. Buzz connected the cables while Zach held the crown line taut. Darcy hugged the sidelines, out of traffic but close enough to record the inflation with her digital camcorder.

"First, the team pumps cold ambient air into the throat of the envelope," she narrated for the audio. "Then, Buzz ignites the propane burner." Lost in the scene unfolding before her, Darcy fell silent but continued recording. Within minutes the red fabric billowed to life, and the balloon rose into the air. Inflated, the envelope stood over seven stories high.

"Bet the Balloonmeister is thrilled because his prayers have been answered," Zach shouted over the chase crew's loud chatter.

Darcy yelled back, "Talking about the weather?"

He nodded, interrupted by the whoosh of a propane burner. "Late last night the weather had us all worried. But the front moved to the east, leaving clear skies and cool temperatures. Winds under ten miles per hour." He motioned toward the Sandias. "Albuquerque is flanked by mountains, which creates what's called a box effect. The winds in the box allow the balloons to travel in different directions and at different altitudes. Fabulous conditions. Go on—walk around, see the sights, but be back in thirty for mass ascension."

"Mass ascension. Sounds like a church function." She blew a speck off her lens.

Zach laughed. "It can be spiritual."

Armed with her camcorder and a new digital SLR camera, Darcy roamed the fairgrounds in search of some perfect shots. A brightly colored balloon demanded her attention. She framed her photo and was about to snap the picture when someone pushed her from behind. She stumbled forward, regained her balance, and spun, ready to admonish the person, but she came face-to-face with a billowing fifty-foot Mickey Mouse balloon. She burst into laughter.

Beside her a half-inflated dairy cow bobbed to life. In minutes the envelope dwarfed Darcy. Sandwiched between Mickey and the cow, she waited for the animals to take flight before she could move again.

Music from the marching band filled the air, the melody muffled by the ferocious roar of propane burners as dozens of colorful balloons blocked the sky. Enthralled, Darcy snapped over fifty stills. She turned to leave, but all around her envelopes had swelled to life, constricting the narrow walking paths to slits. Afraid she'd miss mass ascension, she forced her way through the nylon and polyester forest to the edge of the fairgrounds and jogged back to Colton's launch site.

"Perfect timing," said Zach. "We just finished the pilot briefing."

Darcy wiggled out of her jacket. "Glad I took your advice and layered."

"Told you. Sun comes up and the weather warms in a hurry." He helped her into his tethered balloon. No sooner had she settled into the wicker basket than Ashley squeezed aboard. Zach made a face. "Thought you weren't riding today."

Ashley glared. "You thought wrong."

Zach climbed in.

"Ashley, I'm Darcy McClain." She offered her hand, but Randolph's wife ignored the gesture.

"Call me Al."

An order, not a request.

"Bennett's daughter, right?" Without waiting for an answer, Al said, "Heard Randolph hired you to audit our security setup. Why we do this every five years is a mystery. Flagrant waste of time and money. Guess it keeps someone employed." She smiled sweetly.

Audit? Darcy had no idea what Al meant, but before she asked, Zach whispered, "Later."

Darcy shrugged and focused her camcorder on Randolph's gondola. Beside him in the basket stood Buzz and a young man. "Zach, who's that with Randolph? His son?"

"No," Al snapped. "It should've been Marcus, but Randolph grounded him for bad grades. And for the record, there are penalties associated with rule infractions, but my husband feels he's above the law." She turned her back on them.

Zach rolled his eyes. "Don't know who the kid is. He's been hanging around since the fiesta started, begging for a ride. Just this morning, Buzz told him no. Randolph, however, is a pushover. Hold tight. Liftoff." Their basket rocked from side to side as the balloon took flight.

Aloft, the balloon soared high over the muddy Rio Grande and sailed to the west, slipping past an ocean of rooftops. Coaxed along by a zephyr, Zach soon caught up to the dozens of brightly colored airships that already rode the gentle winds. The tranquil scene captivated Darcy, the visual so commanding, it became easy to tune out the drone of Al's voice as she complained into her cell phone. The balloons reminded Darcy of bubbles escaping from a champagne bottle, each bubble a trapped soul freed.

A blinding flash of light stabbed Darcy in the eye. She jerked her head sharply to the left. Pain shot down her neck, and nausea washed over her. Her sixth sense kicked in. She tensed and prepared—but for what?

Zach touched her shoulder. "Motion sickness?"

"Take deep breaths," said Al. "It'll pass."

Like hell. The feeling had nothing to do with motion sickness, for Darcy knew the sensation well. This always started as an intuitive vibration, similar to an electrical shock, as it crackled through the crevices of her brain and traveled through every nerve in her body. A warning. She leaned away from the roar of the burners and looked about, her eyes searching, but nothing justified the urgency.

The minutes passed.

Lulled by the gentle rocking of the gondola, Darcy suppressed the feeling and concentrated on filming Randolph's balloon as it drifted a few yards away. She zoomed in. The red envelope with its bands of bright yellow and blue appeared close enough to touch.

Another flash of light, and the sound of fabric tearing charged the air.

Uncertain where the sound had come from, Darcy backed up to avoid the strong sunlight and hit the zoom again. Nothing.

And then orange flared from the throat of Randolph's balloon and flames licked up the sides.

"Oh God, no!" Al lunged for the rip cord.

A sharp jolt. Darcy slammed into Zach.

"Easy," he shouted, tearing the cord from Al's hand. "We're going down too fast. We'll crash."

A third blinding flash of light. Darcy shielded her face with her hands.

Boom!

A red fireball lit the sky, and black smoke plumed into the air. Darcy clapped a hand over her mouth to stifle a cry. A powerful roar blasted the peaceful morning. Flames engulfed Randolph's balloon, the searing heat so hot it burned Darcy's face. She turned away, mind grappling with what she had just seen. Blood pounded in her temples, and her breath caught in her throat. Agonized screams filled her ears. In shock she watched the young man who had hitched a ride leap from the torched gondola, fire trailing his body as he tumbled toward earth.

Another blast, and the last shred of red nylon burst into flames as Randolph's charred gondola dropped to the desert floor.

4

Randolph's gondola crashed in a sun-scorched field on private property. Minutes later, Zach set down. Darcy leaped out of the basket and ran across the field, slowing as she neared the blackened heap. Her stomach flipped. She bit her bottom lip to stop it from quivering and peered into the incinerated shell. At first she couldn't tell Randolph from Buzz; their faces were burned beyond recognition, their limbs contorted at odd angles and intertwined. Bile stung her throat. She shut her eyes and swallowed hard.

Death, again. Why, God? Darcy gulped air, a poor attempt to calm her erratic heartbeat. The stench of burnt flesh and singed hair, combined with the pungent odor of steer manure, made her vomit. After the dry heaves, she wiped her mouth on her sleeve and glanced about. She'd better hurry or the law would arrive before she had time to photograph the tragic scene.

Through a blur of tears, Darcy filmed Randolph's smoldering remains, his entire body black except for a patch of blue that protruded from his chest. Part of his jacket, she presumed. The gruesome sight and the putrid smells yanked her back in time to the day she'd stood in the county morgue and stared down at the charred bodies of her parents. She passed a shaky hand over her face, trying to get control of her emotions. Had her father's motto, "Buck up and take your knocks like a man," made her so tough that she refused to let anyone in?

Heavy footsteps approached fast.

Zach rushed toward her. He maneuvered wide to avoid two bulls grazing on a bale of hay and paused far from the wicker basket. "Ambulance on the way. And the cops." He pocketed his cell phone.

Ambulance? Why? "If anyone shows up, shout. I need some shots of the kid."

"Don't know how you can take pictures." He clapped a hand over his mouth.

"It isn't easy." Numb, she stumbled across the pasture to where the young man lay and snapped several frames of his seared body, black from the waist down. When she knelt to examine him, she found a silver chain around his neck. From the tarnished links dangled an unharmed St. Christopher medal. She studied his face: pale, flawless, and angelic. She stood.

In the distance sirens blared.

A ways off hovered Al and Zach, cell phones planted to their ears. So much for warning Darcy about anyone arriving, but it didn't matter now. She joined them just as the chase and ground crews sped up the dirt lane to the pasture. Behind the teams came a station wagon, a Toyota pickup bringing up the rear. The dust funnel that announced their arrival mushroomed into a gray cloud as a squad car wound its way toward the growing crowd. Soon, law enforcement flanked the road.

"Franklin," Zach told Darcy.

"Who?"

"Toyota truck, Don Franklin from homicide. Station wagon, medical investigator."

Above the noise Al barked orders into her phone, more concerned with business than her dead husband. She swore, dropped her arms to her side, and said, "Oh great, Franklin. Zach, do something. I'm in no mood to face him."

"What do you suggest?"

"Thanks. As usual, you're no help."

Darcy fought the urge to grab Al's cell phone and toss it into the neighboring field. Might be the way to get through to her. Words were lost on this woman.

A dented Bronco rumbled up the road and nosed to a stop alongside Franklin's truck. A petite brunette stepped out. She met up with a lanky man—Franklin, Darcy presumed—and the duo headed in their direction.

Franklin wore denim, cowboy boots, and a suede jacket. A wide-brimmed hat shaded his face, and dark sunglasses shielded his eyes. After brief introductions his partner, Lena Gallegos, trooped across the field to the gondola.

Franklin nodded at Zach. "Reconstruct the accident."

The statement surprised Darcy. She expected the detective to question them separately.

"Please, can I join the chase crew?" Al wrung her slender hands. "I can't go through this again. Not so soon. I'll answer questions. Just don't make me listen . . ." She put her fingers to her trembling lips.

Darcy shook her head. Oscar material, all right.

Franklin paused as though mulling over his decision. "Okay, but don't leave the area. I do have some questions."

Al practically ran for the trailers parked outside the barbed wire fence, passing Detective Gallegos as she did. The detective stopped her, and a short conversation ensued before Al continued on.

Zach, Darcy discovered, had an eye for detail. His depiction of the morning's events proved too vivid. Like Al said, once was enough.

"Anything you care to add, Ms. McClain?"

She considered Franklin's query. On only one point did she disagree with Zach's account. She had heard two explosions, not one. "Nothing I can think of." She followed the detective's gaze to her camcorder hanging off her shoulder.

He motioned to it. "Stroke of luck if you recorded the horrible ordeal."

Zach shot her a sidelong glance. "I doubt Darcy had time. Whole thing happened so fast."

Franklin raised his eyebrows. "That true, Ms. McClain?"

She shrugged. "I'm not sure what's on the recording. I haven't viewed it." Zach gave Darcy a dirty look. His reaction baffled her, as did Franklin's response. "Camcorder's evidence," she expected the detective to say. Instead, in an unusually cordial manner for a homicide detective, he said, "I'd appreciate a look. At your earliest convenience. Might give us a clue as to why the balloon exploded."

"Okay." She couldn't think of anything else to say.

Franklin lowered his head as if to study something on the ground. After a few seconds, he straightened and leveled his gaze at Zach. "Everything check out prior to liftoff?"

"Of course. Why wouldn't it?"

"Bit defensive, are we?" Darcy almost said, but caught herself.

"No need to be defensive, Mr. Larson. Just doing my job."

Zach shifted his weight to the other foot. "Buzz is—was—a veteran balloonist. Twenty-five years. Never an accident. Damn shame."

"Who piloted your balloon?"

"Me." Zach's voice rose an octave. His eyes narrowed. "Why?"

"Just asking," drawled Franklin.

Darcy detected a slight Southern accent in the detective's voice. Texas, maybe.

He removed his iPhone from his pocket and typed something into it with his thumb. "How long have you flown, Mr. Larson?"

"Since '72."

Franklin kept his gaze on his cell. "Mrs. Colton . . . did she ever ride with Randolph?"

"In the same balloon?"

The detective looked over his sunglasses, his brown eyes searching. "Uh-huh."

"Never. Personal policy."

"Because of the kids?"

"No, the company. Someone has to play CEO."

"I see." A frown knitted Franklin's brow. "Your association with Mr. Colton, Ms. McClain?"

The CSI team arrived. Two tramped across the meadow to where Gallegos stood.

Distracted, Darcy answered without taking her eyes off the three huddled over the kid's body. "Dad and Randolph had been best friends since college days."

Gallegos circled the corpse and bent down.

"Ms. McClain." Franklin's tone sounded like an order. She faced him. "Were you close to Mr. Colton?"

Tears welled up. She swallowed hard and forced them back. "He was like a father . . ."

Franklin paused as though giving Darcy a moment to compose herself. "Are you visiting or here on business?"

"Visiting." The word burst from Zach's mouth.

Franklin scowled. "For how long? Doesn't matter who answers."

Darcy opened her mouth to respond, but again Zach blurted, "Indefinitely."

A frown creased the detective's brow. "How well do you know Mrs. Colton, Ms. McClain?"

"Met her for the first time today."

Franklin's eyebrows shot up. "Hmm. Just today. Your turn, Mr. Larson. How long have the Coltons been married?"

"Twenty-two years. Around there."

A puzzled expression crossed the detective's face. "And you"—he stared at Darcy—"and Mrs. Colton only just met?"

"She never joined Randolph on his visits to San Francisco. Always too busy," said Darcy as nonchalantly as she could manage.

"Who's the kid? You first, Ms. McClain."

"No idea."

Darcy leaned sideways for a better view of Gallegos. The detective left the boy's corpse and returned to the charred gondola. Had she found something interesting?

Franklin cleared his throat. "Mr. Larson, what do you know about the kid?"

"He showed up the first day of the fiesta. Asked for a ride. Buzz turned him down, so he hounded Randolph. To think that kid could've been Marcus."

"The youngest Colton son?" asked Franklin.

"Yes," said Zach. "He was supposed to ride in Randolph's gondola, but Randolph grounded him for bad grades. His death would've killed Al. She dotes on the brat even though he's twenty."

Gallegos marched over, her stride quick and determined. "Found something."

Franklin closed the gap between him and his partner. After a short consultation, he said to Zach and Darcy, "Join us."

Gallegos glowered, obviously displeased with Franklin's decision to include them, but why? Strange.

"Ever seen this before? Either of you?" Gallegos extended a gloved hand. In her palm rested a small square of purple plastic with a layer of orange embedded in the center.

"Hey, give me that." Zach tried to snatch the object, but the detective's fingers balled into a fist.

"Sorry. Can't. It's evidence. You understand?"

Zach glared. "Where'd you find it?"

"I'm asking the questions, Mr. Larson. Now what's this little square for?"

"It's a computer chip. The project's secret." He looked to Franklin for support, but the detective merely shrugged. "Where did you find it?" Zach repeated.

"In Mr. Colton's jacket pocket. Miraculously, not all of his coat was burned to a crisp," Gallegos said, her tone detached.

"Impossible. He'd never compromise the project. Means too much to the company."

"I only relay the facts, Mr. Larson." Gallegos squeezed the neck of a small manila envelope, slid the chip in, and scribbled something illegible on the front.

"When you're done, I want it back." Zach's remark carried a threat.

Gallegos turned to Franklin. "Want me to question Mrs. Colton?"

He shook his head. "I'll talk to her. Got any questions for Mr. Larson or Ms. McClain?"

"Mr. Larson, you are free to go," said Gallegos. "Ms. McClain, I do have a few for you, but first excuse us for a second."

The minute Gallegos and Franklin moved out of earshot Zach grabbed Darcy's wrist. "Are you crazy?"

Shocked by his harsh tone and behavior, she asked, "What did I do?"

"You offered to show Franklin the video."

"So?" She tried to break his hold, but his grip tightened.

"He can't see it."

"Why? Let go. You're hurting me."

"Keep your voice down." He released her.

"I asked why."

"I have my reasons." He stared at the detectives.

"What I'd like to know is why you told Franklin I was visiting when I'm on the payroll?"

He thumped his temple with his index finger. "Think, Darcy. If it leaks that Colton hired a PI to track down a hacker, we will lose our government contracts, and the DOD will never work with us again."

Condescending idiot. "You could've given him the same story you've given everyone else: I'm auditing your security system."

"Franklin's too smart to buy that."

"Which means sooner or later he'll figure everything out. I don't see any harm in telling him the same fib. Al said an audit's done every five years."

"But not by a private investigator. The term alone conjures up suspicion."

Really? "Fine."

"In the future don't speak to Franklin unless I say you can."

What? Did she hear him right? Great, a liar who wanted her to compromise her integrity to keep his lie. She thought of her promise to Randolph: "For you, anything." So she dropped the issue.

"The balloon exploding was no accident," said Zach.

"Really? How did you come to that conclusion?"

"Trust me. It was no accident," he said with conviction.

She didn't bother to argue the point. "Okay, so any suspects in mind?"

His sharp tone softened. "Let's talk tomorrow, at work, where we have privacy. I should get to the office and inform upper management of what's happened." He walked away in a hurry, leaving her to simmer. Zach's sudden shift in personality confused her. Darcy could only attribute his actions to shock, for she really didn't know him well.

Gallegos advanced on Darcy. "I have a few questions, Ms. McClain. Don—that's Franklin's first name—said you're visiting for an indefinite period of time."

Careful, she's fishing. "Correct."

"However, Mrs. Colton claims her husband and Mr. Larson hired you to audit their security system. She said it's common practice whenever the firm's awarded a contract of the magnitude of "—she looked at her phone—"Enforcer."

If Gallegos expected a reaction to Enforcer, she got none because Darcy had never heard the word before, at least not in this context. "Means nothing. As for auditing Colton's security system, Randolph and I talked about the possibility but hadn't ironed out the details. We planned to . . . later today."

The detective locked eyes with Darcy. "Regarding the audit, during your initial conversation with Randolph, did he mention a problem of any kind?"

"What sort of problem?"

"A security breach at the company."

He'd never mentioned it in exactly those terms, so Darcy said no.

Gallegos shut her notebook with a snap. "A word of advice, Ms. McClain. Withholding information—"

"I know the drill."

"Thought you might. One more question."

Darcy's guard went up. "Yes?"

"What's the name of the security firm you work for, unless you're self-employed?" Gallegos flashed a grin.

Without missing a beat, Darcy fired back, "The Gruet Agency."

A commotion in the lane outside the barricades caught the detective's attention. "Exactly what we don't need. The press."

In seconds a reporter descended upon them. "Detective Gallegos," he said, hailing her as he jogged across the field.

"Not now. I'm busy." Gallegos turned back to Darcy, but the instant the detective opened her mouth, the medical investigator called to her. "Coming," she shouted back. "Thanks for your time, Ms. McClain. And my condolences."

She watched Gallegos cross the pasture to where the MI hovered over the hitchhiker. Darcy would have loved to have eavesdropped on their conversation, but knowing that would never happen, she wandered toward the chase crews, her eyes averted from the yellow crime scene tape and mind occupied with thoughts of Randolph. Part of her wanted to keep walking to anywhere she could be alone, the ache in her heart suffocating, but the detective in her agreed with Zach. The balloon crash was no accident, and the flash of light that had almost blinded her compelled her to investigate, even though her initial thought that someone had fired a long-range missile seemed extremely far-fetched.

She glanced around. The place crawled with law enforcement. Only journalists outnumbered the cops. As she neared the trailers, Al's complaints rose above a drone of muffled voices. "Shit. Hand me another. Got cow crap all over my best boots."

Less than two hours ago her husband had died, but all Randolph's wife seemed concerned about was a ruined pair of boots. Darcy passed Al, seated in a folding chair near trailers, and negotiated a path through the throng of chase crew teams sprawled about the grass. Some sipped coffee or iced tea. Others fanned themselves with newspapers. Two dabbed at their eyes with soggy tissues. All appeared despondent.

A tall woman with long red hair gathered into a ponytail looked up as Darcy passed. "Can I help you, Ms. McClain?"

Darcy turned and paused, puzzled that the woman knew her name. "I need a favor or two."

"Sure, what?" The woman stopped dabbing her eyes with a tissue and slipped on sunglasses. "Karla Sizemore. Friend of Randolph's. He pointed you out earlier this morning."

"About Randolph . . . I'm sorry," said Darcy.

Sadness etched Karla's face. "We all are. You were saying?"

"I need a vehicle for the afternoon, maybe the evening."

Karla dug in her jacket pocket and handed a key ring to Darcy. "Bronze Tundra. When you're done leave the truck at Colton Aerospace, and the keys with the guard. Someone in security can give you a lift back to your hotel. I'll hitch a ride home with the chase crew. Anything else?" Karla swatted at a fly.

"Binoculars?"

"I keep a pair on the passenger seat."

"Thanks." Darcy walked off.

Karla tagged along. "Where are you headed?"

"Not sure yet. I'm looking for something."

"Oh, like what?"

"Tall buildings."

The bright flash appeared to have come from the southeast, and Darcy was already formulating a theory about the source of the explosion.

Karla didn't question Darcy. "That's easy. I grew up here. The two tallest buildings are Skylark Towers and the Santa Clara Savings and Loan. Each a few blocks apart." She gave directions.

Darcy thanked her, climbed into the Tundra, and shifted into drive. Karla waved as the truck rumbled down the dirt lane. Darcy circumvented the crowded salt lick and steered clear of roaming bulls. The brown fields disappeared in her rearview mirror, and pavement opened up as she sped past the fairgrounds to an industrial complex adjacent to Fiesta Park.

She pulled into the drive to Skylark Towers, a twenty-story office building of steel and smoked glass, and hopped out. Silence hung in the air. She headed straight for the entrance and cupped her hands to the reflective glass. Nothing moved in the spacious lobby.

"Help ya?"

Darcy turned.

A uniformed guard holding a paper sack in one hand and grasping his holster with the other beamed at her.

"I'm an architectural buff. Drove by, saw the building, and stopped to take a few frames."

"Really?" The guard sounded skeptical. "Where's your camera?"

"My gear's in the truck. I always scope out the area first, check the lighting." His quizzical expression eased, so she asked, "What kind of business is this?"

He paused as if to weigh his answer. "Pharmaceuticals. I'm afraid you'll have to leave. Without pictures. No one's allowed on the premises after work hours."

"No problem. Thanks." Darcy walked back to the Tundra. In the side mirror, she watched the man knock on the front door. A second guard stepped outside. He stared for a few seconds before the two disappeared inside. Tight security. She wrote off the location.

Her second choice, the Santa Clara Savings and Loan, looked like any other bank on a Sunday afternoon. Deserted. She cruised the ground-level parking first, every space empty and marked Reserved, so she drove to the rear of the building and braked near the mouth of a multilevel parking structure. Her hopes rose. A flimsy metal pole blocked the entrance. She locked the Tundra and hiked the five floors to the rooftop.

On the uppermost level, she leaned against the concrete wall that wrapped the parking lot and studied the valley below. Located on a bluff that overlooked the launch field, the bank building had an unobstructed view of the desert floor.

Thorough to a fault, she started at the far corner and paced off the entire level, working each section like a crime scene. First back and forth in a horizontal course, next back and forth in a vertical route as she walked a mental grid. Hours later she had collected a buck in change but discovered nothing to substantiate her hunch that Randolph's balloon could have been shot out of the sky.

The trek down took much longer. Not only did Darcy inspect the pavement, but she also circled every pillar. On one she noticed a clump of grayish-white fur. She wrapped the tuft in a clean tissue and stuffed the Kleenex in her pants pocket. Not the best way to store a clue, but the situation forced her to improvise. She reached the exit and paused, disappointed her hunch hadn't paid off.

The wind kicked up. The stiff breeze tossed trash across her path. A sheet of black paper slapped her in the leg and landed at her feet. Darcy snagged the tar paper and searched for a bin, but saw no Dumpster, only plenty of garbage.

She tossed the paper into the truck bed. With it came globs of pink bubble gum. She folded the strip in two and dumped it in the Tundra's bed. When the paper landed, it sprang open and fell flat. Something sparkled in the bright light. Streaked across the black paper was a colorful tire track of red sandstone embedded with a pearly white substance.

5

The glaring sun trailed Paco into Old Town. He coasted along the familiar streets, cruised by the Plaza, and inched down San Felipe, which was snarled with tourists. A loud bass vibrated his radio's speakers. He sang along, happy for the first time in years. His thoughts centered on the hit. He wanted desperately to see his handiwork close up, but too many variables played against him. No way could he reach the fairgrounds in time with all the traffic, and to be seen there was too risky.

He parked in the lot off Old Town Road and crossed the square to the church, Bullet at his side. The heavy door shut quietly behind him. As soon as his eyes adjusted to the dark interior, he dipped his hand in holy water, blessed himself, and knelt to pray. Bullet hopped onto a pew. His toenails clicked on the hardwood as he turned in circles, trying to find a comfortable resting place.

Paco knew confession alone wouldn't suffice. Not for this offense. But if God, through Father John, demanded restitution, then somehow Paco would repay his debt. But what penance could he possibly do to atone for murder? On the other hand, why must he recompense anyone, especially when the killings were justified?

Prayer eased his burden but didn't solve his dilemma. After an hour of meditation, he left the church and wandered to the south side of the square where he fed coins to one of the last pay phones in town, his problem still fresh on his mind. When he finished this call, he'd dwell on a solution over a cold beer. Perhaps that would help.

The line at his apartment rang incessantly. Answer, damn it. But no one answered the phone. Where could Billy be? Paco had told his brother not to go anywhere. Maybe he was in the bathroom. Or sleeping late. Paco rehooked the receiver with such force that Bullet growled. "Sorry, boy. We'll try again later. Come on—there's a beer waiting for me."

As Paco neared his dilapidated truck, Bullet sped up. He knew the routine: treats awaited him. Paco dug out his keys and pressed the homemade remote, and the locks clicked open. Nifty. He admired his new invention. Just like expensive wheels. He could afford a new car and a cell phone but had no real need for either one when he could dig deep into his pool of ingenuity and build most things he wanted.

Bullet jumped into the cab and cast those large, soulful brown eyes at his master as Paco produced a handful of dog biscuits. "Sorry. Love to take you, but real people aren't allowed in bars. Only animals. Not that you act the least bit interested."

Bullet devoured his treat, nested in a circle, and sacked out for a long nap.

Paco cut diagonally across the small square to Wanda's Cantina. He slipped between the dusty vehicles crammed in the front lot and mounted the steps to the hundred-year-old adobe. The sign over the door creaked in the soft breeze. The faint perfume of late-blooming flowers interlaced with the pungent scent of sage complemented the spicy piñon smoke that curled from the chimney. He paused on the porch to savor the unusual combination. No need to hurry. Even God rested on Sundays.

Wanda's wasn't his usual hangout, but visiting Bart's Saloon before six seemed risky. Might draw the wrong attention. He checked his watch. Barely noon. Too early to drink, but what the hell. Today's victory called for a celebration, the first of many to come.

He tugged open the oak door to the smoky bar. The joint buzzed with loud chatter, and Garth Brooks crooned from the jukebox. He ambled to a table in the corner and propped his foot on the rail of the chair opposite him. His leg ached like a son of a bitch. He ordered a beer, salsa, and homemade tortilla chips, the house specialty.

"Got some ID, sonny?" The waitress leaned forward, her large breasts testing the resiliency of lace. He tossed his driver's license on the table. She scooped it up. "Dang, you're old enough to shave. You could've fooled me."

"And you're old enough to retire," he almost said, but kept the insult to himself. He didn't need a fight, only a cold brew.

In seconds the waitress returned with his Budweiser. The beer came in a frosty mug and his chips in a plastic basket, the stack piping hot. He rummaged in his pocket for a painkiller and washed the pill down with a frothy swallow. Bastards for doing this to him. He hoped every one of them rotted in hell.

The bar filled. He leaned back, nursed his beer, and surveyed the boisterous crowd. Good, no one he knew. He saw a pencil lying under the table next to him and picked it up. On a clean napkin, he began to sketch the scarred tables and the odd collection of wooden chairs. Wanda must have raided garage sales to furnish her cantina. He titled the piece, "Low Budget" and then hailed the waitress for another Bud.

Two men in blue overalls with "Zephyr Enterprises" embroidered on the breast pockets took the table opposite him. Chase crew, he surmised. He studied them: the Anglo seemed more interested in staring at the waitress's breasts than ordering food, and the Native American kept his face buried in his menu. Neither one even glanced in Paco's direction.

The waitress brought Paco's beer. He sat back and tuned in or out of the men's conversation depending upon the topic. He strained to hear their escapades with various women, but he lost interest when the discussion shifted to nagging wives. How could man respect animals when he had no respect for himself?

"Still can't believe it. Worst accident I've ever seen. Balloon flaring up like that." The Native American made a whooshing sound.

The comment caught Paco's attention. He set his mug down without drinking.

"Randolph Colton dead." The Anglo shook his head. "I mean, the guy was an icon in these parts. Hard to believe he's gone."

Amen. Paco offered up a silent toast.

"At least his kid was spared. Heard he always rides with his dad."

Marcus? Spared? Paco almost gagged on a mouthful of beer. Anger gripped him. Months of planning and he had failed to kill *both* Coltons?

"Crying shame about Buzz Warner," said the Anglo. "Flew with him once in Durango. Best damn balloonist. Can't imagine he did anything wrong. Had to be a tank problem. Anyone identify the kid?"

Paco leaned forward and listened intently to the men's every word. What kid? They'd just said Marcus didn't fly today.

The Native American wiped foam off his mouth with his shirtsleeve. "You mean the hitchhiker? Nah. He asked for a ride last Sunday. I sent him packing. Think of the liability."

Billy? No! Paco threw a bill on the table and hurried to the exit, fighting the urge to run.

"Hey," yelled the waitress.

"Left a twenty on the table," he shouted as he scooted through the door and ran the distance to his truck. Bullet's head popped above the sill. He growled. "It's only me."

On the trip across town, Paco vacillated between worry and fury. "Calm down. Think of something else." He stared through the windshield at bumper-to-bumper traffic. Albuquerque had grown a lot since he settled in the city. Give a developer an acre and he'd carve it into eight parcels. Give him a hundred-foot tract and he'd build an apartment on the land. Just what the world needed—more people.

The gridlock broke, and he blew past a billboard at sixty-five, the ad a gross exaggeration of life at his apartment complex. Ad people. They could dress up anything, even make hell appeal to the most devout Christian. *Sunset Skies.* Dumb name for the rundown cubbyhole he called home. *Lush green landscaping.* The only green he ever noticed were weeds flourishing among the dead flowers in the neglected beds. *Excellent move-in specials.* Ten lousy bucks off his first month's rent. *Quality residents.* Sunny, his next-door neighbor, wore an ankle monitor. Child molester. Phil, who lived on the other side, had been arrested and fined for killing and eating dogs. These days Phil worked at a meatpacking plant. Paco never let Bullet out of his sight. He even padlocked the gate to the tiny, fenced backyard where Bullet did his business, and if left alone too long, Paco blocked all access to the dog door. If Bullet had an accident in the apartment, so be it; at least he was safe.

All in all, he couldn't complain. He lived there by choice, not necessity. He had money but refused to spend a dime unless he had to. Banked every cent because one day he planned to start a new life. Right after he settled a few scores.

"Come on. Come on." He zipped past the car and into his complex, the tires squealing. Bullet joined Paco on the gravel drive and kept up as his master raced up the walkway, ducked under the dead vegetation tumbling from the archway, and skirted the pool. The water cried for a good dose of chlorine. More than once he'd got his revenge on false advertising by letting Bullet swim on hot days. Now if he could only teach his dog to pee in the pool.

A nagging fear hung over Paco as he jogged up the path to his digs. He glanced at the second-story balcony, the sliding door shut and curtains drawn. Bullet brushed by. Paco caught up, slid his key into the lock, and flung open the front door.

"Billy, I'm home." His voice resonated in the confined space. "Billy?" *Relax, he's probably in the shower wasting hot water.* But Paco didn't hear the water running.

He poked his head into the kitchen. A week's worth of dirty dishes had been cleared from the crazed sink, and the worn countertops had been scrubbed a brilliant white. Everything sparkled despite the age of the appliances and pits in the linoleum. He pitched his brother's bank ID on the table and climbed the stairs to his bedroom. The bed was made and the cramped bathroom cleaned to a fault. His heart sank. His brother hated housework and only tidied up to appease Paco, so he could only assume Billy was making up for disobeying orders not to leave the apartment.

"Where in the hell are you, Billy?"

Paco paced, wondering what to do next. What could he do?

No family. No friends. No one to call for help. Alone, like he had been most of his life. Tears stung his eyes. He sank onto the edge of the bed, his head in his hands.

For nineteen years he had searched for Billy. Six months ago he found him. Reunited, the two brothers had spent the past few months planning their future, dreams that years ago had been shattered when their parents deserted them. *This can't happen again. No, God. Please. Anything. I'll promise anything. Just bring Billy home safe.*

He wandered onto the tiny balcony outside his bedroom and leaned on the railing, his eyes fixed on the entrance to his apartment complex. With each hour hope faded. The temperature plummeted. Shivering, he retreated inside.

For another hour Paco kept watch, his nose pressed to the frigid glass, condensation clouding his view. Daylight dwindled. The outdoor lights flickered on. He went downstairs.

Planted in front of the television, he surfed newscasts. So far, the coroner hadn't identified the young man from the balloon crash, but as much as Paco tried to deny it, in his heart he knew the truth. In a trance he stared at the TV as it blared the last of the evening news. Only two words penetrated his thoughts: *William Barnes.*

Sometime in the early morning hours, he staggered into the kitchen for a bottle of vodka and carried it back to the living room. He sobbed and drank himself into a stupor. The liquor dulled the pain eating at his gut, but the void remained. He felt as if someone had crushed his heart to a pulp, the torture worse than the abuse his captors had inflicted.

Dawn broke, and with the new day came reality. The agony ceased, and a moment of calm overtook him. When the tranquil feeling passed, a new emotion absorbed him: rage, so intense it stole his last thread of control. He smashed furniture, shattered glass, and wept. Bullet fled. Above the chaos someone pounded on his door.

"Hey, you okay in there? It's Darien. The manager. Open up or I'm coming in."

"Everything's fine," yelled Paco. "Go away."

"If I get any more complaints, I'm calling the cops."

Paco curled up into a fetal position on the stained couch. His head throbbed, and the room spun. Bullet climbed onto the sofa. Paco took solace in Bullet's presence, but what he wanted the most was his beloved brother Billy.

As the day wore on, the whisper in his tortured mind told him exactly what he had to do. For Billy's murder, someone must die.

6

Darcy pulled into Journal Center, an industrial park on the northwest side of Albuquerque, and parked in an empty spot in front of Starbucks. She dabbed at the corners of her eyes with a tissue and checked her reflection in the mirror. Still puffy, but the redness had faded.

Not in the mood to face a crowd, or Zach for that matter, she waited in the vacant courtyard next to the coffee shop for him to arrive. She would've liked to have driven herself to Santa Fe but thought it more practical to ride along with Zach. He knew the area and had been to the Colton's legal firm on several occasions, or so he said. And why was Al in such a hurry to have Randolph's will read? Pushy bitch.

At a table apart from the rest, she stared across the long hedgerow to the fairgrounds where only the day before hot air balloons had colored the turquoise sky. Today the sunny morning, fresh after a night's rain, had nothing in common with her disposition. Depressed and tired, even after eight hours of sleep and a ten-mile run, she craved only more sleep. And because she detested hotels, she made a mental note to rent an apartment.

Her parents gone. Randolph dead. Her only family was Charlene, and no one called them close. She flashed on her last encounter with her sister during a gray, rainy day at home in San Francisco, hours before Charlene had left for her freshman year at Stanford, Darcy's alma mater.

Charlene had poured coffee for them both before taking her seat opposite Darcy in the breakfast nook. "Well, in less than twenty-four hours, I'm out of here."

"You sound happy."

"Face it, sis. You like your space, I like mine. And you've always hated being saddled with me. Hated the idea eight years ago, hate the idea today. Can't say I blame you. Instant parenthood when you least expected it"—she'd made a face— "must've been a real drag. Believe me, I'm not bitter about the way things turned out. You owe me nothing."

Darcy had felt like slime. "If you're trying to make me feel like crap, you're succeeding."

"Water under the bridge."

True, motherhood was not something Darcy ever considered, no more than she considered marriage. She loved her freedom. Yes, it had been tough to suffer through the sudden deaths of her parents and even tougher to deal with raising her nine-year-old sister. But had she hated being saddled with Charlene? No, never.

"Been waiting long?" Zach's voice snapped Darcy back into the present.

"A few minutes."

He raked his fingers through his ruffled hair. "Had a rough time getting up."

"I can relate."

"Coffee?" he asked, his voice full of tension. Nothing like the friendly tone on the morning of the fiesta.

"Tall latte." She reached for her wallet.

"It's on me." He rounded the corner of the building.

Darcy slid her hands into her pockets to warm them. Something sharp poked her finger: Randolph's business card. He had called her a little over a week ago on a Sunday night to say there had been a breach at Colton Aerospace and he needed her help. The anguish in his voice had concerned her. Not much got to Randolph.

"What sort of breach?" she had asked.

"I'd rather explain in person. Come to Albuquerque. I'm assuming you'll take the case?"

"Of course I will, after everything you've done for us. Let's see." She had checked her calendar. "Give me two days to wrap up business here and line up my house sitter, and another three to drive out as I'll be driving alone. Be there, say, late Friday. That soon enough?"

"The drive won't be necessary. Zach completed the audit on McClain Import Export and is ready to head home."

"Yes, he finished up late yesterday."

"Then why not fly out with him?"

"I have business in Tucson, and I'd like to handle it on the drive out," she fibbed. Actually, the excuse involved economics, but mention that to Randolph and he would mail a check. Until her father's company turned a profit, cash would be an issue. In the meantime, she had allowed Randolph to think she had adequate reserves.

"Fine. See you soon. Have a safe trip."

Zach returned with their drinks and muffins. He slid into the chair across from her. "I spoke to Franklin last night. He's keeping an open mind. Isn't sold one way or the other—accident or murder."

After the episode at the pasture, Darcy weighed her words. "At least he isn't jumping to conclusions."

"Al insisted on autopsies for Randolph and Buzz. Franklin agreed. He ordered one on the Barnes kid as well."

"Has anyone claimed the body?"

"No, and Franklin hasn't located the next of kin, which isn't surprising if you believe Barnes's job app: orphan with no family. But I don't buy it. Something tells me someone will come forward. Only a matter of time."

"What makes you think so?"

"Soon as they realize who owned the balloon, they'll sue."

"According to the news, the bank manager IDed him, right?"

Zach nodded. "Coroner found a paycheck stub in Barnes's pocket, so Franklin contacted the bank and talked to someone named Collins." Zach broke eye contact and took a sip of coffee. Darcy had the distinct impression he was about to fess up about something.

"Yesterday, I'm sorry I spoke to you that way," Zach said. "and sorrier for hurting you. I can only attribute my actions to shock. Randolph and I had been friends and partners for"—his voice cracked—"a long time." He took a sip from his cup. "I thought about the hacker, and well, I lost it. I worked too damn hard and too damn long for some two-bit joker to ruin everything Randolph and I built together."

Darcy wanted to inform him that they were talking about a hacker, not the demise of Colton Aerospace. But she didn't need another episode like yesterday, so she kept the comment to herself, along with the fact that Gallegos and Franklin already knew about the security breach. "Apology accepted. If I still have the job, I'd like to know more about your cybervandal."

"Of course you have the job. Nothing's changed except for Randolph's passing."

"Does Al agree?"

"Yes. I spoke to her last night. She'll honor Randolph's decision to hire you to audit Colton's security system. She knows nothing about the hacker, and I don't plan to tell her, at least not yet."

Honor? How nice of her. "Why doesn't she know about the perp?"

"You met her. Are you surprised? There are a lot of things Randolph kept to himself. This is one of them." Zach broke off a hunk of his muffin and popped it into his mouth. "You asked for the scoop on the breach."

"Wait a minute." She reached for her iPad. "Go ahead."

"The Saturday before Labor Day, someone stole five CR2 lasers from inventory. How the person moved them out of the building is a mystery. Security is extremely tight, and the lasers aren't small." He paused to allow her to type notes.

"Continue."

"Labor Day, someone tapped into our computers and downloaded the schematics for the CR2 lasers. Then, during a routine audit of the parts department, we discovered a long list of missing components, some specific to the CR2, others specific to our patented rangefinder."

"Specific means you can't use these parts to build any other laser model or rangefinder?"

"Correct. The stolen parts are generation specific. What the thief plans to do with them puzzled me because the CR2 lasers he stole are brand new, so why does he need replacement parts? The likelihood of the lasers breaking down is minimal. On the other hand, stealing parts for a rangefinder makes perfect sense because the current model is an old design and prone to failure. However, he didn't steal any rangefinders, so why does he need replacement parts?"

"Are you sure he hasn't stolen a rangefinder?"

"For security reasons, we keep track of every rangefinder we sell. If he had stolen one from us or a customer, we would have known." The conviction in his voice told her not to question him again.

"Up to this point, Randolph found the entire incident irritating, so he put internal security on it and refused to notify the FBI."

She shook her head. "Bad move."

"You know Randolph."

"Stubborn as they come," she said. "Does a rangefinder work on its own or in conjunction with a laser?"

He hesitated. "This one works either way. The weekend after Labor Day, the same person—we presume—hacked into our level-one operating systems and downloaded secret military files. Randolph wanted action. If the DOD gets wind of this, we'll lose our contracts."

"The Defense Department will order an investigation but won't yank your contracts without proof of a security breach. I believe you are overreacting," she said, choosing her words carefully.

Zach smiled. "You have no idea what we're working on."

She didn't pursue the comment. "Can you at least tell me what *kind* of military secrets were stolen and what can he do with them besides jeopardize your government contracts?"

"Can't tell you. Top secret."

Another roadblock. "Okay."

"Yesterday, the reason I acted like such a jerk was that I couldn't let you discuss the breach around Franklin. The word 'hacker' might slip, and it's synonymous with FBI."

Darcy hated to give him the bad news, but there was no

getting around it. He'd find out eventually anyway. "Franklin knows about the breach."

Zach's expression darkened. "Shit."

"And he knows I'm not here on vacation. He's smart. He figured it out on his own. "

Zach shook his head, clearly frustrated. "If the feds show up, then I'm bound to receive a call from the Defense Department."

Again she disagreed. Look how long the feds had allowed Chinese scientists to connect with the Energy Department's computers before they wised up and tightened foreign access. If the FBI took just as long to pull Colton's DOD projects, it would be 2020 before the company saw action. She asked her next question. "Why the reluctance to show Franklin the video I shot?"

"Because the less the cops know, the better. Period."

"The more they know, the sooner they can catch the killer if, as you stated, Randolph's balloon was deliberately shot out of the sky."

Zach gave her a dirty look, so she dropped the subject and asked another question to which she didn't expect an answer. "What type of laser is a CR2?"

"An Nd:YAG. Nd is the chemical symbol for—"

"Neodymium," she said, busy taking notes.

"Should've figured you'd know. So what does YAG stand for?"

"Is this a test?" She looked up in time to catch his smile. "Fine. I'll play along. Yttrium aluminum garnet."

"You're certainly well versed on a lot of subjects."

"On some. You said he hacked into level one. How many levels are there?"

"Colton has three security levels. To date, he hasn't gained access to two or three because the encrypted passwords elude him. Believe me, he's tried. We know that much."

"Are your dates correct?"

"Far as I recall." He pushed his plate aside. "Now you know everything I know about our hacker."

Or all he cared to tell?

"I'm curious—why's Al in such a hurry to have the will read?"

"It's understood, but she wants it confirmed that she's now CEO of Colton Aerospace." He chuckled, a weak laugh. "She feels it's best for the employees to know who's in charge. Randolph was very personable, one of the reasons his managers remained loyal despite some lean years. His death has people worried about their futures. Morale is important. We can't afford to lose anyone at this point. We're about to launch a new product." He leaned forward and said in a low voice, "Randolph landed a contract to upgrade the radar on a bomber Lockheed is building for the Pentagon."

"What bomber? I don't recall reading or hearing about one."

"You won't hear anything about Enforcer for years to come."

How cryptic. Reminded her of FBI days. At least there she was an insider, but now she knew a bit more about the Enforcer contract. "Regarding the audit of Colton's security setup, I think we should get our stories straight in case Franklin pumps me for information."

Zach bristled but recovered quickly. "Definitely. Randolph told Al and upper management he had hired a consultant to review security. No one questioned the decision because, as Al stated, the practice is common, more so after a defense company is awarded a sensitive project. The radar program was top secret. But now that Franklin knows something is up..." Zach sighed. "Tell him the security breach was minor and nothing important was compromised. And do not mention the word hacker."

"So when do I start work?"

Zach polished off his drink. "Whenever you like."

"Tomorrow, and I want to see a CR2 YAG in action."

Again he hesitated, but longer this time. "Okay."

She hadn't expected him to agree.

He stood. "It's still a bit early to leave for Santa Fe, but if you're ready we can kill some time up there."

She glanced at her watch. Close to an hour to kill? Great. She rubbed her tired eyes and pushed back her chair.

Comfortable in the passenger seat of Zach's Lexus, Darcy fastened her seatbelt.

She rode in silence, enthralled by the vastness of the landscape and the intensity of the blue sky as bronze grasslands specked with verdant piñon and juniper flew by her window. The plains stretched to tawny foothills capped in snow. Beyond, craggy red mesas jutted from the desert floor, their chiseled beauty overshadowed by the purple and black peaks of a majestic mountain range. "No wonder Randolph loved this land."

Zach snorted. "Too barren for my liking."

"What? You aren't sold on New Mexico?"

"Nope. Born and raised in Austin, Texas. No finer state. Plenty of green, plenty of water."

"But few mountains."

He laughed. "I think the Chisos in Big Bend qualifies."

"True. I'll have to visit Big Bend, one of these days. Why doesn't Al live in Albuquerque?"

"Too crowded, according to her. She loves Santa Fe. Randolph preferred Taos. Al refused to live there. Too remote and too uncivilized in her estimation. She's an elitist."

Obviously. "Does she come from money?"

He snorted. "Claims to."

"Where is she from originally?"

Zach frowned. "Didn't Randolph ever talk about his

family during all those trips to San Francisco to visit you and Charlene?"

"He brought pictures, but said little about them."

"Not surprising."

Darcy wondered what Zach meant but didn't ask because he had already moved on.

"Al's from the East Coast. Jersey, I'm told. If she ever gives you a straight answer, call me. You'll qualify for an automatic raise."

"How do you feel about her as CEO?"

"I'll manage. Oh, by the way, she's already ordered a name change. We are now Colton Industries."

"But she isn't in charge. Officially."

"Try telling her that. Give the woman free rein and she's off like a racehorse. A bit too impetuous for my liking." He slowed and moved into the right-hand lane. "Remember her on her cell phone yesterday? She was already putting plans into action."

"Figures," Darcy said, her face growing hot as she thought about Al standing in that field, cellphone planted to her ear, probably already making deals.

"She also intends to restructure the company into four small business units: lasers, radar detection, night vision equipment, and new development."

"Will restructuring benefit Colton?"

"Spinning off new development has merit. Martin Hamilton, the department head, was hired by Randolph to be my successor. Someday. Martin's a whiz at dreaming up lucrative products, but most have nothing to do with aerospace. Regardless, Randolph kept Martin and his brainy team. Why? Only he knew."

She smiled. Sounded like Randolph.

"Of course Al balked. She wanted Hamilton fired. Randolph ignored her."

"Will she fire him now?"

He shook his head. "Can't. Hamilton has an ironclad contract."

Zach passed a truck spewing black smoke. Strapped to the bed was a hot air balloon. She diverted her gaze and pushed gruesome thoughts from her mind. "What has Martin invented?"

"His most successful creation? A laser to detect fingerprints. Sold to the FBI in 1980."

"I've used it. Neat invention."

"Of late he created a method to harness solar power for the first solar-driven hot air balloon. Ironically, if Randolph had been flying Martin's invention, he might be alive. The debut launch scheduled for this Thursday has been postponed. He also invented, of all things, HSW, Hamilton's synthetic water."

"Synthetic water? How intriguing."

"Not for human consumption. Yet. But his water is being used in pools, ponds, and fountains around Albuquerque. In another year or two, you may be showering in it."

"No kidding. Synthetic water. I have to see this."

"You will." Zach exited the freeway at Cerrillos Road, wound his way through town, and turned left onto Don Gaspar Avenue. He parked in the lot across from the Hotel St. Francis and locked his Lexus. "We'll leave the car and walk to Weaver's office if you're up for the jaunt."

"I am." She crossed the street and stopped to check the menu at Café Pasqual's, trying to distract herself from thinking about Randolph. Zach continued on. She rejoined him as he rounded the bend on Don Gaspar and headed toward the Plaza. She passed under the portal of the Palace of Governors, glanced at the jewelry displayed on the blankets, and walked on. Another time.

Zach tapped her arm. "We better get moving or Weaver will start without us."

On the stroll north from the Plaza, Darcy half listened

to what Zach had to say, immersed in her own world. She thought of Randolph's love for gardening and paused to admire the withered hollyhocks poking their indigo heads above the adobe walls. Even in sleep, their faded beauty beguiled. A cat sprang onto the stucco wall. He watched her from his perch, his suspicious orange eyes tracking her every move. Sad, she turned her back on the garden, and the cat, and hurried on.

Darcy caught up to Zach and stepped onto the porch of Weaver, Wess, & Wykowski just as a blue Mercedes braked at the curb. Al stepped out, and without a word of acknowledgment, brushed by them in a whirlwind of blond and black, her eyes hidden behind dark glasses.

"Well, hello to you too," said Zach as he ushered Darcy into the lobby.

Weaver's secretary showed them into the library, a room ripe with the aroma of new leather, perfume, and stale cigar smoke. An attractive woman in a purple suit stood as they entered. "I'm so glad to see you." She held out her arms to Darcy. "I must look awful."

The voice gave her away. "Rhonda?" Darcy hugged Randolph's sister.

"I'm not surprised you didn't recognize me. Amazing what exercise and a good diet can do. Now if I could sleep, it might help smooth some of these wrinkles."

Last time Darcy had seen Rhonda she weighed well over two hundred pounds. Why, she must have shed more than eighty. "About Randolph—"

Rhonda's tears bubbled to the surface. "Yes, thank you," she said, cutting the condolence short. "Come, sit by me on the sofa. In this family I need all the moral support I can get."

The door opened and an entourage entered, Al in the lead. "Darcy, hi. So glad you came. Let me introduce my children."

"We aren't kids anymore, Mom, in case you haven't noticed,"

said a tall, dark-haired woman who resembled Rhonda more than Al. "You okay?" the woman asked and plunked herself down next to Rhonda.

Al glowered. "The impudent brat next to Rho is Selma, and this young stud"—Al tweaked the man's cheek—"is my eldest, Randolph Jr. The twins are my babies, Lindsay and Marcus."

If Darcy had to match them up as a family, she'd have grouped Randolph Jr., fair like his mother and guaranteed to break hearts, with his brother Marcus and sister Lindsay, both platinum blondes with pale blue eyes, which gave them a frail, pathetic look. Selma stood out in her own way. She wore her black hair short, streaked red on the right and green on the left. Orange irises and blood-red lipstick completed her garish appearance.

"She looks like a goddamn freak, doesn't she?" said Al.

Selma gave no reaction, obviously desensitized in the same way Charlene was whenever Darcy jumped on her soapbox.

"Artists," Al scoffed. "Those stupid contact lenses you insist upon wearing are only good for one thing—the trash." Selma's red grin widened. "Wipe that smirk off your face. Your father can't protect you now."

"Al, please, not today." Rhonda put a hand to her forehead.

"Where in the hell is Gordy? Running late again?" Al chose a seat next to Randolph Jr. "Darcy, I hope Franklin didn't interrogate you the way he grilled me. He probed into my private life until I said precisely what he wanted to hear."

Darcy took the bait. "Which was?"

"I can deal with Randolph's death, but if Marcus had been on board, well"—she sniffed—"life wouldn't be worth living. Love you, baby." She blew her son a kiss.

What a disgusting display. "If you don't mind my asking, how old are your children?"

Rhonda jumped at the question. "Randolph Jr. is twenty-two, Selma twenty-one, and the twins, twenty."

Darcy knew they were close in age, but not that close. Busy guy, that Randolph.

"Still, she treats them like babies." Rhonda's voice dripped with sarcasm. Al didn't react.

A young man entered the room. At first Darcy thought he might work for the family attorney, but he chose a seat directly behind Al. She leaned back and said something to him. He opened his laptop.

"Who's the man with Al?" Darcy whispered to Rhonda.

"Al's admin. Name's Charles Stevens."

The office door opened, and in walked a short, rotund man with wiry gray hair and a beard.

"Finally, here's Gordy," said Zach.

Strange, all this time and not a peep out of Zach as he thumbed through one issue of *The Harvard Law Review* after another while they all waited for the lawyer to arrive. He seemed preoccupied—worried about the contents of the will, perhaps?

Weaver headed to the only desk in the library. "Hello, everyone. Thanks for coming. I'm Gordy Weaver, Randolph's lawyer and executor." He eased his bulk into a leather chair. "Al asked me to get straight to the point." He opened the bound document he had carried into the room. "So without further ado, the last will and testament—"

"Gordy, cut to the chase." Al whacked the end table with a leather glove. "Who gets what?"

A red hue crept up the attorney's thick neck and colored his pudgy face. "Indeed."

Zach rolled his eyes.

Gordy cleared his throat. "If it meets your approval, Al, I'll read who inherits what in the order listed. Or should I jump straight to the bottom line and read what Randolph left you?"

She glared. "No, read the will in the order recorded."

"Very well," said Weaver. "'To Darcy—'"

"Are you reading in the correct order?"

"I am." Weaver placed both hands on his desk, as if to keep himself from hitting Al. "'To Darcy Elizabeth McClain, I leave the Tierra Blanca acreage.'"

"What?" Al interrupted. "All sixty acres? Randolph gave me that land as an anniversary present. Goddamn Indian giver."

Darcy's face grew hot with anger. What a witch. "You're welcome to have the land back."

"No, she isn't," Weaver said. "The will clearly states, Al is never"—he emphasized the word—"to own the property. If she contests any part of the will, she is automatically disinherited."

"That bastard." She shot Weaver an icy stare and resumed her seat. To Darcy she said, "The land will only bring you grief. Trust me."

Weaver coughed. "Can I proceed?" He didn't wait for an answer. "'To my children, Randolph Edward Jr., Lindsay Lee, and Marcus Alan Colton'"—Al appeared to brace herself for Gordy's statement—"'I leave each 2 percent of Colton Aerospace.'"

"What?" Al leaned so far forward, she almost fell off the sofa. "They're too young and too green to grasp company issues. Why waste a vote on them?"

"Oh please, Al. No more interruptions." Rhonda's lips sealed to a thin line.

Al grunted and then folded her arms across her chest.

"'To my loving daughter, Selma Louise, I leave 4 percent of Colton Aerospace.'"

Al waved a fist at her daughter. "Preposterous. Downright ridiculous. Look at her. Who in their right mind wants a drug-dazed artist voting on corporate matters? She holds your future in her hands, Zach. Hope you have your resume updated."

"Sit down." Rhonda's sharp command silenced her sister-in-law, if only for the moment.

"'To my sister,'" Weaver continued, "'Rhonda Colton Cloverdale, I leave my vacation home in Angel Fire.'"

Al sighed. She sounded relieved. Darcy guessed Angel Fire ranked in a different category than the acreage in Taos. She glanced at Weaver. A smirk pricked the corners of the man's mouth. She prepared herself for more profanity. Less than an hour in Al's company, and any good feelings she might have had for the woman had completely vanished. Why had Randolph married such a shrew?

"Rhonda, your brother also gave you 10 percent of Colton Aerospace."

Al lit up like a firecracker. "That son of a bitch. You aren't serious? There must be some mistake. There has to be."

"See what money does to a person?"

"Shut up, Zach. Your days at Colton are numbered."

He snorted. "Now why doesn't that surprise me?"

Weaver smacked the desktop with his hand. "May I proceed?"

"Do," said Darcy, ready to walk out and leave the bickering behind. Ugly trait, greed.

"To be certain this is clearly understood by Randolph's children, I will state the following stipulation in lay terms. Upon the death of any family shareholder, his or her shares will pass to Ashley Lynn Colton." Weaver glanced at each of Randolph's children. "Do each of you understand?

"Yes," they said in unison.

Al sat back and crossed her arms. "At least, I can thank him for that."

"'To the following charities, I leave . . .'"

Al groaned. "Why bother to list them? No one gives a damn."

Weaver inhaled sharply. "Okay, forget the charities. However, the next reading is mandatory."

"Says who?"

"Randolph said."

Al waved away the remark.

"'To Regina O'Neil . . .'" began Weaver.

Al opened her mouth. Rhonda held up her hand. Al fell silent.

"'To Regina O'Neil, I leave $10,000.'"

Al jumped up. "What? Who in the hell is this person?"

Rhonda leaned forward in her chair. "I'm rather curious myself, Gordy. Who is she?"

"Ms. O'Neil is Randolph's illegitimate daughter."

Rhonda's eyes widened. "Really?"

"Wh—at?" Al sputtered.

A half smile crossed Rhonda's face. "Is that all you know?"

"All I care to divulge. Can we go on with the reading?"

Speechless, Al just stared at Gordy, so Rhonda nodded for him to proceed. He flipped the page, raised his head, and stifled a laugh, the chuckle disguised as a cough. Then he spoke his next sentence so fast, the words took several seconds to sink in.

"'To my wife, Ashley Lynn Colton, and my partner, Zachary Eugene Larson, I leave each 40 percent of Colton Aerospace.'"

When the words registered, all hell broke loose.

7

Darcy parked her 4Runner in a visitor's spot and double-checked the address Randolph had given her. The right address, so she climbed out, pleased by the modern design of the building, from the pink granite to the expanses of turquoise glass banded by chrome to the purple pipe railings on the wraparound balconies. A far cry from the original Colton Aerospace, once housed in an old warehouse in a rundown section of town near the airport.

For a long time, she just stared at the structure, the company now in the hands of seven owners. Sadness swept over her, but she resisted the urge to cave. Budge even a bit, and grief would overtake her. She recalled another of her dad's favorite mottos: "Keep your eye on the goal." And right now the goal was finding Randolph's killer.

Before she went in, Darcy snapped pictures of the building

from every angle as though the structure might change now that Randolph no longer owned the company. But wasn't that true? After all, Ashley had already changed the name.

Darcy pushed the thought aside, placed her camera in a padded section of her daypack, and followed the slate footpath to a marble bridge that spanned a wide moat. A sign along the walk read, "Hamilton's Synthetic Water. Not Real Aqua." She bent over the metal banister for a closer glimpse at the crystal clear pool below. "Looks like real water."

"Hope so. Authenticity is the name of the game."

She turned. Behind her stood a man in his early thirties with windblown hair and cheeks red from the cold. He wore a dark pin-striped suit and a flashy multicolored tie and way too much aftershave. The suit was probably Armani, and the loafers Gucci. She stifled a sneeze.

"Martin Hamilton." His hand shot out. "And you are?"

Her stereotype of a nerdy scientist crumbled. "Darcy McClain."

"Oh, yes. The consultant hired to audit our security system. We must've had a falling-out with Majortech, our former audit team. Bet Al was involved somehow. Going in?" He stepped forward, and the double chrome entrance doors swung open.

Darcy entered the massive lobby, another showstopper, and paused to admire the interior. White marble floors abutted white walls that rose to a vaulted ceiling slanted at a sharp ninety-degree angle to catch the sun's rays. The furniture, purple and chrome, stood out like beacons on a black night. Every wall was owned by a large pastel of sweeping landscapes and huge flowers, the artwork reminiscent of Georgia O'Keeffe. The primary colors dazzled and controlled the viewer. Drawn to the works, Darcy hunted for a signature on a piece titled *Taos in Bloom*.

"Selma Colton? Really? These are beautiful. I've always loved pastels."

Martin raised his eyebrows. "You're familiar with the technique?"

"I am." She inspected the work more closely. "Appears to be chalk on black linen."

"Right on."

"Don't you worry about sun damage to the artwork from all this glass?"

"Not with my high-tech filtration system that screens the sun out. Another one of my nifty inventions. Museums love me." He steered her toward the receptionist's desk. "Sign in. Company policy."

She scribbled her name in the log, and the guard handed her a visitor's badge. "Keep it handy," he said. "You'll need it throughout the building."

"Thanks. Now where's the cafeteria?"

Martin gave directions. "Order an espresso. Good stuff." He pushed up his sleeve. The gold Rolex sparkled. "Check out the time. Gotta run. See you around."

Darcy bypassed the elevator for the stairs and strolled into the cafeteria. Zach sat in a corner with a newspaper spread before him. He looked up as she walked toward him. "Blasted stock market. You back in now that McClain Import Export is in the black?"

"Yes, in a big way. Thanks again. I would've lost Dad's company if you hadn't stepped in."

"Doubt it, but thanks." He stood. "Coffee?"

"Espresso." She slid into a seat at the table.

"You met Martin."

She detected a hint of skepticism. "He seems like a nice man. Definitely not your absentminded scientist."

"Watch him. He's a terrible flirt. And he's married. He'll win your heart, then break it."

Win her heart? Not likely. "Thanks for the warning."

"Anything with your espresso?"

"No thanks." She watched him order their drinks, pay, and head back her way. He could've been Al's brother. Similar wavy blond hair, thin oval face, and large blue eyes. Tall, fit. The only difference between the two? Al shunned sunlight while Zach appeared to worship it.

"Your espresso." He sat down.

She sipped the strong brew. "On the way in, I noticed Al not only changed the company name but also found time to have a marble marquee engraved with 'Colton Industries.'"

"Told you, she moves fast." He drained his cup. "While we're on the subject of Al, I want to apologize for her behavior at Weaver's office. God knows she won't."

"Have you ever seen her act that way?"

"Only when she doesn't get what she wants. Be warned, if two Coltons are present, expect a fight."

"Reassuring." Darcy took another sip. "Were you as shocked as the rest of us to hear Randolph had an illegitimate daughter?"

"Yes, to say the least, but I think he'd only just found out."

"Why do you think that?"

"A month ago he drove up Santa Fe to meet with Weaver on some urgent business and said not to say anything to Al about the trip. He never explained. I think he went up to include Regina in his will."

Possibly. Then she broached a subject that had niggled at her all night. "Between us, doesn't the sum of $10,000 seem rather paltry for a man with billions?"

"I questioned that as well," said Zach. "Seemed odd, especially since Randolph was always known for his extreme generosity. Now if he'd left her a million dollars, that would have been more appropriate, but $10,000?"

He fell silent, as though contemplating the point. "About the investigation," said Zach, "I leaned on Franklin for the autopsy reports. He'll have them later today, along with the forensics results."

"That surprises me. With an investigation underway, I thought they'd seal them."

"Pressure from the right people will get you just about anything in this town."

She figured as much.

"Yep, money talks. But you'll never hear me apologize for having money." He pushed back his chair. "Come on. I'll show you your office. Afterward, the demo you requested."

Good—he hadn't forgotten. She slung her daypack over her shoulder and collected her laptop case.

"Pulling an all-nighter?" He pointed to the Kelty.

"You never know."

"Oh, forgot to tell you . . . along with the name change, Al relaxed the dress code. Business casual from now on. There's a memo, or will be, in your inbox." He punched the elevator button.

A change for the better. "Great. Beats wearing a suit."

"A word of advice. If you tell Al anything, you might as well announce it on the paging system, so when I think the time's right, I'll fill her in on the real reason you're here."

Darcy had no plans to tangle with Al. "Your call."

"There you are." Al's shrill voice sliced the air.

"Darth Vader in drag," said Zach. "I knew the peace wouldn't last."

Al, stunning in black velour, marched up to Zach. "We have a problem. One that needs your immediate attention." She batted her long lashes. "Quinn called. He wants to meet."

"No," said Zach.

"What do you mean, no? I haven't even asked my question."

"Don't bother. Randolph and I vowed never to work with Quinn again. He's a hood. A common criminal."

"Money is money, Zach, and I won't let you dictate—"

"No."

Al's eyes narrowed. "We'll just have to see about that. On another matter, I'm taking Randolph's office." She walked away.

Zach boarded the elevator. "Let's go before she comes back. She has a nasty habit of reappearing, especially if she wants to beat an issue to death."

At the fourth floor, the elevator glided to a stop, and Darcy emerged in the middle of a long corridor. Glass walls stretched the entire length of the hallway and ran along both sides of her. Every twenty feet or so chrome handles protruded from the panels, the only indication an office door existed in the walls of glass.

"Randolph's office is to the left," said Zach, "mine to the right. Yours is down the hall from mine. About the elevators . . . the first question I usually get is why three serve one floor. Because Randolph wanted it this way. The one we exited goes to every floor except the basement. The elevator to the south goes directly to the lobby. The one to the north goes straight to the basement laboratories."

"All floors. Lobby. Basement labs. Where are the stairs?"

"Adjacent to the lab elevator." Zach escorted her down the hall.

Something red caught Darcy's attention. She backed up to take another look, squinting as she peered through the wall of reflective glass into a dimly lit office. "Another of Selma's pieces? Like the ones in the lobby?"

"Yes. Do you want a closer look?" He pulled a key ring from his pocket. "This is Randolph's office. Or was."

Zach unlocked the door, and Darcy entered. Behind a massive mahogany desk hung a pastel of a huge red pansy in a gold frame. "I love her work."

A voice drifted in from the hallway. "It's called plagiarism."

Al strutted in. "Who gave you permission to snoop around my office? Give me your key."

Zach slid the key off his ring and dropped it into Al's outstretched hand.

"Thanks. Now vamoose." She practically shoved them out the door.

Three men in khaki overalls barged past Zach and Darcy.

"Crate them up, guys," said Al. "Every one. Then ship the lot to Rhonda Cloverdale at the Cloverdale Gallery on Canyon Road." She flounced into Randolph's chair. "Comfy enough. The chair stays."

"Ma'am, this piece is nailed to the wall."

"Pry it off if you have to," said Al. "But don't leave any behind. Terrible things." She pointed a red-painted talon at Darcy and Zach. "I thought I dismissed you. No, not you two," Al shouted at the workers. "I'm talking to them."

What a bitch. Darcy walked out, leaving Al to her housecleaning, and followed Zach to his office to check messages. After he sorted through the stack, he showed Darcy to a spacious room opposite the stairwell. It was like the others—plenty of glass, white marble floors, white walls, and purple and chrome furniture—but this one had a rosewood desk.

"Not much of a view, but you have a kitchenette and private bathroom complete with a shower and real water. Not synthetic." He opened the sliding door and stepped onto the patio. A blast of frigid air knifed its way into the heated suite.

Darcy joined him. She scanned the adjacent parking lot. Martin Hamilton sat in a BMW, Selma behind the wheel. "Are they dating?"

"Not to my knowledge. Ready for your laser demo?"

"Lead on."

Before Darcy left her new office, Zach handed her an

envelope. "This password should get you anywhere you need to go on Colton's intranet. Memorize it, then destroy the note."

Darcy memorized the four-digit code, inserted the sheet of paper into the shredder by the desk, and headed for the door with Zach.

The basement elevator landed with a soft thud.

"Quick trip."

"Now you know why Randolph installed three elevators," said Zach. "To get here fast."

At the security checkpoint, Zach fed his ID into a computerized scanner and waited for Darcy to repeat the procedure. Cleared, they proceeded to a door marked Lab X. "It'll take a minute or two for the laser to warm up. Look around if you like, but don't touch anything."

Darcy roamed the room. No different from the office suites upstairs—white and more white. Once again the only color to break the monochromatic decor was purple, the stools shoved under white workbenches. Four floor lasers occupied one wall. Opposite them, glass and steel objects covered a long table. At the very back of the lab, she ducked into a partitioned area for a look. The space, approximately ten by ten, held a desk, two chairs, and shelves lined with empty beakers except for three, which were filled with clear liquid. A few feet from the wall sat a laser, the device about the size of a small riding mower. Bleach laced with ammonia clung to the air.

"Ready?" He put two stools alongside the laser and cleared the tabletop except for a metal box. "Last night I met with Angelo Basini. He runs the computer department."

"The IT department?"

"No, our information technology is a separate entity. Angelo's area is off-limits to most employees."

More secrets. "Go on."

"Like you asked, I rechecked the dates. Angelo's logs show

the hacker broke into our operating systems for the first time over Labor Day weekend."

"First time that you know of."

"True. Once on the Friday. Twice on Saturday. Multiple times Sunday afternoon, and again on Monday. Each time, he searched for specific material but stole nothing until Monday. In one session he downloaded everything he wanted."

"Which was?" She expected him to dodge the question.

"You'd have to ask Angelo. He knows who you are and the real reason you're at Colton, so you two can talk freely."

Zach's comment surprised her.

"I had to clue him in," said Zach, "if you plan to catch this guy."

Finally, he had stopped stonewalling. "Thanks. Makes my job easier."

"And mine." Zach placed his hand on the laser. "This is a CR2, our YAG laser. Only difference between this YAG and the YAG the hacker stole is that this model incorporates our patented rangefinder. It's a prototype for our next generation and the only one of its kind. Until production starts next year."

She sized up the laser/rangefinder. "I didn't expect it to be this large. I mean, I'm familiar with medical lasers, the kind used in surgery."

"For what we're asking this baby to do, well, it needs to be this size," he hedged.

"Were the stolen CR2 lasers comparable in size?"

"Give or take a few pounds. The rangefinder adds relatively little weight or bulk."

Darcy eyed the laser. "He must've had help to steal five of these."

"I'm sure he did. Then he probably cannibalized two or three of the five to build a smaller version. Something easy to transport."

Like to and from the Santa Clara Savings and Loan? "Where would he take a contraption of similar size?"

"To any location within sight of the Albuquerque Fairgrounds. The hacker shot Randolph's balloon out of the sky."

The thought had occurred to Darcy, but a motive escaped her. "Go on."

"You don't sound convinced."

"You haven't said anything to convince me. But let's hear your theory."

"Fact: after he built a downscaled version of our laser, he built a smaller replica of our rangefinder, and incorporated the two."

"Because a downscaled version would be smaller and easier to transport," she confirmed.

"Precisely," said Zach.

"Okay, so a rangefinder's job is to seek," Darcy spoke her thoughts, "which means it located Randolph's balloon, computed the distance from laser to target, and locked on. But locked on to what? I know how a laser target works, but how did the killer specifically locate Randolph's balloon in a sea of balloons? Surely he didn't stare through long-range binoculars to pick out a red dot on Randolph's red envelope? It's virtually impossible to see red on red, never mind at that distance and in bright sunlight."

He paused as if to mull over a point and then neatly sidestepped her question altogether. "Yep, I'm sold—the fire that consumed Randolph's balloon was ignited by a stripped-down version of this baby. Watch." He switched on the YAG and aimed it at the metal cube on the table. The laser beeped. "Don't watch the beam. Watch the digital display. When I press Test, the rangefinder will read the range to target with an invisible beam."

Again, the laser beeped, this time with a higher pitch. "Fifteen feet" flashed on the digital display.

"Now watch." Zach hit the Fire button.

Still no bright light, so what caused the brilliant flash she'd seen seconds before Randolph's balloon ignited?

"Did you see the metal cube on the table shift? Only slightly but still visibly."

She shook her head. No, because she had her mind on the flash of light.

He crossed the room to retrieve the cube and handed it to her. "See for yourself."

She examined the hole.

"I'll bet you when the forensic reports come back you'll find the hole in the propane tank is identical to the one in the cube you're holding."

Not one but two holes. Two explosions, two holes. "No bet because I agree. Something still bothers me."

"What?"

"Minutes before Randolph's balloon burst into flames, a bright light stabbed me in the eye. Remember, you thought I had motion sickness?" He nodded. "Now that I've seen the demo and know the test beam is infrared, therefore invisible, and YAG laser energy is invisible, what caused the flash?"

"Simple explanation. Even with an invisible beam, laser, or rangefinder, both will produce what's interpreted as a blinding flash in the optic nerves. You stood at precisely the right angle for it to zap you."

Three blinding flashes and two explosions. First the flash of a test beam. The other two direct laser hits. Made sense now.

"Seen enough?" he asked. "Or do you want to take a shot?"

"Sure, I'd like a shot or two." She fired the high-powered laser several times and developed a healthy respect for its deadly force. "Another question. If I fired a laser at the propane tank, why would there be an entrance hole, but no exit hole?"

"You can dial in your point of impact. For example, I dialed in a point of inertia for the cube. I wanted to hit the cube, but not have the beam go through it and into the wall."

Which would account for two holes rather than four. Her gaze wandered. "What's the instrument attached to the YAG over there?"

"Beam splitter. Splits a laser's output into two uniform beams of equal power. If you're ever up against a ruby laser, our CR3 for instance, and it's equipped with a beam splitter, throw away your gun. Laser energy's faster than a bullet and a hell of a lot more powerful. Cuts through anything, even titanium. Better run like hell because there's no place to hide."

Chilling thought. "I'll keep it in mind. I'm curious . . . on Sunday, there were over nine hundred balloons in the sky. Two identical to Randolph's. How'd the killer pick the right one?"

"I showed you. Our rangefinder." He switched off the laser.

Something didn't add up, and she was about to question him again when someone knocked on the lab door.

"Come in," said Zach, the relief in his voice palpable.

A man with long hair tied into a ponytail and skin the texture and color of brown leather entered the laboratory. "Heard someone mucking around in here and decided to investigate. Sorry for the interruption, Mr. Larson."

"Perfect timing. Shut the door. Darcy, meet Angelo Basini. Angelo, this is our cybercrime specialist, Darcy McClain."

Cybercrime specialist? Since when? Darcy extended her hand.

"I've heard a lot about you," said Angelo. "Your track record for hunting down cybervandals is impressive. Can't wait to work with you, Ms. McClain."

Someone had fed him a line of BS. "Call me Darcy."

He reached into his shirt pocket. "I'm on my way to a meeting, but stop by after lunch and I'll bring you up to speed on our perp. Here's a map. You'll need directions to find my lab. I live in the basement. Later." Angelo disappeared into the hall.

Soon after Angelo left, Zach and Darcy headed for the bank of elevators at the end of the hall. Neither spoke on the return trip to the fourth floor; Darcy was busy pondering how to push Zach for a realistic answer regarding the rangefinder issue. His remarks just didn't make sense. The doors parted, and there stood an officious looking woman with red hair and a plaid suit, who Zach introduced as his secretary, Charlotte. "Sorry for the intrusion," she said, "but Al has Quinn in her office."

Zach hurried down the hall.

"The reports you needed." Charlotte handed Darcy a manila envelope. "Zach said to make a copy for you the minute they arrived."

Back in her office, Darcy lifted the flap on the envelope and removed the autopsy reports. The results merely confirmed what she already suspected. Despite third-degree burns over 90 percent of their bodies, Randolph and Buzz Warner had died from the impact.

She sorted through the pile of photographs of Barnes's corpse. One was of the pay stub found in his pocket, the bank's name barely legible through the scorched paper. She skimmed the summary. Almost every bone in his body had been fractured. He also had multiple lacerations and contusions. The coroner had attempted to locate dental records to affirm identification, but none existed. Now that raised her suspicions.

She shuffled through the pictures. A black spot directly below Barnes's left earlobe sparked her curiosity. She wrote "enlarge" on a Post-it and stuck the note to the back of the photo. Odd, nothing in the autopsy referred to the mark. Perhaps the spot was a burn and not a hole as she initially suspected. Still, the spot should have been referenced somewhere in the report. She searched every sentence but found no mention of it.

Next, she read the forensics report. On one point Zach was right; on the other, Darcy. The hole in the metal box matched the holes in the propane tanks aboard Randolph's gondola. Holes, plural—her theory of two was correct. The coroner's report noted, "The edges of the cavities were too symmetrical for a bullet from a high-powered rifle." However, he had no idea what had caused the holes.

Darcy reviewed the reports several times and always finished with the same questions. Why had the black spot on Barnes's neck been omitted, and why was there no mention of the St. Christopher medal when two pictures clearly showed him wearing it?

"Wait," she said softly to herself. "What about the computer chip Gallegos found in Randolph's jacket pocket?" Darcy saw no mention of it anywhere in the report either. Sloppy investigation or evidence left out on purpose?

She had encountered this before—the detectives in charge telling her to stay out of their business. Didn't matter if she could help; they wanted to keep the key evidence to themselves. Bet Franklin or Gallegos, or both, had been burned before. Everyone seemed to be more interested in protecting their territory than catching the killer, Zach included.

She logged on to her laptop to probe into Barnes's life. He had lived at 1414 Tramway for six months and had worked as a teller at the Santa Clara Savings and Loan for about the past four. Prior employer, Phoenix Mutual. Parents, Walter and Constance Barnes of Flagstaff, Arizona. Both deceased. Died the year before in a house fire. Ruled an accident. One child. The fifty-year age gap between his parents and Barnes sent up a red flag, so she pursued the hunch. Adopted at eight. She scribbled "Parson's House" on a pad, but all attempts to ferret out information on the Chicago orphanage hit a dead end, so she dialed the number at 1414 Tramway.

"Hello," answered a sleepy voice.

"Sorry to wake you. I'm looking for William Barnes."

"Look, I told you guys. He never lived here. He paid me to use the address. No, I don't know where he lived. Yes, he may have been shacking up. I don't know and don't care." He slammed down the receiver.

When the ringing in her ear subsided, Darcy dwelled on the question that had nagged her since Zach had demoed the CR2. Out of nine hundred balloons, how did the killer pick the right one to blow out of the sky? There had to be more to the equation than Zach's explanation. And what made him jump to the conclusion of murder? She was suspicious by nature, and even she hadn't come to that conclusion immediately.

Thinking the answer might lie in the product's description, Darcy surfed Colton's intranet looking for literature on their rangefinder. She pored over the material for an hour and found no answers, so she delved a level deeper. Suddenly, the screen went black, and the program prompted her for a password. She typed in the access code Zach had given her.

Despite his guarantee it would take her anywhere within Colton's restricted operating systems, she found herself shut out. Strange. Or was it? He wanted her to catch the cyberperp but wouldn't give her the tools to do so. Why? Was he more concerned about the DOD yanking Colton's defense contracts or too busy protecting his own interests to stop the killer? What if she told him he could be next? Would that change anything? Of course she had no idea whether the killer planned to murder again or whether Zach was a target. Or even if the hacker and the killer were the same person—purely speculation on her part. However, too often she had been right on the mark.

Darcy scooped up her cell but decided against confronting Zach about the bogus password. Why tip her hand? Instead, she would bypass him altogether and use her skills to go wherever she wanted. After all, she had worked on the National Security Agency's top-secret cryptographic project: a program designed to maintain the security of government information. For her, deciphering and breaking code had become a hobby, almost as addictive as tracking crack cyberspooks.

Immersed in mathematical computations and key combinations, she took less than an hour to decode Colton's strong digital signature, giving her root-level access to most of the company's proprietary operating systems—a depth restricted to top executives only. And for another hour, she stalked the techno-perp's digital footprints from one proprietary site to the next, at ease in Colton's maze of classified databases. Although he had entered undetected, he had left a trail of electronic traces. But when she tried to reconstruct his exact path, she failed. So she attempted to back-hack the source to his computer. This failed as well. Smart snoop. So smart, something told her his cyberdebut at Colton had occurred long before Labor Day.

For Darcy the first order of business would have been a warrant for line traces, but Zach's mandate to tell no one squelched this idea, so she wrote a program to notify her every time the hacker logged on. Done, she pushed her chair away from the monitor and sipped from her mug. Like the cold black coffee swimming in her cup, Zach's gag order left a bitter taste in her mouth. Frustrated, she decided to confront him on the issue as soon as the opportunity presented itself. She checked the time. Angelo should be back from lunch by now.

Her office door flew open. Darcy leaped to her feet.

"Sit down," bellowed the burly man towering over her. "This won't take long." He ran his hands through his hair, slicking the strands back from his putty-colored face, his rough features contorted with anger. "So Larson hired a friend to audit my system. Well, you won't find any flaws, no matter how hard you try, but while you're searching, sister, remember one thing.

You're on my turf, and I don't take kindly to anyone screwing with my setup, especially a woman. Understand?"

"And you are?" she asked in a calm voice.

"Frank Muñoz, head of security."

"Oh yes, saw your name on an organizational chart."

"Nice to know I still have a job." He kicked the door shut on his way out.

The dysfunctional Coltons, Gallegos the surly cop, Zach the liar, and now, the irate chauvinist. Not to mention a hacker who might be a killer. What had she gotten herself into?

8

A light snowfall mantled the world outside Paco's apartment. He shivered in the bitter cold but lingered on the upstairs balcony to watch the flakes mask the rutted parking lot—nature's beauty disguising man's ugliness. The placid scene calmed his nerves and steeled his heart. His drinking binge had ended last night and with it the abject sorrow that had ripped him apart since his brother's death. Today only anger raged inside—not directed at himself, as deep down he knew it should be, but at the perpetrators of all evil in his life, those he hated as much as they hated him. When his face burned from the icy air, he went inside to prepare for the last assault on his emotions: Billy's funeral.

Bullet scooted around Paco and stretched out on the linoleum floor in the tiny bathroom, forcing Paco to step over the hundred-pound mass of black fur. He downed the last swallow of soda water, but it did little to calm the fire in his empty stomach. He knew he should eat something, but the thought made him ill.

He squeezed a blob of reddish-brown cream into his palm and blended the color over his entire face before he tugged on a wiry gray wig. Bullet growled. "I know, doesn't do a thing for me, but it works." He studied his reflection in the mirror. Perfect. He resembled an old man in old clothes. "Coming?"

Bullet trotted downstairs to the hall closet, where Paco sorted through the packed space for a worn coat, tattered scarf, and a wool hat. He stared at his hands. They shook from too much booze. He wiggled his fingers into threadbare gloves and leaned against the doorjamb. "Hope this dizziness passes."

The problem that had worried him all night sprang to mind. How could he get his hands on a copy of the autopsy reports without revealing his identity? He needed to know what the pathologist had found.

The clock in the hallway chimed. Bullet dodged by. He planted himself by the front door, an expectant tilt to his head. "Sorry. Too risky." Paco reached out to pet Bullet, who smacked his master's outstretched hand with a paw. "Another time. Now remember, no unwanted guests. Do you hear me? The doggie door is for your use only. And stay clear of Phil." The name alone bristled Bullet's hackles. "He's a bad dude, all right. You don't understand a word I'm saying, do you?" Bullet's ears shot up. "Or do you?"

One last hug, and then Paco locked the door and headed down the icy footpath to his truck. His feet felt as heavy as concrete, his knees weak. He wanted to turn back, crawl into a warm bed, and hide from the world, but he owed Billy a final goodbye. His brother would receive a pauper's burial, but Paco promised to make it up to Billy. To bury him properly. This business should be done by January, the perfect time to leave for a warmer climate. He'd take Billy with him.

On the drive across town, the sky turned from pale blue to a somber gray. "Please God, give me the strength to face . . ." He choked back the words, the finality of Billy's death more than Paco could bear.

Snow fell as he entered the half-dirt, half-pitch lot that fronted Our Lady of Guadeloupe Cemetery. He climbed out of his truck and loitered near the sagging gates, reluctant to go in. There were three funerals today; he had checked. One right after the other. Gonzales, Barnes, Montoya. He expected the police to attend and even knew who was assigned to the Colton case, but he didn't spot Franklin or Gallegos among the masses.

With snow in the forecast, large canvas tents had been erected for the mourners. Paco ambled toward the last row of chairs set up for the Gonzales clan and sat sideways in his seat, his head bowed as if in prayer and eyes focused on a freshly dug grave several yards away. White-hot pain radiated through his body and crushed his chest. A sharp gasp escaped his lips. He tried to stifle it. Why bother? In the company he kept, no one cared. As if in response to his agony, those around him echoed his grief. A chorus of sorrowful cries merged with drones of anguish. He wanted to scream "Silence!"

An eternity later, the Gonzales service ended, and the bereaved dispersed. Alone at last, he cradled his head in his hands, but no tears came. He'd shed all he had.

A short man in black walked up to Paco. "I'm Father Paul. Are you here for the Barnes service?"

"No, Montoya."

"Sorry to have disturbed you. Poor chap, Barnes. Seems he had no family." The priest walked off toward the open grave where two men waited.

No family.

He wandered in the direction of the Montoya tent, found a seat in the back, and stared bleary-eyed at the priest as he conducted the solemn ceremony for Billy with only the pall-bearers in attendance. Father Paul closed his Bible and blessed himself. The men lowered the casket into the ground, and the first shovelful of dirt landed on his brother's new home. His shoulders sagged as every ounce of energy drained from him. Had they buried Billy with his rosary and his medal? He would have wanted that. A big brother's job, making sure those things were with him, but he'd failed there as well. His face grew hot as the dirt beat a drum on the lid of the coffin. A hand tapped his shoulder. He tensed.

"Pardon the intrusion, sir. Which service are you attending?"

His eyes met those of Detective Franklin. His heart raced. Had he applied enough makeup? Was his disguise convincing? "Montoya," said Paco.

Franklin looked beyond Paco to the gates where the Montoya procession filtered into the cemetery. Among them was Lena Gallegos, Franklin's partner. Franklin made eye contact with Paco. "Sorry to hear of their daughter's passing."

Paco's gaze never wavered. "Son," he said, thankful he had done his homework. "A good boy killed by some gang." He produced his rosary. The detective got the message and wandered off in the company of Gallegos. They spoke briefly to a priest, who was with the Montoya gathering, and then moved to the edge of the crowd of mourners. Paco nudged his seat companion. "Frederica Montoya, has she arrived?" he asked in Spanish.

"The white-haired woman in the dark suit next to the elderly gentleman."

Paco lined up with several other mourners and waited his turn to offer his condolences to a woman he had never met. Mrs. Montoya frowned but graciously accepted his kind words.

He excused himself and meandered toward the gates; his pace was leisurely, but his heart ran a marathon.

He drove home in a stupor. So many dreams, and they had waited so long. Now everything had been stripped away.

He steered into his complex. A wave of nausea gripped him. He slammed on the brakes and jumped out. Leaning against the bumper, Paco vomited until nothing but dry heaves were left. Shit. Served him right, drinking so much vodka. He wiped his mouth on a crumpled paper towel he found lying in the cargo bed and then walked around to the passenger's side to retrieve a screwdriver from his glove box. Only took him three minutes to swap out his fake license plates for the real ones, but twice as long to warm his hands.

Back in the cab, he ripped off his disguise, wiped his face clean with the scarf, and stuffed the worn coat behind the driver's seat before he stepped out. Blowing snow pelted him. With his head low and his eyes on the slippery path, Paco trooped up the salted walkway to his apartment.

A loud grunt. He raised his head.

Phil blocked his path, an ugly grin plastered on his ugly face. "Hey kid, you look like shit. Where's your mutt? Thought you took him everywhere."

"Touch him and I'll cut your heart out. Feed it to the coyotes."

"Yeah, right. You friggin' wimp. You don't have the balls. Couldn't even kill a fly."

"Think what you want, dick brain." Paco barged past Phil into his apartment and threw the deadbolt on the front door.

"Bullet. Here, boy." He dashed up the stairs and into his bedroom. Bullet had his head on Paco's pillow, his legs in the air and paws resting on the headboard, the picture of contentment. Some watchdog. Relieved that Bullet was safe, he let the dog sleep.

In the kitchen he heated black beans and rice with wilted cilantro. After one bite he put the bowl on the counter and warmed some milk. The tepid drink diluted the acid churning in his gut.

Bullet shuffled into the room. "Where have you been, watchdog?" Paco packed his uneaten meal in a cooler along with water, two colas, and a bag of treats. "Let's go. We've got work to do."

9

Snow clouds pursued Darcy from Albuquerque to the tree-lined streets of Tesuque. Giant cottonwoods, stripped of their summer wear, hugged the creek banks. From their gnarled limbs hung ice masterpieces. Piñon smoke floated through the circulation vents and scented the cab of her 4Runner. She whipped around a corner and braked hard. In front of her stretched tall wrought iron gates. The automatic entrance parted, and Darcy followed the curve of the drive as it gained in elevation and then plateaued. The spacious home overlooked the valley, the land below spectacular in white. She expected a Pueblo-style home with soft earth tones like most of the houses on her drive north, but a white contemporary sheeted in glass rose from the wooded knoll.

She parked behind Selma's Bimmer and stared through her fogged windshield at the vehicle-choked drive. Who wasn't here?

Meeting at Al's home instead of the church irritated Darcy as well as Rhonda, who said, "Control freak," when she'd heard the news from Al's assistant. Bad enough Darcy had to deal with the Coltons at work. Now she had the displeasure of peeking into their private lives. *Just get it over with,* she told herself as she walked up the driveway to the front door.

Before she rang the bell, a young Hispanic man opened the massive entrance and said, "Welcome, Ms. McClain."

"Thank you," Darcy replied as she crossed the threshold.

"I thought I heard your voice." Al appeared in the foyer. "Come in. Join the rest of us mourners." Her voice carried a hint of sarcasm. "You wore black. How ravishing."

And Al thought Selma was strange? Darcy followed her hostess into the adjoining room. The modern exterior didn't carry into the interior. A fire crackled in the hearth. On the mantel, candles flickered. Art decorated the walls, pottery sat on stone pedestals, and Indian rugs cloaked the slate floor; all appeared quasi-traditional. She took in her surroundings, surprised that none of the artwork displayed had been painted by Selma.

"Everyone, Darcy's here," Al announced, her arms held wide.

Rhonda nodded a greeting. She looked tired.

"Take my seat." Zach vacated his spot on the sofa.

"Thanks." Darcy forced a smile. Uncomfortable in their company, she wanted to be anywhere but here, trapped in a room of mostly strangers. To make matters worse, she sensed the tension between her and Zach. After her meeting with Angelo, Darcy had stopped by Zach's office to discuss his decision to keep her purpose at Colton Industries a secret from Detective Franklin. No matter what she said, he'd tuned her out. She had left in a huff.

"What will you have? Vodka? Scotch?" Zach walked toward the drink trolley.

"Water." She fought to be civil.

"Water?" Al questioned. "You sure?"

"Water," Darcy repeated.

Rhonda smiled. "You holding up okay?"

Darcy smiled back. "I'm all right." At least she had one friend in the room. "You?"

"I'll be glad when today is over."

Darcy squeezed Rhonda's arm.

"Randolph, dear, a refill." Al raised her glass. Her son whisked away the tumbler.

Zach handed Darcy her water.

The conversation turned from the weather to Selma's upcoming art show, and as if on cue she waltzed into the living room, elegant in a simple black dress and black heels, and with no jewelry and little makeup.

"Selma, you look wonderful. Come here, dear." Rhonda hugged her niece.

Darcy agreed the transformation was amazing.

Al beamed at her daughter. "So glad you listened, dear. Black is her real hair color. See what it does for your skin? Simply exquisite. I should've been so blessed."

"Mom, you're embarrassing me."

"Don't be. You're a beautiful woman," said Darcy. Only the red rims around Selma's green eyes detracted from her striking looks.

"Thanks for the compliment, Ms. McClain."

"Darcy."

Selma fixed herself a Coke, waved, and disappeared down the hallway.

"I'm glad we're all together at this difficult time," said Al, "to support each other while we grieve. Poor Selma. Randolph's death has been very hard on her."

"At least someone loved him," said Rhonda.

Al's hand flew to her chest. "My goodness, Rho. You know we all loved him. Each in our own way."

The grandfather clock in the hall bonged the half hour.

"We should leave," said Al.

"All of us in one limo? How cozy." Zach buttoned his jacket.

"Come on, be nice—if only for today." Al touched her ear. "Damn. Wait for me. I've misplaced my earring."

"Mom," Selma called from the landing. "I found an earring on the telephone stand. Should I bring it down?"

"Yes, do." She met her daughter at the bottom of the stairs. Selma placed a diamond stud in her mother's palm. "Damn, the other one's missing as well. Was there only one by the phone?"

"Only saw the one. I thought you were wearing the other."

"So did I. Be back in a minute."

"Mom's too wrapped up in appearances," Selma said to Darcy. "She needs to relax, take things as they come. Bet your life doesn't revolve around your looks." She thought for a minute and then added, "I meant that as a compliment."

Darcy chuckled. "I took it as one."

"She's also a control freak," Selma continued. "She hasn't learned there are some things in life you just can't control."

"Like you?" Randolph Jr. piped up.

"Yeah, like me. She's tried everything, but I'm my own person."

"If you are, move out. Quit taking her money," Randolph Jr. shot back.

Selma stuck out her tongue. "I plan to, wiseass."

"Yeah, when?"

Selma's eyes sparkled. "Soon. Aunt Rho thinks my show will be a raving success. If she's right, then I'm out of here."

"I bet Rhonda's right," said Darcy. "From the pieces I've seen, you're a gifted artist. In fact, I have my eye on one of your canvases."

"Really? Which one?"

"Fire Roses."

"Fab choice." Selma rubbed her hands together. "Will you be at my opening? Even Father George from St. Luke's promised to come." She glanced at the staircase. Al crested the landing. "Dragon at twelve o'clock."

"I heard you, young lady. Is she bragging again about that stupid show? Rhonda's idea. I vehemently disapprove." Al slipped into a full-length mink she took from the hall closet. "Selma should make her own way. Kids don't appreciate a damn thing when you hand everything to them. If she wants independence, she should get a job. A real job."

"Sel," Selma said to herself, "don't let her bait you. Walk away." She flung open the front door and dived into the backseat of the limousine parked in the driveway.

To Darcy's relief, they rode in silence to the Cathedral of St. Francis of Assisi in downtown Santa Fe. Parked at the curb, Rhonda slid out and linked arms with Zach, and Al took Randolph Jr.'s arm. While the others made for the reserved pews closest to the altar, Darcy squeezed through the unending flow of arrivals and hovered near the confessionals. She had hoped for a smaller group. This large a crowd made it difficult to observe, never mind memorize faces. Besides, what made her think the killer would show? On the other hand, he may have ridden with them to the church.

She half listened to the eulogies, her attention focused on the assembly. For one very long hour, her eyes roamed the masses, hunting for anything out of the ordinary, but nothing raised her suspicions.

She spotted Karla Sizemore, a knockout in black lamé. Assertive, self-assured, a balloonist—one more for the suspect list? Across the aisle from Al sat Charles Stevens, the administrative assistant within easy reach if Al needed him, but not included in the pews with the family.

Randolph's service ended, and the masses thinned to a handful. Darcy knelt to pray. Thoughts of Barnes dragged her back to the day of his funeral. The afternoon before, Darcy had canvassed the graveyard for a suitable hiding place to spy on the Barnes service and had found a storage shed in the corner of the unkempt grounds. The day of his burial, she returned with a hacksaw and a padlock. She sawed through the thin steel of the existing lock and crept inside to watch.

The morning had dawned cold and gray, but for a spell sunlight washed across the cemetery. The rays painted the crumbled headstones a hot orange, and black shadows licked the frozen ground. She closed her eyes. Ten years hadn't dulled the pain of her parents' funeral. She forced the sad memory from her mind, happy for the intrusion when cars pulled into the dusty lot adjacent to the sagging chain-link gates.

The Gonzales wake had lasted well over an hour. Everyone had something to say about the man. Good for the family, bad for Darcy. Stiff from crouching in one position for too long, she shifted her weight from one leg to another. No relief. She cursed Zach. It was his fault she had to hide from Franklin and Gallegos.

Through binoculars she'd watched the Gonzales gathering depart. She leaned against the wall, extended her leg, and sighed in relief. She conducted the same procedure with the other, careful not to kick over anything in the cluttered shed and draw attention.

Movement to her right. An elderly man left the Gonzales tent and roamed over to the Montoya congregation. For some reason she felt a strange connection to him. She dwelled on the feeling until her concentration was broken by the priest presiding over Barnes's funeral. Twenty minutes and the boy's last rites were over, a sad commentary to his short life.

His gait, mannerisms—something triggered the recollection, but what? Before she had an answer, another interruption distracted her.

Franklin and his partner Gallegos had arrived in a Bronco. She remained by the SUV while he spoke to the elderly gentleman. Darcy zoomed in on the man, snapped several frames, and tracked him in her viewfinder as he walked toward the parking lot. He climbed into a primer-gray pickup with Arizona plates and drove off. At that distance and angle, she could only make out the last three letters of his license plate: *BVN*.

A half hour passed.

Gallegos had crossed the cemetery to her SUV and eased behind the wheel. Franklin sat beside her in the passenger seat. When they sped away, Darcy packed up her gear. She slid the new padlock onto the shed door and made a mental note to mail the gatekeeper the key.

Today, another funeral. Sad times, and she would have loved to forget them, but in her line of work death came with the job. She blessed herself.

A hand closed on her shoulder. Nothing like an unexpected jolt to catapult her back to the present.

"Sorry," whispered Zach. "Didn't mean to startle you. Service is over. We're leaving."

"Be there in a minute," she said without looking at him.

Seconds later she emerged from the dimly lit church to dazzling sunshine. At least the day had brightened. She ducked into the limousine, glad to see Rhonda had saved her a seat.

Befitting Randolph's love of art, Al held the postwake reception at the Siler Gallery off Canyon Road. She preferred the coziness of Cloverdale, she informed everyone as the driver turned onto Paseo de Peralta, but the building wouldn't hold the hundreds bound to attend the public service. Her prediction was right. When their limo pulled into the lot, a sea of humanity clogged the sidewalks and choked the parking area.

The limo inched its way through the masses and stopped curbside. The second the driver braked, Selma bolted from the back door. "Unless you like this sort of thing, come with me." She grabbed Darcy's arm and led her past the hordes of mourners to a fenced area behind the gallery. "I want you to see something. If you don't mind the cold?"

She did but said, "Not at all."

Selma unlatched a pedestrian gate and started across the frozen grass to a man-made pond. Pink, blue, and maroon flowers sprouted from a rock waterfall, and lilies poked their heads above the water's surface.

"They're porcelain. What do you think?"

"Beautiful. Who's the artist?" She knew the answer but gave Selma her moment of glory.

"Me." Darcy heard the excitement in Selma's voice. "John Siler himself commissioned a piece last year. I talked him into letting me sculpt flowers for his pond rather than paint a canvas. Hard sell, but he caved."

"Will your show include sculptures?"

"Afraid not. Conflict of interest. Melanie Skillman wouldn't appreciate the competition, and Rhonda knows it. Melanie's a sculptor. She has a fondness for animals." Selma made a face. "Don't get me wrong—I love animals, just don't dress them in weird garb. You'll see what I mean."

Al approached. "Has she been bragging again?"

Darcy bit back a few colorful insults before answering. "No."

"Then what do you call it?"

"Why are you such a bitch, Mom? I wish you'd show some respect for Dad." Selma stormed off.

"Ungrateful brat!" Al shouted.

The abrupt and distasteful end to an enjoyable moment left Darcy with the almost irresistible urge to smack Al.

"Hey, you two, come inside or you'll freeze to death," Zach called from the patio door.

Without a backward glance, Darcy stepped onto the stone walkway and sought refuge in the toasty gallery.

"Selma asked me to rescue you. Drink?" Zach gravitated to one of the bars set up throughout the gallery.

Right about now, Darcy needed a stiff drink. "Scotch. Neat," she said to the bartender. He poured her a healthy Dewar's. She took the glass and paused near an Allan Houser sculpture to admire his work. Zach joined her.

"If I spent my days with Al," said Darcy, "I'd be an alcoholic. Don't know how Randolph put up with her. Why is she so mean to Selma?"

"Jealousy, I presume. As for Randolph, he traveled a lot, and now you know why. Interested in touring the gallery?" He didn't wait for a response. "A shame the smaller sculptures have been stored. Siler has quite an extensive exhibit of animal pieces. The artist is a local woman."

"Melanie Skillman?"

He laughed. "What a good guess."

"Selma mentioned her."

Darcy passed an Alexander Calder sculpture and strolled into a large room with bleached wood floors. Zach followed. Stainless steel mobiles hung from the ceiling, and wire mesh figures molded into the likeness of the human body lined the walls. Huge pieces of blown glass adorned the marble pedestals, and colored rocks in wooden frames blanketed one section of the floor.

Zach sat on the first bench he came to. Perched on the opposite edge as far from him as possible, Darcy wasted no time discussing the subject uppermost in her mind. "When can I tell Franklin I'm a PI?"

He swirled the contents in his glass. Odd how he appeared calm today when he'd overreacted at Randolph's crime scene and gone ballistic yesterday. "Let's wait awhile, see how the case progresses."

She sipped her Scotch. The liquor didn't temper her anger. "We're wasting precious time."

"What does telling him you're a PI buy us? You've seen the autopsy and forensic results, so you know as much about the case as he does."

She felt her blood pressure rise. "On the contrary, the reports weren't very thorough."

A puzzled expression crossed his face. "What are you getting at?"

"I think Gallegos, or Franklin, doctored the reports."

A frown wrinkled his brow. "Tampering? Why? They had no idea you'd see them and nothing to gain by altering the data."

She folded her hands to keep from smacking some sense into him. "I disagree. I think Gallegos is onto me."

"Are you saying they had something to do with the murder?"

"No, of course not. But often cops can be territorial. They like to keep the evidence to themselves so no one else can solve the case."

"Glory seekers." He sighed. "Let's wait another week before we clue them in on what's going on at Colton."

Darcy seethed in silence, her mind working on a better appeal, but she dropped the subject when Rhonda called out to them. "Sorry for the intrusion, but John Siler would like to speak with you, Zach."

He excused himself, and Rhonda took Zach's seat.

In seconds Selma appeared. "Can I tell Darcy?"

"Sure." Rhonda patted her niece's arm. "Bet Darcy's good at keeping secrets."

If they only knew. "You can trust me."

"Rhonda's celebrating." Selma stirred her Coke with her finger. "Well, not really celebrating."

"No, because that sounds disrespectful to my brother. It's a secret, not a celebration."

"Anyway, I'm busting at the seams." Selma puffed out her cheeks.

Rhonda laughed. She removed a small box from her pocket and lifted the lid. "I'm engaged."

"Five carats," Selma gushed. "Aunt Rho won't wear the ring yet because she's afraid Mom will pitch a fit."

Stunned by the news, Darcy could only say, "Congratulations."

Rhonda pocketed the ring. "A bittersweet occasion, I'm afraid."

"Dad would've been thrilled." Selma squeezed her aunt's arm.

"Okay, I'm dense. Who's the lucky man?" Darcy looked from Rhonda to Selma for an answer.

"I'm sorry. We've done our best to be discreet because Al will flip out when she hears the news," said Rhonda in a low voice, "and I'm in no mood for a fight. Not today."

"Mom still carries a torch for Zach. Unrequited love," sang Selma, her nose in the air.

Shocked, Darcy forced a smile, but she wasn't happy about the news. *Bad choice*, she almost blurted, but now wasn't the right moment to voice her opinion. She'd wait until later and try to talk some sense into Rhonda. And how dare Zach obstruct Randolph's murder investigation and still have the nerve to look his fiancée in the face? Darcy drew long on her Scotch.

The thunderous sound of high heels on wood echoed

through the gallery. Al bore down on them, her face red, arms swinging at her side, and hands clenched into fists.

"Oh no. Here comes the dragon. Wonder what set her off now?" Selma stifled a laugh.

"Rho, I'm really tired of your meddling," Al shouted as she advanced on them. "Putting stupid ideas into my daughter's head. She's not going." Al stomped her foot. "I won't permit it. Cancel her show at Siler New York. Do you hear me?" She wagged a finger in Rhonda's face.

"New York!" Selma said with a squeal. "Oh thanks, Aunt Rho." She threw her arms around her aunt's neck.

"Wag your finger at me one more time, Al, and I'll bite it off." Rhonda's exemplary composure had cracked. "As for your opinion, it isn't worth a damn in my book. Selma isn't a child. Let her decide."

"I won't let you steal my daughter." Al started to cry.

"Oh, Mom, get a life. Preferably your own."

Al shook a fist at Selma. "You can be a real bitch sometimes."

"And you're a vicious—"

"Go ahead. Say it." Al raised her hand, prepared to hit Selma, who backed away from her mother.

"Enough," said Darcy.

Selma moved closer to Darcy. "Just because you've never been happy doesn't mean I can't be. And guess what? Your life is about to get a whole lot worse. The man you've loved all your life is engaged to another woman."

Al paled. "What? What are you talking about?"

"Sorry, Aunt Rho, but I'm at war." Rhonda appeared to enjoy Selma's sadistic moment as much as Darcy. "Steel your balls, Mom. You'll need them. Rhonda is engaged to Zach."

Al lunged at her daughter. Rhonda stepped between them, taking the brunt of the slap intended for Selma. Startled by the blow, Rhonda stumbled sideways. Al flung herself at Selma, grabbed her daughter's hair, and yanked hard with both hands. Selma cried out. Darcy had seen enough ugly family battles in the past two days. When Al refused to back down, Darcy opened her jacket. The Browning commanded immediate respect.

10

Moonlight lit a path through the dark passageways that bisected the deserted salvage yard. On both sides of the narrow walk rose stacks of steel, vehicles flattened to one-fifth of their normal height. Gasoline mingled with the stench of burnt oil and rotting trash. Bullet snorted.

"Don't blame you. The smell ain't fit for man or beast."

Paco arrived at a clearing and hiked through the snowdrifts to the warehouse. He had taken the long way around—anything to avoid people. He kicked gray slush off his boots, spun the dial on the combination lock, and hurried into the cold, run-down building. Bullet scampered around the interior, sniffing every corner for rodent invaders, but lost interest when Paco unwrapped a hamburger.

Bullet drooled.

"Just the way you placed your order. Hold everything but

the cheese, meat, and bread." Paco put the burger in Bullet's bowl and gave him fresh water. "After dinner, a fire. It's freezing in here."

Paco ate his meal. He felt much better than he had this morning. Four aspirins had done wonders for his splitting headache but only added to the inferno in his gut. Wasn't until an hour ago that the burn had cooled and his appetite had returned.

Done with dinner, he built a fire in the rusted stove and watched Bullet claw at his bedding until he bunched the blankets into a large ball. Satisfied with his nest, he settled onto the mound and snored.

Paco looked around the warehouse. Bernardo wouldn't recognize the joint. Years ago the elderly gentleman had run a thriving business out of this dump. Could have today, if his health had permitted. Paco liked Bernardo. The man didn't ask questions. He handled the lease over the phone and said to mail his checks to a post office box.

The first thing he did was rent a Dumpster—in Bernardo's name of course, but Paco paid the bill. Then, with the old man's permission, he tossed out pitted engines, rusted transmissions, and a host of junk accumulated over the years but not worth salvaging. He swept, hosed, and painted for weeks, concentrating on a small space he planned to use as an office. He retreated there now to log on to his laptop.

"Good evening, Master Paco." The greeting pleased him. He typed in his password.

"Processing Incoming Data" popped onto the screen, followed by a tightly woven network of arched and angled lines. He clicked on Print, and the LaserJet cranked out page after page of schematics, everything essential to wire Ravel's key circuits.

Paco worked with a sense of urgency, time his primary concern. When the printer stopped, he gathered the stack of electrical drawings from the hopper and tacked each to a sheet of pressboard nailed to the wall.

After studying the graphs, he collected the parts he needed from the boxes stacked high in the adjoining warehouse and carried them to several folding tables arranged in an assembly-line fashion. He switched on his radio and tuned to a news station.

Throughout the night he soldered, fused, welded, and wired the machine. A sense of power surged within him as his invention took shape. By 3:00 a.m. Ravel had half a body and a partial brain. Paco rubbed his hands together to restore feeling to his cramped fingers. Burned out, he pushed his chair away from his workstation, leaned back, and shut his eyes.

"We interrupt our broadcast to bring you this special report." The newscaster's booming voice snatched Paco from the brink of sleep. "Detective Franklin, what's your take? Was it some kind of incendiary device that blew up Randolph Colton's balloon?"

"No, assholes. I used a laser," said Paco, switching off the radio in disgust. "You have a genius on your hands, not some dumb-ass serial killer murdering for fun. How many assassins do you know who invent their own weapons?"

His voice woke Bullet. He growled, raised his head to check out the noise, and went back to sleep.

Awake now, Paco sucked on a Gatorade and let his mind wander. How different his life would have turned out if his parents had been in his life. All those years in the orphanage, the horrors of abuse, the ugly images indelibly etched in his brain.

He stared at the laser lying within reach, the complexity of its design commendable. It reminded him of his first invention, Zeek, a rudimentary robot. How proud he had been of his creation. He couldn't wait to show it off at the science fair, but his classmates didn't admire his accomplishment. No, they were jealous and called him Zeek the Geek. So he retreated to a world he knew well and one he understood, an electronic universe of algorithms, logic, and science, a world where facts ruled, not subjectivity or emotion.

A low whir. Paco straightened. Outside, the wind had shifted direction. Gusts roared around the draft-ridden building, rattled the tin roof, and threw trash against the walls. During a lull Bullet whimpered with strange chirps: dreams of rabbits or cats.

Paco yawned. Time for bed. In the bathroom diagonal to his workspace, he brushed his teeth. For the first time in weeks, he felt sleepy. Maybe tonight his mind would shut down and his dreams would be peaceful rather than invaded with nightmares from the dark place. Hadn't he suffered enough? Why did they torment him every time he closed his eyes?

He limped to the stove to stoke up the flames. The cold made his leg ache. Bastards. Paco unfolded his sleeping bag, spread it close to Bullet, and pulled a blanket over his head to ward off the icy tentacles threading their way into the room.

Again he was on the tranquil brink of sleep when a deep-throated growl startled him to life. The luminous hands on his wristwatch read four thirty. He raised himself on his elbow and glanced about the dimly lit interior.

Bullet snarled.

A crackling noise, followed by a garbled voice, disturbed the night.

"Quiet. Stay."

Paco padded across the warehouse in slippers and pressed his face to the crack between the double garage door and the jamb. A squad car rolled slowly down the steep hill toward the warehouse. The cop parked under a tall pole equipped with four dead spotlights and climbed out. At one time the motion sensors had lit up the entire yard, but Paco had shot out the bulbs with a pellet gun. Tonight only the moon illuminated the lot. The officer reached into the driver's window.

"Probably radioing dispatch," he whispered to himself.

"Bernardo said the joint's rented to a Ronnie Ravel," the officer's radio squawked. "Seems Ravel repairs cars."

"Thought I smelled smoke," said the patrolman.

A long pause.

"There's a stove in the joint," the dispatcher explained, "but Bernardo said he isn't concerned about fires. I quote, 'Building ain't worth a dime and insurance is paid up. There's sprinklers in the ceiling.' End of quote. Probably nothing. Go home. Enjoy your family, Fletch."

"Thanks, Jerry. Plan to."

"Over and out," the dispatcher said.

Fletch caressed his holstered .38.

Paco rushed to check the stove. The fire had died out—not even embers to give them away. He slipped his hand under Bullet's collar and guided him to the bathroom, the only place they could hide from prying eyes. The dilapidated building, riddled with gaps and holes, was a Peeping Tom's fantasy. He crouched in the shadows with Bullet pressed to his side.

A dull thud.

Bullet stepped forward. Paco's arm circled his chest. A growl percolated in his throat. "Quiet," Paco whispered.

Outside, Fletch jiggled doorknobs, clattered padlocks, and rammed his powerful flashlight into every cavity in the rusty structure but failed to break in. The strong beam landed on Paco's truck parked in one of the bays. Primer gray, dilapidated, and with no license plates, it looked like it hadn't seen the road in years. The sports car opposite it, with a tarp draped over the body and papers piled on the cover, also gave the appearance of an inoperable automobile. In reality, the restored 1969 ZL-1 Corvette was in mint condition.

The light show ended, and an engine roared to life.

As soon as the sound died, Paco gathered their bedding and

carried the pile to the bathroom just in case the cop returned for a second look. Eventually, he dozed off, sleeping until he awoke with a stiff neck at daybreak. Bullet crawled from under the blanket and hurried to the metal door.

"Business first." He rested a ladder against the wall and mounted the rungs. At the top he opened the hatch in the ceiling and checked the surrounding area. "Coast's clear."

On his way out, Paco picked up a gray cylinder lying on his workbench. He strapped the contraption to his forearm with Velcro tabs and extended the inner tube, the metal pipe about the diameter of a pencil and a foot in length. He pulled his sweater over the laser, a prototype he'd designed years ago, and stepped outside for some target practice.

Paco kept Bullet in sight as he loped along the bank of the arroyo, which separated the junkyard from his neighbor, a Native American who made drums.

Bullet sniffed the dirt, sniffed some more, and lifted his leg. His presence disturbed something in the underbrush. A rat scurried up the dry wash. Paco steadied the pipe between his fingers, aimed, and tapped a button on the gray tube. An orange beam shot from the laser. The rat dropped in its tracks.

His business done, Bullet joined Paco as he strolled the edge of the ravine. Billy occupied Paco's thoughts. With a heavy heart, he retraced his steps to the warehouse. There was only one way to avenge his brother's murder: finish building Ravel. Tomorrow he'd complete the circuitry, the laser's nerve center. Next, the real challenge: the brain. For that he had to gain access to level two.

11

Just before dawn, Darcy strolled into a special section of the IT department in the basement of Colton Industries and parked herself before the U-shaped bank of computer screens spread eight wide. Only the subtle hum of machinery filled the ionic air trapped in the windowless room. "This sector has been set aside specifically for you and the task ahead," Angelo had said in his typical formal style when he gave Darcy the tour the day before.

Yesterday he'd also cleared up some misunderstandings on the workings of Colton's YAG lasers. Seemed Zach had told the truth about some things and glossed over others—a sort of need-to-know tactic on his part. Evidently, all of Colton's YAG lasers were equipped with a red HeNe aiming beam for test firing prior to deploying the operating beam.

"Incredibly dangerous using an invisible test beam," Angelo had informed Darcy. "Because Nd:YAG lasers operate outside of the range of human vision, the beams are invisible to the user. A simple and cost-effective solution is to incorporate a low power helium-neon gas laser into our main unit. This gas laser, HeNe, produces a visible red 'pilot' beam for detection. Of course, you can wear infrared goggles to detect an invisible beam, but that doesn't mean they're always readily available. As for how the killer zoned in on Randolph's balloon, as opposed to any one of the hundreds in the air, I have no idea. I'm no techie. What laser stuff I know comes from my association with R&D."

"So the flash I saw could have been a red HeNe test beam?"

"Sounds that way," said Angelo.

Back in the present, Darcy yawned. Even three cups of strong black coffee—high test no less—had failed to chase the cobwebs that netted her fuzzy brain. Thoughts of Randolph, strange surroundings, and unusual noises had kept her awake most of the night. Still, the move from her hotel to an apartment offered distinct advantages, like being able to do her own cooking and, to some degree, quieter digs.

She nursed her fourth cup. Regina came to mind. Although everyone asked, Weaver refused to answer questions about the girl except to say she had been adopted at birth, but by whom, he declined to answer.

Darcy walked down the hall to the break room and gazed out the glass sliding door to the north parking lot. At the moment it was empty, but soon every space would fill. Inventory started today, according to the interoffice memo she plucked from her mail basket on the way downstairs. She slid open the door. A frosty blast stripped away the last veil of sleep that fogged her brain, jarring her senses into high gear.

Dawn broke over the Sandias.

The desk phone rang. She ducked back inside and reached

for the receiver but noticed Zach's extension on the console and decided not to answer. To hell with him and his blasted secrets.

Back in her seat at the computers, she shut her eyes and let her mind sort through the clues she'd found in the bank's parking lot, or what she hoped were clues. It would have been much easier and faster to let Detective Franklin's team analyze them, but since Zach was such an ass, she had mailed the evidence to Testco, a California lab, for analysis.

Testco and Dan Gruet, her former partner at the bureau, had a long-standing contract with each other, and Darcy retained their services from time to time. Thinking of Dan brought to mind her conversation with him the day before. Fed up with Zach's roadblocks, she had contacted Dan to secure a line trace on Colton's phones in the hopes of trapping their perp. And since she had defied Zach once by ordering the tap, she defied him again by contacting Mrs. Collins, the bank manager for the Santa Clara Savings and Loan.

A pleasant and cooperative woman, Mrs. Collins informed Darcy that her association with Barnes had been short. Billy had worked there for less than four months. Model employee. Previous employer, Phoenix Mutual. A call to Phoenix Mutual mimicked Collins's assessment of Barnes as a shy, private, perfect worker.

Mrs. Collins went on to inform Darcy that every employee carried a smart card issued by bank security. The ID functioned as a badge, worn at all times during work hours, and as a pass to gain access to the overhead parking structure, which was shared by two businesses. If the killer had used the rooftop, then he had a card—the metal barrier was intact Sunday when Darcy had scoured the bank lot and was still functional today, Collins had told her.

And according to security, if anyone had been admitted to

the building after work hours, he or she needed prior clearance and had to sign in and pose for the surveillance cameras. No one had worked that particular Sunday. On the other hand, Collins pointed out, the outdoor security cameras may have filmed a person of interest. She promised to deliver copies of those video recordings within the week.

As for business number two—who shared the parking structure with the Savings and Loan—it had been a small CPA firm housed within the bank building. They had moved out two weeks prior and relinquished their ID badges, and all had been accounted for.

In the meantime, Darcy dug deeper into Barnes's past but unearthed little. For years he had lived at Parson's House, a state-subsidized orphanage. Details of his life at the home were sketchy at best, so she emailed Dan, who had access to more resources, and asked if he could probe into Barnes's history.

She checked the time. Much later than she thought. That's what she hated about cracking cybervandals. It took time and plenty of patience.

Still bugged by the question of how the laser had located a single balloon in a sea of aircraft, Darcy logged on to Colton's databases and spent the next hour surfing through a new compendium of information on rangefinders. Nothing in the company's extensive anthology of material answered her question, and nothing corroborated Zach's claim, so she clicked on "Links." The program dumped her off the system. Successive attempts to log on failed. Could Big Brother be monitoring her?

Her cell phone rang. She snatched up the receiver. "McClain."

"Boy, you sound official," said Dan. "Bad connection. Where are you?"

"At Colton. In the basement. By the way, I moved out of the hotel and was fortunate enough to lease a furnished apartment. Not sure how long I'll be here, and you know how I hate restaurant food, not to mention hotel noise. I texted you my landline number."

"Thanks. I'm really sorry about Randolph."

"It's been tough. Can't sleep. Mind won't shut off." Tears pricked her eyes. She changed the subject to keep from breaking down. "Heard anything from Testco about the material I found in the bank parking lot?"

"Yes. Got a pen?"

"Shoot."

"The dog hair, husky-malamute mix."

Darcy sighed. "Probably hundreds in the state, which isn't encouraging. May not even be pertinent to the case. The tire track?"

"As you suspected, the red marks are clay and/or sandstone. The black paper, roofing felt. Nothing unusual there. But the pearly white substance with the sparkle? Never seen anything like it, and neither has Testco. The guys are running additional tests, but it might take a while to nail down the material."

A spark of hope. Finally. "Keep testing. I have to know what the substance is."

"Will do." He yawned. "Excuse me. I'm beat."

"One more thing about the tire track . . . did you notice the unusual wear pattern?"

"I did, but unless we find another track with the identical wear, the observation is of no real help."

"True, but who knows? I may get lucky. What about Barnes's past?"

"Oh yeah, almost forgot. Parson's House closed years ago, and no one can locate any of the staff or the records."

"Of course. It would be too easy otherwise."

"But we haven't given up. I gave the assignment to Steve."

Darcy liked Steve, Dan's best skiptracer. Nose like a

bloodhound, tenacity of a pit bull. "What about the chase and ground crews? Did you check them out?"

"Sure did. Hold a second." Paper rustled at his end of the line. "Nothing significant to report on any of them, except Karla Sizemore."

Not expecting even this bit of news, Darcy said, "Oh yeah. Go on."

"Want facts or rumors?"

"Both."

"Karla Ann Sizemore. Thrillseeker. Bungee jumper, skydiver . . . the list goes on and on. Taos-born model meets Dallas industrialist Blake Sizemore. Trophy wife. Fifteen-year age difference. Blake, a balloonist, gets Karla hooked on the sport. Industrialist dies of a heart attack, leaves wife filthy rich. Those are the facts."

Her pen went dry. She tossed it in the trash and rummaged in a drawer for another. "Now the rumors."

"You sure?"

"Come on."

"Okay. According to the Colton rumor mill, Randolph and Sizemore had a brief affair."

"How brief?"

"Don't know."

"Okay, so he had an affair. Who wouldn't, married to Al?" Darcy ran her index finger down the list of clues collected at Randolph's crime scene. "Wish I had my hands on that computer chip."

"Me too. Zach's secrecy is setting off warning bells in my head. Do you think it's possible he killed—"

Darcy responded with a definite no. "He's only guilty of being an asshole, and withholding information, I feel, might be pertinent to the case."

"His motive for doing so?"

"He stated it himself, and I believe him. As close partners, he and Randolph built Colton into a billion-dollar defense company, and he's afraid of losing his legacy if the wrong party, the DOD, gets wind of a serious security breach. In some ways, he is overreacting, but he's trying his damnedest to protect his interests, and those of Colton by throwing up every roadblock he can conjure up, but his secrecy doesn't help me solve Randolph's murder case."

"Before I hang up, anything else cooking?"

"Seen Charlene lately?"

"Yesterday. We spent hours walking the beach and talking. She's sorry about not coming out for the memorial service, but she's really broken up about Randolph and is having a hard time dealing with his passing. Feels everyone she loves ends up . . . deceased."

"Poor kid. Tell her I understand and not to feel bad about skipping his funeral. I think she made the right decision. Why subject her to more death than she's already been subjected to at her age? Thanks for being there for her, and for me. At least we can count on you."

"Happy to help. If you need anything at all, call." He hung up before she could thank him again.

The desk phone chimed and she picked up. "Forget something?" Instead of Dan, she got an earful of deafening static. She held the phone away from her ear until the noise cleared, and an anxious voice came on the line. "Muñoz, get down here on the double. The asshole ripped us off again. This time he stole CR3 parts. Muñoz? Hey, who is this?"

Darcy yanked the telephone console toward her. The caller ID read Chris Rodriquez. She thumbed through an employee list. Rodriquez worked in manufacturing. She snatched up her visitor's badge and ran down the hall to the guard post. She flashed her ID at security, cleared the metal detectors, and proceeded to a wall-mounted pad. The second the LED lit up, and she punched in her access code. A loud click. She raced into the south wing and followed the signs to the next checkpoint. With her fingertips on the wall panel and her face aligned with a mirrored circle, she said, "Darcy McClain. ID 222."

"Voice, fingerprint, retinal scan confirmed," said a tinny voice."

Darcy jogged down the long corridor.

A man turned the corner. He froze in his tracks and gaped at her as though he had seen a ghost. "Who in the hell are you, and what are you doing here?"

"McClain. Security consultant. I'm looking for Chris Rodriquez."

"Let's see some identification." He held out his hand.

She showed her badge.

Even after inspecting her badge, he still acted suspicious. "At the end of the hall—hang a right."

Darcy rounded the bend. A short man in khaki pants and demin shirt stood at the other end of the hall.

"Can't believe this shit," he said to his companion, a dorky kid in jeans and a sweatshirt. "We're supposed to have the best freaking security in the aero biz. Who screwed up? That's what I want to know." He dragged his hands over his shiny pate. "Well, don't just stand there, find out."

The kid disappeared down the hall at a fast clip.

Darcy cleared her throat and the man turned. "Who in the hell are you?" he shouted.

"Darcy McClain."

His frown faded. "Oh. Sorry, Ms. McClain. You're the security consultant, right?"

"I am."

"Chris Rodriquez. Can I see some ID?"

Again Darcy handed over her badge.

Unlike the first man, Chris took his time examining her ID before handing the badge back. "Have you seen Frank Muñoz? He's head of security. Been trying to reach him all morning."

"Not today." Nor did she care to. One encounter sufficed for a lifetime. "I just heard you yelling for Munoz on my office line."

Chris flipped open his cell phone. "What's your office extension?"

"I wasn't in my office but a sector of IT. The extension there is 1318."

His head bobbed up and down. "Okay. Explains the mistake. Muñoz's is 1319." He looked her over. "Randolph hired you to audit the laser project, right?" Without waiting for an answer, he asked, "So you have nothing to do with catching our thief? For that matter, do you even know about him?"

"If I answer, I breach security."

He pointed a finger at her. "You're good."

"However, now that I know about an intruder, tell me what I've missed."

A smile crossed his face. "What's your clearance level?"

"Bit late to ask, don't you think?"

"Still."

"Five."

His brows shot up. "Five?"

"What security level gives you access to this floor?"

"Five." Chris laughed. "I see what you mean. If you didn't have the proper clearance, you wouldn't be standing here right now."

"Precisely."

"Like your style, McClain." He glanced at his phone. "Thought that might be Muñoz, but no." He unlatched a metal door but didn't go in. "Kevin, keep trying to raise Muñoz," he said as he ushered Darcy inside. "About our intruder, the first time the asshole—excuse me—stole from us, he ripped off five

CR2 lasers and enough parts to build several more. CR2 is our YAG laser, in case you didn't know."

"What'd he steal today?"

"Last night," he said. "Got here this morning and first thing I discovered was a shortage of CR3 components. I knew that couldn't be right because we replenished CR3 inventory two days ago. Stocked enough parts to manufacture thirty units. Now I'm down to twenty-five. The CR3 is our ruby laser."

"So he can build five units."

"Not yet. As it stands, he can't even build one. In order for the laser to be fully operational, it requires a nervous system and a brain. The minute I noticed the basic parts missing, I entered a special password into the system and recoded all of the nerve and brain components. These parts are kept in a different location for security reasons. If he does manage to steal them, he still can't complete a CR3 without the schematics. Should he attempt to download them, the computer is programmed to shut down, which automatically dumps the information. We can reload later. Backup drives are in the main vault. No one gets in there. He won't succeed like he did with the CR2."

Famous last words. "What does a CR3 do?"

Chris smiled. "Vaporizes. Human flesh, steel, anything you can dream up."

"What does the laser do in a military capacity?"

"If I told you . . ."

Another Zach. "I've heard the line before. Do you think the thief's a man?"

He made eye contact. A frown creased his brow. "As opposed to a woman?"

No, a eunuch. Patience, McClain. "Yes, a woman." Al, for instance, but Darcy didn't voice her suspicion.

He seemed cagey. "Maybe, but I'm more inclined to think our thief's a man."

"Oh? Why?"

"Because stealing a CR2 takes . . ." He must've thought better of his answer, because he finished with, "Trust me. The thief's a man."

Trust me. One of her least favorite phrases. Always made her antennae go up. "Is Zach Larson capable of building the lasers you mentioned?"

He fidgeted. "Hell, yes. He helped design them. In conjunction with Randolph. But the initial plans came from Zach."

"What about Al?" She wondered when he would halt the interrogation.

"She knows more about lasers than most people give her credit for."

Darcy was about to call him on this when he said, "If you're dead set on nailing a woman for the crime, I'd focus on her."

She resented the accusation but let the comment go. She wanted the facts, not a debate. "So you think Al could build a CR2 or a CR3?"

Chris paused. "With a little help, sure. She's buds with a lot of the techies in manufacturing. She'd have to buy their silence or threaten them, but come to think of it, she's good at both." He snickered, a poor attempt to make light of a serious allegation. "And, of course, there's her following. Loyal fans who'd do almost anything for her, especially when she could fire them if they didn't do what she orders."

Darcy watched him closely, interested in his reaction when she asked her next question. "What about Martin Hamilton?"

His eyebrows shot up. "Sure. Guy's a scientific wonder. He could build anything he set his mind to."

Another suspect? "What time did you leave Colton last night?"

A broad smile. "Me? Seven-ish. Lot of prep work to complete prior to inventory."

"And you arrived at what time this morning?"

"Six sharp. Am I a suspect?" The prospect seemed to amuse him.

"Better yet, can you build a CR3?"

He screwed up his face. "Good point. Strike me off your list."

"I'd like to see the parts department."

He waved her forward. "You've got the proper clearance, so follow me."

Chris skirted the assembly lines, headed down a narrow passage, and stopped outside a locked door. He slid his card key into the slot above the handle and held the door for her to pass first. She stepped inside, taken aback at first by the vampire seated behind the counter. Then she remembered Halloween was less than a week away.

"Kevin," said Chris, "this is Ms. McClain, our security consultant."

"Where's your costume?" He sneered at her with blood-stained fangs, although his teeth weren't as intimidating as his body piercings and his tattoos.

She answered with her own question. "Bit early for Halloween, isn't it?"

"Sure is," said Chris, "but with Randolph gone, Al moved the company party up by a week because she has plans for Halloween. Starts at five in the cafeteria, if you're interested." He unlatched the door to the stockroom.

"Thanks. Why aren't you in costume?"

"I am. I'm me." Chris walked the aisles of shelving. "We never locked up our stock until two years ago when an employee developed a fetish for SCA lenses."

"Which are?" Her gaze roamed the inventory.

"UV lens filters for another product of ours. You can screw an SCA onto a camera just like a lens protector. Lost hundreds."

"Some people will steal anything."

"Amen." He walked to the end of the hall. "Here we are. Both sides of this row are dedicated to CR3 parts. Stay as long as you like. I want to check with Kevin, see if he located Muñoz. Be back in a few. Not saying you would, but don't take anything. All parts contain a sensor that will sound the minute you exit the building." He started to leave.

"Wait. Are the sensors easy to remove or disarm?"

"No. They're embedded into the construction material and then activated after manufacturing. They remain activated while product is in inventory. On shipment day we disarm the sensors just as the products leave our dock. How the hacker disarmed them is beyond me." He disappeared.

Alone, Darcy opened cardboard boxes, studied the contents, and returned them to their respective places. Nothing but shelf upon shelf of nuts, bolts, and metal components that resembled nothing she had ever seen before. She picked up a conical section of steel. Something white slapped her arm and fell to the floor. She put the part back into its carton and then stooped to retrieve the object.

"Find something interesting?"

Darcy shot up as if someone had stabbed her with a hot poker. Chris stood in the aisle. He reached around her. "Forgot my cell. Hey, what's that in your hand, and where did you find it?"

She heard the apprehension in his voice. "Latex glove. Inside a cone."

Chris stepped closer. "Which one? Show me."

She pointed to the lower shelf, taken aback by the urgency in his voice.

He pushed her aside and mumbled an apology. "One, two,

three. Shit. Should be five. Short two. Freaking A, he's building a brain."

"He? Who? The hacker?"

"Yes." Chris broke into a run.

Darcy ran after him.

Outside a closed door, he skidded to a stop. His shoulder whacked the metal frame. He swore, fumbled for the handle, and yanked open the door. "Kevin! Kevin, how many people are working inventory?"

"Six. Why?"

"No one goes in or out of the stockroom until I find Muñoz." He looked at his watch. "And no one clocks out without my permission. Understand?"

"Yes, sir."

Chris charged down the hall to his office and grabbed his phone. "Where in the hell is Muñoz?" He paced the small room, the receiver to his ear. He hit redial.

"What did he steal?"

"Told you. Parts to build a brain." He rubbed a hand over his face as if trying to pull himself together. "Relax, Chris. The jerk needs schematics. Ain't no way he'll get them. No friggin'-ass way." He slid into the chair in front of his PC, the phone cradled between his shoulder and ear while he typed in his password.

In seconds a menu of CR3 schematics materialized on the screen. He scrolled to one and punched Enter. A tightly woven network of gray and black lines crisscrossed the monitor. He duplicated the procedure with a number of other files. "Thank God." Chris set his phone down. "Nothing's missing."

Muñoz broke into the room. "Heard our hacker's up to his old tricks."

"Where have you been?" Chris asked with an edge to his voice. "I've been calling all over the place."

"I'm here now."

Chris frowned. "Who told you our hacker broke in again?"

"Kevin." Muñoz finally noticed Darcy. His dark, bushy brows dived to an angry *V*. "What's she doing here?"

"Talking." Chris looked from Muñoz to Darcy, a perplexed expression on his face.

"If you'll excuse us, McClain. We've business to discuss." Muñoz shoved her from the office, one hand clasped on her shoulder and the other pressed to the small of her back. He shut the door with a bang.

Darcy twisted the handle. Locked. Fuming, she walked briskly to the elevator and rode to the fourth floor. How dare he treat her this way, especially in front of Chris? She strode into her office, took a seat at the computer, and typed in Chris's password. Worked on the first try.

A sea of lines filled the display. "Hard to believe something like this was used to build anything." She scrolled through the line items. For a long time, she sat motionless, her eyes fixed on the monitor, seething about Muñoz. Her thoughts drifted to the cracker, whom many had already dubbed The Holiday Hacker. "Well, you're too early for Halloween."

Sunlight streamed across the tile.

Darcy swung her feet onto the desk, her eyes glued to screen, and sipped cold coffee. In the lower right-hand corner of the terminal, the schematic that blanketed the display faded from black to a chalky gray. Her feet hit the floor, and she leaned in closer, her nose inches from the monitor. The solid lines fractured into a thousand segments and gradually began to disappear, pixel by pixel. For a split second, she stared in total disbelief as something gobbled up the lines. She lunged for the telephone and dialed.

"Chris, McClain here. You near your computer?"

"Sure, why?"

"Something strange is happening. I accessed your file—"

"You what? You can't breach security, McClain. You can't go around stealing passwords."

Muñoz yelled in the background. "Tell her I'll have her fired!"

"Shut up and listen," she said. "While we yack, the CR3 schematics are disappearing before my eyes. One pixel at a time."

"What? Quick. Hit Escape. Get back into the menu."

Above her own typing, she heard him pounding keys. "Done."

"What do you see?" Chris asked.

Her pulse rate shot up. "No change."

Silence.

"Chris, are you still there? Chris?"

"Page Angelo!" Chris screamed into the receiver. "Now. I'll try to shut him down. Hurry."

The tension in his voice made her heart quicken. She hit the disconnect button and dialed the operator. "This is an emergency. Page Angelo Basini. Hurry."

Her door flew open. Muñoz barged in with Angelo steps behind.

"Move!" Muñoz shouted.

She leaped out of her chair, and Angelo slid into her seat. For a long time, the only sounds in the room were rapid key clicks. The noise stopped.

Angelo smacked the keyboard with both palms. "Son of a bitch!" he yelled. "Asshole locked us out. I can't kill the system. He's stealing every goddamn schematic right before our eyes."

Muñoz looked over Angelo's shoulder. "Shit. He's on this floor. Larson's office."

Their horrified expressions propelled Darcy into a run. She sprinted into the hallway and down the corridor, Angelo and Muñoz close behind her. She drew her 9mm and slowed outside Zach's door. "Stay in the hall. Both of you."

Muñoz grumbled a response but didn't obey. He stuck close to Darcy as she leaned against the frame and peered into the dark room. She heard only silence, so she reached in and flipped a switch. Light flooded the empty suite. "All clear. Muñoz, check Al's office."

"I give the orders around here, not you, McClain."

"Suit yourself."

Angelo was about to open his mouth, probably to tell one—or both—of them to cool it, when he looked past Darcy. His eyes widened. "Hey! Stop!" he yelled.

Darcy spun.

A figure cloaked in a white sheet burst from Al's office and dived into the elevator.

Darcy sped past Muñoz toward the stairwell and descended the steps two at a time. Behind her Angelo followed. "He jumped on the south elevator, right?"

The thud of their footfalls almost drowned out his answer. "Yes."

She remembered the south elevator went directly from the fourth floor to the first, so she didn't bother to search the other levels. At ground she tugged open the heavy metal door. A crowd had assembled in the lobby, their excited chatter adding to the tension-charged air. Two security guards with guns drawn stood near the elevators. She elbowed her way through the noisy gathering to a large muscular man at the front.

"You McClain? The security consultant?" said the uniformed guard.

"Yes." She showed her badge.

"Tom Benevides," said the guard.

Darcy scanned the crowd. "Where's Muñoz?"

"Fourth floor. He radioed. Gave us the lowdown. He's staying up there in case the guy goes back up."

Her suspicions grew. "Why would he?"

"The guy keeps hitting the pause button, so the elevator travels up and down between the first and fourth floor but won't open at either one. At the moment he's headed our way. He can play this game all day. Doesn't matter to us. We've got men on both floors, every exit, and everywhere in the building. He's going nowhere."

"Incoming!" someone shouted.

Benevides cocked his Smith & Wesson. "Jim. Denny. Heads up."

The elevator chimed, and the doors opened. A ghost shot from the enclosure. In his haste he tripped on his sheet and crashed to the floor. Inky globes stared up at them through the slits in his disguise. A muffled objection filtered from underneath the costume.

"Stand up, and no funny stuff." Denny aimed his firearm at the sheeted figure.

The gawking throng moved closer, and the low hum of speculation grew louder. The ghost tossed off his costume. A brief, stunned silence preceded the chorus of startled cries. No one appeared more shocked by the entire ordeal than Martin Hamilton.

12

Martin Hamilton was their mystery man. The murmur of questions from the astonished crowd reverberated throughout the lobby.

Denny holstered his Colt. "Get up. You've got some explaining to do."

Martin scrambled to his feet and tore at the sheet clinging to his arm. "*I* have some explaining to do?" He thumped his chest with his finger. "Me? I think you have that reversed, buddy. You owe me an explanation. And make it good, because no one treats me this way. No one."

Benevides took charge. "What were you doing on the fourth floor?"

"None of your business."

"Why don't we talk in private?" Darcy motioned with her

head to the curious crowd loitering in the entry, a hundred pairs of inquiring eyes trained on the spectacle.

Benevides nodded. "I see what you mean. There's a conference room down the hall. Come on, Martin."

"I have no idea what this is about," said Martin, his tone terse, "but I won't say another word until I speak to Al or Zach."

"Jim, contact one of them. We'll be in the R&D room. And Denny, tell them to get back to work." Benevides pointed to the gawking workers. "I don't want Al showing up with this crowd loitering in the entry. She'll flip out." He escorted Martin down the long corridor. Darcy and Angelo brought up the rear.

Martin stopped in midstride. "Darcy, you strike me as a straight shooter. What in the hell's going on?"

"Muñoz won't appreciate interference," Benevides cautioned her.

Martin turned to Benevides and shook his head in disgust. "I know your boss is a jerk, Tom, so I can't blame you for protecting your ass, but someone please tell me what's going on."

"I'll do the talking and, if necessary, take the heat," said Darcy.

Benevides looked skeptical. "Well, okay."

Martin sighed. "Finally, someone with balls."

Benevides scowled. As she passed him to enter the room, he said in a soft voice, "Hope you can defend yourself."

"What?"

"Nothing."

She chose the chair at the head of the table with Martin to her left and Benevides on her right. Angelo lingered in the doorway. "I've never been one to dance around an issue," Darcy began, "so I won't start now. Martin, what do you know about Colton's cracker?"

Benevides's eyes widened. "Who told you?"

She shrugged off the comment. "Martin?"

"Had a feeling this had something to do with him." He reclined in his chair. "A month ago, Randolph said someone had stolen CR2 parts and downloaded schematics for this particular laser. He told me to keep watch and report anything suspicious. I questioned him about the problem, but he wouldn't go into detail. Said he'd fill me in when the time was right and not to discuss the matter with anyone, especially Al."

Angelo spoke up. "Approximately ten of us knew from the beginning."

Ten? And Zach had made the breach sound like a well-guarded secret? "The beginning being when?" Darcy asked.

"Labor Day weekend. Far as I know," said Angelo.

"Which ten?"

"Muñoz, Benevides, Denny, Jim. I'll make a list."

"Thanks. Be sure it's complete and at your earliest convenience."

Benevides shook his head.

"Is there a problem?" she asked.

"No," he mumbled.

"Good." Heat hissed from the vents. Darcy slid off her jacket, and Martin's gaze moved to the holstered Browning. "Martin, what were you doing on the fourth floor?"

Fixated on her 9mm, he said, "I'm working on a project for Al. Something she wants kept secret."

"Secret from whom?"

His gaze roamed over each of them before he answered. "Zach."

"Why? They're partners."

"He'll consider it frivolous and kill the project without even a cursory glance at the data. Check her in-basket. You'll find my proposal. Worked all night on the darn thing."

"When Angelo shouted at you to stop," she continued, "you hopped on the elevator. Why?"

Martin chuckled.

"What's so funny?" Benevides said. "This is a serious matter, in case you haven't noticed."

"Ease up," said Darcy. "Well?"

Martin laughed. "Seems childish. Downright stupid now. Every year I refuse to wear a costume to Colton's Halloween party. Every year I get flack. For once I jump into the spirit of the holiday and look what happens."

"I'll attest to the costume thing," said Angelo.

"We have a contest," Martin explained. "Identify the person wearing the disguise. I wanted to fake everyone out. They'd never guess it was me because I don't fall for this kind of crap. I ran from Angelo to protect my identity."

Benevides raised his eyebrows in disbelief and grunted.

"Told you. Sounds stupid even to me." Martin plucked lint from his jacket.

"Less than an hour ago, our perp downloaded schematics to the CR3." Darcy let her bombshell settle.

He finally found his breath. "Shit. Not our ruby," Martin blurted.

The door to the conference room flew open. The handle crashed into the wall and stuck in the drywall. Everyone jumped. Muñoz's large frame filled the doorway. The veins on his meaty neck bulged, and his glazed eyes shone like black glass. "Angelo, back to work. Benevides, take Martin to my office and stay there until I return. McClain, don't move."

The room cleared in the blink of an eye.

Muñoz latched the door. "Think you're smart, don't you?"

She kept the table between them. Benevides's warning rang in her ears: *Hope you can defend yourself.* Although brief, her first encounter with Muñoz had left Darcy with the distinct feeling he loved to push women around, verbally and physically. Fine, this sucker had met his match.

"Where have you been, Muñoz?"

"Sit down." He leaned across the table.

Composed, she spoke in an even tone. "I don't take orders. Not since I quit the bureau."

"No wonder they fired you." He inched toward her.

"I resigned." She rounded the corner of the table, putting more distance between her and Munoz.

"Colton is my turf. Hear me?" His voice rose. Meanness darkened his face.

"If you don't like the way I do business, talk to Zach."

"Nepotism. I love it."

"Wrong. We're not related."

"Might as well be." Muñoz leaped at her. His chest hit the tabletop with a loud splat. He reminded her of a blowfish floundering in a tank with no water. But in that single action, he managed to catch her off guard. His massive hand tore at her shirtsleeve, restraining her long enough for his other hand to seize her wrist. He held her like a vise, her flesh burning beneath his iron grip. He yanked hard, trying to drag her over the hard surface. Only when his feet landed on the carpet did he gain any momentum. Both hands firmly on her forearm, Muñoz hauled her to the center of the table.

Strong son of a bitch. She popped the snap on her shoulder holster with her left hand. "Let go, Muñoz."

"I'll teach you to fuck with me, you bitch." He panted, winded from the capture.

"I'm warning you."

"What's a woman—"

She drew her 9mm.

"Yeah right, McClain. Go ahead. Shoot me. See if you leave the building alive."

She cracked him on the knuckles with the pistol grip. He roared in pain. Another tap on the wrist bone. He wailed.

"Works every time."

He wrenched his hand away and snared the Browning with the other. He flung the gun aside, dragged her toward him, and pinned her to the table with his enormous paunch. "When you sweat, bet you smell as good as you look." He grinned, his stained teeth revolting.

She tried to squirm free, but her efforts failed. He lowered his face to within inches of hers and licked his lips. "Yep, you smell good, all right." The strong scent of musk cologne gagged her. She coughed. The veins on his fleshy neck pulsed, the skin slick with perspiration. She shuddered, repulsed by the idea of what she was about to do, but what choice did she have? Her eyes closed, she bit him in the jugular.

He whipped his head backward. She felt his skin tear. Her gums tingled from the jolt of his pulling free. He howled like an injured animal. Darcy jumped to her feet. When he turned to face her, she kicked him in the groin. He collapsed on the floor, agonized groans spewing from his mouth. She rubbed her teeth on her shirtsleeve, retrieved her Browning, and holstered the handgun.

"If you screw with me again, Muñoz, I won't kick you in the nuts. I'll bite them off, tie a pretty pink bow around them, and hang them from my rearview mirror." She stormed from the room.

In the elevator she leaned against the wall of the compartment, took a deep breath, and exhaled slowly. Anger shook her from head to toe. The doors slid open.

Angelo paged her. He'd have to wait.

She marched into Al's office, plucked Martin's proposal off the stack of correspondence, and reboarded the elevator for the basement. Cleared by security, she knocked on Angelo's door.

"You okay?" he said. "Muñoz is an idiot."

"He's dangerous. Definitely shouldn't be head of security."

"This is why I paged you." Angelo walked out of his office and up to a computer terminal, one of dozens in his high-tech lab. "Watch." He touched the mouse. A single sentence flared from the screen, the letters bright orange on a black background. The message said: You were tricked, I was treated.

"It's on every terminal in IT. No exceptions. By the way, when you discovered our cyberpunk, he had already downloaded seventeen of the twenty schematics he wanted."

"And how many by the time you dropped the line?" She assumed Angelo's immediate reaction would be to pull the modem to disconnect the computer.

He smiled. "How'd you know I dropped the line?"

"Good assumption."

"By then he had eighteen and nineteen. Number twenty? No loss. He'll work around the inconvenience and succeed in spite of it. He's too damn smart not to."

"How do you get rid of this?" She pointed to the sentence plastered on the screen. "Can you reboot?"

Angelo typed in several commands. "I've been trying but can't close the program."

"Think he planted a virus? Maybe a logic bomb?"

"Don't know yet. Entire department's working on the problem. Won't finish inventory today."

"Any idea when we'll be back up and running?"

"Might be a lot sooner with your help, which is why I paged you." He pulled out a chair.

The compliment boosted her confidence, but hours later neither Angelo nor Darcy had succeeded in removing the cryptic message.

Angelo paced. "He's got us by the balls until he's ready to let go."

"I'm afraid you're right. I have some calls to make. Is there an office nearby? I'd prefer to stay in the area so I can be close to the command center."

"Think he'll try for number twenty?"

"No. Like you said, he's too smart and he doesn't really need the schematic, so why risk it?"

"Use my office. I'll be out here for the next couple of hours." He nodded at the document under her arm. "Martin's proposal?"

"Found it in Al's mail basket exactly like he said."

Angelo smiled. "Good."

The minute she slid into Angelo's chair, Darcy went over Muñoz's head and called Sue in the video department to request the surveillance tapes. She wanted to see who had signed in and signed out of Colton over the past six months.

"No can do," Sue responded to the request. "Not without Benevides's or Muñoz's permission."

She contacted security, exhaling with relief when Benevides, rather than Muñoz, picked up.

"Security."

"Tom, it's Darcy."

"What's up?"

"Are you alone?"

A pause. "Yes. Muñoz had an errand to run."

"Need your help."

"With what?"

"Go to the surveillance department and pull every videotape from the past six months. Then ask Sue to lock them up. No one is to check them out or view them without my permission."

"All right." His voice lacked commitment.

"You okay with that?"

"Yeah, sure."

"Thanks." She dialed Sue's extension. "Benevides gave

permission. After you hear from him, lock up the tapes until I request them. If anyone wants to see them, please call me first."

"Yes, ma'am."

She dialed the next extension. "Denny? McClain. At the end of the day, I'd like the security logs for the past six months delivered to my office."

"Someone has to okay it. Like Mrs. Colton or Mr. Larson."

"Call Larson."

"Yes, ma'am. If he agrees, I'll drop them by after inventory clears out."

At five fifteen sharp, after Darcy called Sue and requested the surveillance tapes, Tom Benevides knocked on her door to say the tapes could be viewed in the surveillance room, which was two doors down from Angelo's lab. As she headed in that direction, Angelo stepped into the hall. "The front desk said this just came for you." He handed her a square envelope.

"Thanks." Good, the Barnes recordings. But she'd have to wait to view those. Her first priority was the surveillance footage from Colton Industries. Maybe she'd get lucky and the hacker would slip up, show his face. And she wanted to see what Martin Hamilton had been doing in his free time.

Benevides waved her into the room. Video display terminals stacked four high and a dozen wide ran wall-to-wall, exposing every cranny in Colton's stronghold. The constant movement on the blue-gray screens gave her a headache. She couldn't imagine an eight-hour shift of spying. The luminescent glow alone was a visual drain.

After two tiresome hours, Darcy was surprised Benevides hadn't mentioned Muñoz's intrusion on Martin's interrogation.

The last tape ended, and Benevides flicked a wall switch. "Not even a rule infraction."

She squinted, the bright light momentarily blinding. "Do you buy Martin's explanation?" she asked, curious to hear his input.

"Now I do. I mean, everything he said checked out. Including the proposal in Al's mail basket. Thanks for bringing it down. Martin's been with the company a long time. Why rip us off now?"

Why the sudden benevolence toward Martin, she wondered, but let the issue drop.

Benevides retrieved the tape from the machine. "Any questions?"

"I investigated a case once where the intruder removed himself from a surveillance video. What I mean is—"

"I know exactly what you mean," he said. "He manipulated the software. Takes talent, but our hacker's got it. Only downside is, if he screwed with the software and cut himself off the tape, you'd see a blank frame on the video. Didn't come across any. How frustrating when we know he was in the building."

"Do we?"

He looked at her. "Do we what?"

"Know he was in the building. Maybe he downloaded off-site."

"But last night he stole CR3 parts. You can't steal them from a remote location."

She considered the statement but disagreed. Colton's hacker could've figured out a way.

"Besides, Muñoz told me the hacker used Zach's computer, which means he had to be in the building. We should check the security logs."

If he was in the building, how did he slip past the guards? She kept the question to herself. "About the logs . . . already asked Denny for them."

"Oh?" He sounded surprised.

She looked at her watch. "Actually, he should be delivering them to my office right about now."

"Want me to catch him and have them brought here?"

"Good suggestion. I might have questions you can answer." She got up to lower the room's thermostat. She wanted to remove her jacket—the warm room was uncomfortable—but had no desire to explain her torn blouse or the ugly bruise on her forearm.

Benevides replaced the receiver. "Denny's running a little late."

She inserted a USB into a computer and pulled up the footage.

He sat down. "Looks like a bank. Where'd this come from?"

"Santa Clara Savings and Loan. You're watching William Barnes sign in. Now sign out."

After five sign-ins and sign-outs, the dates and times of which were recorded along the bottom of the digital recording, she froze the frame and zoomed in. Benevides spoke her thought: "Not much help. Other than the fact he's left-handed."

"So he doesn't look familiar to you?"

"No. Should he?"

"I heard that several people at Colton bank there and thought you might be one of them."

"Nope."

Denny arrived pushing a utility cart piled with logs. Benevides wheeled it into the room. "We have a system," he said as he opened a log. "Green log, visitors' signatures. Blue, employees' signatures. Red logs, workaholics. Weekend warriors."

"How many sign-ins today?"

Benevides flipped the page. "Two hundred and ten. Want the log?"

"No, hand me the red one."

"Workaholics. Whatcha looking for?"

"A pattern. Who works late at night often and who works holidays."

He kept her company for over an hour as she pored over signatures and noted dates and times, all an act of futility.

"If we're done," he said, "I'd like to be in my office when Muñoz comes back."

"I understand. Thanks for your help, Tom. I'll return the favor if you need me."

"I appreciate the offer." He smiled. "I'd do just about anything for Mr. Colton."

"Know how you feel."

Long after Benevides departed, Darcy remained seated, contemplating something he had said. Perhaps her disdain for Muñoz clouded her judgment, but she wondered what kind of errand he was running.

13

The next morning, Darcy arrived at Colton Industries to find a phalanx of law enforcement roaming the building, from FBI agents to telecom engineers to the local police. Among the plainclothesmen crammed into the lobby mingled Gallegos and Franklin. Darcy approached them.

"What's going on?" she asked before Franklin spoke.

A frown knitted his brow. "Hoped you could tell me."

From his expression, Darcy surmised that the gig was up. Damn Zach for putting a gag order on her, but it didn't matter now, because the damage had already been done. Made her look like a liar. Would Franklin trust her from here on?

"Muñoz, Colton's head of security, has been a busy man," said Franklin. "Evidently, something's been brewing at Colton for some time." His dark eyes searched hers for an answer. "Nowhere I know can you get a warrant for a wiretap overnight, especially in New Mexico. Nothing moves that fast here but time."

Shit. "Wiretap?"

The detective glared at her. "Yes, for line traces. Muñoz claims Colton has a hacker. His solution? A full-scale sting operation."

Her face grew hot and her hands quivered, a sure sign Muñoz had tripped her anger switch. She wanted to strangle the man. When an operation got that big, word of it always got out somehow. Difficult enough to trap a cracker but nearly impossible if you broadcast the news to the general public. He would either go underground or change his strategy.

Franklin looked around the lobby. "Gang's all here. Fifty to be exact. Including Colton's chief counsel, Anthony Lucas."

Funny, Muñoz had known about the cracker since May and had shown little concern until Darcy invaded his turf. Then he went into crackdown mode. "Where's Muñoz?"

"Behind closed doors. Or so I'm told." Franklin toyed with the brim of his Stetson.

Tires squealed.

"Look out. Here she comes. Now the entire gang's here." Amusement rang in Franklin's voice. "Think I'll hang around and watch the fireworks."

Colton's glass entry doors flew open, and in burst Al. Her shrill voice sliced the buzz of discourse like the high-pitched blast of a whistle. "What in the hell is going on?"

The naive stared. The experienced scattered.

Zach barged into the lobby, his hair tousled and necktie loose. He advanced on Darcy. "Indeed, what is going on?"

"Ask Muñoz."

"Couldn't you stop him?"

He works for you, not me, came to mind, but why fuel the

fire with all these employees looking on? "He said he was taking charge, but I had no idea he'd go this far."

"So you weren't party to this—this mess?" Zach waved an arm around the room.

Condescending jerk. "No," she said emphatically.

Franklin put on his hat. "Had you clued us in from the start, we might have saved you the publicity."

Not to mention the embarrassment.

"I made a decision, and at the time it felt right." Zach walked toward Denny. "Clear the lobby," he told the guard.

The employees vacated the room.

Franklin turned to Darcy. "Why didn't you clue us in?"

"Sorry, I'm not the one calling the shots."

Al, engaged in conversation with Zach, shouted, "Hacker? What's all this talk about a hacker? Who has a hacker? Colton?" She backed away from Zach as though he had a contagious disease. "Tell me this isn't true."

"I'm afraid it is," said Zach.

"Shit, shit, shit." Al stomped her foot on the tiled floor. "How long?"

"Two months, more or less."

"Oh, fabulous. When did you plan to tell me?" Al commandeered several of Colton's guards. "Find Muñoz and escort his butt out of the building. He's fired."

Fired? Finally, someone had come to their senses, and Al, of all people.

"Come on." Al pumped the elevator's call button with her thumb, climbed aboard, and held the door with her foot. "Well, what are you waiting for, Darcy? Get moving. We have to talk to Angelo. One of you has to close the hole in our firewall. Pronto."

Zach stepped onto the elevator. Darcy followed.

Al flipped open her cell phone. "Angelo, meet me in my office. On the double. He's what?" She snorted air. "Doesn't matter. Hop on an elevator and get upstairs. Now. I'll handle things from there."

"Something wrong?" Zach asked.

"Yes, Zach. Something is wrong. That asshole Muñoz is in my office. Who in the hell does he think he is? And be careful, you are on my shit list for not informing me about the hacker in the first place."

"Randolph's call, not mine."

"To hell with Randolph. He's dead, and I'm in charge. Either you keep me in the loop or . . ."

"Or what, Al?"

Her voice softened. "It's in *our* best interests to work together."

"Amen," said Darcy. Her remark triggered glares from both. She hoped they had come to their senses about all this fighting. Darn annoying and counterproductive.

The elevator doors opened. Angelo lurked in the corridor.

Al sprang from the enclosure like a freed cat. She darted down the hall, her arms at her sides and hands balled into fists. She jingled the knob to her office suites. "It's locked." She looked astonished by the realization. "Break the damn thing down."

"Why don't you try knocking first?" Zach pounded on the door. Startled voices came from within, followed by silence.

"Okay, we tried it your way. Where are those damn guards? Here, page them." Al thrust her phone at Angelo.

"Wait." Zach stepped in front of Al. "Muñoz, it's Larson. Open up, or we'll break down the door."

As soon as Al heard the click of the latch, she forced her way in. "You ingrate. Were you out of your goddamn mind, contacting the feds?" She slapped Muñoz across the face so hard, she almost lost her balance. The men seated at the conference table leaped to their feet. The five looked more like members of the mob than the law.

"You can't treat me like this you, you bitch." Muñoz raised his hand.

Instinctively, Darcy stepped forward. "I wouldn't tangle with him. He likes to slap women around."

"Not me he won't." Al held her ground.

Munoz turned to Darcy. "Mind your own business, McClain. I forgot—you can't. You're a born snoop."

"Shut up, Muñoz," Al said. "As for you five, scram. Now." The feds hurried from the room, and Al shut the door. "Before I really lose my temper, Muñoz, what do you know about the hacker?"

A smile crossed his lips. "Randolph knew someone had been waltzing through our systems as early as Memorial Day weekend, the hacker's first appearance."

Darcy met Zach's gaze. He shrugged. "News to me. You sure, Muñoz? Angelo?"

"News to me as well," said Angelo.

"Well, it's true," the head of security barked. "He visited again on July 4, which is why we dubbed him The Holiday Hacker. Labor Day weekend, Randolph and I watched him go from browsing sensitive material to stealing the schematics for the CR2."

Incredulous, Darcy asked, "You *watched* him? He wasn't on any of the tapes I viewed."

"Maybe someone altered the video."

"Okay, but you saw him and did nothing?"

Muñoz turned his back to her and addressed his comments to Al. "Early on I tried to convince Randolph to contact the FBI. He refused. He said the company couldn't afford the publicity. Feds poking around would hurt Colton's reputation and jeopardize future DOD contracts. Hey, I told him he was making a big mistake. His reply? Simply not worth the bad publicity, especially if the hacker turned out to be some punk having a little fun and not the big threat everyone thought. No, Randolph always knew better and preferred to handle things his way." The statement dripped with sarcasm. "Instead of notifying the bureau, he hired his bud McClain to track down our cyberspook." Muñoz's officious tone ended on a caustic note.

Al placed her hands on her hips as she eyed Darcy. "Now why doesn't that surprise me? How long have you known about our hacker?"

"Since the end of September."

"Wonderful. But you, Zach, didn't know about the May break-in? Liar."

Muñoz spoke up. "He and Randolph were in cahoots. Whatever your husband knew, Larson knew. Haven't you figured that out?"

"Shut up, Muñoz!" Al screamed. "Okay, Zach, admit it. You've known since Memorial Day."

Zach avoided Darcy's piercing stare. "Okay, so I knew." Betrayed, Darcy fumed in silence.

Al stomped her foot on the floor. "Great." Then she started to pace the room. "Not our YAG. This is serious. Damn serious." She sank into a chair and wrung her hands, a pensive expression on her flawless face. "Doesn't matter now. Not since Muñoz blabbed to the entire state. At the moment I'm only interested in three things: how much damage the hacker's done, can he be stopped, and how soon." A loud sigh broke from her lips, followed by a sharp command. "All of you. Sit."

Everyone took a seat but Darcy.

"Angelo, has he done any permanent damage to our operating systems?" asked Al.

"Don't know, and frankly, I'm worried. This guy's a genius. First cracker capable of penetrating our firewalls. He could infect our systems' software, then burrow so deep into our network we may never trace him."

"Speak English. Has he planted a virus? Yes or no. And how soon can we lock him out?"

"He may have planted a virus. I really don't know."

Al swore. "Does anyone in this room know anything? What about you, Darcy, since Angelo's no damn help."

"If this guy can hack his way into your restricted databases and steal classified material, then he's obviously a pro. Therefore, he's capable of hiding his tracks. He may have planted a virus that can copy itself from program to program, one impossible to locate and erase. Or he may have planted a logic bomb, a program designed to lie dormant for months, then erupt at some future date." *There. Chew on those facts for a while, and lay off attacking Angelo.*

"Since no one will speak English, answer this question. Can you lock him out?"

"Tried," said Angelo, "but he keeps finding a hole."

"Wonderful. We're supposed to be a high-security defense contractor with encrypted passwords, guards with guns, even biometrics, but we can't keep a hacker from breaking into our computers. I told Randolph all this high-tech crap was a waste of money. You better have a plan to catch him."

Angelo leaned his elbows on the tabletop. "Won't be easy. To make the charge stick, you have to arrest him while he's in the middle of a hack."

Al let out an exasperated growl. "Can't you record his activity?"

"Piece of cake," Muñoz said. "Angelo can modify our software to alert us anytime a suspicious person logs on. The system will record his keystrokes."

Angelo deferred to Darcy, who said, "Won't work. He's too smart. He'll notice the software changes, realize we're watching, and might go berserk. He could trash your databases as revenge."

Al pressed her fingers to her temples. "Could you paint a gloomier picture?"

"Give us a day or two to hash out a plan," said Angelo.

Al pounced on Angelo. "You've known since May and have the nerve to ask me for time to work out a plan? There should be one in progress."

"Zach may have known since May, Muñoz as well, but no one told me," Angelo fired back.

"Good for you," Darcy said under her breath. "Stand up to the witch."

Al put her hands on her hips. "Do you have something to say, Darcy?"

She shook her head, eyes fixed on the flesh-colored Band-Aid that hid her teeth marks on Muñoz's neck.

"Two days, no more. As for you, what have you done to catch him, Muñoz?"

The head of security sucked in his gut and threw out his chest. "Got a warrant for line taps. I estimate it will take a couple of days to set them up, a day to track down the hacker, and two weeks at the outside till he's behind bars."

"Won't need the line traces." All eyes landed on Darcy. "Trap's been set." Their astonished stares amused her.

"What are you talking about?" Zach's irate expression pleased her.

"Since when?" asked Al.

"Days ago." This time she looked them straight in the eyes.

"Really? Wonderful." Al rubbed her hands together in glee. "Glad someone had the smarts to move on this. Why didn't you speak up earlier?"

"Ask Zach."

"Whatever." Al pushed her chair away from the table. Feet from the door, she whirled and screamed, "Shit!"

The loud curse caught Darcy off guard. Angelo dropped his pen. Zach turned to face Al.

"Shit," Al said again, this time through clenched teeth. "ABL." She waved a fist at Muñoz. "You flaming asshole. You'll pay for this."

"Which is exactly why I kept the whole hacker issue a secret," said Zach.

"What's ABL?" asked Darcy.

"The largest defense contract in the history of our government." Al spat out the words. "We won the bid for the airborne laser because our security procedures are superior, or were, to the other aerospace firms competing for the top-secret program. Now Muñoz blabbed to the Feeb, which means the DOD will yank the project and Colton will lose trillions."

"Trillions?" Darcy repeated.

"Yes, trillions, McClain. You heard correctly." Al's arched brows knitted, and beads of perspiration formed on her upper lip. The frown disappeared, and a strange serenity crossed her face. Darcy recalled something Zach had said: "When Al raves and rants, I ignore her. When she grows calm or intent, I run like hell."

Al's hand slid into her coat pocket.

"My God. She's got a gun." Angelo ducked under the table.

"Christ." Muñoz vaulted to his feet and reached for his gun.

"Easy, Muñoz." Darcy unsnapped her shoulder holster. "Al, put away the gun. It won't help your cause."

Al laughed, crossed the room to where Muñoz stood, and pointed the pistol at him. "Kneel." His knees struck the floor with a thud. She pressed the barrel to his temple. "No one fucks with me and gets away with it."

Darcy stepped forward.

"Back off, McClain," said Al. "This isn't your fight. As for you, Muñoz, start praying for forgiveness."

"You're out of your fucking mind," said Muñoz, his voice heavy with fear.

"Am I?" Al laughed as he pleaded for his life.

What a humiliating sight. A bully with a coward's heart. Darcy drew her Browning. "Okay, this has gone far enough, Al. Drop the gun."

"Hope you're a good shot."

"Drop the gun," Darcy ordered.

Al put the barrel to her head and squeezed the trigger. "Wimp," she yelled at Muñoz. "The gun's not even loaded. You're fired. Vacate the premises in ten minutes. As for you, Darcy, you're my new head of security. Do whatever it takes to catch our hacker. Just remember what a crazy bitch I can be, so don't cross me."

14

Paco stared at Bullet, sleeping contentedly on their mattress in the warehouse. He hated leaving his best friend behind, especially when he needed Bullet's support emotionally, but the risk of taking him was too great. Eye-catching and memorable, the breed drew stares like metal to a magnet. Not good when he wanted to be inconspicuous. Nor would Bullet's reaction be welcome if anyone approached their truck while Paco hid inside the gallery. Territorial, the giant schnauzer would go ballistic, drawing the attention of everyone close to his property.

Paco gently lifted the ruby laser sitting on his workbench and packed it in rigid Styrofoam before setting it into its metal carrier. The fragility of the CR3 series was the laser's downfall. He had a fix for the problem, but his job involved destruction, not repairs. Better to leave such mundane things to less creative minds.

Ready to leave, he patted Bullet's head and headed to his pickup parked in the adjoining garage bays. He strapped the metal case to the cargo bed, locked the fasteners, and covered the container with a waterproof tarp. He preferred to keep the laser inside the cab, but the steel carrier resembled a gun case. If the cops stopped him, the laser would certainly draw attention, and the officer would probably search the vehicle.

Before he took the wheel, Paco pored over the list attached to his clipboard. Good, everything accounted for. Still, he went through the items again, ticking off each as he located them in the cargo compartment. Too late for glitches.

He raised the rusted garage door and surveyed the outdoors. Ice crystals coated the dormant grass, and a full moon cast ghostly shadows on the crushed vehicles stacked high in the abandoned salvage yard. He coughed, the frosty air thick with the smoke of piñon fires. His mind wandered to the task at hand. And the dangers. He worried not for himself but for Bullet. If anything happened to Paco, who would care for him? The thought of his best friend in a shelter, or euthanized, tore at his heart.

A loud bark snapped Paco back to reality. "I'm here, boy. Come."

Bullet trotted in the open bay, his cropped ears down and his docked tail wagging at rattlesnake speed. Paco hugged him. "Be good while I'm gone." He led Bullet a safe distance away so he could back out of the garage and then put him on a sit/stay. His heart swelled with love as he watched him immediately obey.

Reluctantly, Paco backed out of the garage, shut the door, and drove south on Tramway—not the quickest route to the interstate but the safest at this hour. Less traveled and with fewer cops. He hit green lights all the way. Shortly before sunrise, he sped up the ramp to the I-40, Albuquerque disappearing in his rearview mirror. He cruised through Tijeras Canyon at fifty-five, well below the posted speed limit. Sunlight fired the slopes of the Manzano Mountains. Their rugged peaks brushed a teal sky streaked with fluffy white contrails.

He exited onto the Turquoise Trail, the long way to Santa Fe. Wasn't often he visited the town. Too many tourists in the summer. Too many skiers in the winter. Besides, the galleries and shops held no appeal. Too expensive. What brought him to the city today? Business. Creative business. In a land where artistry thrived, he had found his niche, not on canvas or in clay but as the creator of finality.

Everyone who migrated to New Mexico seemed to have capital, and Paco was no exception. Only his assets came in the form of talent and an IQ of 160. What a shame brilliance didn't guarantee happiness.

The bitter memories came pouring back. Days after his tenth birthday, his father died, and with no mother to care for him and Billy, he had no choice but to wait for someone in the family to answer his letters. When no one did, he called. Everyone was too busy to raise another child, never mind two. So the state placed him and Billy in an orphanage. Already feeling abandoned, Paco suffered through a new nightmare: the dark place. He forced the sick thoughts from his mind and dwelled on his brother.

He had prayed hard for Billy to find a good home—anything to spare him the torment Paco had endured—but soon after the adoption, Billy's new family moved two thousand miles away, and the separation was more than Paco could bear. He consoled himself with the fact his brother had escaped the horrors that had scarred Paco for life. For this he remained grateful.

The years wore on, and the constant rejection from prospective parents who found him too bright to be normal or too distant a personality turned Paco into a hostile introvert. He trusted no one. In the lonely stillness of the night, unable to sleep, his mind working overtime, he came to grips with the realization he would never have parents again. A new emotion filled the void in his heart: revenge.

He spent hours in the school library, using their new computer to plan his escape. On his sixteenth birthday, he gave himself the best present he'd ever had. In town for a field trip, he strayed from the group, blended into a crowd, and boarded the right train: the coach to freedom.

For a month he kicked around the alleys of Chicago, lost, hungry, and frightened. He dug through Dumpsters for food, slept with the homeless, and stole from street vendors to eat. One day he robbed the right man. He ripped open the wallet, eager to count his take. He couldn't believe his good luck. A hundred bucks. But as much as he wanted to, Paco couldn't rationalize stealing from a priest.

He should have mailed the wallet to Father Gregory, but he had no money and his sense of morality wouldn't allow him to touch a dime of the hundred. He chuckled. After all these years, he still remembered the expression on the priest's face and the glee in his voice when he'd placed the wallet in Father's outstretched hand. Heck, Paco had no choice. The priest caught him standing on the rectory steps, bent down and trying to stuff the billfold into the mail slot on the door.

Father Gregory fed him, asked few questions, and didn't pry. "You have a home at St. Ann's for as long as you like, provided you stay in school and make good grades." Paco accepted but remained aloof, afraid to trust anyone. He studied hard, cared for the grounds, and helped Father in the church and the community. In the evenings he whiled away the hours on the office computer.

"Time you had one of your own," Father Gregory later said as he led Paco into the tiny dining room. On the table sat several boxes wrapped in red bows. "Happy birthday."

The following year, Father put Paco on the payroll. With the money he treated himself to the latest electronic gizmos, which won him the nickname Gadget-head. New technologies fascinated him and gave him a purpose.

In his senior year in high school, he won a scholarship to St. Mark's College. It was a bittersweet day for him as he waited on the platform for the train to arrive, his arm around Father's shoulders and eyes leveled on the sad, wrinkled face of the only person who had ever cared about him. The breeze ruffled the priest's gray hair, and his hazel eyes shone with tears—that memory would forever be etched in Paco's mind.

"Bless you, my son." Father hugged him goodbye.

Paco swallowed hard, the lump in his throat about to choke him. It was the most emotion he had felt in years. He boarded the northbound without looking back, not knowing he would never see Father Gregory again.

Now, he yanked a tissue from the box on the truck's console and wiped the tears trickling down his cheeks. He still missed the padre.

On the outskirts of Madrid, he steered to the shoulder of the road and climbed out to stretch, as well as gather his thoughts and his emotions, so he could prepare himself for the task ahead. This was where he always watered Bullet. He smiled at the thought of Bullet prancing along the greenbelt, exploring new smells, searching for the perfect pee spot, and then leaving new scents of his own. He slid behind the wheel and drove on, the window cracked open to clear the veil of condensation that blurred his windshield.

Minutes later he exited at Cerrillos and crossed over the I-25. At Beckner he pulled into the right-hand lane and steered into the outlet mall's vacant lot. Parked far from the entrance with the nose of his truck facing incoming traffic, he hooked a crazed mirror over his steering wheel, smeared a thick layer of reddish-brown cream over his entire face, and wiped off the excess. Next, he applied bushy eyebrows and a mustache. He hated them. The hairs tickled his nose, and the spirit glue made him sneeze, but today's event required maximum coverage. Lastly, he added a few finishing touches to his makeup and pulled a gray wig onto his head.

A van entered the lot. It stopped abruptly near a construction site on the fringe of the mall, and four men came out. Music blasted the frosty morn. Paco checked the time. The mall didn't open until ten, and some eagle-eyed worker might report him as a suspicious person, so he shifted into gear and threaded his way through traffic to the Plaza.

He cruised past the shops and restaurants that dotted the thoroughfare. The rancid smell of burnt grease snaked its way through the ventilation system. He opened the passenger's window to clear the air. A cold breeze laden with spicy piñon floated into the interior. He slowed as he neared the intersection, cruised through the yellow light, and crossed over the Santa Fe River.

After parking in the first available space he came to, Paco fed the meter and started up Alameda, limping slightly. The leg hurt. Blasted cold. He kept to the sunny side of the street, avoiding the shadows of the massive cottonwoods that flanked the riverbank. The drone of vehicles dropped several decibels as he hiked the gradual incline to Canyon Road. Ahead, a small group of people chatted and sipped from Starbucks cups. He flipped up his collar, not to ward off the sharp wind but to hide his face—a reflex.

At this time of year, the gallery-studded street lacked the allure of spring when lilacs in bloom draped adobe walls and drooped over carved gates. Although they were long gone, he could still smell their sweet perfume. Spring seemed a lifetime ago. In the summer the streets hummed with tourists and locals as they meandered from one art show to the next. In the fall the chamisa blossomed. All beautiful, but he loved Christmas best: adobes warmed by the ever-present piñon fire and thousands of farolitos outlining the rooftops and bordering the streets. A magical season.

Today the monochromatic landscape had begun to melt, revealing patches of blue, yellow, and red. Artificial, all of it. Retailers called the metal forms yard art. Paco called them a poor substitute for real flowers.

Ahead, the gallery popped into view. He walked slowly past the adobe, which looked no different than it had on his last visit weeks ago—an old home converted into a fine arts establishment. A white picket fence enclosed the front courtyard, the garden a mixture of browns and black. Over the gate bowed a nude tree, its branches arching to a cloudless sky. On one limb a cluster of dried leaves rustled in the soft breeze. In the center of the courtyard, the twisted vines of a dormant lilac choked a concrete Neptune placed among dead monarda. Water pooled on the flagstones at the feet of a kinetic sculpture, the focal point of the garden.

Through the tall glass panes of the hundred-year-old structure, Paco saw vivid pastels and showy flowers, the canvases dwarfed by life-sized statues. He bent forward. The freshly painted sign nailed to the fence post served as an invitation to a showing of two new talents: Melanie Skillman and Selma Colton. "Join us from 5:00 to 8:00 p.m."

A green Kia approached from behind him. The sedan pulled into the dead-end street alongside the Cloverdale Gallery, and a blonde climbed out. Paco recognized Melanie from photos taken at various art shows but had never met the woman—nor did he care to. The less people knew about him, the better, and thankfully Selma could keep a secret, so his identity was safe with her. He averted his gaze and moved on, his head low as he passed Geronimo Restaurant. Two men unloading cartons called out greetings. He waved his reply.

Initially, he'd planned to arrive in Santa Fe in the afternoon, but an unforeseen complication required a second inspection of the stakeout site before he arrived at the gallery. If the Cantfield home on Acequia Madre had sold and someone now occupied the house, then he could flush months of hard work down the drain. He couldn't risk being seen loitering near the back of the gallery. Someone might become suspicious and call the police. He sighed. He could only control so much.

As he neared the corner, his pulse rate shot up and increased with every step. The muscles in his body tensed. He held his breath as he drew closer to Cantfield compound, a four-lot family homestead. Years ago, old man Cantfield sold the back two tracts to art galleries, one of which was the Cloverdale Gallery. On the corner of the two front parcels stood the original Cantfield home, and adjacent to the house Cantfield had built a three-car garage. The doorless bays faced the back of the Cloverdale Gallery rather than the street.

Paco saw the signs first. One bore the realtor's name with "Sold" in red. The other warned, "Private Property, No Trespassing." He surveyed the area as he walked up the road. The upscale neighborhood lay silent, dormant like winter. In a bold move, he mounted the steps to the front porch of the Cantfield home and peered into the picture window. No curtains. No furniture. Elated, he felt his heart skip a beat. Sold but not occupied.

He crept down the side drive that ran the length of the house until he reached the enclosed patio at the back. Through the wrought iron gate, he noticed paint cans, buckets, and an assortment of trash stashed in one section of the yard. Cleanup crew.

He crossed from the corner lot to the adjacent weed-infested tract where the three-car garage stood. Inside the open bays, he moved deeper into the shadows and studied the abutting parcel that housed the Cloverdale Gallery. All appeared quiet—too early for any activity—so he continued down Acequia Madre, looping back to Canyon Road, where he searched for a pay phone.

The Realtor, Monet Waverly, answered on the first ring. "Who is this?" she asked for the second time.

"Supervisor for the cleanup crew at the Cantfield place."

"Oh yes, hi."

"We're scheduled to clean the house this afternoon."

"What?" Her high-pitched response almost deafened him. "The house should've been cleaned last week. The new owners are moving in Monday morning."

"Sorry, ma'am. Must've got our wires crossed."

"Whatever. How soon can you finish the job?"

Paco paused. "Tomorrow."

"You have the key, right?"

"Yes."

"Good. Just get it done."

Paco hung up and dialed the gallery. The minute Melanie answered, he delivered his canned message about a family emergency and immediately broke the connection. By the time he retraced his steps to his parked truck, she would probably be on her way home.

He fired up his Ford and cruised Canyon Road, surprised and dismayed to see two vehicles parked in front of the gallery. Why was she still there? He pulled to the curb. Fire burned in his stomach. He swallowed an antacid, the short wait grueling on his raw nerves.

Melanie stepped onto the narrow portal, overlapped her coat, and wrapped her arms across her chest. Her head low, she rushed to her Kia. Tires squealed, and the car zipped by Paco's truck. He watched the vehicle disappear in a blur up Canyon Road before he pulled out onto the lane that led to Cantfield's vacant house. He drove past it to the lot next door and backed his truck into the open three-bay garage. Engine off, he waited to be sure Melanie didn't return. Working in broad daylight was dangerous, but he had no other option.

Paco thought about Bullet, safe in the warehouse—at least safer than in their apartment. Cops had arrested Phil again for cooking dog meat after a neighbor had complained of seeing a strange carcass in the trash. How many times would he beat this rap?

The minutes ticked into the half hour. The sky grayed. He removed his disguise, swabbed his face clean with makeup remover pads, and snapped on latex gloves. Over them he slipped on a pair of leather ones.

With a daypack slung over his shoulder, he gathered his invention into his arms as if it were a month-old baby and cut a path through the chest-high weeds, cringing as the crisp grasses crackled with his every move. Although faint, the rustling noise sounded loud enough to alert the entire neighborhood. Something wet hit his bare neck. Snow. Shit, bad timing. Maybe it wouldn't stick. After all, the weather had been unusually warm.

On the portal he shifted the ruby laser to his other arm and whacked the metal door of the gallery with gloved knuckles, as he had numerous times before. It creaked open.

Selma, her bare shoulder against the jamb, hip jutted to the left, surprise written on her beautiful face, then amusement. He never read her right, so he never tried.

Firelight from the kiva backlit her shapely frame and warmed the scent of citrus. The fragrance, one he knew well, captured his senses. He fought the urge to pull her into his arms. That too he had done more times than he could count. Only she managed to wipe away the pain and bitterness of the dark place. Only she could draw him out of that hell and make him feel normal.

But as life would have it, Selma broke the spell. She furrowed her black brows in a manner that reminded him of the one person in life he despised the most. *Good,* he thought. Made the nasty job easier to do.

"What are you doing here?" she asked.

He moved closer to her, the turmoil in his brain building as his thoughts swung from reality to fantasy. Sometimes he could barely separate the two.

"Come in," she said. "You must be cold. I'll put another log on the fire. What's that thing you're hauling around? Looks heavy." Talk broke the anger building within him, but too much talk made it difficult to focus on the task at hand. Her soothing voice, if it continued, would win him over, stopping him from going through with his plans. *Stop.*

"Actually, I'm glad to see you," she rattled on. "Put your stuff down. Sit next to me." She slid onto the *banco*, her body stretched full length on the bench, black stilettos propped on the edge of the fireplace. He eyed the six-inch heels and wondered why women inflicted such cruelty upon themselves, all in the name of fashion. "Come on. Sit."

The command sliced through his ruminations. He placed the laser on the telephone stand, tested the table for sturdiness, and lowered his backpack to the tile. "Awfully hot in here." He eased his frame to the cold floor, his back resting against the *banco*.

"I love hot." She ran the tip of her tongue over his ear.

A chill slithered up his spine. "I can see why. You aren't wearing much."

A salacious smile sprang to those ruby-red lips. "Take off your gloves."

"My hands are cold."

"Show doesn't start for two hours. Can you think of anything to kill time?" Her black fingernails dug into his arm.

His heart raced. "Where's Melanie?"

"Family emergency, which is really bad timing. The call came a few minutes ago. I hope she makes the drive to Los Alamos without any problems. Heard it started to snow on the Hill about an hour ago."

Good. The call had worked. "I'm sure she's driven in snow."

"But we were drinking while we set up. Only a few glasses of wine, but Melanie's a lightweight. We planned to nap before the show."

"She'll be fine."

Selma moved closer to the fire. Orange flames flickered from the kiva. Their brilliance danced off her black hair and made her porcelain skin radiant. Why someone as beguilingly beautiful as she was had set her sights on Paco mystified him, yet the opportunity had proved a godsend. He cast sidelong glances at her, wanting desperately to numb his feelings with booze or drugs, but such a decision could prove fatal. It took every ounce of strength he owned to suppress his desires. Afraid he'd surrender, he blurted, "Strip for me."

She slid off the bench, a seductive slide, and an eager smile sprang to her full lips. "Now you're talking, big guy." Selma always belted out the same song, but every time, the melody sounded as it had the first time. He gasped when the skimpy black top that barely covered her small firm breasts hit the Saltillo tile. No man could ever tire of a body as exquisite as hers. She giggled. "You okay?"

He cleared his throat. "I will be."

"You always say that." She unzipped her skirt and wiggled out of the leather mini, revealing black lace panties and a black garter belt. "Everything?"

"No." The word shot from his mouth. "I'll remove the rest."

"With your teeth, I hope?"

He averted his gaze, purposely avoiding eye contact. Every inch of him burned with passion, a sensation he'd thought dead until he met her. He unzipped his backpack and removed two pieces of rope corded from red silk.

She extended her arms. "Kinky. Okay, guard, tie me up." She stuck out her tongue and ran the tip of it over her lips, her eyes fixed on the ties encircling her wrists. "Silk, no less. Classy. And next to black, you know how much I love red." She kicked off her heels. One shoe crashed into the wall and spun across the slick floor. "What are the metal hooks for?"

"You'll see." He tugged gently on Selma's bound wrists, drawing her toward a wall where two sculptures once hung. He tied her to the large picture hooks bolted to the drywall and tested the silk cords. "That should hold you."

A smile broke on her face. She winked. "You really are kinky today."

"The fun's just beginning." He removed two scarves and a handkerchief from the pack. "I'm going to gag you."

"You'll miss those delightful squeals."

"I'll suffer in silence."

"Suit yourself." She laughed. The throaty giggle percolated from the depths of her being. A sound he had come to love. The realization triggered a strange conflict, a battle between his emotions and his pledge for revenge. Never had he questioned his decision. Until now. *Hurry*—the words blared in his brain—*or all is lost*. His gaze devoured her flesh. The ache intensified. *Concentrate. Stay focused.*

"Hey, big guy, what's the holdup?"

Funny how Selma could cast a spell and break it all in the span of a nanosecond. "Open your mouth."

"Yes, master." She winked salaciously.

He stuffed the handkerchief into her mouth. Over her lips he tied a scarf. Her dark eyes shone with anticipation. Not a shred of fear. For that he rejoiced. He wanted it to be as painless as possible, which was why he opted against duct tape. "Be patient, okay? I'm a bit nervous, even though I've played this fantasy over and over again in my mind. Can I blindfold you?"

A nod.

His hands shook as he placed the scarf over her eyes, blocking the trust that shone through. A chill coursed through him. He had to finish the job before he bungled the opportunity. Oh God, how he wanted to keep her, to savor their time together, but . . .

He unpacked the laser. It felt lighter this morning. Now it weighed a ton. He uncapped the lens protector, dialed in the strength, and chose his focal point. The red LED flashed and then pulsed as the power surged to the indicated level.

Selma groaned. A guttural protest.

"Be patient. I'm taking off my clothes."

The laser's palpitating light mesmerized him as his brain crossed that invisible threshold from sanity to a world where few went or should ever go. Heads flew at him, decapitated spooks who'd haunted him all the days of his life. In a catatonic trance, he aimed the ruby-red dot at her forehead and tapped the Fire switch. An angry burst of energy shot from the laser and cored a minute hole in her skull. Her brain ruptured. Her knees buckled, and she convulsed. With every twist of her body, a sickening swish filled the room as her stockinged feet dragged across the concrete floor. She sagged.

Silence filled the room, the sound welcome.

Reality penetrated his fantasy. She was dead. The finality consumed him. He fought off the tears that pricked at his eyes, but unsuccessfully. They spilled onto his cheeks, wet his shirt, and then completely clouded his vision. His hands shook uncontrollably. He raked his fingers over his face, clawing at the stream of tears with such ferocity that a ragged fingernail cut a long, fiery scratch across his cheekbone. *Get a grip on yourself. Remember the source.* The thought calmed him, reenergized him.

Refocused on the task, he increased the power on the laser's delivery system, amplifying cauterization to full intensity, and adjusted the point of inertia to prevent damage to the walls or the artwork. Holding the laser like a firearm, he made six precise, bloodless cuts: feet severed at the ankles, calves at the knees, and thighs at the hip joint. Like Ronnie, Ravel performed with surgical precision, and as always, Paco remained in awe of his inventions as though someone else had masterminded them.

He set the ruby laser on the telephone stand before he began stacking the limbs away from the torso. The odor of burnt nylon wafted up to him. A small section of Selma's black tights had caught fire. He slapped out the spark with his glove and then took a short break. The next chore required time, skill, and persistence.

Feet apart to steady himself, he aimed the laser at the base of her neck. This was the ultimate test as to how well the ruby would perform. The bright red beam traveled vertically down her body and terminated at the pelvis. After five painfully slow minutes, he managed to slice the trunk in half without creating a gusher. Blood spattered the wood, but the spillage was minimal.

He stepped forward to view Ravel's handiwork. A six-inch-wide black strip bifurcated her milky-white torso. The laser had seared a clean cut through skin, bone, and muscle, cauterizing tissue on both sides of the channel. The overpowering stench of cooked flesh filled the hot room. He stuffed tissues in his nose, adjusted the latex liners under his leather gloves, and carved up the remainder of the body into manageable sections.

After he caught his breath, he searched the back storeroom for the sculpture he had helped Selma build during his previous visits. He located the piece buried behind a stockpile of Melanie's animals and hauled the heavy sculpture to the display area. Time to create his own artwork.

15

Rhonda lived off Canyon Road on a quiet street of upscale adobes whose occupants spared no expense to protect their privacy. She seldom saw or heard her neighbors unless she wandered close to the tall compound walls that shut out prying eyes. Behind her house wound the Santa Fe River, its banks lined with giant cottonwoods. On a normal day, she could hear a pin drop in her home, but today the house bustled with activity. Flowers arrived by the van load, and delicious smells wafted from the kitchen. The hired help lingered in the dining room checking floral arrangements and place settings, working around one another as they carried out their assigned chores.

Rhonda retreated to the parlor where she lingered in front of a large pastel, a captivating one in vibrant colors, but lost in thought she didn't see Selma's work. She and her niece shared a strong bond, which was why today had to be extra special for Selma. Not your ordinary art opening, but a grand affair. So

Rhonda had done everything in her power to ensure its success. She had contacted everyone in her extensive address book as well as Selma's and invited all to stay on for the surprise party after her niece's debut show. The response had overwhelmed her.

She could just imagine Selma's reaction when the family returned to Aunt Rho's for a quiet dinner. She laughed, pleased with herself. It had taken months to organize such a gathering, especially with Selma's friends scattered across the US. Of course, Rho bought each guest a plane ticket and provided a free place for them to crash while in Santa Fe. Struggling artists and writers—never a buck to their name. She empathized, so much so that years ago she had formed a foundation to bring the gifted to the attention of agents and publicists who otherwise might have overlooked some of the best talent in the nation.

Yes, she identified with them. At one time she too was the best, at least in her estimation, but she had lacked the self-confidence and the determination to stick with her dream. If only her parents had had money or the right contacts, she told herself. When money came at a much later date, the contacts followed, but by then she had given up on the idea of being an artist and instead had purchased a partnership in the Cloverdale Gallery.

Soon afterward, she married her partner, Carson Cloverdale, a wealthy entrepreneur. She divorced him a year later. Money did not bring happiness. Instead, wealth only brought grief, just as it had caused her brother nothing but sorrow.

"Ma'am, are you all right?"

Rhonda turned. "Fine," she told her butler. "Simply admiring Selma's newest piece. A birthday gift."

"Beautiful."

Rhonda rattled off some last-minute instructions and mounted the stairs to her bedroom to shower and change.

She wanted to return to the gallery early to spend time with Selma before the crowds converged on them.

The hot shower spray eased the cold rooted in her bones. She'd never been fond of fall or winter and had often thought of moving to a warmer climate, but her ties to Santa Fe kept her here. Bare trees, snow . . . downright depressing. Just like today. Every detail had gone perfectly, except for the threatening weather. In fact, the only thing that would've made the occasion absolutely perfect was if Randolph had been alive to enjoy it. How she missed him. To some degree, Zach filled the void, but little could replace the bond between a brother and sister.

Randolph's illegitimate daughter popped into Rhonda's mind. She made a mental note to press Weaver for more details. Now with her brother gone, she felt compelled to reach out to the child to make sure she had been placed in a good home with loving parents.

Wet from her shower, Rhonda slipped into a silk robe and sat at her dressing table. She scooted the vase of flowers away from the mirror. Why had Al sent them? The card said, "A peace offering for the terrible way I acted at Randolph's memorial service." Funny, no flowers after she made an ass of herself at the reading of the will or the time . . . she dismissed the other times. Thinking about them only angered her and drained her spirit.

She chose a blue silk suit and matching blue suede boots, which she put in a canvas bag before she searched the closet for galoshes. She had learned her lesson after ruining a pair of expensive heels while walking home in an early-season snowstorm. She wouldn't be caught unprepared again.

Dressed in a calf-length wool coat and with a scarf tied loosely around her head, Rhonda slipped out the front door and strolled leisurely down the lane. The short jaunt from her house to the gallery rejuvenated her tired body. She hadn't slept well since Randolph had died. She rounded the corner at Camino del Monte, crossed the parking lot that served Geronimo Restaurant, and walked down the hill, wondering if the new owners of the Cantfield properties would finally do something about their vacant lot with the dilapidated garage. She wished they would sell the land or at least mow the knee-high weeds, which were a fire hazard in the summer.

A white limo braked in front of the gallery. Rhonda's good mood faded. With the arrival of her adversary, she could kiss peace goodbye. The vehicle's door opened, and out stepped Al decked from head to toe in . . . white? It had been years since she'd worn any color except black. The change raised Rhonda's suspicions. Everything about her sister-in-law shouted ulterior motive. She pushed the concern to the back of her mind. "Hi. Early, aren't you?"

"I wanted to be here for Selma. Help her over her jitters."

"Selma? Jitters? That'll be the day. She's the most confident person I've ever known."

"You should know. You two spend enough time together."

Rhonda ignored the comment. Her easy gait became a fast walk. She wanted to distance herself from Al, if even in a small way, but Al was right on Rhonda's heels.

"Guess I'll have to ask. Did you receive the flowers?"

"Yes, thanks." Rhonda opened the gate and hurried up the stone path to the gallery as if she could shake herself free of Al.

"I acted terribly. Forgive me. The news came as such a shock. You and Zach engaged. We've been friends a long time. I feel like I'm losing a brother."

Rhonda directed her ire at the doorknob, her grasp so tight her knuckles turned white. "Strange, the door's locked." She knocked on the window next to the massive oak doors.

"Surely you have a key."

A comforting thought sprang to mind. Technically, Al was

no longer her sister-in-law, the tie severed with Randolph's death. "It's a shame that what's technically true doesn't reflect reality," she said aloud.

"What does that mean?"

"Nothing," said Rhonda as she unlocked the door and entered the old adobe, once the grandest house on Canyon Road. Today little remained to remind visitors that this landmark had been a home. The ten-room structure had undergone a major renovation, eliminating all traces of a kitchen and bath that now served as storage. Only the adobe walls, pine floors, and weathered vigas were representative of the original building.

Rhonda paused in the living room. The poorly lit interior puzzled her. When she'd left earlier, a fire burned in the kiva, and every light in the room blazed bright. Now candlelight flickered from the *nichos* carved in the plastered walls, and the embers in the grate glowed a bright orange. The fire had died down.

"Why are we standing in the dark gawking at a fireplace?" Al had seized the opportunity to do what she did best, bitch. "It's always so damn black in here no matter what time of day. When you remodeled, why didn't you consider more windows or replace the old ones? What stinks? Do you smell that? Selma, where in the hell are you?"

A door at the back of the gallery banged.

Rhonda ran down the narrow hall to the rear of the building. Behind her Al's high heels clattered on the wooden floors. The racket drowned out any noise Rhonda hoped to hear. "Watch your step. We store art supplies in here." Her foot kicked something and sent it spinning across the warped boards.

The back door stood open. Beyond the wooden deck with its plastic chairs stretched Cantfield's weed farm and the old garage, most of the structure stolen for firewood or a more worthy cause.

"Who was it?" Al leaned closer so she could look out the door.

"I didn't see anyone. Nor could I hear anything."

"Probably a boyfriend of Selma's. You caught them, and they took off. She'll be back in time for the opening."

Took off? No—Rhonda knew differently. A professional, Selma ensured that nothing interfered with her art career, least of all male friends. Plus, she wouldn't leave lit candles or a smoldering fire unattended in a gallery with over $2 million in art. She had too much love for her craft and too much consideration for her aunt to risk a rift in their relationship if the place burned to the ground. In fact, Selma constantly bugged the city about Cantfield's weeds and the fire hazard they posed.

Rhonda threw the deadbolt and stumbled through the blackness back to the living room, the entire area dedicated to Selma's art. She sniffed the air. Beneath the stench, she swore she detected the scent of citrus, a fragrance blended for her personal use. Normally, she wore perfume on every occasion, but in her haste to return to Cloverdale, she had forgotten. Only one other person loved the scent as much as Rhonda: Selma.

Rhonda slinked along the wall to the nearest light panel. She flipped one switch after another, but nothing happened. She yanked her hand away as though she had received an electrical shock. From the moment she learned of Randolph's death, she wanted to believe that the tragedy was a horrible accident, but standing here in the murkiness, the truth hit home. He had been murdered. Now with Selma missing, worry escalated to fear.

"Oh God, no, please." Rhonda fished through her purse for her cell phone.

"What?" demanded Al. "Are you okay? Who are you calling?"

Rhonda said, "9-1-1."

"What in the hell for?" Al threw her arms over her head in protest.

Again, Rhonda sniffed the warm air. The repugnant odor Al had complained about minutes ago had grown stronger. Feeling faint, Rhonda leaned against the wall. "Hello, 9-1-1? Yes. The Cloverdale Gallery. Canyon Road. Hurry." She set the phone on the mantel before the emergency operator spoke another word and moved quickly toward her office.

"Damn it, Rho," Al stomped her foot. "What's wrong? Are you ill?"

"Something terrible has happened."

"What in the hell are you talking about?"

"She's here. Somewhere. I can sense her. Feel her." Tears welled up.

"You're making no sense."

In her office Rhonda flung open the door to a small closet and climbed onto a stepladder to reach the top shelf. She took down an oil lamp and handed a flashlight to Al.

"Good idea. Maybe we blew a fuse," said Al. "Where's the junction box?"

"In the storeroom." Rhonda rushed down the corridor to the back door. She noticed a dark spot on the floor and stooped to touch it. Whatever the substance, it had dried.

"See what happens when you overindulge your kids."

"Shut up." The harshness in her own voice startled Rhonda.

Al's eyes widened. "Well, excuse me."

"I'm trying to concentrate."

"Very well." She snorted. "I won't say another word."

Rhonda placed the lantern on the telephone stand and hunted through the drawer for a putty knife to pry open the rusty junction box. The hinges creaked.

"Hand me the flashlight."

"Here." Al handed it over.

"Tripped breaker. This should do the trick." She flipped the 110, but still no lights.

In the distance sirens blared.

"Finally." Rhonda sighed.

"Hope you have a good explanation for calling them."

"Let me worry about it." She took the lamp and headed for the front door. Halfway across the room she froze, her eyes riveted to the wall sculpture hanging opposite the kiva. She staggered backward. Red streaks trickled down the white wall. The room began to spin. The lantern crashed to the floor. She tripped over something hard and looked down. A muffled cry reverberated in the crevices of her mind. Gradually, the wail grew louder until her own voice shattered her eardrums.

"Sel . . . ma!"

16

Darcy drank in the scenery as she walked briskly up Canyon Road, excited about attending Selma's art show. The day, cold but sunny, provided perfect lighting for snapping shots with her new camera. As she neared the old adobe, she paused, baffled by all the vehicles that choked the narrow road. Rhonda must have invited half the state and then called in the police to direct traffic. At a distance this seemed to be the case, but as she neared Delgado, Darcy saw barricades and several officers holding back curiosity seekers. Maybe Rhonda had invited her movie mogul friend or the governor of New Mexico or some foreign dignitary. After all, the Coltons were connected.

She approached the cops posted behind the wooden barrier. "What's going on?"

"See some identification?"

The request piqued her interest. She produced her driver's

license. "I'm supposed to attend an art show at the Cloverdale Gallery."

"Gallery's closed for the day."

Closed? His comment stopped her. "Can someone contact Rhonda Cloverdale, tell her I'm here?"

The officers gave her a quizzical look, but one radioed someone stationed at the gallery. After a brief exchange with the person, the officer let her pass. A few feet up the hill, she glanced back. The policemen watched her. Something in their expressions triggered concern. Her thoughts drifted from dignitaries to burglary, but as she crested the rise, reality dashed her hopes of anything so minor.

Yellow crime scene tape scalloped the white picket fence and draped the compound wall. Her gut feeling told her to get ready for the worst.

"Hi." Franklin stood by the front gate, his Stetson in his hand. His tone said bad news. "It's ugly inside."

Her last shred of optimism died. Murder, in her book, qualified as the worst. "Thanks for the warning. Who?" Sadness clouded his face. She sunk her teeth into her bottom lip, yet nothing prepared her for the truth.

"Selma."

Her stomach flip-flopped. A knot formed in her throat. "How?"

Franklin looked her square in the eyes. "He mutilated her."

"Oh, no."

"If you prefer not to go in," he said in a soft voice.

"No, just give me a minute."

"Take your time. I'm out for some fresh air." He headed up the walkway to the portal.

She followed. "Who found her?"

"Mrs. Cloverdale. And Mrs. Colton." Franklin's shoulders slumped forward.

Poor Rhonda. "What a shock. Where are they now?"

"Hardy sent them home. Mrs. Cloverdale has a nurse with her."

"Who's Hardy?"

"John Hardy's my counterpart in Santa Fe. Mrs. Cloverdale contacted the police. Hardy, in turn, called me."

"You got here fast."

"Already on our way. My partner asked for an invite."

"Oh?"

"To follow a hunch." He stared off.

"If you don't mind my asking, what's her hunch?"

"A family member killed Randolph."

Before she could reply, Franklin said, "Ready?"

Darcy took a deep breath, but nothing equipped her for moments like these.

"Through here. Used to be the parlor when the Sanchez family owned the house." He ducked under the low archway.

Halogens mounted on tripods lined the perimeter of the living room. Their bright light glinted off white plaster. The floorboards creaked and groaned with their every footfall. Large canvases and metal sculptures hung on the walls, each piece given a generous space and each spotlighted, but the bulbs were dead. A slightly built man in a dark suit, two officers beside him, and a lanky Hispanic with a Canon slung over his shoulder all stopped to stare at her as she entered the room.

"We brought in lamps," said Franklin. "Power's out. Haven't located the problem. Someone's working on it. No phones either."

The odor of burnt flesh and singed hair hit her, smells Darcy recognized all too well. She pinched her nose and breathed through her mouth. An officer passed her, handkerchief to his nose. "Gets worse."

Darcy glanced around the room. "Where's the body?" She followed Franklin's gaze to the far wall. She moved slowly toward the gruesome sight, the stench of charred flesh repulsive. "Jeez." She turned away.

"You okay?" Franklin touched her shoulder.

She held up her hand. He backed off. She felt eyes upon her and composed herself, somehow mustering the strength to inspect the bizarre sculpture. Killing a person was bad enough, but mutilation? This killer had taken the act of murder to the cruelest point of all.

At first impression it appeared the "artist" had wrapped white fabric around soft objects approximately eight to ten inches in length and then attached the sections to a bed of nails. But upon closer examination, it became apparent that the white mounds were milky-white flesh with the edges seared black as charcoal, the cauterized body parts squeezed tightly against each other. Severed limbs framed the outer ledge, fingers and toes tucked behind carved sections. She felt ill and weak, all energy sucked out of her. "The . . . head?" The word stuck in her dry throat.

"Under the sheet." Gallegos motioned with a nod.

Darcy hadn't noticed the detective's presence until now. She let out a long sigh, the urge to vomit compelling.

"Fell off the sculpture," said Franklin, "according to Mrs. Cloverdale. The holes in the skull confirm her statement."

The man in the dark suit stood up. "But we aren't sure."

"Darcy, Lou Dominquez, medical investigator."

He gave her a weak smile. "The mutilation occurred post-mortem."

After death. Dear God, Darcy hoped so. Cutting her up like this was savage enough.

"And if it's of any comfort, she died instantly," Lou added.

Some, but not much. "Cause of death?" asked Darcy.

"Cerebral hemorrhage."

She baited him. "Caliber?"

Franklin, his finger poised over his phone, said, "I think you know that no gun killed her."

"Laser?"

"To be exact, a ruby laser. Had a long talk with Larson. He's in the front office. Hardy's questioning him. Now we're sure Colton's hacker is our killer."

"A solid conclusion." She stared at the sculpture. Cold. Calculating. Cruel.

"You sound skeptical."

"Keeping an open mind." *Tread lightly, McClain.* She was only an observer. Franklin and Hardy were the detectives in charge. Step on the wrong toes or say the wrong thing and they might shut her out like she had them at the onset of the investigation, although unintentionally. She wondered if Franklin would be as cooperative if she wasn't a family friend and if the Coltons didn't carry so much clout.

She stared at the gory artwork, not out of morbid curiosity but for a purpose. Clues. The sadistic bastard had created a wall hanging from a sheet of plywood approximately four feet by three feet. The person had painted the board white and hammered nails into the back of the board, spacing them, she estimated, an inch apart. "Must be over a thousand."

Franklin appeared at her side. "I'll leave that ugly task to Lou."

Darcy leaned closer to the sculpture, the scent of singed flesh revolting. "Galvanized screws, not nails," she mumbled.

"Astute observation." He texted something into his phone.

"Too many weekends in my dad's workshop. Find any fingerprints?"

"Might be some on the wall hanging. Waiting for Lou to give us the okay. In the gallery itself, not one, but we found a tire—" Franklin broke off in midsentence.

A large man with brown hair and a reddish beard entered the room. "Go on, Don, tell her. The way I see things, if she can help solve the case and put this psycho behind bars, then more power to her. I'm not after glory, only justice."

A slight smile curled the corners of Franklin's thin lips. "Darcy, John Hardy."

Hardy bowed. "So you're the PI."

"We found a tire track out back, inside the neighbor's garage," Franklin said. "Follow me."

Gladly. She needed a breath of fresh air.

Franklin paused on the porch behind the gallery to flip up his jacket collar. Large dry flakes swirled through the arid air. Gallegos and Hardy appeared on the patio. Hardy called to one of the lab boys, who looked over his shoulder and pointed to the makeshift path they were to follow. Someone had extended a string line from the portal to the crumbling garage.

"Not standard procedure for roping off an area, but the guys ran out of tape." Hardy took the lead. She tramped along behind him through the tall dead grass, breaking stride by a metal post that once supported a chain-link fence.

"The post marks the property line between the gallery's property and the neighbor's yard," said Hardy. "The fence was hauled away, from what we can tell."

"Know anything about the neighbor?"

"Plenty, but nothing that helps our investigation. Cantfields. Their house is on the corner." He pointed to the home. "He owned Cantfield's Produce off Water Street. The family fell on hard economic times and sold the home and business last week. Moved back to California."

"Is the house vacant?"

"Until Monday, when the new owners move in."

"Wonder if the killer knew?" Realtor. She made a mental note.

"Probably. It's no secret." Hardy raised his head to the sky. "The snow's stopped."

Darcy reached a section in the dirt drive where the area

had been swept clean. She stooped to study the terrain. Something sparkled in the intense sunlight.

"Tire track's in the garage." Franklin walked ahead, Hardy with him.

"Be there in a minute." She knelt to scrutinize the white blob shimmering through the watery surface of a large puddle. Her pulse rate spiked. The glittery substance looked identical to the white pearly smear she had seen on the black roofing paper from the Santa Clara Savings and Loan parking lot.

"Find something?" Gallegos hovered over Darcy.

"No, only a clump of ice."

Darcy hated keeping the truth from Gallegos and Franklin, but she was still debating whether or not it was a good idea to tell them the truth. After all, withholding prior evidence from the police could put her back in the dog house again—and shut out of the investigation.

The detective's black eyebrows shot up. "Ice? It isn't cold enough for snow to stick."

"You're right. I'm mistaken."

"Come on. The tire track's real," said Gallegos, her voice heavy with sarcasm.

Real? The word registered like a slap in the face.

A long strand of yellow tape circled a three-bay garage that had no doors. Holes in the few adobe bricks that remained near the base of the foundation emitted spears of light, the beams strangely reminiscent of those from a laser. *Hyperactive imagination, McClain.* Franklin lifted one end of the tape, and she ducked under it.

"Don't touch anything," said Hardy. "The lab boys haven't lifted the track yet." He lowered his huge frame to a crouch.

Darcy squatted between Franklin and Gallegos. The latter shot sidelong glances at Darcy, who wondered if the detective used the silent treatment as a form of intimidation.

"Funny that he missed this track." Hardy grunted and shifted his weight to his other leg. "From what we can tell, he swept his footprints off the walk leading to the back patio. He even defaced the tracks on the driveway but forgot this one in the garage. It is fairly dark in here, which could account for the oversight. Well, what do you think of our only clue?"

"As you pointed out, it's too dark in here to get a good look, so I'd be interested in reading the forensics results," Darcy said. "Assuming they're available to me." And accurate.

"Hell, yes." Hardy tapped her on the back.

Franklin offered Hardy a hand and helped him to his feet. The two men walked off toward Acequia Madre, leaving Darcy and Gallegos alone.

"Think they'd mind if I take a few shots?" Darcy uncapped her lens protector.

"Hardy's all but offered you the keys to the city, so why not take a pic or two?"

Darcy shrugged off the catty remark and took her stills. "Place smells more like a barn than a garage." The comment failed to draw Gallegos into conversation. Instead, the detective dissected a twig. Darcy framed a close-up of the tire tread. A perfect match. She sighed and pulled her camera away from her face. It was time to come clean. Catching this bastard was more important than her protecting her own ass. "Looks identical to the one at the Santa Clara Savings and Loan." That got a reaction.

Gallegos dropped the stick she was maiming. "What one at the Santa Clara Savings and Loan?"

Darcy lowered her camera and looked up to find three pairs of eyes staring at her. Franklin and Hardy had returned.

"Can't wait to hear this explanation," said Gallegos. "Withholding evidence critical to a murder investigation is a crime."

She emphasized the word "crime." "By the way, Hardy knows about Colton's hacker. I filled him in."

"You can blame Zach for all the secrecy," she said. "If anything, were the circumstances different, I might have quit the investigation, but considering the situation, I couldn't."

"Why not?" said Hardy.

"I took the case for one reason, and I'll finish it for one reason: Randolph Colton." Darcy weighed her words. She didn't want to make a bad situation worse by saying something stupid. "Sorry we started off on a bad note. I hope we can get beyond it."

"Apology accepted," said Franklin, a bit too quickly for Gallegos, who grumbled something unintelligible. "Now I'd like to know why you kept the tire track a secret even after Muñoz blew your cover."

"I had every intention of discussing the case, but if you recall, all hell broke out at Colton." The excuse sounded lame, even to her.

Franklin's dark eyes bored holes in her. Darcy prepared for a lambasting.

"At this stage of the game," Franklin said, "I'm more interested in justice than retribution."

Hardy hesitated, then agreed. "Likewise."

A vein throbbed in Gallegos's slim neck. She merely nodded.

"Now back to the tire track at the Santa Clara Savings and Loan." Franklin slid his hands into his pockets. "How'd you come across it?"

"Standing in Perriman's Field, I thought, what if I planned to shoot down a balloon? Laser or high-powered rifle. Where would I fire from? Decided to start with the tallest buildings within a half-mile radius of Fiesta Park. The Skylark Towers and the Savings and Loan fit the criteria. Security's tight at the

Skylark. Too tight to shoot from their rooftop. And the building has another drawback."

"Oh?" Hardy said.

"No parking structure. I'll explain in a minute. On the other hand, the Savings and Loan has a multilevel lot. I walked every floor but found nothing of interest until I found the track near the entrance." She recounted her find in more detail, letting them know the track was made on felt paper and not on dirt, which was why she couldn't cast it and had to send the tire track to a lab to be lifted.

Hardy frowned. "What makes you think he fired from the parking lot and not the bank itself?"

"Sunday. Bank's closed. But the biggest problem's the laser. The design is too bulky and heavy to cart to the top floor. He probably loaded it into a truck bed and drove the truck to the rooftop."

Hardy grunted. Franklin nodded. "Makes sense. Where's the evidence now?"

"I sent the tire track to a detective friend in San Francisco, who gave it to Testco Labs for analysis."

Franklin typed a note into his phone. "Your friend's name?"

"Dan Gruet. The track at the bank was a Bridgestone P225, all terrain. A best seller for them."

"Small truck or SUV," said Gallegos. "Anything more?"

Darcy nodded. "Testco confirmed the soil. Red clay and sandstone on black roofing felt."

Gallegos shook her head. "Found anywhere in New Mexico, especially around Abiquiú."

The clump of ice in the driveway came to mind. "The lab did find something unusual embedded in the clay. Some kind of a pearly white substance that glows." Darcy had their attention.

Gallegos frowned. "In sunlight?"

"Light isn't a factor. It's luminescent day or night. Testco's running additional tests, but I haven't seen a report. I thought it might be a substance indigenous to this area. Maybe white clay like caliche or some other soil."

Hardy shook his head. "None I'm aware of. Wonder if Mr. Larson can shed some light on the substance. Shame he left. I'll ask him."

The wind kicked up. Darcy moved to the back of the garage. The others followed. She used the interlude to test her hunch that the reports had been altered. "I'd like an undoctored"—she emphasized the word—"copy of the autopsy reports as well as the forensic results."

She didn't get the reactions she expected. Franklin didn't even flinch. Gallegos maimed another twig. Hardy studied the sky.

"Should I fax or scan and email them to you?" asked Franklin.

"Whatever is easiest." Darcy handed Franklin her business card with her apartment landline written on the back.

"You moved from the hotel?" Franklin asked.

She nodded. She'd bet that the "real" reports did reference the burn mark below Barnes's left earlobe, the St. Christopher medal Barnes wore, and what happened to the computer chip Gallegos found in Randolph's jacket pocket. The next hurdle was how to butter him up for a front-row seat at Selma's autopsy, but before she spoke her request, Franklin said, "I'd like something in return."

"Go ahead."

"I conducted a background check on you."

Over the years, who hadn't?

"Your expertise as a former FBI agent, not to mention your track record as an ace profiler, might help us crack this case. I'd like you to attend Selma's autopsy."

Gallegos brushed snow from her parka. "If you think you can stomach it."

Darcy dismissed the snide remark. "I'll be there."

Franklin checked the time. "Ready, Lena? We have a ton of paperwork waiting. John, good to see you. Sorry it had to be on a case."

"I'll walk you out." Hardy chatted with Franklin about the weather on their way to the front of the property.

Darcy and Gallegos brought up the rear. Her hand closed on Darcy's arm. "You'd have found us more cooperative had you been honest from the beginning."

"Not my call," said Darcy.

"I disagree. You strike me as being your own person. If you had clued us in Sunday afternoon, our lab boys could have combed the area before half of Albuquerque stomped over the rooftop." Gallegos made sure everyone heard.

"Let's go." Franklin shepherded his partner out the gate.

"Mind if I poke around a bit?" Darcy asked Hardy.

"Sure. I'm going home for dinner."

"Thanks." She waited on the porch until Hardy climbed into his car and Franklin's truck rambled up Canyon Road.

Alone in the backyard, Darcy rested one knee on the wet ground and leaned forward. The white lump sparkled through the pool of water. The all-important clue lauded in mystery novels. The killer had tried to erase his tracks, but melted snow had turned the New Mexico loam into thick, sticky mud nearly impossible to completely camouflage with only broom bristles.

"He should have used a hoe, not a broom."

Startled, Darcy looked up. She hadn't heard the man approach. The bluest eyes she had ever seen stared back at her.

"He must not have planned on snow," said the man. "You can sweep dirt, but not mud. Sticks to everything and dries as hard as concrete." He removed his glove and extended his hand. "Name's Seldon. Aaron Seldon. Forensics."

She stood and shook his hand.

"Finding you here has brightened this dreary day."

Darcy stifled a laugh. She'd heard worse pickup lines. "The tire tracks along the drive—"

"Weren't worth much. Lifted a few, but when our killer couldn't rub them out with a broom, he used the handle to deface them."

"Seems he's good at mutilating things. Guess they're a total loss?"

"Yes, as far as forensics is concerned. Ironically, the best track, the one in the garage, would have been the easiest to erase. Dry as a bone in there."

"He was probably interrupted," she said more to herself than him.

"I came to the same conclusion, which supports Mrs. Cloverdale's story that she heard someone leave by the back door as she and Mrs. Colton entered the living room. Or what used to be the living room."

"The room where they found Selma?"

He nodded. "But Mrs. Cloverdale didn't actually see anyone."

"A shame they didn't come out to the back deck. They may have seen the killer leaving or defacing his tracks."

"I thought the same thing."

"Has anyone questioned the neighbors?"

"Door-to-door. No one saw or heard anything within a two-block radius, which isn't unusual. I'll show you." He trudged through the tall grass to Acequia Madre.

"Broad daylight, yet no one saw anything?" she asked.

"Like I said, not surprising. Almost every home is adobe. Thick walls make for great insulation. Bad part is, they block or muffle noise. The high compound walls don't help either. To top it off, four families are part-time residents. Two of the four are only here in the ski season, and both are in Colorado this week. What are the odds?" He shook his head.

"I'm confused about the layout. Who owns this lot with the three-car garage?" She wanted to confirm Hardy's information.

"Cantfield. He owned two parcels. The one closest to the corner"—Seldon pointed to the house—"where he built his territorial home and this one with the dilapidated garage. Said he planned to give the garage lot to his son someday. Unfortunately, it has served as nothing more than an eyesore. People constantly complain about the knee-high weeds as a fire hazard."

He walked out into the street. "The lot with the house butts up to a pop art gallery on Canyon Road. Closed at the moment. Owners are remodeling. The garage tract, as you can see for yourself, backs up to the Cloverdale Gallery. Killer must have come down Acequia Madre, the street we're standing on, into the dirt drive, and into the garage."

"The drive appears to be well used."

"Teens. Popular place to make out."

She scanned the street. The house across from her, the only one without a high compound wall to block the entrance, had three large picture windows. "Surely they saw something."

"The Gimballs. I bet our killer knew they spend winters in the Caribbean. They leave the first week of October and return around mid-April. They have a housekeeper—not a live-in one, though. Lucky jerk, our killer."

"Indeed. Doesn't Rhonda Cloverdale live around here?" Of course she knew but wanted to hear what Seldon had to say.

"Two streets up and four over. Beautiful adobe. Well maintained." He headed back down the lane to the rear of the gallery, Darcy in step. "Hope he isn't sending us a message."

"What do you mean?"

"Next week's Halloween."

"Thanks for the reminder." She walked toward the puddle,

stopping within a few feet of the evidence. "The tire track in the lane . . . think I found something."

Those blue eyes sparkled. "You sure? We looked at the impression, but he did a real number on it by gouging the tread marks with a broom handle."

"I know, but I'm more interested in this." She crouched next to the track, Seldon beside her and closer than necessary. "See that shimmery white substance swimming in this pool of water?"

"Yes. Have you seen it before?"

"Yes, on a tire track in Albuquerque." She stood. "Do you have a flashlight handy?"

He shot her a quizzical look and then shouted to one of the forensic guys to bring him a flashlight. With the light in hand, he followed her to the garage.

She squatted beside the tire track. "The one I saw in Albuquerque . . ."

"Don't tell me you think they're a match?"

"I most certainly do."

"You sure? I mean, the tread's fairly common. An all-terrain tire sold by Bridgestone. Popular seller."

"Tread might be common, but the wear marks aren't."

The evidence against the killer confirmed what Darcy had suspected. Now, all she had to do was catch him.

17

Al had awakened that morning tired and depressed. And even an hour-long sojourn at the spa had done nothing to boost her spirits, so she rode home in a huff, ignoring her chauffeur's efforts to cheer her up. She pushed open the back door of the car with more force than necessary, darted out of the Bentley, and stormed into the house.

Carter swooped in behind her. He handed her hot coffee spiked with hundred proof vodka and disappeared. Al gulped the hot brew, savoring the burn while she studied the row of family portraits gracing the fireplace mantel. Nasty habit, this drinking in the morning, but with Randolph dead, who would rag on her? She had to find a distraction: someone tough, impervious to bad manners, and comfortable with authority. Someone young, sexy, and disposable.

Another swig. So far she had fought a good battle, staved

off the tears, and buried her emotions well. A noble public display, but in privacy she gave in to the torment, the guilt, and the sorrow that haunted her. The mistakes. God, she had made so damn many. Young, she had rationalized every one. Older, she recognized that the enormity of those bad decisions had manifested themselves in irreversible ways—like the men in her life, all nothing more than stepping stones to what she really craved. Money. Power. And what had both bought? Grief.

As for children, she'd never wanted any. Even the notion of motherhood drained her. But she appeased Randolph, sacrificed her figure, and bore him a son, the heir to Colton Industries. Over the years, husband and son became inseparable, shutting her out. Robbed of their love and friendship, she retaliated. Stupid damn mistake, getting pregnant a second time.

She stared at Selma's portrait. Tears spilled down Al's cheeks, blurring the vision of her daughter, innocent and sweet. Al had resented Selma's carefree attitude toward life. Her daughter had no idea what the word "struggle" meant. But Al had no one to blame but herself for driving her daughter away. Still, she hated Rhonda for stealing Selma and blamed her sister-in-law for making her want to get pregnant a third time.

Al set the mug down hard. The sharp clap rang through the drawing room. Carter appeared out of nowhere with a refill and vanished without a word.

Idiotic mistake, thinking children could fill the raw ache in her heart, but the twins had. She picked up the photo of the two cradled in her arms and kissed the picture. Poor frail Marcus. He needed her. Depended upon her. "The only emotional depth I've ever seen you display has been toward them," Randolph once commented.

Al leaned against the wall and wept deep, mournful sobs for Randolph, Selma, their brutal deaths, for everything wrong in her life. What had Randolph said? "No matter how strong you think you are, something will always bring you down. Death, love . . ." When the emotional maelstrom that drowned her ended, she showered, dressed, and treated herself to a spirit lifter.

Artwears, a trendy shop on the Plaza in Santa Fe, greeted their richest client with exuberant enthusiasm. Al loved the attention, a good reason for patronizing the establishment. In the dressing room, she shed her running suit for an ankle-length cashmere dress and inspected her reflection in the full-length mirror. Exquisite. She'd never looked so beautiful. So young.

"I'll take the dress," she sang out, thrilled with the workmanship of the garment. Such detailing. "Carmen." She tapped her stockinged foot and waited. Silence. Al yanked open the stall door, almost chipping a nail in the process. She immediately examined her manicure. Good, no harm done. "Carmen!" Al shouted, angry that the saleswoman had deserted her post.

Rapid footsteps. "Sorry, Mrs. Colton, but I'm shorthanded this morning."

Al wagged a red talon at the woman. "If you want my business, don't let it happen again. I'm in a hurry. A big hurry."

"Yes, ma'am." The response was almost a whisper.

"How much?" Al ran her hands down her trim frame.

Carmen snagged the label dangling from the back of the garment. "Two thousand."

Al threw her arms into the air in jubilation. "A steal."

"On a hanger?"

"No, no, no, dear girl. I intend to wear it. Cut the tag."

Carmen snipped the plastic tie. "Beautiful fit. You look radiant."

"Young," Al said. "I should. I plow enough bucks into this old bod." She admired herself in the mirror. "Gosh, when was the last time I wore blue?"

A bell sounded.

Carmen remained rooted to the spot, her inquiring eyes on her client.

"Oh, go. See who it is, but don't dally. As soon as I gather my stuff, I'm leaving."

"Debit your account?" Carmen glanced over her shoulder toward the door.

Al reached into her bag and removed her makeup kit. "Yes, whatever."

Outside the fitting room, loud male voices intermingled with Carmen's protests.

Al ignored the ruckus and concentrated on perfecting her mascara job. Done, she slipped out of the dressing room.

At the cash register stood Carmen and two men. "Franklin? Hardy?" Al shouted. "What are you two doing here?"

Carmen's shoulders sagged. "I tried to cover."

"Which is interfering with an investigation," said Hardy.

"Why are you here?" Al repeated as she went back into the stall to retrieve her coat.

Franklin's reflection appeared in the mirror to her right. His slim frame blocked the doorway. "Mrs. Colton, we'd like you to come down to the station and answer a few questions."

She pursed her lips and mulled over the request. "About?"

"The murders."

Al whirled around. "This is a bad joke, right? Come now, you don't think I had anything to do . . . oh please, I've probably killed four flies in my lifetime."

Franklin backed up, out of striking distance. Al smiled, amused.

"No joke, ma'am. We would have preferred to talk at the house, but you left early."

"What you mean is, you couldn't trap me there because no one would let you in. You'd have no luck at Colton Industries either, which means you followed me here. To make a fool of me in public. Well, I hope you're ready for a lawsuit, guys. No handcuffs. You might ruin my new dress." She slipped on her gloves and headed for the exit.

"You aren't under arrest," said Franklin. "We only want to ask you a few questions."

"Ask away. Who cares if Carmen hears? The whole damn state will know by day's end."

Hardy opened the door. "If you'll come with us, please, Mrs. Colton?"

"Okay, okay. Suit yourself. Thanks, Carmen. The dress you chose . . ." She gave the woman a thumbs-up.

Al waited on the sidewalk in the dour company of Franklin while Hardy went for his car. She refused to walk the block. If they wanted her, they'd have to come to her.

"Where's your ride?"

"None of your damn business." Her hand dived into her purse for her cell phone. "Lucas, meet me at the police station. Yes, now darling. So it's Sunday. Who cares?" She dialed again. "Zach, Al. Round up McClain. Get her to my place. I know it's Sunday. Just do it. It's urgent." She pressed auto five. "Victor, when McClain arrives, bring her straight to the police station. No, I'm fine. It'll take more than these two clowns to upset me. Later, I'll ring for a ride." She dropped the phone into her bag.

Hardy pulled to the curb. "Sorry for the delay. Traffic's a bitch."

Franklin opened the back door, and Al slid in. "Hope you're getting a vicarious thrill arresting me in public."

"No one's arresting you," said Franklin from the passenger seat.

"Well, ain't this cozy?" she crooned. "Three of us together in a rundown sedan. Okay, who am I supposed to have killed?"

She sat at one end of the seat, extended her long slender legs, and admired her shoes. A fluke, but the perfect choice of outfit.

"I can think of four," said Hardy. "Let's start with your husband."

"Me? Kill Randolph? Whatever for? What's the motive?"

"Money. Power." Hardy braked abruptly and cursed. "Blasted tourists."

"Ridiculous. You call a measly 40 percent of Colton motive? Hardly worth the effort . . . 60 or 80, maybe." She laughed. "Hell, why put my neck in a noose when his doctor warned him he'd probably keel over by seventy? I'm patient. Shouldn't you read me my rights?"

Franklin shook his head. "I told you. You aren't under arrest."

"Oh, right." She wanted to smack him for talking to her as if she were some dumb blonde. "As for Buzz Warner, I loved him. Peach of a guy. I had no reason to want him dead."

"Barnes?"

"Don't use that tone with me, Hardy. Never saw the kid until the balloon fiesta."

"Actually," said Franklin, "we aren't interested in Barnes or Warner. We figure both happened to be in the wrong place at the wrong time."

"If my math serves me correctly," Hardy butted in, "Selma had 4 percent of the vote. And Randolph Colton's will states you inherit the shares of all deceased family members."

"Which adds up to 44 percent," Al said. "I said 60 or 80, not 44." She sighed. "This conversation is as boring as sex with Randolph." Franklin cleared his throat. Hardy almost ran a red light. Their reactions pleased her, if only for a moment.

Hardy regained his composure. "If you count Randolph

Jr., Marcus, and Lindsay, you'd have an additional 6 percent, which adds up to 50."

Al leaned forward. "I said 60."

"Rhonda has what, 10 percent?"

"Careful, Hardy. I don't like where you're going with this." What started as a lark had escalated into something more serious.

Franklin must have read her thoughts. "Perhaps you shouldn't say any more until Lucas arrives at the station."

"Nonsense." Al sounded calmer than she felt. "I'm not worried about incriminating myself because I'm not guilty. Only thing I've done is made some bad choices."

"Such as?" Hardy entered the lot diagonal to the precinct, whipped the sedan into an empty space, and killed the engine.

"Marrying, for one. Having kids, for another. Personally, I detest the little buggers. A drain on the body and the soul." Al shoved open the door and got out. She took Franklin's advice and kept her mouth shut as she rode the elevator to the third floor. Hardy, the epitome of a good host, showed her to the best seat in his office, a worn sofa, and offered her what resembled muddy water. He called it coffee. She declined with a grimace. "Stains my teeth."

"We've got tea."

"Yuck. Worse."

Franklin excused himself. Hardy shuffled paperwork. Al thought about her morning in the drawing room. She missed Randolph. He had been good to her. Never complained about anything. And buying a new dress hadn't helped as much as she'd hoped. Maybe a vacation. Some place exotic, like Fiji.

Al checked the time. Where was McClain? All those trips Randolph made to San Francisco to see his other girls—Al should have gone along. *But why bother?* she'd thought at the time. *No payoff in getting to know Darcy.* But now she could use a friend.

Since Randolph's death, she had constantly wondered who Regina's mother was and if Darcy knew but refused to tell, although she appeared as shocked as the rest of them when she'd heard the news. Al had pressed Weaver for answers, but nothing she'd tried worked. She'd wondered if the whole scenario was nothing more than a fabrication until she found a diary locked in Randolph's desk drawer. She had Colton's maintenance man break into the desk. Along with the diary, she'd discovered a photo album. He had indeed fathered the child.

Randolph's death did solve one problem: his extramarital affairs. How many, she had no idea, nor did she want to think about his infidelity. He had taken a lot of trips over the years and always came home too darn happy. For months afterward Al lived in a constant fear, expecting that at any moment he would demand a divorce. Randolph had powerful friends in high places. He'd take Marcus. Leave her a pauper. Al had worked too damn hard clawing her way to the top to let him hand Colton Industries to any woman who spread her legs for power or money.

Franklin walked in, along with a tall gray-haired man impeccably dressed in a dark pin-striped suit.

Al sprang to her feet. "Lucas. Darling. Thanks for coming."

"What seems to be the problem?"

Her attorney acted as bored as the detectives. His contract ended next month. Maybe Johnston, the new kid in town, might be a worthy replacement? Ashley Johnston. Nah, bad idea. Perhaps she'd make another play for Zach? A more intriguing challenge.

"Al." Lucas folded his hands. "What's the problem?"

"They're arresting me for the murders. Please clear up this

mess. Quickly. I'm due at the office. I don't have time for this crap."

Lucas looked at the detectives. "What's going on?"

"We wanted to question her. Nothing more. She came willingly," said Hardy.

"Then continue."

"Lucas." Al squirmed.

"They're within their rights. The sooner they start, the sooner we leave." Her attorney sat beside Al on the sofa.

"Fine, but someone better state the evidence against me or I'm walking. Not circumstantial crap—I want cold, hard facts." She folded her arms across her chest.

Darcy knocked on the open door.

"Finally, a friend." Al waved Darcy in.

"Is there a break in the investigation?" asked Darcy.

"Franklin seems to think so, but he's wrong." Al pouted.

"Al"—Lucas tapped his watch with a finger—"the sooner we start, the sooner we leave."

"Yes, of course."

"Please continue, Detective Franklin," said Lucas.

Franklin deferred to Hardy. "The cold, hard facts. We found a computer chip in Mr. Colton's down parka—a chip only a handful at Colton had access to: Randolph, Larson, Hamilton, two people in R&D, and Al. We've ruled out everyone except you."

"Why me?" asked Al.

"Because the evidence points to you."

"Nonsense. I've read the forensic reports. Even the Testco results."

Darcy glanced at Al. "Really?"

Al hid the blunder by moving the conversation along, not allowing Darcy the opportunity to question how she had seen the Testco results. "The tire track from an SUV," said Al. "Hell,

I haven't driven since I married Randolph. Why bother? I have a chauffeur. As for the dog hair, I hate dogs more than I detest kids, so why would I own a husky-malamute mix? At least brats don't shed. As for motive, what would I stand to gain by killing three people?"

"Four. Remember Selma?"

"Careful, Hardy," Al warned.

"What you stand to gain is voting power. That motive, plus the diamond studs, is why we're interviewing you."

Al frowned. "Studs? What studs?"

"Yes, what studs?" asked Darcy.

"Three to be exact," said Franklin. "Forensics discovered two at the gallery—one in the storeroom and the other when the MI examined Selma's body. The third was found in Randolph's jacket pocket inside a metal box, a container frequently used at Colton to store small laser components. On one of the prongs, we found a strand of black wool, but no one in the gondola wore black wool. In fact, no one in the Colton party, including Darcy, wore black wool the day of the balloon fiesta."

"Where on the body did you find the stud?" asked Darcy.

"Impaled in Selma's upper ear," said Franklin.

"I don't recall . . ."

"When you arrived at the gallery, the head was lying on the floor, cheekbone pressed to wood flooring. You wouldn't have seen the diamond."

"The stud was forced into the cartilage." Hardy studied the pad in front of him. "This diamond also had a strand of black wool snagged in one of its prongs. Both strands of black wool belong to a jacket owned by Mrs. Colton."

"I own lots of black wool jackets. So does Rhonda. It proves nothing." Al jutted her chin into the air.

Franklin checked something on his phone. "The samples

matched only one jacket. A Herman Koss." His brows shot up. "Hmm." He grunted and blinked. "Retail $8400."

"So what?" Al put her hands on her hips. "Not everyone is poor, Donald."

"Evidently," said Franklin.

"Go on," said Lucas.

"The Friday prior to Randolph's murder, Al was seen at the Sandia Hills Country Club wearing her husband's down parka, the same one he wore when he boarded his balloon on Sunday. She had the perfect opportunity to plant the chip."

All heads shifted in Al's direction.

"Chip? I thought we were talking about diamond studs. All this talk proves only one thing. I wore his jacket because I left mine in the limo. Nothing more. What you should ask is, where was the parka all day Saturday? Did anyone else wear it besides me? Selma, perhaps? She always borrowed my jewelry, my clothes, and anything else she damn well wanted."

"What are you insinuating?" Hardy placed his elbows on the tabletop. "That Selma killed her father, then killed herself?"

"Asshole." Al said.

"Easy, Hardy," Lucas said.

Al put her hands on her hips. "Maybe Selma conspired with someone to kill Randolph, then the killer murdered her to shut her up?"

"Franklin," Darcy interrupted, "have you shown the studs to Al?"

"Not yet." He grabbed an envelope sitting on Hardy's desk and opened the flap. Two earrings slid onto a sheet of paper. "I don't have the third diamond, only a photo of it. The stud won't be available until after the autopsy."

Lucas laid a hand on Al's arm. "Watch what you say."

Darcy took the photo from Hardy and placed it next to the

diamonds lying on the sheet of paper. "Same setting in all three. Same size diamonds. And all three look identical to the one Selma handed Al the day of Randolph's funeral. And, if I recall correctly, Al returned wearing emeralds, not diamonds. Take a look at these. Remember the earrings you misplaced the day of Randolph's funeral service?"

Al smiled. "Thanks for reminding me. Three missing. No wonder I couldn't find a matching pair, so I wore emeralds." She placed a finger to her cheek, and a frown furrowed her brows. "Or did I wear rubies?"

"Minor point." Hardy waved away the question.

"You wore emeralds," said Darcy. "Do you own only one pair of diamond studs?"

"No, I own two. Stupid move at the time, but I loved them and was afraid I might lose one. I can be very careless. Randolph told me to buy a second pair. Expensive, but it's only money."

"The question remains, how'd one get in Randolph's pocket, one in the storeroom at Cloverdale, and one in Selma's ear?" Hardy drummed his fingers on the desktop.

"They were stolen, of course," said Al, her tone indignant.

"By whom?" Hardy said.

"Hell, anyone, anywhere. At home, at Colton. Every time I answer the phone, I take one off and leave it on my desk, nightstand, or office in the house. I'm lucky they don't end up in the trash."

"Indeed." Hardy cast a skeptical eye.

Her eyes narrowed. "I'm getting the distinct feeling someone's trying to frame me."

"I wouldn't worry." Lucas placed his hand on Al's arm. "You have an alibi the afternoon of Selma's death."

"Who?" asked Darcy.

"Carter. Al's cook," said Lucas. "He signed a sworn statement."

"Selma had moved out by then, correct?" Hardy skimmed his questions.

"Not officially. We fought the night before. She packed a bag and drove to Los Alamos to stay with a friend. That dreadful animal artist."

"Melanie Skillman," said Darcy.

Al nodded.

"If we rule you out"—a slight smirk curled Hardy's lips—"do you have any idea who the murderer might be?"

"Whoever he is, he's awfully clever."

Hardy raised his eyebrows. "We've come to that conclusion."

"Are you mocking me, Mr. Hardy?"

"No, ma'am."

"Since we're dealing strictly with fact and not supposition," Darcy said to an obviously attentive audience, "perhaps someone can explain two facts."

"They are?" Franklin straightened up.

"The diamond stud in Randolph's pocket . . . why would anyone put it in a metal box, one specifically designed to store laser components?" She let the question sink in. "And why two studs at the gallery?"

A long hush ensued.

Franklin broke the silence. "In Randolph's case, maybe to prevent fire damage or loss?"

"Go on," Darcy said.

Franklin cleared his throat. "As for the two at the gallery, the killer brought two to be certain someone found at least one. He put one in the storeroom, rethought the move, and decided to force the other into Selma's ear, making the earring impossible for us to overlook."

Darcy had the last word. "Which leads to my conclusion: all three studs were plants."

18

Darcy's apartment complex faced the snowcapped Sandias, their slopes dusted heavily and low after a new fall. She braved the frigid morning and rested her arms on the icy railing of her upstairs balcony. Below, people walked gingerly across the ice-sheeted parking lot. Sometimes she missed those days at the bureau and would have welcomed returning to her old job, especially today. She could think of a million things better than attending an autopsy.

A woman with black hair and about the same height and build as Selma came out of the downstairs rental. Darcy had noticed her the day she moved in, her resemblance to Randolph's daughter striking. When someone dear died, you wanted the entire world to stand still and take notice, for everyone to feel your pain and honor your loved one's departure, but it didn't work that way. Life went on as though nothing had happened.

"Hey, Della," a man yelled.

The woman spun and slipped on the wet step. Her briefcase hit the ground. Glass shattered.

Darcy leaned over the railing. "Are you all right?"

Della looked up and smiled. "Yes, thanks. Chalk up another thermos gone. One of these days I'll get smart and move to a warmer climate."

The man rushed to her side. "Sorry. You okay? You forgot your lunch."

Darcy's phone rang. She closed the glass sliding door and grabbed her cell phone off the kitchen counter. "Hello."

"How are you holding up?"

He didn't have to identify himself. "Dan, hi. Okay."

"Heard about Selma on last night's news. So sorry. I'm flying out."

"No, I'm okay. Honest."

"I'd rather see in person. Besides, I'm going your way, in a manner of speaking. I have a job in Cruces."

"Really? You'll have to fill me in."

"Can you meet me or should I rent a car?"

"No," said Darcy, "I'll pick you up."

"Good, because I'm calling in-flight. I land in an hour."

"An hour? I'm still in my bathrobe."

"Take your time. I'll hang out at the Admiral's Club."

"Albuquerque doesn't have one."

"Okay," said Dan, "curbside, at your convenience." He hung up.

Showered and with a towel wrapped around her dripping body, Darcy walked into her makeshift office and replayed the Barnes's recording. "Not much help," Benevides had commented. At the time she agreed, but something kept her coming back to the surveillance video. She repeatedly played the short take, studying every nuance, but nothing jogged her memory. She returned to the bedroom to dress.

She opened the closet door. "Rangefinder," she said aloud. "Locates distance to target." She wiggled into a pair of jeans. "Laser shoots target out of the sky." Over the turtleneck went a wool sweater. "But how does the shooter pick one out of a sea of balloons?" She combed her wet hair. The equation continued to nag her. Done dressing, she checked the time and walked back into her office.

On the whiteboard she purchased yesterday, she wrote, "Computer chip found on Randolph. Chip or homing device? Barnes. Coincidence or plant? Barnes and killer partners? Or could Barnes have been the homing device? Suicide mission?" The questions persisted all the way to the airport.

Darcy had no trouble picking out Dan from among the crowd loitering at the curb. Tough to miss a man six foot four and 220 pounds. Intimidated by his size and aloof personality, most "G-bies," Dan's term for FBI new hires, considered him unapproachable, and she certainly received her share of condolences when the bureau chief partnered her with him.

Their first year together, she agreed with the rumors. A loner, Dan was as emotionally detached as any person could be, but the day Darcy shot and killed an escapee from death row, she saw a side few had ever seen. Standing over the body and racked with sobs, she was stunned when he drew her into his arms and held her until she stopped crying. She expected him to brag to the guys, to be the butt of their jokes, but he said nothing to anyone. He gained a lot of respect from her that day. As Charlene had said, "He's the brother we never had."

"Hey, hi." Dan dumped his bags in the backseat and slid into the passenger's side. He hugged her but offered no condolences. He knew her well enough not to. Any form of kindness would only make her cry. "Mind if we stop for a muffin and coffee? Something along those lines? I'm starving."

"Will Starbucks do?"

"Perfect."

They talked about the investigation as Darcy motored north to Journal Center. As she pulled into the parking lot, snow started to fall. She located a table in a quiet corner of the coffee shop while he ordered breakfast.

"Any news on the white substance?" she asked after he settled into his seat.

"Lab promised a report later today. I asked them to fax or email the results to your apartment."

"Good," said Darcy. "Can't wait to find out what it is. Thought the substance might be white clay, indigenous to the area, but Hardy said no."

Dan cocked his head, as though trying to remember some detail. "Hardy?"

"He's the Santa Fe detective working with Franklin. Said he plans to ask Zach about the substance."

"Sounds like Hardy knows something we don't."

"My thought exactly. Think I'll beat him to the punch and question Zach the first chance I get."

"Good idea." Dan opened his laptop. "You asked for some background checks. I had Jan summarize the key points. The full reports I emailed to you this morning."

"Good. Thanks."

"Check Zach's background first. You'll find the data interesting." Dan slid his laptop toward her.

She skimmed the summary. "You're kidding? Zach consulted for Whitton Healthcare?"

"Same company you worked for, right?"

"Yes, owned by Francine Helen Whitton. My first job after

resigning from the Feeb. She hired me to find the person who had leaked their blockbuster drug to the competition."

"Small world. I don't recall what they manufactured."

"Ophthalmic drugs and devices such as medical lasers. Some switch. First Zach fixes people up, now he blows them up. Wait a minute. What's this? He graduated art school? The teachers said he wouldn't cut it in the art world because he produced outlandish, if not bizarre, sculptures that aroused disdain among his fellow artists. Have you seen pictures of his work? Are they wall sculptures?"

"Let's see. I have some additional data on my iPad." He scrolled through the pages with his thumb. "Only one showing. Ever. Julian Gallery, Boston. A failure. I sent Rick to poke through their photo archives."

Rick's name brought a smile. If anyone could dig up information, it was Dan's skiptracer. "Can't wait to see what he turns up."

"Nor I."

"This is interesting," said Darcy. "Muñoz and Martin, both fired from their last jobs. Muñoz for insubordination. Not surprising. Martin, on the other hand, is a surprise."

"His former employer wouldn't talk, but a coworker said Martin's departure involved selling company secrets. Other than the one accusation, his record is exemplary."

"Selling company secrets? That's serious. Can you dig some more?"

"Already am, or at least Rick is."

"Not much here on Al."

"Because I couldn't dig up much," said Dan. "Even the basics eluded us."

"Really?" Darcy clicked on the folder. "Zach said she was born in Jersey of wealthy parents, if he has his facts straight."

Dan shook his head. "He may, but we couldn't find a birth certificate."

"Odd."

"Again, I put Rick on the job. If there's anything worth discovering, he'll root it out."

She sipped her coffee, her mind working. "Wonder what Al's hiding?"

"I wouldn't read too much into any of this. There's probably a simple explanation."

"With Al, not likely."

He checked his watch. "What are your plans for the day?"

"Selma's autopsy at two in Santa Fe."

"Mind if I tag along?"

"No. I could use the support, but I have a stop to make before the autopsy."

On the ride north, Darcy relayed all the events that had taken place in the investigation so far.

"Talk about a dysfunctional family," said Dan. "On another note, do you remember Kendall?"

"Of course," said Darcy. "Worked with him in the think tank."

"He retired and owns a spread in Española. I thought about calling him. Maybe the three of us can knock back a few beers together. Interested?"

"Love to." Darcy liked the way he always included her when fraternizing with the guys. "Where's Española?"

"Between Santa Fe and Taos."

The name sparked her interest. "Know anything about Taos? Randolph left me land there."

"When? You never mentioned this. In the city?"

"I just found out at the reading of the will. His attorney said sixty acres, so I don't think the land is in the city."

"Wow. Maybe we can check it out if there's time."

Dan filled her in on his case in Las Cruces and concluded as Darcy exited on St. Francis en route to downtown Santa Fe. She weaved her way through traffic and then zipped up Alameda and onto Ortiz. "Love GPS."

Dan laughed. "Me too."

Darcy braked outside a salmon-colored adobe and hopped out. The structure housed two businesses: a Realtor's office and a title company. She stepped into Waverly Realty. The scent of heavy perfume made her eyes water. She hoped for a quick interview and a fast exit.

The blonde with the cell phone glued to her ear motioned for them to sit on the *banco* sculpted in the mud-colored wall. Light from three strip windows danced across her cluttered desk, highlighted the woman's tanned face, and washed over the Gorman prints that hung cockeyed on the stucco walls.

"Oh yes, darling, I understand. Completely. You'll love Santa Fe. Promise. Meet one person and before long you'll know half the town. Yes, yes. No one in their right mind retires in California, dear. No one with money." Her hand patted her ample chest. "Gotta run, I have clients. Yes, we'll do lunch. Monday next? I promise."

The Realtor swung around the corner of her desk. She was short, thin, laden with silver, and clad in denim decorated with a montage of flowers. "Monet, like the artist, Waverly."

Darcy shook the diamond-studded hand Waverly extended. "Darcy McClain," she said, fighting the urge to say, Darcy, private investigator, McClain. "And this is Dan Gruet."

"How can I help you?"

With her quick exit in mind, Darcy got straight to the point. "Last month you sold a house on Acequia Madre."

"The Cantfield home." Waverly beamed with pride. "If you're interested, I have a fabulous house on Garcia. Listed at $1.2 mil, but the sellers are motivated."

"Only $1.2 mil?" Dan looked thoughtful, as though mulling over the possibilities.

"Actually, we aren't interested in purchasing real estate," Darcy said. "My partner and I are investigating the Colton murders."

Waverly's hand landed with a hollow thud on her chest. "What a terrible tragedy. Poor child. Disgusting, the way they cut—"

"Yes." Dan rescued Darcy from an ugly visual.

"How can I help?" Waverly reclined in her chair, folded her sienna-colored fingers, and eyed one of her diamonds.

"Police believe the killer used Cantfield's side lot to gain access to the rear of the Cloverdale Gallery." Darcy searched the woman's face for a reaction.

"Oh, I'm sure he did. Less than an hour ago a Detective John Hardy paid me a visit. I told him everything I knew," said Waverly. "How I hired a crew to clean the Cantfield house because the new owners—well, the woman—wanted the place spotless. I scheduled the cleaning for last Wednesday afternoon. The new owners plan to move in today. Saturday I got a call from someone saying he'd clean the house first thing that morning. I saw red. I was so furious, it didn't dawn on me until I hung up. The voice sounded nothing like Jimmy, the guy I hired, so I called him back. He hadn't called me at all on Saturday. Said he completed the job early Thursday morning. Suspicious, I drove to the house. I thought someone might be casing the place to burglarize or vandalize it. Thankfully, nothing looked disturbed. Just spick-and-span."

"Did you check the grounds?"

"Definitely. I even contacted the police and asked them to patrol the area until late yesterday when the movers were supposed to arrive. You'd think with the police cruising the streets the killer . . ." Waverly let her sentence trail off.

The phone rang and Waverly let it go to voicemail.

"Sorry, but that's all I know. Hope you catch The Carver before he strikes again."

The Carver! Darcy cringed. "What made you call him that?"

"Everyone is. Didn't you see the morning news? I forget the anchorman's name. He started it. Said there's a serial killer loose. Half the town's terrified to go out at night."

Great. More complications. She stood, ready to leave.

"I'll walk you out. After our conversation I need some fresh air." Waverly gathered up her shawl, the fabric a collage of flowers, and wrapped the garment around her.

She wasn't the only one who needed fresh air.

"Such a wonderful man, Randolph Colton," said Waverly. "Very generous. You name the charity and he'd lend his support."

Darcy escaped the dank office to a sun at high noon. The intensity blinding, she slid on sunglasses. While Waverly pumped her hand, Darcy freed her lungs of perfume. "If you think of anything else, please give me a call." She handed the Realtor a business card.

Waverly smiled. "Al sure has come a long way since we first met."

Astonished, Darcy almost choked on her words. "You know Al?"

"Oh, yes. We go way back. Well over twenty-five years. Pre-Randolph days. She's certainly done a lot better in life than me. In every aspect."

"Where'd you two meet?" asked Dan.

"Trapa."

Darcy treaded lightly. People tended to clam up if she came across as an interrogator. "I've heard of the town but don't recall in what context."

"The village is home to New Beginnings."

"Which is?" She did her best to sound nonchalant.

"A haven for battered women."

19

"Well, what do you think of Waverly's bombshell?" Dan opened the driver's door for Darcy.

"I'm curious as hell."

"Where is Trapa, anyway?" He climbed into the passenger seat.

"Haven't a clue."

"But you told Waverly . . ."

"I lied."

Dan tapped the "Maps" app on his iPhone. "Northwest of Santa Fe. About an hour's drive."

"Interested in heading up there after the autopsy?"

"Might be too late. I have an idea. Española is along the way. I'll call Kendall, see if he's available for dinner. We can spend the night in town and head out first thing in the morning."

"You're on."

During Dan's lively phone conversation with Kendall, Darcy tuned out as she tried to prepare herself for the miserable business ahead. She had seen her share of autopsies, but how someone could carve up a person (to use Waverly's words) when it wasn't for the purpose of determining the cause of death defied reason. She recalled the killer's moniker, The Carver, and shuddered.

Dan touched her hand. "You okay?"

"No. This won't be easy. I'm glad you flew out."

"Me too."

Darcy suppressed the tears pricking the corners of her eyes. If she gave in, they wouldn't stop. She had been on the brink so many times since Randolph died but had managed to fight breaking down.

"Kendall can't wait to see us. His wife operates a B&B on the delta. We can stay there tonight." Dan made light conversation during the short trip from Waverly's to the county offices. His lively tone lifted her spirits, a bit.

She parked near a one-story adobe plastered in dark brown with white portal posts. Without a word Dan led the way into the building.

In the hallway stood Franklin, a look of anticipation on his face. "Hi, been expecting you." His gaze moved from Darcy to Dan. "Who's your friend?"

"Dan Gruet," Dan said.

The men shook hands.

Franklin's expression said he disapproved. "Don't know how Hardy feels about visitors."

"Visitors?" Hardy marched down the corridor. "Well, I'll be . . . Thought I heard a familiar voice. What in the hell brings you to Santa Fe? How'd you find me?"

Dan hugged Hardy. "Strictly by chance, my friend."

Darcy thumped Dan on the arm. "You knew all along."

"All along, no. But when Waverly mentioned his full name, I knew I had the right person. For a brief time, Kendall and Hardy were partners," Dan explained. "Long before you joined the bureau."

Lou, the coroner, walked in.

The levity died.

"We're moving next door," said Lou as he ushered the small group into an adjoining room that overlooked the autopsy suite: three walls of glass with the fourth dedicated to AV equipment. "This way you won't have to suit up."

"Suits me." Hardy chuckled. "Hate wearing protective garb." To Dan he said, "Normally, we'd do the autopsy in Albuquerque, but Al insisted upon doing it here even though she will not be in attendance. She said she wanted to avoid screw-ups."

"This room is equipped with video and audio," Lou continued, "so we can communicate back and forth as well as see everything."

Darcy swallowed, the lump in her throat constrictive. She moved away from the glass. Already emotionally compromised, she tried hard to act cool and collected.

Franklin cornered her. "Got some interesting news."

"Oh?"

"About the latex glove you found in Colton's parts department, the one Muñoz ended up commandeering from Rodriquez . . . we found two sets of prints. One belongs to Kevin, the guy in the vampire costume, the other to Martin Hamilton."

"Interesting."

"Gets better. Kevin called in sick this morning. Rodriquez tried to reach him on an unrelated matter. When he couldn't get him on the phone, he went by his apartment. The mailbox was crammed with letters and bills. Landlord hasn't seen him since last Friday."

Which meant nothing, but she repeated, "Interesting."

"As for Hamilton, he called his secretary late Saturday. At home. Said he had a personal emergency. He's officially on vacation for three weeks."

"Three weeks?"

"My response exactly. I drove by his place. No sign of life. His neighbor is watching the house. If you hear anything, I'd like to know."

His way of reminding her to keep him informed. Franklin took a seat across the room. Gallegos sat beside him.

Someone flicked a switch. Darcy blinked. The bright lights in the morgue intensified the throb in her temples. She glanced sideways at Dan. He smiled and nodded reassuringly.

Classical music, joyful and light, masked the emotionally charged atmosphere, but nothing, not even the glass enclosure, camouflaged the stench of death. It clung to everything, alive or dead, a parasitic odor immune to sterilization. She concentrated on the sonata and took solace in Dan's presence. Her thoughts drifted to the crime scene at the Cloverdale Gallery. She had grown fond of Selma in their short time together. In some ways she reminded Darcy of herself, a tomboy and a maverick.

Lou, a slim man obsessed with cleanliness, walked by the glass. He wore pressed scrubs and three covers over each shoe and had scoured his hands beyond the requirements for a surgeon, never mind a pathologist. He snapped on two pairs of latex gloves, adjusted his plastic face shield, and waited for Mickey, the morgue attendant, to retrieve the body.

Mickey, a large man with his head shaved clean and the longest, thickest mutton chops Darcy had ever seen, breezed past the refrigerated drawers to a heavy stainless steel door. He opened it and disappeared inside, emerging minutes later shrouded in a vapor cloud. He plunked the wall sculpture onto a gurney. Beside the bed of screws, he set a stainless steel basin covered with a white cloth.

"Gosh. No body block. Nothing to measure. No sew up. Getting off easy today." He wheeled the corpse to the autopsy table.

"Mick. Please. Show some respect." Lou scrutinized his instruments before placing them on a tray.

"Respect for who?" He looked about. "Oh. Sorry." He leaned over the sculpture. "Don't see a toe tag or an ID band. In fact, I can't even find a foot or a hand. Wait, here's a toe—nail polish gave it away—and a tag."

"Butcher," Gallegos said softly to Franklin, but they all heard.

Mickey toyed with a knob on the microphone suspended from the ceiling. "Ready?"

Lou nodded.

A hush fell as Lou pried the first body part off the bed of galvanized screws and laid it on the porcelain dissecting table. "Clean cut. Edges cauterized," he dictated.

The grayish-white body parts with their edges charred black were, as Lou said, clean until he cut into the seared tissue to free the severed organs. Blood spurted onto his gloves and scissors. Then came the trickle of Selma's precious fluids dripping down a white drain. After Lou dissected each quarter of the torso, he stacked the organ parts in neat piles: liver sections in one heap, kidney in another, and so on.

"Hmm. Liver's in four."

"Mickey." Lou's voice carried a warning.

But Mickey didn't heed the hint. "Won't need the saw. Chest cavity's slit in two. Clean. Precise. You thinking a laser like the news said?"

"Mickey, the knife."

He handed the breadknife to Lou. With one long sweeping action, the pathologist sliced into Selma's heart, the only organ still intact. He recorded his observations—all normal—made several crosscuts with a scalpel, and put the segmented heart into a stainless steel basin.

With a bloodstained hand, Mickey picked up a marker and scrawled a number on the whiteboard, the eight a smear of bright red. Acid churned in Darcy's stomach.

Mickey whispered to Lou, but the microphone amplified his voice. "Want me to start on the brain?"

"No, I will. Pickups." Lou took the forceps in exchange for a plastic basin.

"Great. Gut cleaning." Mickey carried the container to the sink.

"Remember. I want samples of everything." Lou stretched.

"Way ahead of you." Mickey motioned to the plastic cassettes, each labeled and lying open. After he weighed and measured the severed organs, he sliced postage stamp-sized samples from each, sealed them in the cassettes, and placed them in a jar of formalin for fixation.

"Oh, and Mickey, we need a count on the screws." Lou removed the last chunk of flesh from the crude wall hanging and rested it on the dissecting table. "This is interesting. Hardy."

Everyone gravitated to the glass wall. "On the monitor can you see these charred sections? Here and here." Lou touched the black spots with his knife.

"Sure do."

"Notice the powder on this one?"

Hardy grunted. "Yeah, white against black makes it obvious. Powder from surgical gloves, maybe?"

"Thought so at first, but close up what looks white is actually pale yellow. Never seen anything quite like it." After a pause Lou continued. "You might want to hit each section with a laser light for fingerprints. I think he tried to erase something by burning it off."

Hardy scratched his head. "Clever guy. Thanks."

Lou removed the cloth from the steel basin that sat on the gurney and lifted out Selma's head. Darcy fought the impulse to vomit. She unwrapped a stick of peppermint gum and chewed with a vengeance, but the worst was yet to come.

"Small perfectly circular hole burned into the forehead." He measured the cavity. "It's .20 inches in diameter. Edges cauterized. Bruise on temple, cheekbone. Postmortem."

Hardy spoke up. "Head fell off the sculpture onto the tiled floor, remember?"

"Yes," said Lou, then continued dictating. "Four puncture wounds. One temporal. One nasal. Two cranial." He rolled the head onto its side. "Three earrings. Two pearl. One in each lobe. Diamond in the left. Diamond stud impaled into the flesh, not pierced. The bruised and lacerated tissue, postmortem." He removed the earrings and put them on a piece of gauze.

A cool breeze seeped into the room and with it a malodorous odor, followed by the unforgettable stench of gastric acid. Mickey had finished his organ samples and stood at the sink, passing one section of intestine after another under running water. He set aside the pieces he wanted and dumped the discarded parts into a biohazard bag ready for incineration.

Gallegos coughed. "Too bad we aren't protected from the smell."

Hardy rubbed his nose with his index finger as if to ward off the repugnant odor. Franklin passed the VapoRub—a bit late to mask the rankness, but the ointment helped, at least for a few minutes.

Between the fetid smells, the wafts of formaldehyde, and the camphoric balm stuffed up her nose, Darcy's senses caved in to the onslaught. Bile refluxed. It burned her throat. The floor rose to meet her. She whispered to Dan, "Water." She looked around the room, wondering if anyone was watching her, but everyone seemed preoccupied with his or her own discomfort.

Gallegos plugged her nose with tissue. Franklin had his hand to his face, Hardy a handkerchief.

Dan returned with a paper cup. The sips cooled the fireball flaring in Darcy's stomach. Now for the real test.

Lou reached for a Stryker electric saw. Wielding it like a composer waving a baton, he made several incisions around the equator of the cranium. Darcy tensed, anticipating the sucking sound as he lifted off the calvarium. Lou cursed loudly.

Mickey leaned around Lou. "Jesus. Never seen anything like this. Still want the jar?"

"Yes, damn it. And pickups."

Franklin and the others formed a tight circle around the monitor, Darcy behind them, her view obstructed. Gallegos covered her face with her hands and backed away, leaving an opening for Darcy at the screen.

Lou was bent over the cracked skull, probing the cavity with forceps. He removed a black mass that resembled a lump of coal and waited for Mickey to tilt the save jar for better access.

Hardy screwed up his face. "Lou, what in the hell is that? Some kind of tumor?"

"Brain matter," said Mickey. "The entire organ fried to a crisp."

20

Morning dawned cold but clear.

Tired after a sleepless night, Darcy drove to Trapa in silence. Dan didn't seem to mind. He settled into a comfortable position in the passenger seat and snored.

On the last leg of the trip, he sat up. "Didn't sleep worth a darn last night. That's why I don't like bed and breakfasts. Too small and too noisy. "

"I know, but at least the rooms were free, which was nice of the Kendalls."

"And I enjoyed our evening. She's a great cook."

"She is." Darcy eased her 4Runner over a wooden bridge and descended into a valley. A slow-moving creek cut a brown trail through tall cattails as the stream meandered amid towering cottonwoods.

"You okay?" asked Dan.

"Been mulling over Lou's findings, hoping something will help me profile the killer."

"Your experience at the bureau should come in handy. I remember the first time I saw you in action. Said to myself, this woman has an uncanny knack for reading a crime scene."

She punched him in the arm. "Bet you said 'broad,' not 'woman.'"

"Might've."

Darcy slowed. "Almost missed the road." She made a sharp turn into a gravel drive that cut through dense piñon and followed the dusty lane to a large clearing fringed with boulders.

New Beginnings was housed in an old barn painted blue. As soon as they parked, a woman in baggy jeans and an oversized T-shirt appeared on the front porch. "You the folks who called?"

"Yes, ma'am. Dan Gruet and Darcy McClain," said Dan as he headed up the path to the front porch.

The woman flipped a dish towel over her shoulder and rubbed her palms on her pants but didn't shake hands. "Kat Whistler. Come in."

The place reminded Darcy of a cheap motel. Bedroom doors ran down both lengths of a dark corridor, the carpet a muddy brown and the air tainted with mildew. A door creaked, and a woman with stringy black hair gaped at them from around the jamb.

"Just visitors," said Kat. She proceeded through an open glass sliding door and into a huge sunroom, the bright sun a welcome sight and a spirit lifter after the dark entry area. Kat sank into a rocker. "Now what's so important we couldn't discuss this over the telephone?"

"We're investigating the Colton murders," said Darcy.

Kat gave them a blank stare. "Oh?"

"I'd like to know why Ashley Colton once lived here."

Kat turned to Dan. "Is she a suspect?"

"No," said Darcy.

"For the same reason all my charges come to New Beginnings—to escape a batterer."

"Who beat her?"

Kat smiled at Darcy. "I think you should ask Mrs. Colton." The rocking chair squeaked.

"I wanted to spare her the pain of the past," said Darcy. "After all, she has enough to deal with at the moment."

Kat shook her head. "Nasty business, the murders—especially the daughter."

"And I hope it ends there."

"You think Al's next?" asked Kat, her voice devoid of emotion as she rocked.

"Don't know."

"I'll give you a lead, then the rest is up to you. Frank Peters."

"Who is he and where do we find him?" asked Darcy.

"I told you who. The rest is up to you. You'll find him in Las Vegas." She leaned forward, prepared to stand. "Now I've got cleaning to do."

"Las Vegas, Nevada?" asked Dan.

"New Mexico. I'll see you out." Kat escorted them to the front door. She nodded her goodbye, and Dan thanked her.

Darcy swung onto the running board of her 4Runner and slid behind the wheel. "She's watching from the window. Hope her info isn't bogus. She gave him up rather easily."

"I agree. Our best bet is to go back to Santa Fe, then head east to Las Vegas."

"Okay." While she drove, Dan searched for an address for Frank Peters.

"Two H. Peters," he said, twenty minutes into the trip. "One in a retirement home, the other owns or runs a B&B. On the map the B&B comes up first."

"Address?"

"Working on it." He typed away on the keyboard. "Place is in the boonies. Stay alert or we might become very familiar with the area."

"As in lost?"

Dan chuckled. "Yes. Wonder who Peters is."

"I wondered the same thing."

At noon Darcy motored through the outskirts of Las Vegas. She drove across town and out into the countryside. Brown hills undulated into green valleys, and stately ponderosa pines replaced the scraggy sagebrush. She sped past pastureland dotted with grazing cows and gained in elevation as the road zigzagged into the dense forest.

"A sign up ahead," said Dan.

Darcy braked. "Peters B&B. Glad you saw that." In low gear she rolled off the highway and onto the dirt easement, the road uneven and the sides thick with vegetation. She almost missed the drive and had to back up. The house, tucked among the foliage, gleamed white in the strong sunlight. The instant she parked, a man emerged from the garage at the back of the circular drive.

Darcy alighted first. "Mr. Peters?"

"Call me Frank," said the man. "Guess you found the place okay. Margie is fixing hot cider. Best in the state. Don't bother with your bags. Someone will bring them up after you settle in."

"He thinks we're guests," said Dan, leaning into Darcy's 4Runner to retrieve his cell phone.

"Bet he won't be as hospitable when he's finds out who we are and why we're here," she whispered. Deception bothered her, no matter whom it benefited, but sometimes necessity made it inevitable.

"Come in. Sit down." Peters led them into a spacious living room. Grayed vigas, massive and commanding, stretched the length of the ceiling. Darcy gravitated to the stuccoed kiva and sat close to the fire, thankful for long pants—not because of the cold but because of the cowhide upholstery on her chair. She hated fur unless a live animal wore it.

Peters slipped off his parka. Without the bulky jacket, he appeared much smaller. His red scalp shone through his thinning white hair, and the dark circles under his blue eyes lent him a feeble persona.

Dan shot Darcy a questioning glance, a look that said, "This man can't be a beater." She'd come to this deduction as well. She couldn't visualize Peters and Al as a couple, and Al wasn't the type to take crap from anyone. Said so herself. Hell, if anything, she probably would have pistol-whipped this guy more often than he slapped her around.

"Mr. Peters." Darcy started to explain the reason for their visit, but a woman entered the room.

"Welcome. Glad you found us without any problems," said the petite brunette in a white eyelet apron and a floral dress.

Peters introduced his wife Margie; then she excused herself, giving Darcy a second chance to get the ugly business over with. "Mr. Peters—"

"Frank, Ms. McClain, and I'll save you the embarrassment of explaining who you are and why you are here. Monet phoned me yesterday. And this morning, Kat Whistler."

Margie returned. She handed out cups of steaming cider and curled up next to her husband on the couch.

"Kat never thought I beat up Ashley Colton."

"Not again." Margie sighed. "You tell me, does Frank strike you—pardon the pun—as the type to hit a woman?" She smiled at her husband. "Floor's all yours, dear." She leafed through a magazine while Peters launched into his story.

"One dark winter day, literally, Al came into my life. She glommed onto me like glue. What she saw in me, I don't know." He shrugged and shook his head.

"Oh, please, you're a wonderful man," Margie said without taking her eyes off the page.

"I'll spare you the book version. When Al and I met, I worked at Los Alamos as VP of R&D. The attraction? My position, my money, my contacts. Every person has two sides. Al was no exception. Indulge her every whim and she adores you. Deny her and she'll beat the crap out of you. Why I married her is a mystery I no longer contemplate." He rested his hand on Margie's leg. She smiled.

Peters took a swig of cider. "We stayed together until a bigger fish came along. LANL signed a contract with Colton Aerospace. A month later, Randolph became a fixture on the Hill. At the time Al worked for the head of accounting. I got her the job. Almost every night she would provoke a fight, flying into violent rages. I'd fend her off, and she'd end up bruised."

"Did you ever hit her?" asked Darcy.

"No. I may have grabbed her arm or wrist to keep her from hitting me, but I never struck her. After these fights she'd flee to Whistler's place and cry on her shoulder."

He paused. "Soon thereafter, we divorced, and Al accepted a job at Colton. Later she married Randolph. I married my secretary." He kissed Margie on the cheek.

"Mind if I ask a few questions?" asked Dan.

"Not at all, Mr. Gruet. I have nothing to hide."

"The only marriage certificate on record was Al's and Randolph's."

"Not surprising. During one of our fights, Al said something about erasing her past, not letting anyone dig up dirt on her once she married the all-powerful Colton. Those were her words. 'Have-nots hate the haves,' she constantly informed me." Peters nudged the envelope across the coffee table. "A copy of our marriage certificate. It's yours."

"It might help our investigation," said Darcy, "if you told us everything you know about Al's past. As you may have guessed, she made good on her threat."

Frank smiled. "With Randolph's connections, nothing amazes me. In retrospect, I knew very little about her. A big mistake on my part. She claimed to be born in New Jersey, raised in Philly. If I asked questions, she'd change the subject."

"Did you have children with Al?"

"Good Lord, no," Margie answered for her husband. "A blessing. I've heard how she treats her kids. You'll excuse me. I must tend to our guests. Will you stay for lunch?"

Darcy thanked her but declined.

"Last question," said Dan. "Do you know Al's maiden name?"

"Her maiden name wasn't the only thing she changed."

"I don't follow."

"Her real name is Lindsay Lee Turner."

21

Back in Albuquerque, Darcy ran up the steps to her apartment, Dan at her heels. "Can't believe Al named her daughter Lindsay Lee. How strange, especially if she wanted to bury the past."

"So where did the name Ashley come from?" He shut the front door.

"Beats me," said Darcy.

In her office she scooped a stack of documents off the fax machine and carried them into the kitchen, where Dan sat at the counter.

"Someone's been busy." She thumbed through the sheets. "Great, Testco. And let's see, the autopsy and forensic reports Franklin promised. Plus, a picture for you. A bit grainy, but passable." She placed the snapshot in front of him without a close look at it, more intent on reading the Testco results.

Dan studied the photo. "Larson's art isn't radical. Erotic, yes, but not extreme. Does he seem the type?"

Engrossed in the report, she said, "Who? What?"

"Zach Larson. Does he strike you as a sex fiend?"

"I don't know him that well, nor do I care to. Forget my clay theory. According to Testco, the white substance is a mixture of argon bromide powder and hydrofluoric acid or, as the lab terms it, ABH. Benign in its quiescent state unless mixed with cyphosolene, a volatile binary gas. Then ABH gives off argon fluoride gas. When you pump electricity into the argon gas to excite it . . . it goes on and on. The important part is we now know what the substance is." She sorted through the pages. "However, Testco still can't identify what causes the sparkle."

Dan hit speed dial on his cell phone. "Calling Rick. The sooner we get a line on Lindsay Lee Turner, the better."

"Good idea. About the white substance . . . I thought Testco would be more specific."

"If you want specifics, ask Zach if Colton is experimenting with an ABH laser. If he says yes, then he knows what the substance is and what it's used for."

"Will do. Coffee?" She drained the contents of the coffeepot and warmed the decaf in the microwave.

He pinched his nose. "You aren't going to drink that, are you?"

"Picky, picky. Do you want coffee or not?"

"Fresh brewed, sure. Reheated, no." Into the phone he said, "Emily, hi. Sure, I'll hold." To Darcy, he asked, "What'd you think of Peters and his wife?"

"Soupy but cute."

"What?"

"Too gooey for me."

"You are no romantic, McClain."

"Guilty as charged." She ground beans, filled two mugs

with hot water, and slid a half-eaten apple pie onto the butcher block.

Into his cell Dan said, "Have Rick call as soon as he's back. Thanks, Emily." He hung up.

"Is Emily subbing for Jan?"

"No, I promoted Jan to fieldwork."

"Good move." Darcy poured water into the coffeemaker, switched it on, and logged on to email via her iPad mini. "Only one message."

"Anything important?" Dan helped himself to pie.

"Nothing concerning the case, but much appreciated." She slid the mini toward him.

"'Miss you,'" he read aloud. "'Stay safe. See you soon. Love, Charlene.'" He smiled. "She's coming around."

"We're working out our differences. Sure makes life a lot easier." Darcy met his gaze. "Don't say it."

"What?"

"Don't even open your mouth except to put pie in it." She cut herself a generous slice.

"Your guilty conscience is working overtime?" He reached for the sugar.

"Believe me, I know I caused the rift between Charlene and me, but I'm doing everything in my power to fix it. Well, I'm trying."

"Told you a hundred times—forget the past, move on. You did your best, McClain."

Dan's cell chirped. "Hmm. Really? Thanks." For a long time, he said nothing, his spoon clanging against the walls of his coffee cup.

"Well, do you plan to clue me in?"

"Oh, yeah. Sure. Rick has a lead on Al's past."

"What? Already?" She dried her wet hands on a dish towel.

"The kid's good. The search for Turner points to California. Berkeley, to be exact."

"Darn. Bit of an imposition. Guess I better start checking flights."

"No need. My business in Cruces won't take more than a day or two. Why don't I pursue the Turner lead? You stay here in case something develops."

"I thought you had a ton of work waiting."

He held up this thumb and index finger. "A small ton. I'll assign someone. Besides, I liked Randolph. I want his killer caught as much as you do."

"Thanks. Keeps me where I'm needed."

"Regarding the case, I've been kicking around a few thoughts."

Darcy slid onto a bar stool. "Let's hear them."

"Hardy wondered if the killer did the hit, then drove to Perriman's Field to see his handiwork up close. I told him I didn't think so."

"I agree," Darcy said. "If he wanted a firsthand look at the charred gondola to confirm his hit, who would he mingle with? The chase crews? Too late to join them, because everyone on Randolph's crew had to preregister. Then they were checked off when they arrived at the launch site. If he showed at Perriman's Field, he'd risk being spotted. No outside crowds to hide among."

"Plus, there's no way he'd risk driving around town with a laser in his truck bed, covered or uncovered. About the truck . . . I assume that's how he moved the laser from point A to point B."

"I agree." Darcy poured refills.

Dan's wireless chirped again.

"Mind if I put you on the speaker? Yes, just me and my partner Darcy."

"Thanks for returning my call," said Dan. "Darcy, I have Martha on the line. She worked at Parson's House. Years ago."

Darcy spoke in reassuring tone. "Hi, Martha and again thanks for contacting us.""

"Hi," Martha answered, her voice low and unsure.

Darcy ran to her office and pulled a file folder from under her desk protector. On the cover she had written "Killer Profile." Inside, the first page read, "Barnes and killer—partners?"

"Your message said you wanted to know about William Barnes," Martha was saying as Darcy reentered the kitchen. "Unfortunately, Billy left the orphanage about two months after I started work at Parson's House. The Barnes couple adopted him."

Darcy shoulders fell with disappointment.

"On the other hand, I knew his brother fairly well."

Dan's eyebrows shot up. "Brother?" he said.

"What can you tell us about him?" Darcy fought to sound calm. She drew a line through "partners" and scrawled "brothers."

"I believe Paco was ten and Billy eight when they arrived at the orphanage. Paco spent most of his free time in the kitchen keeping me company while I cooked. A sad young man who internalized a lot."

"What happened to their parents?"

"Deceased, of course. Not sure how. Paco wouldn't talk about them. If I mentioned anything regarding parents, even my own, he excused himself to do homework. For a while I thought I'd made progress. He started discussing the future—plans for himself and Billy. Then the Barnes couple adopted his brother, and Paco clammed up. During the months that followed, he still wandered into the kitchen to keep me company, but he sat for hours and said little or nothing at all. Definitely not your average ten-year-old. He brought a book with him—not something he did before Billy went away."

"What kind of book? Science fiction? Nonfiction?"

"A diary. I only saw the cover, never anything he'd written. He guarded it well. I wanted very much to read some of his thoughts. Maybe I could have helped him open up."

"Surely Billy kept in touch with his brother?"

"Not according to Paco. Said he never heard from him again because the Barnes couple wanted it that way. This all could have turned out differently if only I'd acted sooner."

The sadness in Martha's voice touched Darcy. She glanced at Dan.

A frown creased his brow. "What could've turned out differently?"

"We, my husband and I, decided to adopt Paco."

Something in Martha's statement made Darcy ask, "What triggered your decision?"

A long sigh traveled over the line. "I had my suspicions but no proof. No one would talk, least of all Paco." Her voice went from a calm, even tone to upbeat. "I was so happy to arrive at work that morning and hunt him up. Couldn't wait to tell him he'd finally have a good home and loving parents. I looked for him everywhere. No one had seen him. And no one gave a damn if they had seen him."

The fervor of the last statement and the curse word caught Darcy's attention as well as Dan's. Swearing didn't fit Martha's demeanor.

"I discovered Paco's letter tucked between two cans in the pantry. He knew I fixed pork and beans on Mondays. He had run away to find Billy. I was sick about it. A month later, I resigned."

Dan frowned as though he didn't make the connection between the two events. "Why resign?"

"I told you. The abuse."

Darcy shook her head. Dan too was shaking his head. No, Martha hadn't mentioned abuse until now.

When she continued, Martha sounded on the verge of tears. "I couldn't prove anything, so I contacted a friend in Child Protective Services. They investigated, but no one would come forward."

"What kind of abuse?" Dan asked.

"Personal abuse. You know. And beatings." Martha choked out the words. "One Monday he hobbled into the kitchen, with no explanation for why he was limping." She cleared her throat. "I begged him to tell me why he appeared to be in pain. I wanted so badly to help. Excuse me." She blew her nose, then came back on the line. "Sorry."

"About the abuse"—Darcy chose her words carefully—"are you certain?"

"Positive. If you had seen the look in his eyes."

The anger in Martha's voice told Darcy to drop the abuse questioning or risk having the woman hang up. "Was Paco a nickname or his real name?"

"I don't remember anyone calling him anything but Paco. However, I do remember his last name. Cunning Owl."

22

On the third swipe, the alarm clock hit the carpet. Half-asleep, Darcy kicked off the covers and padded into the kitchen to brew coffee. She and Dan had stayed up until 3:00 a.m. rehashing clues in the murder case. During their conversation he triggered an idea long forgotten. Dredging up an old investigation, he had planted a new lead in Darcy's weary brain. She wrote, "Accounting. Check contract numbers for laser parts," on the notepad kept by the telephone and poured beans into the grinder.

"Paco Cunning Owl," Darcy repeated as she puttered around the kitchen. Strange combination of names. Dan had agreed. Paco must be a nickname.

In the other room, the fax machine whined. Darcy started toward the sound. Her mobile chimed. The number wasn't familiar. "McClain."

"Franklin." The detective sounded too cheerful for this time of the morning. "I faxed the reports."

"Got them. Thanks."

"Have you read them?"

"Yes." And nothing in them was noteworthy.

"I sent you an update. You might want to read it at your earliest convenience." The tone of his voice piqued her curiosity. "Been calling you but haven't been able to reach you." He paused as though expecting her to explain. She didn't, so he said, "We found Kevin."

"Oh? Where?"

"In a casino in Taos. The mail stuffed in his box was unpaid bills. He's addicted to gambling." Papers rustled at Franklin's end.

"What about Martin Hamilton?"

"He hasn't turned up. On another note, thought you might want a firsthand look at the evidence we've collected to date."

"Yes, I would."

"I'll be in all day. Drop by. Lena completed her interviews with Selma's boyfriends, and I should have her report by then. I'll make you a copy." More paper shuffling. "After you read my fax, you should have a talk with your friend Larson. We've tried but failed."

She opened her mouth to respond, but a dial tone droned in her ear. For a long time, she stared into space, the phone pressed to her ear, mulling over Franklin's statement.

In her office she grabbed a highlighter off the desk and skimmed the five-page fax, scanning the paragraphs for something pertinent to the case. Losing patience, she recapped the highlighter and tossed it on the tabletop. The pen landed at the same moment her eyes locked on the word "chip."

"'Purple in color with an orange center,'" she read aloud,

"'the computer chip is a—'" Darcy's feet hit the floor. "'Homing device?'"

She tossed the document on the desk. She'd been right. Randolph had a *homing device* in his pocket when he went up in that balloon, not just a computer chip, as Zach claimed. Stolen from Colton Industries, planted on Zach's boss, allowing the killer to find his target in a sea of hot air balloons.

"Damn you, Zach. Bet you knew all along, but instead you had to feed me a line of BS." Zach's desire to protect company secrets was bordering on obsessive. How was she supposed to solve a case when the guy who hired her held back key evidence?

She calmed down enough to skim Selma's autopsy report. According to Lou, Selma had shed her clothes willingly. No sign of a struggle, which meant she knew her killer—and well.

"What about the hole in her head?" Bad habit, this talking aloud, but the practice helped her think.

She hunted through the report. The hole in her forehead was inwardly beveled and circular, which could attest to a gunshot entry wound. However, no lead snowstorm—the pattern the result of a disintegrating bullet—and no bone plug in the brain matter that would indicate a cylindrical object, such as a bullet, had penetrated the skull. In conclusion, no projectile had created the wound.

"'We know'"—she moved to the next paragraph—"'all body parts belong to the same person.'" Reassuring.

"'And no seminal fluid in the vaginal canal.'" She pitched the report into a wire basket, her emotions running high, and pulled out a page with Hardy's name on it. Lou's suggestion of hitting the body parts with laser light had revealed two prints, both marred by cauterization. As for the powder he found on the body parts, he was right: it was yellow and didn't come from latex surgical gloves. Substance unknown.

Her gaze darted from the subject of gloves to the words

"diamond studs." The sequence jogged another thought. On a tablet she wrote, "Glove found in Colton parts department. Planted like diamond studs?" But who would want to frame Martin Hamilton or Kevin? Darcy rubbed her forehead. She felt a headache coming on. Perhaps the hacker was merely trying to throw investigators off the scent so they'd be too busy chasing false leads to find the real culprit?

Darcy took a seat at her desk, logged on to her laptop, and accessed Profiler, her software program for profiling serial killers. For hours she studied the evidence, fired up by the gory details and flashbacks to Selma's autopsy. As the pieces fell into place, a haunting image emerged, one all too familiar. She tried to drown the words with uplifting thoughts, but the vicious scenario dragged Darcy into her and Charlene's past.

Damn shrinks had done more to turn her sister against Darcy than to help. That's where Charlene learned her favorite line: "Neglect your children and the results can be criminal," a sentence she often screamed at Darcy when she didn't get her own way. No murder investigation had ever proved as challenging as her responsibilities as Charlene's guardian. She should have resigned from the bureau the day her parents died, but Darcy couldn't bring herself to give up a promising career.

On the other hand, how stupid she'd been to think that shipping a ten-year-old off to boarding school would solve all of her problems. Only made them worse. Much worse. Charlene retaliated by joining an elite gang of juvenile delinquents who justified their existence by robbing the rich to help the poor. Female Robin Hood or not, her sister broke the laws Darcy had vowed to uphold and proved a big disappointment to a family who prided themselves on integrity. Today, Darcy grappled with the impact of her mistakes—ones that would probably take a lifetime to correct, if at all.

She sipped cold coffee and listened to the silence, full of

regret and guilt. Abandoned—that's how Darcy had felt when her parents died. Now Randolph was gone, and her relationship with Charlene could best be described as strained but improving.

"Okay, forget the pity party and get back to work. Charlene did *not* turn out to be another Paco. Not even close, so stop kicking yourself for past mistakes and be glad you did get her help when you did."

Hours later, satisfied with her depiction of the murderer, Darcy printed a hard copy of the profile report and went into the adjacent room to dress, glad that Al had relaxed Randolph's strict dress code. The thought of wearing a skirt in zero-degree weather was a poor incentive for leaving the warmth of her apartment. Humans should hibernate.

On her hike through the snow to her 4Runner, she noticed a tall figure in black and called to her. "Hey, Della. Hi."

"Oh, hi. Haven't seen you lately. Been on vacation?"

"Working." Darcy still couldn't get over how much Della, her apartment neighbor upstairs, reminded her of Selma. She brushed the sad thought away.

"Oh, what kind of work do you do?"

"Freelance writer. Doing a feature article on Albuquerque."

"Cool. Well, I have to run. I take night classes. Have to study for an exam." Della made a face. "I hate tests."

"Who doesn't? Good luck."

"Thanks. Be careful. Roads are treacherous."

The drive across town took twice as long as usual, the streets coated in ice. Behind her chugged a cinder truck. Darcy avoided the freeway: nerve-racking enough keeping to the thirty-mile speed limit. Still, irate drivers honked or cursed as they flew by.

"Go ahead. Kill yourselves."

She steered into the lot at the third precinct and parked in an empty space near the front door. Pea-sized hail pelted her as she ran from her Toyota into the hot lobby.

"Can I help you?" asked an officer.

"Detective Donald Franklin." Darcy slid out of her parka. A pool of water formed on the floor. Darn, she forgot to kick the snow off her boots. She looked up to see Gallegos staring at her. "Oh, hi Lena."

The detective smiled, but there was no warmth behind the expression. "Been waiting for you."

"First time I've driven on ice. An experience I don't care to repeat." She combed her windblown hair into place with her fingers.

"It'll melt by the time you leave. I notice you don't wear a hat. Bad idea at this altitude. Bad for your skin."

"Thanks for the advice."

"Don had a personal emergency, so he asked me to meet with you. This way." Gallegos escorted Darcy down the hallway to a small vacant office sparsely furnished with only one sofa, one desk, and one chair. On the wall behind the desk hung a framed quote by science fiction author Lois McMaster Bujold:

Children might or might not be a blessing, but to create them and then fail them was surely damnation.

To Darcy the words certainly hit home. She stared at the quote for some time and didn't look away from the framed piece until Gallegos cleared her throat and said, "Have a seat." Then she shut the door.

Darcy sat on the edge of the couch. "What did I do to piss you off?" she asked. "Had to be more than withholding information or not telling you why Randolph hired me." She had an inkling Gallegos knew from the beginning Darcy was a PI, and she wanted to say so but reconsidered. Might sound too adversarial.

"You're right," said Gallegos. "A whole lot more than

withholding information. You robbed us of your talent. We had leads you didn't, but you had information and experience we needed. Together we could have arrested the killer before he murdered Selma."

The big guilt trip. "Do you really believe that?"

"Doesn't really matter what I believe." Gallegos immediately changed the subject. "Anyway, we appreciate your keen observation at the Cloverdale crime scene. Seldon filled me in on the white material. If it weren't for you, the lab boys might have overlooked the substance entirely." The detective launched into another topic. "Heard you're a hotshot profiler, and that you worked for the FBI's Behavioral Science Unit."

"For a short time, and I did okay."

Gallegos snorted. "Better than okay. Coworkers dubbed you The Ace. Let's hear your profile of the killer." She perched her diminutive frame on the edge of the chair, which was centered under a barred window.

Darcy leaned back against a sofa cushion. "Before I do, Franklin said you thought the killer might be a family member."

"I did, but not after Selma's gruesome murder. I can't envision anyone in the family doing something this evil. Go on. Let's hear your profile."

"Male. Physically and/or verbally abused by his father, mother, maybe both, or someone in or outside the family. Neglected. Perhaps even abandoned." She relayed the details with confidence, as Martha's information had confirmed the profile Darcy had compiled.

"Abandoned at what age?"

"Seven to ten."

"Abused at what age?" Gallegos asked, her expression pensive.

"Same. Seven to ten."

"Motive for murder?"

"Hatred. Revenge. Both. He harbored a lot of rage to kill in such a malicious way."

Gallegos nodded and appeared to relax. "I agree. Dismemberments are rare. It took sadistic rage to mutilate Selma, which says he can't relate to women."

"As for profiling the killer, part of me wonders if we might have another Ted Bundy on our hands."

Gallegos nodded again. "A murderer who defied profiling because he didn't fit a specific type. You might have something there. The mutilation a hidden desire to shock, to offend."

"I agree."

"He's mentally ill. A hard-core psychopath, don't you think?"

"Hard-core psychopath, no." Darcy spoke without thinking. She could've kicked herself for saying it just when Gallegos had opened up, but the comment didn't seem to offend the detective.

"Okay, then let's hear your take." She motioned for Darcy to proceed.

"We could debate whether he's a sociopath or a psychopath all day, but I feel he leans more toward being a sociopath."

"What makes you say that?"

"While genetic and hereditary factors create a psychopath, environmental ones are responsible for making a person a sociopath. A sociopath's personality disorder is an effect of a negative upbringing, including parental neglect, and/or poverty. And don't forget hyperintelligence. The killer's knowledge of lasers and his ability to penetrate Colton's operating systems suggest he's no dummy."

"And you already mentioned abuse, neglect, and/or abandonment, any or all of which would cause him to shut down emotionally and gradually withdraw from society. Continue."

"Usually, if a sociopath hurts others, he—or she—attempts to do so emotionally and not physically. I believe he sees killing as attacking his victims emotionally more than physically."

"You're right—we could debate this issue all day."

"I don't think he's a threat to the public as a whole. He's not a random serial killer who will kill anyone for any reason—he's limited his killing spree to the Colton family. Motive? Not sure."

Gallegos pondered the point. "There we concur. Regarding the abuse issue, what's the link between Randolph and Selma and the killer's abusive past?"

"Good question. Haven't a clue."

The detective stood. She looked as tired of the discussion as Darcy was, for no amount of debating was as important as catching him before he killed again.

"Don said to show you the evidence we've gathered so far," said Gallegos, moving toward her office door. "Down the stairs and to your right. Be with you in a minute."

Darcy waited at the bottom of the steps. Soon Gallegos appeared, a key ring dangling from her hand. She unlocked a door along the corridor and stepped inside.

"Hey, Lena." A burly officer greeted them.

"Eddie, hi. Almost time for your break. Thought you might be gone already. This is Ms. McClain, a private investigator. She's helping with the Colton case. Show her what we've got from Perriman's Field and the Cloverdale Gallery."

"Through here." He led them into the property room and slid the log toward Darcy. Gallegos chatted with the man about another investigation while Darcy signed in.

White cartons marked "Evidence" lined the walls, the boxes stacked five high. Sandwiched between the tall columns was a black door. It opened, and a man walked out, his arms full of packages wrapped in brown paper. On top of them sat a cluster of Ziploc bags. He set the lot on the table, waved to Gallegos, and made his exit. Eddie went with him.

The two reappeared with several cartons and two propane tanks. "That's everything," said Eddie.

Instead of hovering as Darcy thought Gallegos would, she sat on a stool and continued her conversation with Eddie. Occasionally, as Darcy examined the evidence, Eddie called out a comment or two. "Those are the propane tanks from Colton's gondola. The holes are close in diameter to the hole in the female victim's forehead. Tissue, of course, is elastic, while metal's not. Means the diameter may vary slightly." Same conclusion Darcy had come to.

The photo enlargement of Barnes's head and neck came to mind. "What about the black spot below Barnes's left earlobe? What caused it?"

"Superficial burn, but not a laser burn," Gallegos said. "No puncture associated with the mark."

Eddie left his seat, reached across the table, and retrieved a small manila envelope. He raised the flaps and held it over a piece of white cardboard. "The diamonds." Three studs slid out. "Two had a strand of black wool snagged in the prongs. Franklin said you already discussed the studs."

"Yes, earlier at Hardy's office." Darcy turned to Gallegos. "Where's the computer chip?"

"Ah, yes, the computer chip, which is really a homing device, but Zach won't confirm our findings. And the more we press him on the subject, the less information we get. He keeps insisting it's nothing more than a computer chip. Eddie, where is it?" The detective held out her hand. He put a pair of tweezers in her palm. Out of another envelope and onto another piece of cardboard slid the notorious chip. Barely a quarter inch square, it glistened in the bright light. "Pretty little thing," said Gallegos as she placed it under the Zeiss microscope, zoomed in, and adjusted the focus. "Take a look."

Darcy cupped an eye to the lens. Perhaps the chip was patented and Zach was trying to protect proprietary information?

Theoretically, she understood that, but realistically, his secrecy was killing people.

"I'm done." She purposely avoided the objects wrapped in brown butcher paper. She knew exactly what they were and had read the results in Lou's report. Why subject herself to the sight of Selma's defleshed and degreased bones?

She recalled her first autopsy. "Bad timing," the coroner had mumbled as he sawed the end off a femur, bone dust floating into the cool air. "I usually save these tasks for Friday nights or weekends. Once you smell the stench of boiling body parts and bone dust, the odors never leave you."

How true. Darcy pushed the gruesome memory aside. "Did you receive the Testco report?"

Gallegos smiled. "Yes, thanks. Almost forgot, I have a copy of my interviews with Selma's boyfriends, all two of them. Everyone knew she'd been dating on the sly. Really took a lot of digging to come up with names and descriptions, but the information is not much help, I'm afraid. However, the reports are yours if you want them."

Darcy recalled seeing Martin and Selma in her BMW at Colton Industries and wondered if Martin could be one of Selma's boyfriends. But if he were, Gallegos probably would have come right out and said so. "Their names?"

"Matt Davis and David Shuts. Both are artists at the Siler Gallery."

Darcy reentered the detective's drab office. For the first time, she noticed a three-shelf bookcase, the top cluttered with photographs. "May I?" She picked up one before Gallegos responded.

"Sure," said the detective, her face buried in an open file folder.

Darcy set the picture down and chose another. All of the

same child—a boy of four or five, a mass of dark curls on his head, his eyes wide and inquisitive. "Your son?"

"No." Gallegos sorted through a pile of documents. "My nephew. I don't have the patience, the time, or the inclination to raise a child. Wonderful little creatures, but in all honesty I don't have what it takes to be a good parent."

"Today few do." Darcy replaced the photo, the layer of dust a giveaway as to where the frame had sat.

"How true. Take a look at my desk. About 70 percent of the offenders are juveniles. Only this morning Don said, 'See what happens to cast-off children of irresponsible parents?'"

More shrink spiel, but the words cut close to home.

"At last." Gallegos wrenched a document from the stack. "My interviews."

Darcy scanned the sheets. "In the police and autopsy reports, I don't recall any mention of Barnes's ID card, the bank-issued smart card."

"Because we never found it. Nor do we have any idea where he really lived. We spoke to Jason—don't remember his last name—at the complex on 1414 Tramway, but he was no help. Barnes covered his tracks well. We're doing a background check, but everything moves slowly. Too much red tape. If you find out anything, we'd appreciate the information."

Darcy nodded and smiled. "I won't make the same mistake twice."

"Thanks. I'll walk you out." As she led the way down the hall, Gallegos asked, "Are you and Dan just friends?"

Darcy laughed. "Yes, just good friends."

"How long?"

"Fifteen years. But the years don't matter as much as the time we've spent together. You get to know a person well after months of twenty-hour stakeouts."

"Your bureau days, right?"

"Yes, and occasionally we collaborate on cases."

In the lobby Gallegos extended her hand and Darcy shook it, pleased the encounter had ended on a positive note. She zipped up her coat, ready to brave the cold. A uniformed officer burst through the door, his arms full of newspapers. He dropped the load in a chair and walked to the watch desk. A headline snagged Darcy's attention. She snatched up the paper.

"Take it. They're for recycling," the officer called out.

Darcy thanked him, jogged to her Toyota, and spread the front page across the steering wheel. The headline read, "More Mutilations."

23

Darcy devoured the newspaper article. Thank goodness the mutilations alluded to in the headline of the *County News* had nothing directly to do with . . . The Carver. In fact, the fatalities were bovine in nature and not human. She tossed the newspaper on the passenger seat. Still, something in the article bothered her, and she planned to pursue her theory as soon as she logged on at Colton. According to the rancher, someone was killing his livestock with a laser—a preposterous assumption, said the local police.

She drove painfully slow across town. Gallegos was wrong. The ice hadn't melted. It had actually grown worse by the time Darcy departed the police station. She arrived at work just as fresh snow fell in blinding sheets. Leaning over the seat for her emergency duffel bag, she examined the contents: sleeping bag, wool blanket, and down pillow. She'd spend the night at

Colton if need be. No way she'd drive back to the apartment in this weather. Tortellini's Pizza lived by the same motto as the US Postal Service: guaranteed delivery in all forms of weather, and Colton stocked plenty of coffee.

Darcy negotiated a safe route across the ice-slick walkway and entered the warm lobby. FBI agents were sprawled over the furniture. She walked briskly past the agents and marched up to Jim, the security guard posted near the elevators.

He opened the logbook. "FBI geek hunt." He spoke in a low voice. "The rest are on a break. Must be forty all together. Telecom guys, cops, agents. Heard them say something about a dragnet to catch the techno-perp. Exciting stuff." He popped a mint, his eyeteeth adorned with gold. "Want one?"

"No thanks."

He handed her a badge. "They're glaring at you."

"I'm used to it. What's this for?" She studied the ID.

"New security regulations for visitors. You have to wear one at all times when you're in the building. Notice the turquoise star in the lower right-hand corner? Highest clearance ever given a visitor. You obviously carry some clout."

Darcy pinned the badge to her lapel and took the stairs to the lower level. "Here to see Angelo Basini," she said to the guard outside R&D.

"Angelo Basini?" he repeated as though she spoke a foreign language. "New shift hours. He won't be in until nine tonight. Some major changes going on in his area and R&D in general."

Darcy jotted a message for Angelo, gave it to the guard, and climbed the stairs to the fourth floor, taking the long way around. She wanted to avoid Al and Zach until she was ready to confront them about the computer chip. She slipped into her office without being seen.

The phone rang. The security guard's extension appeared on the caller ID.

"McClain."

"Darcy, it's Al. I asked Jim to alert me the minute you arrived. There's a note in your in-basket about the . . . about Selma's memorial service." Al sniffled. "Excuse me."

"Thank you." She started to hang up, but Al continued to talk.

"Angelo works nights now. If that asshole hacker shows, call me immediately. Jim put my extension on your speed dial, okay?"

"Okay."

Another sniffle. "Anything new with the case?"

Darcy eyed the completed report sitting on her desk. "You'll have my update by week's end."

"Randolph believed in you. I do too."

Wow, a compliment from the dragon lady.

Darcy switched on her computer, fixed coffee, and logged on. She typed in the website listed in the newspaper article and downloaded one document after another from the National Institute of Discovery Science. Absorbed in the data, she lost track of time.

A sharp knock on the door startled her.

Zach entered. "Been here long?"

Next time she'd lock the door. "Perfect timing."

"Oh? I haven't seen you in days. Have you made any progress on the case?" He removed the newspaper that was sitting on the visitor's chair, set it on the desk, and sat down.

"You'll have my report Friday. In the meantime, I have some questions." She thumbed through the material Detective Franklin had faxed. "Let's start with the computer chip found in Randolph's jacket pocket, the one that's really a homing device."

Zach calmly crossed his legs. "I'll tell you what I told Lena Gallegos. It's a computer chip, not a homing device. Whoever dreamed up that explanation is reaching."

"Liar."

He flinched, obviously surprised by her comment and her tone of voice.

"Why would I lie? I want to catch Randolph's killer as much as you."

Darcy really lost her temper. "Damn you. After everything that has occurred, and you are still in damage control mode, trying desperately to protect your damn job and the company's proprietary information." She unfolded the newspaper from the third precinct.

Zach peered at it, his brows coming together. "Bovine Mutilations? What the hell does that have to do with Randolph's murderer?"

"Nothing. But it has everything to do with you denying that the computer chip found in Randolph's jacket pocket was indeed a homing device. To find its target, the laser has to lock onto something. And it does. It locks onto a homing device."

He leaned forward. "What are you driving at?"

"I'll only hit the high points. Fact: three bovine mutilations in three months. All in Taos County. Full necropsies were conducted on two cows and one bull followed by toxicological, histological, and chemical analysis. Findings? Holes a half inch in diameter in the craniums. In the bull, a second hole in the chest. The margins of the cavities were charred. Internal hemorrhaging, yet not a trace of blood in the pastures where the carcasses were discovered. The bull's heart shredded but the pericardium intact. The animal's brain matter desiccated. Evidence of high heat or cautery in all three."

"Where's this leading, McClain?" His lips sealed tightly.

"I'm almost there."

"Make your point soon."

Her hands balled into fists, nails biting into flesh. "It would be in your best interest to listen."

In a gesture similar to one Al used frequently, he threw his arms into the air. "Okay, play out your little drama."

"Fact: witnesses testified they saw a green light flying in the area on the night of the bull's death. Gouge marks in the field, some five to six inches deep, were noted by the experts at the NIDS." She pointed to the report she'd downloaded from the National Institute of Discovery Science. "In some places the grass appeared uprooted, but no footprints were found in the waterlogged meadow. The rancher who owned the bull said he suspected a laser beam killed it." She dropped the report on the desk.

"On this same issue," she continued, now fired up, "last but not least, a sparkly white substance with a yellow powder was detected in the hole and on the surrounding tissue. Yellow powder? Similar to the yellow powder found on Selma? I wonder. Shall I go on?"

"Don't bother. I've heard enough."

She scooped up another document. "Ever heard of RBTI?"

"In this state, who hasn't? The air force's Realistic Bomber Training Initiative. Training flights for aircrews flying B-1B and B-52H aircraft out of bases in Texas and Louisiana. Approximately three thousand low-level flyovers in northern New Mexico alone. Two counties in particular, Taos and Colfax. No secret there. The flights are a major source of contention among the residents. Hell, the *County News* runs an article or editorial about the issue at least once a month. So what?"

She pulled a sheet from the stack. "I got this off the DOD's website. 'The ABL, Airborne Laser Program, started in 1997. It tests low- and high-powered lasers over White Sands Missile Range and regions north of Los Alamos. Firing of the high-energy, long-range equipment will involve destruction of target missiles during the test phase.' Hmm. Wonder if some of our young top guns are having fun with the local ranchers by taking out a few bovines instead of concentrating on military objectives?"

"So a bunch of hotshot flyboys are practicing on bovines. What's your point, Darcy?"

"My point is that I'm sick of all the secrecy."

"Maybe if you calmed down, you'd make sense."

"My point is that you've known all along that the computer chip is really a homing device and you flat out lied to me. Had you been honest rather than wasting all of this time protecting our damn job and the company's proprietary information, I could have stopped the killer."

"You have a fabulous imagination. Ever thought about putting your talents to work with the Roswell gang?"

The statement fueled her ire. "I'm tired of playing games, Zach. There's more at stake here, like avenging Randolph's death, and I won't stop until his killer is brought to justice."

24

The heating unit kicked on, warding off the chill in the basement command center where Darcy kept vigil. Two doors down, the boys had taken up residency. Their plan of attack was textbook FBI. Regardless of the bureau's involvement, Al had insisted that Darcy stay on the case because Al never had much faith in the government or law enforcement in general.

Stretched out and prepared for a long wait, Darcy pondered her conversation with Zach. After this latest encounter, she had lost all respect for him. Despite his promise, he hadn't done everything in his power to help solve the murders. Instead, he had become a stumbling block. She understood he walked a fine line between protecting Colton's proprietary defense contracts and providing information to crack the case, but Randolph had trusted her with the company secrets, so why not Zach? Darcy hated mind games. Waste of time.

Warm air stirred the smell of pizza, the empty box stuffed in the trash can under a collection of soft drink cans. Dinner from hours ago. Her stomach growled. She unzipped a pocket in her backpack and rummaged for change, then collected the Coke cans stacked on her desk.

Silence followed her down the hall. She dumped the cans into a plastic box marked "Recycle" and walked on. Near the stairwell stretched a wide selection of vending machines. The clink of coins sounded like gunshots in the still of the night. She popped the tab on a ginger ale and strolled back toward her workstation. Dead as a morgue now that Al had done away with the night shift for most of Colton's employees. Whereas hundreds once roamed the corridors, now only a handful did. Seemed strange not to hear the drone of equipment and the sound of people laughing, all normal during a shift hard at work.

Somewhere an elevator door opened and a cleaning woman rounded the corner. With her floated the sharp scent of ammonia intermingled with bleach. She nodded a greeting and then slipped into the restrooms, a trash bag in hand.

Darcy reached the end of the dog-legged corridor, stopped abruptly, and whirled around, surprised by the sound of footsteps behind her. In the hallway stood Karla Sizemore, her red hair flowing around her shoulders. She looked like an apparition in the dimly lit passage and even more so when she didn't move or say anything until Darcy spoke first. "Karla?"

"Darcy, hi."

"I thought Al did away with night shift," said Darcy, puzzled by Karla's presence, and at this hour.

Karla came closer. "I had to pick up some lab reports for Al." Her gaze fell on the documents stacked in her arms. "How's the case going?"

"Slower than I'd like."

"Well, good luck." She turned around and hurried back in the direction from which she'd come.

Puzzled by the entire encounter, Darcy proceeded to the command center, closed the door, and headed straight for her laptop. She had mail. Al's message brought a chuckle. "I've been researching how hackers work. Can't you log on to their networks, check their bulletin boards, and make them talk?" Darcy hit Delete.

Email. Not a bad idea. Maybe she'd find something of interest in Zach's correspondence if she could crack his password. And she stood a good chance of doing so, for sometimes she found it easier to decode corporate passwords than to crack personal keys. After an hour of random combinations, she had Zach's code: Lonestar, spelled 12, o, 14, e, 19, t, 1, r. Of course, knowing he was from Texas helped her break his password.

She scrolled from one boring message to another, none pertinent to the case until "ABH" in the subject line jumped out. The email read, "Case of ABH stolen. No need to panic. Checking into the matter." Randolph had sent the memo to Rodriquez and Muñoz and copied Zach.

She opened another email and read aloud: "'Switching vendors from Ultradine to Aerodynamics. Effective 9/30. Submit final statements to . . .'"

The email jolted her memory. Earlier, before Zach barged into her office, she was about to log on to Colton's accounting databases to follow the lead Dan had brought to mind during their brainstorming session. She had a sneaking suspicion the hacker was somehow using the company's automated systems to steal what he needed, which meant she needed to research contract numbers for laser parts. The only problem then was she'd had no idea how to access the data without a code. Now she had Zach's code, assuming the same random access worked here as well as for his email account. Too often, people used the same passwords for numerous accounts, this being simply easier to keep track of but not safer.

On a pad she scribbled "Aerodynamics" in one column, "Ultradine" in another. Then for hours she traipsed through Colton's maze of operating systems, pried into credit records, and snooped through vendor accounts, concentrating specifically on Aerodynamics and Ultradine. She signed out of accounting and connected to the sales department to verify Colton's use of contract numbers for their laser parts. If her theory was correct, then she knew precisely how the cracker had moved the lasers out of Colton Industries without detection. Close to being convinced, she needed to confirm her premise by searching Colton's shipping logs.

The hair on her neck bristled. This was what she loved about cybersleuthing: the thrill of discovery. Her fingers flew over the keyboard. Armed with Zach's email password, she logged on to Colnet, Colton's high-security database of defense contracts, but a firewall locked her out of the proprietary sector. Undeterred, she ate up an hour trying random combinations until she penetrated the electronic barricade, only to find herself staring at another wall, this one more formidable than the last. Challenged, she persisted in her quest.

The night dragged on. Unable to circumvent the second firewall and with nothing better to do, she returned to Zach's email to comb his folders. Bored after twenty minutes of trolling, she groped for her empty coffee mug. Time for a caffeine fix. Out of the corner of her eye the letters *PL* leaped off the screen. She stopped in midair, her hand suspended over the cup. Her pulse raced.

"The PL chip (purple/orange) is an integral component of the ABH long-range, high-energy laser incorporated into the B1-B and B-H52 bombers used in the RBTI sorties over Colfax and Taos Counties."

Boldface liar, that Zach. Those flyboys *were* using Zach's chip for target practice. She speed-read the document, stopping when she reached "A highly refined silicate material, SL32, is crucial to the chip's workings. Without it—" Odd, someone had deleted portions of the text. However, the paragraph ended with "SL32, a space-age micaceous white compound, disintegrates to a yellow powder when exposed to high temperatures."

Yellow powder. The killer hadn't been careless. Just the downside of the job, which he knew and had tried to erase.

Her temples throbbed, the rush of discovery exhilarating. She skimmed the next sentence, her eyes devouring the words. "SL32, the primary property in the PL chip, is sparkly white when cold. Excited by an electrical current, SL32 glows orange, indicating that the laser seeker (homing device) has been activated."

"Homing device. Homing device," she repeated aloud. "Hmm. Rangefinder, laser, laser seeker." The final piece of the equation fell into place. "Damn you, Zach. You knew all along."

Footsteps in the hallway.

Darcy quickly signed out, but not before "ABL, Airborne Laser Program" and "Aerodynamics manufactures B-1B and B-52H bombers" glared from the monitor.

Someone knocked. The door opened. Light blazed into the room. "Darcy?"

"Kill the lights."

"Sorry, didn't mean to blind you." Angelo shut the door and drew up a chair, his face lit by the ghostly glow from the LED. "Why are you working in the dark?"

"I concentrate better."

"Thought I'd find you logged on."

"Disconnected a second ago."

"How are things going?"

"No sign of him."

Angelo looked at her laptop sitting open next to the bank of computer screens. "What's with the flowchart?"

"Been working on the project for days, but only tonight has everything sort of come together."

"What does all of this mean?"

Although she was unable to crack the second firewall to confirm her theory as to how the cracker stole the lasers, she decided to share her premise with Angelo and get his reaction. "It's about the method he used to steal the CR3 computer parts. He stole them without ever setting foot in the building."

Angelo stared in disbelief. "Are you sure?"

"Yes. For weeks I've racked my brain wondering how he pulled off the heist without being caught on Colton's surveillance cameras. Now I know. If we hadn't been watching for him, he might have gotten away with it altogether. Or we might have only discovered the theft during an audit of the CR Project, which doesn't take place until next July. By then the damage would've been done and our hacker long gone."

Angelo rubbed his hands together. "Don't keep me in suspense."

"I've asked myself a million times, how does anyone rip off lasers practically the size of a VW Bug—a slight exaggeration—without being caught. Simple. For the hacker, that is. I'm not as familiar with Colton's lasers as you are, so correct me if I'm wrong."

He nodded.

"The CR Project encompasses all phases related to a particular line of lasers: the CR2 YAG, CR3 Ruby, and the soon-to-be-released CR4L lasers. All phases were assigned the same contract number. Bad idea because this only made it easier for him to steal CR2 models and parts for the CR3 lasers. Different contract numbers may have slowed him down."

"Whether we assigned one or twenty," said Angelo, "I have

a feeling it wouldn't have mattered with this guy because our rangefinder had a different contract number, and he stole those parts as well."

"Good point."

"Still, it is too bad no one wised up after the YAG theft and implemented new contract numbers," said Angelo. "As you said, different numbers may have slowed him down and allowed us to catch him."

There Zach had dropped the ball, but Darcy said nothing. It had no real relevance now.

Angelo continued. "On the CR project alone there are over a thousand vendors, which makes it hard to keep track."

"No kidding. And he relied on that fact." She thought of the hours she'd spent poring over vendors' accounts.

"Plus, accounts expire and new ones are activated. Easy to hide things in a sea of paperwork."

"And our cyberperp counted on that as well and used it to his advantage. Moving on. From my research, after a dozen lasers are built at one time, they're shipped directly to a company called Ultradine."

"Used to be. We have a new vendor now. Aerodynamics," Angelo said.

"But it used to be Ultradine."

"Right."

"And Ultradine fabricated a special housing for the CR2."

"Right again."

"Once the special housing was installed, Ultradine sent the entire laser to Aerodynamics. Aerodynamics manufactures jet fighters for the DOD. Ultradine declared bankruptcy two months ago, but Colton was in no hurry to find a new vendor for the special housing because Aerodynamics planned to purchase the housing assembly from the defunct Ultradine," Darcy said.

"Wow. You've done some research."

"Our hacker broke into Colton's accounting databases, reactivated Ultradine's account—a cinch because he knew the contract number—shipped the lasers he wanted to the defunct address, and stole them from the Ultradine premises. Lax security, I discovered, is the only reason Ultradine went belly-up." She reclined in her chair. "A breach our guy used to his advantage."

"Which means he knew about the Ultradine/Aerodynamics switch. Inside job?"

"Yes, I think our hacker works for Colton. Actually, stealing YAG lasers was the easy part."

Angelo's eyes widened. "Oh? Go on."

"Unlike the fully assembled CR2 lasers shipped to Ultradine, the CR3 lasers require parts and parts only because they're built on site. Why? Because the housing for the CR3 is specific to that generation of laser. No parts, no matter how small, are shipped to anyone but Ultradine, so when our hacker needed components to build his CR3 he got real smart. He broke into an independent credit agency, Ace Credit."

"Not affiliated with Colton in any way," Angelo commented.

"Correct. He listed his fictitious company on a register and gave himself a triple-A rating, the highest available. He knew accounting would verify his credit. Then he hacked into Colton's parts department. He created a real paper trail, a way of covering his tracks. Equipped with a parts list, he connected to the sales department where he placed an order. Next, he jumped to accounting and paid the invoice. Logged on in shipping, he typed a delivery manifest. The delivery address? Ultradine's. For Colton the paper trail was complete. You have an order, a paid invoice, and a delivery manifest; Ultradine's credit rating is tops, so everything checks out okay. Until next year's audit, he goes undetected."

"Ingenious, not to mention doggone smart on your part. Darcy McClain, diva of cybersleuths."

"I wouldn't go that far. Something still puzzles me. Munoz claimed the hacker was using Al's PC when he downloaded the CR3 schematics from Colton's database, but the only person we found in her office was Martin Hamilton. And in my opinion, he is not a suspect."

"Every computer in the company has a user's ID number. Al's is fifty-two. Zach's is fifty-nine. Yours, eighty-two. If he works here, then he knows this. He simply used the codes to fake us out. Even off-site, you can create a program to switch codes, which is probably what he did. It's the simplest thing he's done so far. His only reason for doing so? To screw with us. He wanted us to think he was in the building." He shook his head. "Scary how a high-security defense contractor can be this vulnerable. On the other hand, the average Joe wouldn't know what to do with stolen CR3 parts unless he had the schematics and the know-how to build a laser."

"Everything our hacker possessed."

Angelo sighed as he stretched his neck. "But what are the odds? Less than one in a million? As for Colton's vulnerability, hell, we pale in comparison to some of the security breaches at Los Alamos. Not only do the Chinese have our military secrets, but we can't even account for every pound of plutonium. The enemy counts on someone falling asleep on the job."

"No." She yawned. Her elbow brushed her mouse, and the computer woke up. It beeped several times. She sat upright. "Our cracker is signing on. I installed an intruder-detection program to alert me."

Angelo slid into the seat beside her. "He's reading emails."

"Searching. Going through them fast. Probably to see if we mentioned him in any of our internal chatter."

"Holy shit. He deciphered five encrypted passwords in a matter of minutes. You have to admire this guy."

"He's nervous. Every five to ten minutes he stops reading and issues a command to tell him if anyone's logged on. He's afraid someone's watching," Darcy said.

"Now he's hunting to see if we've made any changes in our operating system."

"Smart." She forced herself to blink, her dry eyes burning.

"This blows my mind. He's using our computers to dial Livermore Labs. But why? I mean, what can you learn in a two-second phone call?"

"He's not trying to learn anything. He's showing us that he can—that he has the smarts to bypass our security as well as Livermore's, which is a hell of a lot harder to break into."

"Now he's cracking Sandia Labs."

Darcy reached for a notepad.

"Shit. He's gone," said Angelo.

"What?" She swung back to her computer.

The door opened, and a coworker of Angelo's barged in. "Sorry, but the feds need you to fix some kind of glitch in the system."

"Be back in a minute." Angelo left the room with his co-worker.

Tired, Darcy stood in the doorway, her back against the jamb, and watched Angelo disappear down the hall to his lab. As soon as he returned, she'd have him babysit the hacker while she went upstairs for her sleeping bag.

Angelo reappeared in the corridor, his sneakers screeching on tile. "He's back. Hurry."

The shout galvanized Darcy. She ran to Angelo's lab. "There." He pointed to the bank of computer screens. "Jerk came online the minute I fixed the so-called glitch. A hiccup caused by the hacker."

Nothing on the displays aroused her suspicions. "What's he doing?"

"Reading email."

"Again? Are the feds tracing the call?"

"Yeah." Angelo pointed his thumb at the massive glass window that separated his lab from the FBI's nerve center. The four agents Darcy had seen earlier draped over the lobby chairs stared back, grins plastered on their pasty faces. She couldn't hear a word they said, but by their smug expressions she suspected that something was going down.

Suddenly alarm wiped the grins off their faces, and two agents gestured frantically to the rest.

"I have a bad feeling," said Darcy.

Angelo snatched his telephone off the desk. "Do you have a location? Better get him now or he'll be gone." He hooked the receiver over his shoulder. "No trace yet."

The display in front of Darcy dissolved to gray, then black. The one next to it did the same. "Quick!" she shouted. "Something's going on. The screens are going black."

Angelo whipped his head around. "Holy shit." He hammered on the glass partition. Startled, two agents jumped up. "Hurry. Trace the goddamn call. He's not on email anymore."

Darcy swept the bank of monitors, relieved to see a tangle of crisscrossed lines displayed on each. "What's wrong?"

But the instant Angelo glanced at the screens, he screamed, "Trace the fucking call or I'm shutting down. Shit. He's downloading every schematic. Quick. Bottom left. Give me a number."

"Thirty," said Darcy. She held her breath as the count increased.

"If he gets them all, Colton will be ruined. Our military secrets broadcasted to the world. Fucking A. Only two to go." The phone slipped from his shoulder and crashed to the floor. He pounded the glass with both fists.

An uproar ensued in the adjoining lab as several agents dived for telephones while others gathered before a city map tacked to the wall. An agent jotted an address on a whiteboard. The trace. They had their hacker. And she had his address. Darcy shoved her chair away from the computers and ran for the nearest exit.

She slammed into the release bar on the door closest to the north parking lot and charged out into the cold night. The air vibrated with the shrill sound of Colton's breached security alarm. She reached her 4Runner just as Franklin pulled into a space several slots away.

"Darcy?" he shouted.

"Hurry. Hop in."

Franklin crossed the lot in quick strides, ripped open the passenger's door, and swung his tall frame into the seat. "What's up?"

"Think we located our hacker."

25

"I don't want this to come across wrong, but are you comfortable driving on ice?" Franklin asked as Darcy steered cautiously toward the main entrance to Colton Industries.

"Not really," she said gently. She rolled to a stop and traded places with Franklin.

"Thought I'd offer since I'm used to these conditions and I know the area."

"Thanks." She tossed him her car keys. "A whole lot easier on my nerves and probably yours as well."

He laughed.

Darcy shot him a sidelong glance. In no way did he resemble her childhood vision of a cop: shaved head, big muscles, and practically every word barked, not spoken. The kind of man who reminded her of her boss at the bureau, a Napoleonic drill sergeant. None of these traits fit Franklin. Calm, soft-spoken, and reflective, he acted self-assured and confident in his conclusions, basing them on fact, not assumptions.

"Address?" said Franklin, interrupting Darcy's evaluation of him.

"It's 1818 Coors."

"Strange, holed up in a salvage yard. Thought our hacker would pick swankier digs like an apartment, a house, even an office."

"Is that where we're headed? It does seem odd."

On the outskirts of town, Franklin cut through a residential neighborhood and emerged on a back street. Thunk, thunk, thunk. The tires churned up mud and flung it out of the wheel wells.

"Shortcut," he said. "Fewer signal lights to slow us down and less ice to fight."

Darcy was about to comment when her 4Runner skidded sideways, glided a few feet, and then regained traction. She stared out the window. Nothing but murky black. Dark shadows specked the roadside. She squinted at the forms. Construction vehicles. "Sharp bend ahead."

Franklin plowed around the curve, swerved to avoid a truck abandoned on the shoulder, and narrowly escaped collision with a backhoe parked on the opposite side. "Sorry, didn't expect anything there. It's a no-park zone."

Darcy blew out a lungful of air. "I'm okay—1818 is coming up. Next one. There." She pointed to the sign, the metal digits tarnished by harsh weather.

He downshifted. "Get ready. This bank could be tricky."

The Toyota descended the embankment into the salvage yard. Franklin steered left, then right, to keep the 4Runner on the steep grade and away from the crushed vehicles that bordered the entry. With less than a car length to go, the Toyota fishtailed. His hands planted firmly on the wheel, Franklin guided the vehicle into a skid and coasted to a stop in front of a sprawling galvanized structure. He appeared calm and composed. Darcy wished she felt the same way.

He opened the driver's door. Icy air gushed into the warm cab. "Want me to go first with you as backup?"

The offer sounded genuine, not macho. "Sure." Besides, this wasn't the time to prove who had bigger balls. At the bureau Darcy's track record spoke for itself. Older now, she didn't need to prove anything to anyone, except on occasion to Charlene.

The full moon cast suspicion on the piles of jagged steel that buffered the perimeter of the lot. Like being trapped in a metal tunnel. Franklin stopped near an electric pole with dead spotlights mounted to the top and scanned the area before him. Darcy did the same. Silence. And with the night being so cold, the air held no smells.

His gun drawn, Franklin approached the service bays. He motioned for her to keep to his left. On a prior case, when Darcy had cautioned a CEO to stay put, he'd said, "Come on. How dangerous can a hacker be?" His gunshot wound had taken months to heal.

Franklin peeked through the gaps in the sheet metal walls and then backed away. He nodded for her to take a look. A blue-gray glow filtered from one corner of the inky interior. She couldn't make out what it came from.

He tapped her on the shoulder before he crept down the side of the building and squeezed through an opening in the chain-link fence that encircled the backyard. A foot or two behind, she watched his back.

Darcy passed a huge dirt hill, paused, and then walked on, arriving alongside Franklin at the rear of the building. He tried the knob to the pedestrian door. A slight twist and it opened.

He stepped in, Darcy at his heels. He located a switch. Light flooded the interior.

Other than a row of cardboard boxes jammed against the far wall and an abandoned monitor in the tiny office, the place was empty.

"He must've split in a hurry."

"What's the distance from Colton to here?" asked Darcy.

"Didn't clock it, but ten minutes, tops."

The blue-gray glow didn't come from a computer as Darcy suspected but from a black light sitting on the desktop. Franklin knelt on the floor. "No hard drive. No printer. Only a cheap monitor, and not even plugged in."

"Setup," said Darcy.

"Exactly. He redirected the call." Franklin dug through the trash. "Nothing."

"You have to admire this guy's intelligence. Too bad he doesn't put his talents to better use."

"I prefer to admire him when he's behind bars. Look at this." Franklin stood before a chalkboard. The single sentence said, "Trick or Treat." Franklin shook his head. "You're right. It's a setup. Wonder what's keeping the feds."

"Wondered the same thing," she said from the tiny bathroom at the back of the building.

"How come you beat them here?"

"They did me a favor. Not knowingly, of course." Darcy explained how the agent had jotted the address on their whiteboard. "Saved me from running back to my lab to get it."

"Two line traces—what a waste of time and money. At least $59K each."

"A hundred grand for both sounds about right. There was no reason for me to have a separate wiretap. The one for the FBI would've sufficed, but Al insisted." Something black drew

Darcy's attention. She retrieved the ball of fuzz stuck to the anchor bolts on the toilet and wrapped it in tissue paper.

"Any luck?"

Darcy showed him what she'd found. "Maybe nothing."

"Can't hurt to run it through the lab as soon as we're back. I'll be over there." Franklin headed for the service bays.

Darcy walked over to the rusted stove near the back door and probed the ashes with a metal poker. A patch of white caught her eye. She changed positions to block Franklin's view of the stove, then pulled a small book out of the ashes, its edges and spine burned but most of the pages intact. After browsing a few paragraphs, she shut the diary and pocketed it. The disgusting descriptions of physical abuse turned her stomach.

She should've given the book to Franklin, but once the police had it, she couldn't be sure they would allow her to read it.

"Find anything?" he called to her.

"Fire's cold."

"Come over here and check this out."

She joined Franklin in the deserted bays.

He flicked his penlight beam over the pitted concrete corners. The strong shaft landed on a wide tire track. She knelt alongside the impression, the dull red-orange tread marks easy to make out against what was once a layer of black mud, the clay now rock hard. She opened her penknife and speared a tiny blob of white material embedded in the sandstone. The frozen sample sparkled under the brilliant torchlight.

Franklin smiled. "Look familiar?'

"Sure does. Argon bromide powder and hydrofluoric acid. ABH for short."

"How did you know what it was?"

"Only found out hours ago. No chance to call you, but I'll fill you in on the way back."

He seemed to accept her explanation. "Is this stuff dangerous?"

"Benign in its current state. Here, hold this for a minute." She handed him her knife, then crossed the garage to the cardboard boxes.

"Already checked them. Empty. Every one."

Darcy pushed a carton over. A thick film of white the consistency of dried caulking, and easily mistaken as such, coated the bottom of the box. Only the telltale sparkle told her it was something else. The stolen case of ABH? She righted the carton. "Why don't we check the yard before the feds show?"

"Good idea." Franklin wrapped the knife in a clean latex glove he took from his pocket. "I'll return your knife later."

"No hurry."

Conscious of the time, Darcy led Franklin directly to the dirt hill she'd spotted on the way in.

He shook his head. "What's so exciting about yards of fill?"

"The fact it's red clay or sandstone." She fanned the ground with her flashlight. The same wide tire tracks crossed and crisscrossed the area approximately ten feet in width and twenty in length. They ran from the base of the red hill to the rear of the building. With only one entrance and one exit to the yard, a vehicle had to drive past the pile of red clay whenever he entered or left the yard. Rain or melted snow must have washed the eroded soil across the entry in the chain-link fence, which meant their hacker couldn't avoid driving through the red clay coming and going. She squatted. Franklin knelt next to her. She shone her penlight on the tire track.

"Identical wear marks," said Franklin.

"Uh-huh. Identical wear marks on the tire track found at the bank parking lot and the tire track in the drive behind the Cloverdale Gallery. Our hacker, killer, gets around."

The drone of engines filled the night.

"Feds," said Franklin. "When we're done defending ourselves, how about coffee somewhere? We'll both need one."

"Love to, but I can't. Have to be up early."

"Must be important."

"Selma's memorial service."

"Strange date to pick."

"Why?"

"Tomorrow's Halloween."

* * *

South of Albuquerque in the town of Socorro, Paco backed his truck into a warehouse on the west side and slid out of the driver's seat. He called to Bullet, who leaped into the cargo bed and watched while his master loaded supplies into the dilapidated Ford.

Fat snowflakes tumbled from the sky. Bullet snapped at them as they twirled toward him. Soon, he went from being black to covered in white. He shook, jumped out of the truck, and trotted to a blanket spread on the cold garage floor. Paco followed.

He wrapped his arms around Bullet and hugged him. Paco took comfort in knowing Bullet was still young, for when he went to the Rainbow Bridge, Paco's world would crash. Tears stung his eyes, not at the thought of losing Bullet but at remembering his first giant schnauzer, Manny, stolen out of his backyard at six months old. Not knowing her fate tore at his heart every day.

All his life they had stolen from him, taking everything he held dear, including his ability to love. They stole his childhood, his dreams, his life, his dog—even damaged his soul, which he'd never recover from. He'd planned to live life through Billy, but they took him as well. He wiped away the tears and held Bullet closer. Then as quickly as it came, the fog in his brain lifted.

He checked the time on his phone. "FBI should be entering the yard right about now."

Bullet cocked his head.

"Give them five minutes, and they'll know I've kissed them off. Come on, guys. Do you really think I'd let you trace my call? I don't make mistakes—" He thought of Billy, cold in a grave in Albuquerque, and snapped his mouth shut. The anguish in his heart flared anew. He brushed at the tears. Hurt dissolved to anger. Paco stood. "Let's go," he said, his tone sharp. Bullet sprang off the floor and ran outside.

Paco tied a tarp over the truck bed and cinched the lines taut with unnecessary strength. He hated venting his anger at Bullet.

"Okay, okay, I'm sorry I raised my voice at you."

Bullet poked his head around the corner of the truck. Paco laughed the minute he saw the ice balls stuck to Bullet's beard and eyebrows. "Hop in." He held open the passenger's door.

Seated beside Paco, Bullet rested his muzzle on his master's thigh and dozed during the trip back to town. Paco spent ninety grueling minutes fighting icy roads and worrying about getting into an accident at one in the morning. Distracted by the weather conditions, memories of Billy, and the job ahead, he failed to notice the 4Runner until he cut in front of it, afraid he'd miss his off-ramp. The driver leaned on the horn. The SUV veered into the next lane, sailed over the icy surface, and careened into a snowbank. Paco exited the freeway and drove home.

26

In the warmth of her living room, Darcy massaged liniment into her sore shoulder before limbering up for her morning run. Stiff from head to toe from last night's accident, it took longer than usual to ease the kinks in her tight muscles. Bruises covered her arms and legs, but she hadn't been badly hurt when the truck forced Franklin off the road and into the snowbank. Thankfully for them both, his attention was focused on driving, and hers centered on first the vehicle, a primer-gray pickup, and second on the license plate. Again she couldn't make out the numbers, but she had no trouble seeing the letters: *BVN*. Same truck she saw at the cemetery the day Barnes was buried.

She filled a water bottle, pocketed her keys, and glanced at the status report lying on the kitchen counter. She decided to email the report to Zach rather than hand-deliver it. The less she saw of him, the better.

Darcy started her routine with a fast walk around her complex before she broke into a steady jog, her sights set on the nearest exit from the gated community. A cinder truck and a snowplow lumbered by, both working north on Tramway, so she opted for the southerly route, its streets already clear of snow and ice. More traffic, but nothing compared to San Francisco.

The cold, crisp air stung her throat and froze her cheeks. She tugged on her turtleneck until the high collar covered her ears and overlapped the edge of her wool cap. Cars whizzed by. Every vehicle warranted a stare. Maybe she'd spot the primer-gray truck with Arizona plates.

She dodged a group of pedestrians mingling on the sidewalk. No matter where, running in the city was like negotiating an obstacle course. Ahead loomed fast-food row. The aroma of coffee brewing wafted through the air, chased by burnt grease. Darcy passed a chicken franchise. A man loitered in the doorway, a stogie hanging from the corner of his mouth. "Nice day," he yelled.

She waved and shot up a side road that led past a string of apartment buildings, each cheaper to rent than the last—this evident from the age of the structures and the neglected grounds. She circled the cul-de-sac and jogged back up the dead-end street. As she neared the main drag, Darcy decided to cut her run short—not for physical reasons, for she had a high tolerance for pain, but for emotional ones. What really ached this morning was her heart. Randolph. Selma. Her parents.

Hot tears trickled down her cheeks. She fought them back and ran faster, but speed couldn't block the ugly images. Randolph's charred body, contorted and crammed into the bottom of his gondola. Selma carved into pieces like a slaughtered animal. Darcy's parents burned beyond recognition. When they died Randolph became her emotional safety net, her proxy father. Now she had only Charlene . . . and Dan.

Building to a lung-bursting speed, Darcy pounded the pavement with resounding thuds. She maintained the pace as she sprinted past the Sunset Skies apartments, slowing for a few seconds at the corner of the street before running on.

High-pitched yelps blasted the serene morning, the cries so loud and painful that Darcy winced. Spurred by anger, she propelled herself over a low hedge beside a nearby apartment complex and rounded the bend at a fast clip. She saw something red standing near the fenced-in swimming pool and stopped in her tracks.

Tied to the wrought iron fence, on a very short leash, was a large black dog. A few feet away stood a man in a green-and-red plaid bathrobe. "You worthless piece of shit," he screamed, and then kicked the wet animal with his cowboy boot. Snarling, the dog tried to lunge at the man. He raised a baseball bat over his head and swung.

"Hey, stop. Now!" Darcy shouted.

"Get screwed," the man shouted back. "I'll do whatever I want to my dog."

"I won't tell you again." She closed the gap between them.

The dog thrashed on the tight lead. The nylon leash broke, and the animal bolted. The man paused as if to size up Darcy as a threat and then fled.

She pursued him to the rear of the complex, arriving in time to see him scale the stone wall. She raced to the nearest pedestrian gate, but it was locked, so she grabbed hold of the wrought iron and hoisted herself to the top. The man skidded down a bank and disappeared among the houses in the adjacent neighborhood. She wouldn't catch him now, so she retraced her steps to the front of the apartment complex and went looking for the manager.

His appearance did nothing to inspire confidence: short, with wet hair (what little he owned), faded sweats, and a protruding belly. The moment he opened his mouth, he angered her. "Don't see a problem. Dogs are allowed in the pool area, but not in the pool or in the spa."

Darcy hadn't said a word about the dog being in the pool. "That's not my complaint. I'm trying to find the dog's owner."

"Don't know anyone, not off the top of my head, who wears a plaid robe and has a big black dog, but I can check around. You sure he wore plaid?"

"Yes," she said, losing patience.

He chewed on a toothpick. "Like I said, I'll ask. Can't say I blame him for being pissed. Dogs aren't allowed in the pool."

"I heard you the first time." And no animal deserved such treatment. She wanted to smack him. Instead, she asked for a pen and paper to jot her name, apartment address, and phone number. "If you find the owner, please contact me—" He snatched the note from her hand and closed the door.

Fuming, Darcy looped the complex twice, searching for the dog. In many ways she had more regard for animals than humans—definitely in this case. She made a mental note to check animal shelters, veterinarians, and groomers to see if she could find the dog. Hopefully, the animal would not return to his owner.

She jogged out of the main entrance toward the nearest thoroughfare. Several blocks ahead she noticed a crowd gathered at the curb of a busy intersection. Her pace slowed. As she drew closer, she saw black legs jutting from beneath a blue parka lying in the street. "Excuse me." She pushed the people aside.

"You a vet?" asked a boy in the crowd.

Darcy knelt to examine the dog. He whimpered and tried to stand. "Easy, boy. Easy." Blood oozed from a nasty gash on his right flank.

"Ran right in front of a car, and the car kept going," said the boy.

Typical. Darcy looked up at the boy standing beside her. He had a pained expression. "I'll take him to a vet. He'll be fine."

Darcy tried to flag down a car, but everyone flew by. Frustrated, she returned to the injured animal. No way could she carry him any distance on foot. "Can one of you stay with him while I go for help?" No one in the gawking crowd immediately volunteered, so she offered to pay someone to stay. No sooner did a man agree than a car made an illegal U-turn and braked a few feet away. Della, her upstairs neighbor, stepped out. Darcy could hardly believe her good luck.

"You okay?"

"Boy, am I glad to see you. I need a vet."

This time, without her asking, two men in the crowd helped put the dog into the backseat of the car and Darcy climbed into the passenger seat.

"There's a vet on Broadway, not far from here," said Della as she sped off.

Five minutes later, Della braked hard in front of the animal clinic. "Injured dog," she yelled to the man standing on the steps.

"Della? Hi. Bringing me more strays?" He peered into the back seat and his brow furrowed. "That's no stray."

A woman opened the door to the clinic and looked out.

"Connie, I need a stretcher and some help. Big one."

Darcy breathed a long sigh of relief after the vet and a tech laid the dog on the table in the examining room.

A woman in a white jacket entered. "What do we have, Grant?"

"Hi, Sue. Hit and run," Della answered.

The vet examined the dog's legs. "Lacerations. Possible fracture of the femur. Let's pull X-rays."

The dog whimpered and tried to stand. "You'll be fine, boy," said Grant.

Della paced. "Hope so."

Grant didn't respond, as he had a stethoscope on the animal's chest. "He's in remarkable shape. Strong heartbeat. Excellent muscle tone. Swimmer, aren't you?" Again, the dog attempted to stand. Grant restrained the animal.

"Unfortunately," said Darcy, "swimming got him into this mess. Before the car accident, I caught a man beating the dog because he'd had the audacity to go for a dip in the apartment pool."

"I'll take a closer look as soon as I sedate him. Be back in a minute."

Connie entered. "We'll phone later and let you know what we found and when you can take him home."

"Home?" Della eyed Darcy. "I have a cat. I mean, I don't own him."

"Maybe you can put an ad in the paper and hopefully find the owner," said Connie, helping a tech restrain the dog.

Della's eyes widened. "No, not the owner. He's the one who beat him. Right, Darcy?"

"He said he owned the dog, but I'm not sure."

"What about his collar and tags?" Connie asked.

"He had one but yanked free of it during his struggle. When I leave here, I'll go back to the apartment complex and see if I can locate them." Darcy stared at the dog. *Be realistic, McClain.* How could she nurse a dog back to health and conduct a murder investigation? And afterward, what? Take him home? To a house in the city?

Darcy put her hand on the animal's neck, and he looked up at her with baleful eyes. Lots of people in San Francisco owned dogs. Besides, not twenty minutes ago she would have done anything to find him.

Connie petted the animal's head. "He's a beauty. You don't see many giant schnauzers."

"So that's what he is." Darcy stroked the dog. He licked her hand.

"High energy. Expensive. Stubborn. Or so I've heard. I'll make a few calls. Groomers, kennels, other vets—I'll see if I can locate the owner. If I do, I'll contact you. If he's the beater, I'll handle the matter. If not, he'll be home where he belongs."

Handle the matter how? Reprimand him and give the dog back? No, Darcy would make her own inquiries. "When he's ready to leave, call me please, whether you know who the owner is or not." She jotted down her contact information and offered to pay the bill, but Grant stopped her before she could get out her wallet. "Don't worry about it," he said. "I've got a soft spot for good Samaritans."

Outside, Della lingered on the steps, her eyes raised to the sky. "Sorry, but I'm already breaking the rules by owning a cat. The thought of moving . . ."

"Hey, I understand. Believe me."

"Maybe if he were a small dog, but he must be a hundred-plus pounds." Della leaned against her Mazda, her expression serious and pained. "What if the beater is the owner?"

Darcy patted Della's shoulder. "If he is, I won't let him keep the dog. Every dog deserves better."

27

The first to leave Selma's memorial service, Darcy arrived early at Rhonda's home on Canyon Road. The butler ushered her into the drawing room, a PPG masterpiece. Light splashed from the skylights, washed across the black marble floors, and bounced off walls of reflective glass—one, an expanse of beveled mirrors interspersed with strip windows, the other a series of French doors. The transparent presentation impressed and commanded, and was made more dramatic by the world of white outside.

A minimalist, Rhonda had furnished the room with an S-shaped, butter-colored leather sofa. Opposite it stood matching chairs dotted with turquoise and coral pillows. On the black lacquer end tables sat hand-painted plates filled with magnolia blossoms, their lemony scent tantalizing. Over the granite mantel hung a large picture of a lilac bush in full bloom in a whitewashed frame, the piece signed by Selma.

Drawn by the view, Darcy wandered to the French doors and tested the handles: all locked. The backyard sloped to the Santa Fe River, the dormant lawn cloaked in white and the trees stripped of their summer wear, sad in winter gray. Soon the room would abound in a similar somber color as the mourners filed in, and Darcy was no exception.

She studied her reflection in the mirrored wall. The outfit Charlene had mailed on such short notice was stunning. That Charlene had volunteered to help meant Darcy had come a long way in mending the rift between them, although Darcy had been reluctant at first to accept. What a nineteen-year-old called fashion often clashed with what Darcy considered wearable. To her surprise, Charlene had made an excellent choice, and because they both wore the same size, the dress and jacket fit perfectly. Her sister's comment? "Wait until you get the bill."

Her thoughts drifted to the memorial service and Selma's remaining siblings. Like their mother, they had shown no emotion during the eulogy, while she and Rhonda cried throughout the ceremony. Seated apart from the family, Rhonda made her escape the moment the priest descended from the altar. Where she disappeared to, no one knew.

Somewhere a clock chimed twice, and the house came alive with voices, wonderful smells from the kitchen, and the clatter of high heels. A woman in a white starched apron entered the room. A member of the catering staff, Darcy presumed. "Drink, Ms. McClain?"

Before Darcy answered, Rhonda walked in with a Scotch in each hand. "Thanks, Sil. I took care of the drinks." Rhonda placed the glasses on an end table and sank onto the couch. She sighed loudly. "Today being Halloween . . . never occurred to me."

"I don't think the date's important," said Darcy, even though intuition told her otherwise.

Rhonda sipped Scotch and dabbed at her swollen eyes with a tissue. She was taking her niece's death hard.

A shrill voice broke the sad vigil. Al barged into the room, wineglass in hand. She acted as though she'd been invited to a party, not a wake. Ignored, she toured the room.

Darcy had disliked Randolph's wife from the day they met but had always managed to tolerate her carping and vitriolic personality. Until today. Why bother to put on a show? Only Randolph would have cared, and he was gone.

Rhonda pulled a Kleenex from her pocket. "Not even a tear for her daughter. Now you know why I detest her. Excuse me. I should check on the caterers."

Zach entered the room, along with a steady stream of guests. On their heels the waitstaff toted an endless supply of hors d'oeuvres and drinks. Darcy traded her Scotch for sparkling water and drifted to the sidelines. She sneezed. Heavy perfumes entwined with tobacco smoke played havoc with her allergies.

She studied the gathering crowd—a macabre group shrouded in black. Actors with painted smiles, artificial concern, and forced cordiality. The majority attended out of obligation or to further their own agendas, Rhonda informed Darcy. Selma's friends and select family members would attend a private memorial service next week.

The sun vanished, and the room grayed. The hired help switched on lamps and retreated. Snow fell from a darkening sky. Darcy watched the mourners break off into groups.

Lindsay, pretty in a lavender dress and black jacket—not the outfit she'd worn to the church service—slid onto the sofa beside her twin brother Marcus. He put his arm around his sister and said something into her ear. She nodded but said nothing in return.

Randolph Jr. walked up to his mother. Al brushed her son's

forehead with a kiss and linked arms with him as they headed toward the bar near the French doors.

Bored, Darcy circulated among the growing throng of guests, keeping to the fringes and observing but not engaging anyone in conversation. She didn't need or want the distraction. In one of the beveled mirrors, she saw Zach bearing down on her.

"We need to talk," he said.

"Not now."

He grabbed her arm. "Let me explain."

"I said, not here."

His grip tightened. People began to stare.

Darcy smiled at the gawkers as she broke free from Zach's grasp.

"Okay, but for your information . . ." he said.

Darcy half listened, her eyes trained on a priest hovering in the arched entrance to the living room. He looked lost in a group where almost everyone knew somebody. He removed his spectacles and wiped them with a handkerchief. Something about him seemed vaguely familiar, but what exactly eluded her.

She walked away from Zach and elbowed a path through the sea of bodies. "Darcy McClain, Father." She put out her hand. He ignored the gesture and continued to scrub his glasses. "I'm a friend of the family. Something to drink? Or eat?" She motioned to a waiter.

"Thank you, my child. Water. I'm Father Gregory from St. Luke's." He looked sideways. "The snow's stopped. And there's the sun."

Preoccupied, she could think of nothing better to say than "A welcome sight."

"Pardon the interruption," someone said from behind Darcy. She turned. "Oh, Gallegos, Franklin. Hi."

"Al invited us," said Gallegos. "You're probably wondering why. We wondered the same thing."

"Not at all." An invite coming from Al did surprise Darcy, but she didn't mind having the detectives here.

"You okay after last night's mishap?"

Gallegos shot Franklin an inquiring gaze. He explained.

"I'm fine," said Darcy, watching Father Gregory blend into a crowd of men discussing their golf games. "People cut you off in traffic all the time. At least in San Francisco they do." She scanned the room.

"Who you searching for?" asked Franklin.

"The priest I was speaking to."

Franklin hailed a passing waiter. He handed a wineglass to Gallegos and took one off the tray for himself. "Drink?"

"No thanks."

"Why the interest in the priest?" asked Franklin.

"Something he said didn't ring true, but I can't recall what." When Gallegos had interrupted Darcy's conversation with the priest, the thought had fizzled.

"Think I'll circulate," said Gallegos.

"I'll come with you," said Franklin.

The detectives wandered off. Alone, Darcy went over the short exchange between her and the priest. His speech, personality, dress: something didn't jibe. Even his reappearance—he shuffled his way from the hallway back into the living room—failed to trigger her memory. Three women homed in on Father Gregory and a conversation ensued. The women chatted and laughed loudly, but the priest's stone face never changed.

Al waltzed up to Darcy. "Beautiful service, don't you think?"

"Sad." Darcy kept a watchful eye on the priest.

"We'll miss her terribly." Al blotted a tear with a lace handkerchief, a useless creation—just like its owner.

The priest saw Darcy staring and waved.

"Who's the padre?" Al asked.

She didn't know? Darcy's guard went up. "I was about to ask you."

"Rhonda did the invites. There are a lot of people I've never met. Nor do I care to. So typical of the way Selma led her life. She and Rho"—Al crossed her fingers—"such a tight little duo. They shut me out years ago. I've always resented Rho for stealing my daughter."

Darcy changed the subject. "The priest said he was Father Gregory from St. Luke's."

"St. Luke's has three. John, Paul, and I forget the third. Could be Gregory. Not sure. Three priests. Almost unheard of these days with the shortage of men entering the priesthood. I mean, why forego a lifetime of great sex for celibacy and masturbation?" On that note, Al departed.

To appear less obvious to the priest, Darcy mingled with two women swapping recipes. At first they acted standoffish but soon included her in their stroganoff debate.

The priest moved from group to group, said little, and nodded often. He drifted toward the sofa where Lindsay, Marcus, and now Randolph Jr. lounged. The eldest Colton acknowledged the priest with a smile. The three moved to one end of the couch, and Father Gregory sat down. Darcy relaxed. He removed his hands from his pockets. The motion fired her synapses. He wore gloves and had since he arrived. His hand shook when he waved. Suspicious, she walked nonchalantly toward the sofa, being careful not to scare him off.

The Coltons stood, then the priest. He patted Lindsay's shoulder, spoke to Randolph Jr., and hobbled away, looking back as he paused near the French doors. A faint smile curled his lips. Instinctively, Darcy caressed her Browning. Suddenly, it registered. The walk. The old man at Our Lady of Guadeloupe Cemetery. The priest. Both walked with a defined limp. What had Selma said about her art show? "Even our priest from St. Luke's promised to come." Father George. Not Gregory.

Rapidly, she started to close the gap between her and the Coltons, working a path through the tight groups of chatting guests. She fought the urge to shout, "Get the hell out of my way," because she didn't want to cause a panic.

Randolph Jr. scooped up a glass sitting on the end table, took a sip, and set it down. When he turned his back on his brother, Marcus grabbed Randolph's drink. Darcy looked at Father Gregory, the priest's eyes wide and mouth agape. Fear propelled her into a run. The loud clatter of her high heels drowned out the startled cries from stunned guests as she shoved them aside. Sunlight burst through the skylights. In its strong rays, she immediately noticed the orange glow that radiated from the bottom of the highball glass.

"Noooo!" she screamed the instant she recognized the SL32 chip.

The cry came too late. In one swallow Marcus drained the contents of the glass.

Darcy reached him and grasped him tightly by the shoulders. "Vomit."

Shocked, he gawked at her. "What?" he said, the question barely audible.

"Put your fingers down your throat. Make yourself vomit. Now." Darcy pivoted. "The rest of you move as far back as you can. Go, go, go."

"Are you crazy? Leave my baby alone." Al descended on Darcy, her talons extended. She elbowed Al in the ribs; the woman groaned and recoiled. Marcus forced his fingers into his mouth. He choked. A sickening gurgle filled the air. He gagged.

"What in the hell are you doing?" Al screeched.

Darcy searched the crowd for the man dressed as a priest.

He stood by the French doors, yanking on one handle after another. When he discovered them locked, he shed his heavy black overcoat. A wicked smile sprang to his face. To Darcy, the grin translated as a warning. "God damn it, Marcus, vomit. Now." She ran to the French doors, ready to tackle the imposter.

A loud detonation sounded.

Darcy whirled, her arms up to shield her face. Marcus cried out in agony, his hands clutched to his abdomen. The powerful blast had blown him apart, the detonator creating a cavern in the core of his body. Bloody tissue and organ fragments spewed high into the air, and hysterical screams echoed through the room. Those closest to Marcus clawed frantically at their faces and arms, repulsed by the bloody flesh that rained down on them. In shock, Al stood over the remains of her son and sobbed uncontrollably.

The killer forged through the dazed gathering to the front door. Gun drawn, Darcy disengaged the safety on her Browning, kicked off her pumps, and chased after him. Zach and Randolph Jr. also gave pursuit. The man dodged one caterer but collided with another. Glass shattered. Shards skipped over the tile and banged into the baseboards. Wine puddled on the marble. She steered clear of the pools and maneuvered around a man leaving the kitchen, Franklin.

"The killer!" she shouted.

"Here, take this." Franklin thrust his glass at the man next to him.

Zach overtook Darcy. "No, stay back," she called out, but Zach didn't listen.

He cornered the priest in the foyer. The man pulled a small apparatus from the folds of his loose-fitting tunic and aimed.

"Laser!" Darcy yelled.

A green dot materialized on Zach's pant leg. He wailed, and then crashed to the floor.

"Stop or I'll shoot," she ordered, but the killer had already yanked open the front door and had disappeared.

She leaped over Zach and ran down the icy stairs with treacherous speed. Mud churned up by the man's shoes pelted her legs and spattered her dress. Her soles burned from the cold and her cheeks smarted, but she kept pace, chasing him around the corner of a building and down a side street.

When he vaulted over a low retaining wall, Darcy gained on him. Inches away, she dived for his back. Fabric tore between her fingers. He broke free. Behind her, rapid footsteps resounded in the alleyway. Over her shoulder, she saw Franklin. Good. Backup. She fired a shot.

The killer jumped sideways. The bullet ricocheted off a metal Dumpster. He flung himself over a row of trash cans, sprang to his feet, and continued on. The moment Darcy had a clear shot, she squeezed the trigger. Again, he managed to dodge the bullet. He stumbled, regained his footing, and ducked behind a huge cottonwood.

Before Darcy had a chance to catch up, Franklin yelled, "Down!"

She noticed the green dot traveling up her leg and dropped hard, the wind almost knocked out of her as she hit the frozen ground. Dirt and stucco showered her.

Franklin discharged a round, missed, and fired again, but the laser struck its target the first time. An angry roar vibrated in her ears, and Franklin went down. The murderer darted from his hiding place and took off.

"You hurt bad?" asked Darcy, stopping long enough to check on Franklin.

"Think my leg's broken. Get the bastard."

With her back to the wall, she crept along the compound to where she'd last seen the killer. Nearby, an engine started. She squatted and peeked around the trunk of the cottonwood. A primer-gray pickup sat in the rutted alley, the killer slumped over the steering wheel and the engine idling.

Gun drawn, she tiptoed toward the vehicle, ready to drop if he fired. He saw her in the side mirror and threw the truck into gear. Darcy squeezed off a round at the fleeing assailant, blowing out his back window. The Ford vanished up Canyon Road.

"Damn." She lowered her head to her chest.

From the asphalt a silver object glinted in the fading light of day. She stooped, hooked her finger through the chain, and lifted the St. Christopher medal off the pavement.

28

"An all-points bulletin on The Carver? Already? Fast work." Paco snickered as he checked his rearview mirror. Not a soul in sight.

He raised the volume on his truck's radio. The police had a description of his pickup and the fugitive priest who killed one and wounded two during his flight from the Cloverdale mansion. Three dead Coltons. Three to go. The thought warmed him and made his body feel strangely alive.

In his mind he replayed the events of the day. Strange that what worked in theory didn't always pan out in reality. His plan had taken him years to implement. He had to track down the criminal, infiltrate his world, and then mastermind justice. But no one, not even the best strategist, could control everything. How would he have known Marcus had been grounded and that Billy, a balloon enthusiast, would defy his orders to stay away from the fiesta? Still couldn't believe that old man Colton let Billy hitch a ride.

And who would've guessed the drink intended for Randolph Jr. would be polished off by the very person Paco had targeted in the first place? Marcus should have died with his father, not Billy. But in the long run, it didn't really matter. As long as he killed them all.

He thought of Darcy and his narrow escape. He never thought that Randolph, a stubborn man who never admitted his mistakes, would have the smarts to hire a crack cyberspook to electronically track Paco through Colton's classified databases. And she had done a good job. She had forced him to master his cyberarena. Now, every time he went after a techno-haul, he had to battle the hotshot cyberwarrior to avoid detection. On the ground she was equally formidable. He laughed; the real world was proving almost as fun as the virtual.

Several miles south on the interstate, Paco exited onto Highway 285 and kept to the posted speed limit, watchful for cops, worried one might notice his shattered window. He steered into a private drive and killed the motor. Outside the warm cab, snow flurries swirled through the icy air and settled over the rusty hood. The flakes melted into spidery streams and rolled off the hot metal. Contentment washed over him, a euphoric feeling. He had faced his enemies, and one by one was conquering them.

After a quick look around, he eased out of the pickup, his leg stiff. The cold, the chase—both had made the pain worse. He paused alongside the cab and again checked his surroundings. Seeing no one, he limped to the pipe gate. If the Mortons were home, the gate wouldn't be locked. He snipped off the padlock with bolt cutters and drove onto the property.

The easement snaked around a mesa and emptied into a grassy meadow dotted with cholla cacti. A double-wide trailer fanned by low-hanging tree limbs sat alongside the stock pond. Nearby, cattle grazed. He parked next to the abandoned well house and ducked into the tiny building to change clothes, the switch made in record time because of the blistering wind.

Dressed, he stopped for a few minutes to catch his breath and then doused tissues with alcohol to scrub his face clean of the dark foundation. The second the astringent touched his neck, the skin burned like fire. A long scratch ran from his ear to his chin. His St. Christopher medal was missing. Saddened by the loss of his father's gift, he stared at his chest in the side mirror as though he could will the medal to reappear.

He checked the time, slung a backpack over his shoulder, and hiked up the road to the main house. No time for emotions; he had to focus on finishing the job.

Years ago, the Mortons hired him to help with the livestock. The couple trusted him so much they put him in charge while they made their annual trek to California. Right about now, they'd be eating dinner in Needles at Jerry's Diner. Nasty things, habits.

Playing it safe, he knocked on the front door, not expecting anyone to answer. When no one responded, he walked to the rear of the barn where Morton kept a steel drum for burning trash. He threw everything flammable into the container, soaked the lot in gasoline, and lit a match. When the flames died to a smolder, he headed for the detached garage where Morton stored his Chevy.

The pickup had a full tank. Paco tacked two hundred-dollar bills to a pegboard over the workbench and inserted the ignition key, which he'd duplicated in a Madrid hardware store weeks after the Mortons had hired him.

Back on the highway, he drove below the posted speed limit. Cars whizzed by, most with Texas license plates. Ah yes, Texans—New Mexico's tolerated tourists or future unwanted landowners. He drifted to the shoulder to allow a van to pass. Part of him wanted to follow the convoy to the Lone Star State, maybe even to Mexico, a great place to blend in with the locals and let the past be just that—history. Soon.

At Clines Corners he steered into the truck stop, parked behind the nearest Dumpster, and tossed everything that wouldn't burn in Morton's oil drum into the trash. An hour later he arrived in Albuquerque. He chose a busy motel close to the I-25, locked Morton's truck, and walked the mile to home.

Every step brought a mixture of pain and pleasure. Up one minute for striking a fatal blow to the enemy, down the next when his father drifted into his thoughts. Instinctively, his hand caressed his neck where the medal once hung. Why had his father left them? They'd loved him so much.

In his apartment Paco removed the long black box from his backpack and placed the laser gently on the coffee table in the living room. Thanks to the foam insulation, it had survived the chase as well as the trek home. He'd test-fire it later to be sure the internal workings weren't damaged.

"Hey, Bullet. Some watchdog I own." He mounted the stairs two at a time, but Bullet wasn't stretched out on the bed or on his blanket next to the dresser as Paco expected. His heart pounded as he descended to the first floor. No way Bullet could have gotten out. Paco had blocked off the dog door and padlocked the back gate, unless . . . Darien.

Paco hurried into the kitchen. The back door stood wide open. Fear gripped him. If anything had happened to Bullet, Darien would pay dearly. Paco didn't bother checking the levels on his liquor bottles. He knew why Darien had been there.

Sick at heart and fighting a rising panic, he jogged down the walk to the pool, terrified his neighbor Phil had made good on his threat. "Catch him running free and I'll drown him," he'd said. With every step Paco prayed. A knot formed in his throat, making it hard to swallow. No way Phil could drown Bullet by himself. But with Darien? No, dear God, no. Hadn't he suffered enough?

A thorough search of the pool revealed nothing. Relief flooded over him, then fear. He scoured under bushes and behind shrubs, in case Phil had dumped Bullet. The thought alone was enough to paralyze Paco. He clawed through the Dumpster, the stench overpowering, his hands grimy and disgusting. Dear God, don't let Bullet be at the bottom under all this garbage. He pushed the thought from his mind and prayed harder. The longer he hunted, the greater his fear. The day wore on, and hope faded. He rinsed his hands in the spa. Time to pay Darien a visit.

The note tacked to the manager's door incensed Paco. "Gone for a few. Phil in 333 is in charge." Phil? The hatred Paco harbored for the dog-eater boiled to the surface. If Bullet had been harmed, both morons would pay. A few zaps from a laser might solve Darien's habit of stealing booze and Phil's habit of eating dog. Or make them sterile for life.

He passed his apartment without stopping for the laser. He wanted to, but he couldn't trust himself to control his temper. An unplanned murder might mean his own demise. He clenched his fists and counted to twenty. Useless exercise. Fucking psychiatrists, they hadn't helped. Just kept repeating the same old line: "When a person suffers a series of psychological traumas, such as you have . . ." So, in the end, he'd resorted to his own and best form of therapy: revenge.

Phil came up the drive. Paco hid until the front door shut and then sneaked around to the back of the apartment. Tall hedges enclosed the small porch and the five-by-five-foot patch of lawn some called a yard. Paco slipped through the gate. Meatpackers must make good money. Only ten apartments had yards.

Crouched next to the back door, he stared into the kitchen. Thirty-eight degrees out, and Phil had the door wide open. Only a flimsy screen separated Paco from the dog-eater. He pressed the black knob protruding from the handle and pulled. Locked.

Phil shuffled into the room, ugly in red slippers and a red-and-green plaid bathrobe. The dog-eater opened the refrigerator, lifted out a package wrapped in brown butcher paper, and carried it to the kitchen table. He slit the strings with a filet knife, sliced off a huge chunk of raw meat, and ate it.

Paco cringed, the urge to vomit overpowering. When Phil speared the knife into the bloody carcass a second time, something snapped in Paco's brain. He crashed through the Teflon netting on the screen door and plowed into Phil. The knife soared through the air and lodged in a cabinet door. Paco yanked it free and straddled the bewildered man. "Where's Bullet?" He pressed the blade to Phil's wrinkled throat.

"How would I know?" He sputtered like a dying engine. "Please don't hurt me."

"My hand's shaking, and this blade's sharp. Hate to slip and puncture your jugular. Accidentally, of course. Now where's Bullet?"

"Told you, I don't know."

"If, if . . ." Paco shot a sidelong glance at the table.

"You thought—" Phil's head whipped from side to side. "No, no. Beef. Stole it from work."

"Where's my dog?"

"I saw him this morning," Phil said, sniveling. "By the pool. I shouted at him, but he ran off."

"How did you see him by the pool when I locked him in my apartment?"

"I don't know. The doggie door maybe?"

But Paco had locked the dog door on purpose. To prevent

something just like this from happening. He pressed harder on the blade.

"Ouch, that hurt. I told you everything I know. Honest."

Blood pounded in Paco's temples, and rage bubbled within him. It would be so easy to kill this parasite. He laughed. Phil started to cry. Paco laughed harder. Not a jovial outburst, but a cackle. From the expression on Phil's face, the sound also scared him. The rasp of his own voice yanked Paco from the dark abyss and back to reality, but only after Phil howled in agony did he notice the laceration along the moron's jawbone. He jumped off the wailing man.

"My God, I'm bleeding. Really bleeding. I'm going to die." Phil danced around the room like a madman.

"Don't tempt fate. I still have the knife." Paco brandished the weapon. Phil cowered. "I'll be watching. If you've lied, you'll pay." Paco stabbed the blade into the kitchen table and flung open the back door.

Hidden in the bushes beside Phil's place, Paco watched him tear a sheet of paper off the refrigerator door. The magnet hit the floor. "Fucking asshole. Scaring the shit out of me like that." Phil disappeared upstairs, returning minutes later with his coat on and a dog collar hooked in his index finger. The tags jingled.

Paco's heart lurched. He slunk down the side of the house to the front door, anger mounting with every step as he stalked Phil from their apartment complex to the surrounding streets. At first Phil checked his back often, but soon he relaxed and walked on without a backward glance, making Paco's pursuit easier.

Phil neared the pricey apartments of Sutton Way, the rooftops framed in the shadows of the snowcapped Sandias. Paco had considered leasing here, but $800 a month for a studio ate too deeply into his wallet. Phil crossed the street and headed down the quiet, tree-lined lane, his steps slowing to a more casual pace. He skirted the rough stucco wall that enclosed the grounds and dropped from view.

Afraid he'd lose him, Paco jogged over the damp green-belt to the fenced complex. About ten feet ahead lurked Phil, his hand to his forehead, sheltering his eyes from the waning sun. He ducked between the buildings and hooked a right in the fork in the sidewalk. The dog-eater certainly knew his way around the joint. He followed as Phil turned the corner. Paco froze in stride, surprised to see Phil loitering beneath a staircase.

A black Mazda zipped into the parking lot. Phil squatted. A shapely dark-haired woman alighted from the car, a grocery bag nestled in her arms, and went into the downstairs apartment.

Phil waited a few minutes, wrenched off his sneakers, and ran up the stairs to the second-story apartment. He hung the dog collar on the knob, punched the bell, and descended in a blur, scooping up his shoes as he bolted.

Ten minutes passed. No one came to the door in the upstairs apartment. Fifteen minutes. Twenty. Paco tiptoed up the flight and reclaimed the tags. As he suspected, the collar belonged to Bullet. Weak in the knees, he hesitated on the small landing for a few minutes, wondering why Phil had left Bullet's collar on a stranger's front door.

On his way down, a door creaked somewhere. He heard voices. The sounds died. He crossed quickly to the apartments across the way and hid in the shrubbery.

The dark-haired woman Paco had seen earlier opened her door and stepped onto her front porch. Immediately, he zeroed in on the leash she held in her hand. "All clear," she called to someone inside the apartment after she glanced around. "Come on, boy," she coaxed in a soft voice. "You can do it. You know"—her tone rose an octave—"I'm not sure this is working. Here, you're better with him than I am."

To Paco's amazement, Darcy appeared on the patio and took the leash from the woman's hand. "Glad I live above you. I'd hate to move him across the complex."

"I should've called a friend. Someone with big muscles." The woman chuckled. "Tell me again what Grant said. Sorry, I was half listening. Busy day at work."

"He asked if the dog was crate trained. He forgot I don't own him. The dog has to sleep sprawled out, with his leg extended. He'll be stiff for a while. Don't let him chew on his cast or stitches. Come on, big guy. Let's get up those stairs. Dinner awaits."

A black dog hobbled onto the porch. Paco's heart soared. He saw the bandaged leg and wanted to run to Bullet, comfort him, and take him home.

Darcy started for the steps. She tugged gently on the leash. "Come on. You can do it. Della, get on the other side of him in case he trips. We don't need another mishap."

"No kidding. Come on. Darcy has treats for you."

The women scrambled up the stairs, Bullet between them. Each had an awkward hold on him. They reached the top and sat down on the landing to rest, both breathing hard. Despite the injured leg, Bullet seemed content to have two people doting on him.

Della, hands firmly planted on Bullet's haunches, pushed him gently while Darcy coaxed the dog until he crossed the threshold into the apartment; then Darcy shut the door.

Paco felt light-headed and drained. He sighed. At least Bullet was safe, and he appeared to be in good hands. "I'll come back for you soon, boy."

But first business—and ugly business at that. For the time had come to murder the source.

29

Darcy opened her eyes to large brown ones staring back. Startled, she sat upright and blinked. The dog cocked his head. He rolled over and tried to stand, but his bandaged leg wouldn't cooperate, so she helped him off the bed.

"Ouch. My aching feet." Her body had taken a real beating these past two days.

She shuffled into the kitchen to fix coffee. The dog limped along behind her. While a fresh pot brewed, she eyed the manila envelope sitting on the counter. Inside was the diary she had fished out of the stove at the salvage yard. Revolted by the few pages she'd read yesterday, Darcy had put the book away to read later. Later meant now, for the book might hold clues valuable to the case.

Armed with a strong cup of black java, she sat on the sofa, snapped on latex gloves, and opened the journal. The charred edges crumbled and speckled her bathrobe. For the next hour, she read every word the cracker had written, a difficult task when so much of the content disgusted her. Bullet watched from his post in the bedroom doorway.

Her mind began to wander, so she read aloud: "'Stupid counselor. What does she know? She told me to write down my thoughts and feelings. Said it would help me heal. Well, her advice hasn't helped one damn bit. The pain, the hatred, runs too deep. The anger is consuming. I've lost everything. My family. My childhood. My innocence. My dreams. You stole everything from me. I loved you, trusted you. I hate that this has happened to me. You crossed the line, invaded the boundaries. Parts of my life are total blanks because there was only one way to survive—to shut down. Withdraw.'"

She sipped from her mug. The French roast tasted bitter.

On the next page, scrawled across the entire sheet in bold letters, was "The Dark Place." Disgusted, Darcy forced herself to read one account of abuse after another, sickened by the horrors the cracker had suffered in the abandoned wine cellar at the orphanage. Halfway through the fourth vile encounter, the words far too graphic, a tidal wave of nausea overtook her. She ran for the bathroom.

Back in the living room, she checked on the dog. He slept quietly on the living room carpet, his injured leg extended. She placed a throw pillow under his head. He grunted, a sound of contentment. She returned to the diary and read on, sad at heart and ill in the gut. "You soon learn that the world is a dangerous place. Your sixth sense kicks in to defend you. A sort of built-in radar. You tune in, know where they are at all times, and when they'll strike again. So much rage, but now I know how to control my feelings. I must remove these cankers from the world, save all innocent children from infection."

She put down the book. *He's a murderer, McClain. Someone*

you should despise, not pity. But at the moment, she felt only deep empathy and compassion for him after the hell he had lived through and anger at those who had inflicted the abuse. Needing a break, she stripped off the latex gloves, entered her office, and pitched the gloves into the trash can.

Seated at her desk, Darcy sorted through a stack of folders, found the one she wanted, and emptied the contents onto the desk. Last to slide out was a close-up of Barnes's battered neck with his silver St. Christopher medal resting on his scorched chest. Beside the enlargement she placed the medal the killer had dropped in the parking lot on Canyon Road. Distinct detailing dispelled any possibility of a coincidence, not to mention the same date engraved on both: 1954, long before Barnes's birth.

She pulled up the surveillance footage from the Santa Clara Savings and Loan on her laptop. She had memorized Barnes's every move but kept playing and replaying the video, hoping to catch something new, something she'd overlooked.

On the screen Barnes made his way from the front of the bank building, through the lobby, and strutted up to the security desk. He signed in, chatted briefly with the guard, and boarded the elevators. She watched the recording again, still stumped as to the connection between Barnes and the killer and the Colton family.

Deep-throated growls filled the apartment. Through the open bedroom door, Darcy saw her rescue stagger to his feet and bark. She dashed into the foyer to quiet him, afraid someone might hear and complain to management.

The dog limped down the hall to the front door and leaned against the wall for support. Growls rumbled from deep within him. Darcy placed her eye to the viewer. Dan stood on the landing. She opened the door. "It's all right. He's no threat," she said, trying to reassure the dog. "Go on, give him the sniff test." The dog planted himself between Darcy and the threshold.

"Where'd you find him, and what happened?" Dan maneuvered around the dog and motioned to the cast.

"Cracked femur. Hit and run." She shut the door and relayed an abbreviated version of the rescue.

Dan bent down. "You got a name, handsome?"

The dog growled.

"I'm calling him Big Boy until I find the owner."

"For a minute there I thought you'd adopted him. Good-looking dog, but not very friendly."

"About the adoption issue—not so fast. About being friendly, well, he likes me."

Dan punched her affectionately in the arm. Big Boy growled again. "Okay, okay, sorry. I won't touch her. Promise."

"Coffee? I have a fresh pot brewing." Darcy put two mugs on the butcher block. "I didn't expect to see you so soon."

"Nor I, but I wrapped up the Cruces job in record time, flew to Oklahoma, then caught a puddle jumper here to give you my news in person before heading home."

"Hope you have good news."

"Patience." Dan used his favorite word on her. "Let me get organized." He opened his laptop.

Another growl.

"Come on, boy. Really, he's no threat." Darcy patted the dog's head. He licked her hand.

"He seems to have taken to you." Dan logged on. "Now this is rather a strange coincidence."

"What are you referring to?"

"The black hair from the bathroom in the salvage yard." He looked at the dog.

Darcy set down the coffeepot without pouring. "You're kidding? Same breed? You sure?"

Dan nodded. "I'm sure he isn't the only black giant schnauzer in Albuquerque, but what are the odds? The breed certainly isn't common, which leads me to wonder if the beater and the hacker are the same person."

Darcy limped to the cabinet by the stove for the sugar bowl. "The beater didn't strike me as smart enough to break into a piggy bank, never mind hack into Colton's operating systems. Only thing he's ever scaled is a fence, not a firewall." She slid onto a stool at the breakfast bar. "Maybe the beater wasn't his owner. Maybe he was just a jerk, and Big Boy's owner—our hacker—was somewhere else at the time." Big Boy moved closer to Darcy, his large brown eyes fixed on Dan.

"Are you limping?"

"Who? Me or him?"

"You." Dan laughed. "Never seen you so tied to an animal."

"He's good company. About the limp, I burned my feet on freezing rough pavement." She recounted her chase with the killer, as well as the events at Selma's service and the accident. "Rounded the corner and saw the hacker behind the wheel of a primer-gray pickup with Arizona plates and *BVN* in the license number. Same truck as I spotted at Our Lady of Guadeloupe Cemetery the day Barnes was buried, and identical to the truck that forced me and Franklin off the I-25 a couple of nights ago. Franklin ran the license, but the trace led nowhere. Probably stolen from one of the cars in the salvage yard."

"Any more news?"

She updated him on the investigation, finishing with, "The priest limped. The old man limped. Broken leg, perhaps? Remember, Martha mentioned beatings, plural? And don't forget about the St. Christopher medal."

Dan gulped his coffee. "Cold-blooded bastard, killing his own brother."

"I don't think he did. Just a tragic mistake," said Darcy.

"Mistake for who? Barnes?"

Darcy made a face. "No, for Paco. He had no idea Billy had hitched a ride with Randolph."

"What makes you think he screwed up?"

"Because he loved his brother. Wouldn't have done anything to hurt him."

Dan frowned. "You sound awfully sure."

"I have his diary. Found the book in a stove at the salvage yard. He talks about 'us, dreams we had.'"

"Could be a woman."

"Don't think so."

"So you found the book recently?"

She nodded, her mouth full of coffee.

"Have you read the diary?"

"Every word. Disgusting. The abuse is far too graphic." Darcy sucked in air to compose herself, the foul thoughts still fresh in her mind. "On another note, if he likes killing for fun, he had the perfect opportunity at Selma's service. He could have mowed down half the crowd with a stroke or two of his laser."

"You're right."

"He isn't an indiscriminate killer. He's targeted certain people and is going after them—and them alone. He wants revenge, but why on the Coltons I'm not sure. Not yet."

"Question," Dan said. "If he's so smart and methodical, why would he screw up and leave his diary behind for someone to find? I would've hung around until the book burned to ash."

"Maybe leaving it behind is a cry for help. He wants to be arrested. Or he wants someone to understand why he committed such despicable acts. It's a means of clearing his conscience. Or he's lost everything and had nothing left to lose. He simply doesn't give a damn anymore."

Dan nodded. "All valid points."

Darcy winced as she flexed her arm.

"Your shoulder?"

She nodded. Years ago, while hunting Solis, a rogue CIA agent she was assigned to bring in alive, he had shot her in the back. She knew that if they crossed paths again, he wouldn't miss a second time.

"Now let's hear your news."

"I might have some answers."

Darcy sat down, eager to hear them. "Well, don't keep me in suspense."

"Hopefully, something Rick discovered will help."

"Go on. Anything you have, I want to hear it."

"Rick traced Al's past from Berkeley to Oklahoma, which is why I was there." He typed something into his computer. "Born in Summit, a small town on the Texas-Oklahoma border. Population eight hundred. Never set foot in New Jersey or Pennsylvania. Never had the money to travel, even in the US. In fact, many times during our search, people referred to her parents as trailer trash or poor white trash."

"I hate the term."

"I know. Al certainly knew poverty. Parents lived on the outskirts of town in a mobile home fit for demolition. Birth name Imogene Lynette Smith. Her father was Parker Dean Smith. Mother, Alexandra—no middle or last name. Al dropped out of school at fourteen and hitched a ride to, of all places, Kingman, Arizona, where she worked as a waitress at a truck stop. There, she met Ronald Allen Cunning Owl, a full-blooded Hualapai Indian."

"Go on." Darcy leaned her elbows on the counter and cradled her chin.

"Cunning Owl's profession? Potter. Good one, from what I've seen." He slid some photos across the counter toward her. "He has pieces in the Dallas Museum of Art and the O'Keeffe Museum in Santa Fe. Back to the story. Al linked up with him and moved to the reservation. Here things get sketchy. Our next lead finds her in Berkeley—her, Cunning Owl, and two kids."

Darcy reached for his wrist, knocking the photos to the floor in the process. "Boys?"

He retrieved the pictures. "Easy. Yes, boys. One weekend they drove down to San Francisco. Al went to the restroom. Never returned. Cops, FBI, an all-out search, but she was never found. Search was called off."

"Desertion."

"Then a year later," Dan continued, "Ronald committed suicide, and the boys were placed in an orphanage because no one in the immediate family would take them."

"Desertion. Suicide. Institutions. Abuse. Been through a lot."

"I hear the wheels spinning." Dan scrolled to another file.

"The two boys have to be Paco and Billy. It's too much of a coincidence. Paco Cunning Owl, and Al's ex-husband having the same last name."

"Not 100 percent sure, but Rick did discover some additional information on them."

"Go on."

"Parson's House shut down about two years ago. When the place closed, people began to talk. Allegations of sexual abuse. Shortly thereafter, the abandoned structure burned. Arson."

"Interesting."

Dan doctored his coffee with more sugar. "Remember Connie and Walt Barnes?"

"Yes."

"They died in a house fire."

"You're right," said Darcy.

"Barnes wasn't living with them at the time."

"Burying all connections to the past, maybe?"

"Could be. From Parson's House, Rick traced Paco to St.

Ann's in Chicago where he lived until he completed high school. The pastor who took him in? Father Gregory."

Darcy stood and stretched. "You don't say."

"Thought you'd find that interesting."

"Did you interview the priest?"

"He's dead. Years ago."

She groaned. "Figures. Natural causes?"

"Yes. Let's see. Paco attended St. Mark's College, graduated *summa cum laude*. Major, computer science."

"Not surprising. Work history?"

"One minute." He accessed another file. "Five years at Mitre."

"Cybersecurity?"

Dan nodded.

"Impressive." She sat down.

"You'll love this. He also did a stint at the National Security Agency."

"What? He worked for the NSA? When?"

Dan scrolled to the bottom of the page. "Five years after you left."

"For how long?"

"Two years. Then one day he dropped out of sight. Quit work at the NSA without even giving notice. Simply disappeared. A few months later, he used their computers, Mitre's and the NSA's, to link to other sites."

"Which ones?"

"Missing persons."

Darcy slid off the stool and paced the small kitchen. "Looking for his brother."

Dan poured himself a refill. "I think you're right." His cell phone vibrated across the countertop. He retrieved it. "Gruet. Rick, hi. Good, good. Okay. Thanks."

"Good news?"

He smiled. "William Barnes's real name is—was—William

Ryan Cunning Owl, and Paco's birth name is Parker Allen Cunning Owl."

Dan's words made Darcy's heart race. "So they *were* brothers. Go on."

"I don't think this has any relevance to the case, but friends called Ronald, the father, Ravel."

The name meant nothing to her. She walked to the patio doors, drew aside the sheers, and stared at the snow-clad peaks of the Sandia Mountains. "Cold as a cadaver."

"What?"

"The day—cold as a cadaver."

"Odd comparison."

Deep in thought, Darcy didn't comment.

"I can hear those wheels turning," said Dan. "What are you thinking?"

"Something in the killer's psyche has changed, which is why he's becoming careless. With his brother dead, he may feel he has no reason to live. Showing up at Rhonda's house was sloppy. Trying to murder a Colton with so many people present, downright stupid. He knows we're closing in, so I suspect he'll kill again, and soon."

Dan nodded.

"To me, Randolph always came across as a kind and loving person who wouldn't hurt anyone intentionally," said Darcy.

"I agree, so where is this line of thought going?"

"Patience," she said, using Dan's favorite word to her on him. "I hate to sound prejudiced, but the problem here, in my estimation, is Al. She deserted her children. For obvious reasons we can rule out Billy as having any real part in the murders. So Paco is our killer-cracker, and he wants revenge. Revenge for being deserted and then being institutionalized where the staff hired to care for him inflicted such horrific physical abuse that even I—and I've certainly seen my share of horrendous crimes—can't stomach to read about or even contemplate going through what he did."

"I haven't heard you say so much at one time in ages."

She threw a napkin at him.

He ducked. "So Al's probably his next target?"

"Three Coltons are still alive, and two currently work at Colton Industries—Al and Randolph Jr.—so I'd bet one or both are next on his target list."

"I agree, but how do we ferret out one employee among the thousand who work there?"

She leaned on the counter. "Call my idea far-fetched, but I'm running out of them."

"Okay, unload."

"If I'm right and our hacker-killer works at Colton, then who better to root him out than his own dog?"

"Actually, that's not a bad idea. Besides, what do we have to lose?"

She dug her sore feet into her running shoes and snagged Big Boy's harness off the coat rack. "Help me put this on him."

"I assume we're headed to Colton?"

Darcy snatched her keys off the kitchen counter. "Yes. Time to play my hunch."

30

Despite the growling Big Boy had done, the giant schnauzer seemed comfortable with Dan lifting him into the hatch of Darcy's 4Runner. "I'll drive. You watch him."

"Thanks." She looped her hand through the harness she had bought for the dog.

They rode in silence until Dan broke the hush. "What's on your mind?"

"I've been wrangling with motive. I don't believe anyone in the Colton family sexually abused Paco."

"I agree. On the other hand, in many abuse cases, the line becomes blurred between who actually committed the acts and who the abused feels was responsible."

"Precisely what I was about to say, which means he blames Al for ruining his life," said Darcy.

"Then why kill everyone in the family?"

"Just part of his revenge?"

Dan grunted, his eyes on the road ahead. "Hold on. This icy patch looks treacherous."

The SUV lost traction. She held tight to Big Boy's harness, concerned that he might reinjure his leg if they had an accident. Grant had said to watch him, not drive him all over town. The 4Runner glided over the slick surface to dry pavement without incident. The traffic light ahead turned red. Dan braked gently. A few minutes later, he steered into the parking lot at Colton Industries and drove to the front of the building.

"Roads weren't too bad."

Darcy let out a bottled-up sigh. "Bad enough."

Dan lowered Big Boy to the ground and helped him into the lobby where Jim, the guard, did a double take when he saw the dog. "Sorry, Ms. McClain. No animals allowed. No exceptions."

"The atrium." Darcy pointed to a glass-enclosed section off the main lobby and said to Dan, "Take him there until I settle this." She handed him the dog's lead, and he started for the atrium. Surprisingly, Big Boy followed without any resistance.

"Sir, sign in first, please," Jim called out.

Darcy grabbed the log, had Dan sign, and scrawled her own signature on the next line.

"Ma'am, the dog has to go. The atrium doesn't qualify as out of the building," Jim said.

"Can I use your phone?" She reached for it.

A quizzical expression creased Jim's face. He handed her the receiver, and she dialed Al's extension.

"Mrs. Colton's in the lab," said Jim. "She doesn't want to be disturbed. Orders."

"Which one?"

"X. She isn't taking calls either."

X, the YAG lab. "Where's Randolph Jr.?"

"Shipping and receiving. Inventory. But Mr. Larson's in his office."

She phoned Zach. His assistant put Darcy on hold. A queue of employees impatient to sign in formed behind her. She moved aside so the workers could autograph the logbook.

"I'm in the lobby," said Darcy when Zach came on the line. Mindful of the employees gathered around her, she lowered her voice. "With a friend and a dog. Yes, a real one. No, he's not a guide dog. Yes, there's a good reason for bringing him here. Imperative," she answered when he asked if the dog had anything to do with the case. "Yes, I know the rules."

Regardless, Zach rattled off a list of areas off-limits to animals. She tuned him out and studied the logbook, noting signatures as each employee signed in. The person beside her autographed the book. He looked familiar, but a name escaped her. She smiled. He smiled back and headed for the elevators. She reached for the log to check his signature when Zach interrupted her train of thought by yelling over the line, "Are you listening? Darcy? Damn it. Answer me."

Loud, excited barks drowned by angry commands demanded her attention. She turned abruptly toward the atrium, confused by the commotion. Dan struggled to control the giant schnauzer as the dog fought frantically against the constraints of his harness.

"What's all the commotion?" Zach yelled into the receiver.

Darcy wondered the same thing. What was driving Big Boy crazy?

The elevator doors parted, and the Colton employee barged inside, his hands in his coat pockets. The doors closed.

The slight limp. Left-handedness. The resemblance to Barnes. Dyed hair. It all struck home. Al's assistant—Charles Stevens! Stunned by the revelation, Darcy dropped the telephone on Jim's desk. The startled guard reached for his firearm.

"Dan!" she screamed, loud enough to burst eardrums. "Jim, alert security. The killer's in the building," she shouted as she shoved her way through the crowd to the elevators. No wonder the dog had kicked up a ruckus.

"Dan, Lab X. Leave the dog," she shouted before she ripped open the stairwell door and descended the basement steps two at a time, holding onto the railing to prevent herself from falling. At the bottom of the staircase, she tore open the door and unsnapped her shoulder holster as she ran to the first security station.

"Hacker's in the building," she yelled and drew her 9mm, keeping the pistol at her side.

"Ma'am, your biometrics," the guard said, hand on his revolver.

"In a hurry. Let me through."

"Can't."

"Alert security. Now." With no time for biometrics or punching pass codes into a computer to verify her identity, she flashed her visitor's badge and veered around the guard. He bellowed something unintelligible as she sprinted to the glass door and yanked open the bullet-proof entrance to the subterranean level.

The cavernous tunnel twisted around a corner, leading her to another security station. At the post three men in white lab coats huddled in a circle, the group waiting for the guard to complete a telephone call. The men glanced at her, looked away, and looked back again, the Browning the focus of their wary stares. She walked past them.

"Hey, we were here first."

Darcy ignored the protest, leaped the low barrier several feet outside the security kiosk, and scurried along the corridor. In her wake chaos erupted. An alarm blared, and angry threats echoed off the walls, but she ran on, her feet barely touching the tiled floor. As she distanced herself, the din gave way to silence, the soft thud of her footfalls the only sound in the sterile passage.

She zipped by a doorway, saw someone inside the room, and came to a dead halt. A pregnant woman sat on the edge of a desk, her hands to her face and shoulders heaving with sobs. Beside her hovered a disheveled Martin Hamilton. He noticed Darcy at the same time she spotted the gold band on his finger. So he'd disappeared for personal reasons. Not surprising. She hadn't pegged Martin for a murderer.

"Randolph's killer might be down here. Lock the door." She spoke quickly and moved on, anxious to alert Al, then Randolph Jr., who was at the other end of the building. If she couldn't make it to shipping soon, she'd call security from Lab X.

Darcy sprinted around the bend. She placed her thumb to the biometric door lock to Lab X and waited for the soft click. No response. Someone had activated the manual override. She jiggled the knob. Locked. "Al. It's Darcy. We have to talk." She knocked. No answer, so she pounded with her fists until the door opened automatically. She entered slowly, her guard up and the Browning grasped firmly in her hand. "Al?"

Nothing had changed since her last visit. She stole through the lab past the floor-mounted YAG laser; it was the same one from the demonstration, for she recalled the short serial number. Near it stood the other YAG, the one equipped with a beam splitter. She glanced under the workbenches, purple stools stowed in a neat row, then up at the shelves that ringed the perimeter of the room: jars, beakers, and vials were arranged in an orderly manner.

"Al?"

At the far end of the laboratory, behind the ten-by-ten partition of obscure glass, someone dragged a chair from one location to another, the shadowy figure unidentifiable. "Al, is that you? We need to talk." Cautious, Darcy moved closer to the partition and peered around the corner.

Al sat on a stool, her back to Darcy, poring over a pile of computer-generated documents. After a long silence, she snapped, "Yes, McClain. What do you want? Can't you see I'm busy? We aren't done with inventory, in case you didn't know. Why won't people listen when I say no interruptions?"

"The killer's in the building."

Al spun. Her elbow clipped a stack of glass slides sitting near a microscope. The specimens skittered across the tabletop, toppled over the edge, and shattered on the tiled floor. "Shit. Now look what you've done. Are you serious?"

"Dead." Darcy crossed the room in a hurry, cell phone in her hand to dial Jim, when the lab door opened and Charles Stevens slipped in. He appeared surprised to see Darcy standing before him but recovered quickly. With a sadistic smile plastered on his face, Stevens reached behind him and threw the deadbolt on the door with a soft click. Calmly, Darcy sized up her options. She couldn't go forward without a physical confrontation, so she weighed her next move, working on a plan until Al broke the silence that hung heavy in the room.

"What now, Charlie?" Al demanded in a stern voice. "My message clearly stated no interruptions. Is this some kind of joke? Why in the hell are you wearing that garb? Halloween's over."

Dressed in combat boots, black pants, and a gray shirt opened at the neck, Stevens looked nothing like the insecure assistant Darcy had met at the reading of the will or seen a few times around Colton glued to Al's side. No longer a blond as he had been weeks ago, his black crew cut gleamed under the strong lights. And today his blue eyes were a cold dark brown. Why hadn't she suspected him? Probably for the same reason she didn't peg Martin as a killer. Neither one fit the profile.

Quit kicking yourself, McClain. Even Al hadn't made the connection during the two years Stevens had worked for her, and he was her son.

Face-to-face with him and knowing he had killed his half siblings in such a savage fashion, she felt her pity for him dissolve to concern. Not fear, but a healthy respect for the brutality he could inflict on his victims. Her eyes riveted to him, Darcy watched Stevens roam the edge of the lab as though plotting his next move. He acted composed, confident, and methodical—just as she felt, for she knew it came down to kill or be killed.

"McClain, Colton's cyberdiva. Pleasant surprise. And Al, the source of all evil. Two adversaries in one room. But neither one's any challenge. For I am the liberator of tortured souls."

Al started toward him. "What in the hell are you talking about?"

"Shut up." He faced Darcy. "Almost forgot. Another challenger waits in the wings. Assuming your buddy Gruet can break into the lab."

Al moved closer to Darcy. "What is all this gibberish?"

"Meet Paco," said Darcy. "One of the sons you deserted years ago."

Al gasped. "Can't be."

"And Billy. Billy's dead." The word exploded from Paco's mouth.

"Dead? No, not Billy." A sob broke from Al's lips. "You have no idea how often I prayed my babies were safe."

"Oh, please, stop with the theatrics," said Paco, his voice heavy with sarcasm and his eyes fierce with rage. "You call yourself a mother? You don't know the meaning of the word. You deserted two small children because you only cared about yourself. We thought you'd been abducted. All those nights we prayed and wept. The agony Dad went through. So distraught. You killed him."

"He committed suicide," said Al, "because he was weak."

"Shut up. I pity you. You had it all. Not once but twice. And both times, you threw everything away because the only person you ever loved was yourself."

"Not true." Al wiped at a tear trickling down her cheek. "My poor baby, Marcus. And Selma. So brutal. Why?"

"Because while I carved her up, I pretended she was you. Besides, you never gave a damn about Selma. If I spared anyone, I should have spared her. Stupid plan, killing off the Coltons one at a time—just like you killed off my family. I should have started and ended with you. I was dumb enough to think you loved your family, that killing them one by one would be the best way to torture you. I should have taken the laser and burned holes in every inch of your body—one for every time you caused us pain. A slow, agonizing death."

"You don't understand." Al wrung her hands.

"Oh, I understand perfectly. For eight years, almost every night, I was gang-raped in that fucking orphanage."

Al flinched as though he had slapped her in the face. "I—I . . . oh no, Paco," she mumbled, her voice heavy with emotion.

"The gun, McClain." He held out his hand. "Set it on the floor and kick it toward me. Gently." A faint smile twisted his lips.

Darcy's grip tightened on the Browning.

"Before you get trigger-happy . . ." He tapped a switch on the floor laser. "Look around the room. See anything?"

"No," said Darcy.

Al grabbed Darcy's arm. "Wait." She scooped up the erasers from the wall-mounted blackboard and clapped them together. Chalk dust scattered into the air. As the particles settled, the fine dust illuminated a network of white shafts. The mesh work resembled a spider's web, only with thicker strands. "Invisible laser beams, harmless until the energy builds. Takes a few minutes, but you'll see them soon enough."

Still time to fire off one round.

"I wouldn't," said Paco, reading Darcy's mind. "You might get off one, but even that's unlikely because you've overlooked something important." He raised his right hand. A thin leather sheath covered his forearm. Strapped to the underside, a long white tube forked into three as it crossed his palm. "If the YAG doesn't get you, my ruby will. One false move and zap—no arm or worse."

Two death rays against one 9mm. She remembered Zach's comment. "If you're ever up against a ruby laser, our CR3 for instance, and it's equipped with a beam splitter, throw away your gun."

A glimpse of red from the corner of her eye drew Darcy's attention. The color spread until all of the chalky white webbing glowed a bright crimson. No trouble seeing the lethal beams now. Suddenly, the ugly red mesh that separated Paco from Darcy broke, split, and divided again, manifesting its death rays in not one network but dozens of giant spiderwebs until the entire room was netted from floor to ceiling, Paco on one side and Darcy and Al on the other. No place to hide but the small ten-by-ten area where she'd found Al working on her slides.

"Beam splitter?" Darcy asked Al.

"Yes."

"How does it work?"

"In this case," Paco said, "the laser is equipped with a dual beam splitter. The beams bounce off mirrors. So if for some reason you can avoid the YAG, which I strongly doubt, you'll force me to use this." He pointed to the far wall and tapped a button on his wristband. A magenta shaft shot from the hand-held laser. The ruby beam landed on a stainless steel table and sliced a neat line through solid metal. Sawed in half, the table collapsed and with a loud clang crashed to the floor.

"Self-explanatory, McClain? One more time, give me the gun. Nice and easy. Set it on the floor and kick it gently toward me."

Darcy drew her pistol. "Never let anyone take your firearm," Dan had told her during training. Good advice, but with only one exit and the door blocked by the laser web, now what?

"Quit stalling, McClain."

One false move and she'd sacrifice a limb. High stakes. In a bold move, she shoved Al, removing her from the line of fire, then squeezed off a warning round. Anticipating retaliation, she dived through the doorway into the partitioned room at the back of the lab. Plastered against the wall, she searched for a place to hide, but how do you hide from a laser?

Glass shattered. Slivers pelted Darcy's back.

"Last warning, McClain. Next time I mean business. Hand over the gun."

"Darcy!" Al shouted frantically. "Take off your jacket. Acid!"

Noxious fumes choked the surrounding air. Darcy coughed and rubbed her eyes. She clawed at the garment, the padded shoulders exposed where the chemical had dissolved the fabric. She wiggled out of the jacket and tossed it aside. Her face shielded with her hand, she looked up at the shelves directly overhead. A ruby-red dot scanned the empty beakers. One exploded.

She threw herself under a workbench. Across from her, Al crouched beneath the desk, her hands over her ears while Paco popped off one container after another, the sound deafening. Where in the hell was Dan?

The beaker rampage ended, and only the constant drip of liquid filled the still air.

Darcy's heart lurched and thudded. Slowly, the throb in

her chest settled to normal, allowing her to think more clearly. The only cover between her and the killer was an opaque wall of glass. The large pane rested on steel partitions sheeted in fabric. The core was probably Styrofoam. She didn't stand a chance against Paco's weapon, and he knew it.

A low hiss. The sound came from Al. "Hopeless," she said.

Darcy shook her head. Prone on the cold tile, she slithered to the opening and peered from the jamb into the adjoining lab. Paco hadn't moved. Something wet rolled off her cheek and onto her hand. Perspiration. Moisture sheeted her forehead. She steadied the Browning and aimed. She hesitated slightly before firing and paid dearly for the distraction.

"For you, Father." His words slapped sense into Darcy. She fired, but he shot first. Glass exploded. The blast echoed in the confined space. The stench of burnt flesh permeated the enclosure. Blood spattered the floor. The laser had nicked Darcy in the shoulder. She swallowed, screwed up her nerve, and framed Paco in her sights.

"Darcy!" Al screamed, but the cry was barely audible over the ringing in Darcy's ears. "Look up!"

The laser beam cored a horizontal line across the top of the metal panel and zigzagged downward as Paco searched for Darcy's location. She leaped from one section of the small room to the other as the beam tracked her moves. She slid under the desk and crouched against the wall to escape him, but not for long.

The laser cracked a crooked line across the floor, chips flying into the air as the tile fractured. To avoid the beam, she flung herself across the partition to the other side, accidentally slamming her injured arm into the center support under a workbench. She saw stars. As soon as her vision cleared, she captured him in her gun's sights and discharged a round. A bloodcurdling wail ricocheted off the walls. "You bitch."

A hush ensued, followed by a maniacal laugh.

Crack. The glass wall closest to Darcy crumbled. Jagged shards showered the floor. The central heating unit switched on, the drone masking faint sounds. She crawled to the opening of the partitioned room. Paco leaned against the wall. Blood stained his shirt. He had his head bowed as he checked something on the laser remote. She squeezed the trigger. His agonized howl roared over the whoosh of the heater.

A flash. Darcy ducked for cover. Too late. Fire coursed up her leg. She winced. Scorched flesh fouled the air. She rolled over, dug her fingers into the slit the laser had cut in her pants, and ripped the material apart to examine the wound. A black line snaked down her thigh to her knee, the skin charred but not a drop of blood. "Shit."

"You fucking, fucking bitch!" Paco bellowed.

From the sound of his voice, Darcy knew she had inflicted a serious blow. She risked a peek. His left arm hung lifeless by his side. Blood spurted from his hand, dripped off his fingers, and pooled on the tile. He'd bleed to death if he didn't get help. Maybe now he'd rethink his plan to kill them.

"Ready to bargain, Paco?"

He swayed, unsteady on his feet. "Fuck you."

Damn him. He's losing a lot of blood. "Paco, please. Give yourself up."

A tinny sound filled the room.

Darcy tensed. She looked at Paco. He too had heard the noise. It came again.

Light sneaked under the lab door, and the knob glowed a bright orange. Paco slowly raised his right arm, the ruby laser trained on the lab door. The handle fell off, bounced on the tile, and skipped across the polished surface. Jim and Denny burst in, guns drawn. Behind them stood Zach and Dan with Tom Benevides in the background.

"No, go back!" Al shrieked.

Paco sneaked a quick look toward the partition and then faced the guards. Denny froze. Jim collided with Denny, lost his balance, and pitched forward, catapulting into the beams. The Ruger hit the floor, spun in a circle, glided across the room, and smashed into the baseboard, Jim's severed hand still clinging to the pistol's grip. His tormented cries seemed to go on forever but probably lasted only seconds. Jim fainted.

Paco howled with laughter. "Come on. Come on. Who's next?"

The red puddle at his feet widened. Guilt pricked at her. She wished he hadn't given her a reason to shoot him.

Big Boy tottered into the lab.

Before Darcy could act, Paco screamed, "Down! Down!" But the dog walked under the first beam. The smell of singed fur wafted through the lab. Calmer yet firmly, Paco ordered, "Bullet, down, boy."

The giant schnauzer obeyed, easing awkwardly to a reclining position.

Dan aimed but never fired off a shot. Paco reeled sideways. Blood soaked his pants. Hunched over, he sucked in mouthfuls of air and exhaled. Red seeped into the white grout and traveled in a steady stream toward Darcy. She stood, prepared to rush him now that reinforcements had arrived. He had lost so much blood, she expected him to black out. His head moved from side to side. He appeared to be blinded by pain, unable to focus. He leaned against the wall to steady himself.

"Come on, Paco. Let me help you. Please. Time's running out," Darcy pleaded in a low, soothing tone. Damn. He was bleeding to death before her eyes. She fired at the YAG, blowing away a chunk of the unit, but not disabling the laser as she had hoped.

Paco rocked forward and then fell back against the wall.

"I'll save you, Billy. I'll save you." His delirious cries echoed through the lab.

Bullet started to howl, a soul-shattering sound that racked Darcy to the core.

Paco launched himself off the wall. The forward motion threw him into a spin. Weak from too much blood loss, he collapsed, his legs giving way beneath him and careening his body into the spidery red web. The laser beams cut him to shreds.

31

Snowflakes fluttered through the icy air and speckled Darcy's black coat. She stared at them as though she had never seen snow before, her brain numb and her heart sick. Father Paul opened his Bible. She bowed her head, her eyes on the frozen ground, but not a word the priest uttered registered. She tried to block the ugly memories, but the images, the voices, were all too recent, too vivid, too raw. Paco's decapitated body torn apart. The bloody trail Bullet left to reach his master. The dog's soul-piercing howls as he lay on Paco's mangled corpse, a torso without any limbs. Al's gut-wrenching sobs. In a trance Darcy saw Dan deliver two shots to the YAG's control panel. The laser sparked, then died. The beams vanished.

"Our Father, who art in heaven . . ." said the seminarian who had accompanied Father Paul to Our Lady of Guadeloupe Cemetery.

Her mind wandered from Randolph to Selma and Billy to Paco. Randolph's promise tripped through her hazy brain. "I'll make time. We'll talk." But time had run out. For the dead Coltons. For Billy and Paco. The Carver.

"Holy Mary, Mother of God . . ."

A hand touched her shoulder. "You did everything possible, my child."

Darcy glanced sideways. "There was no reason for him to die."

"Perhaps he had no reason to live," said Father Paul. "Imprisoned as an adolescent, only to suffer imprisonment again as an adult." He shook his head. "No life. At least now he is finally at peace." The priest nodded toward Billy's gravestone. "With his brother. Both are home at last."

A deep sense of loss pervaded Darcy. His life shouldn't have ended this way. "His St. Christopher?"

"Around his neck, along with his brother's medal."

The first shovel of dirt landed and fanned out across Paco's coffin. Father Paul grasped her by the elbow and steered her from the gravesite. She didn't resist. At the gate to the cemetery, he patted her arm. "God bless you, my child." He climbed into his vehicle and left.

Outside the cemetery, Darcy leaned against her 4Runner and brushed away the tears. For a long time, she just stood there and watched the snowfall blanket her vehicle before she grew too cold to linger any longer. So she slid behind the wheel, fired up the engine, and drove back to her apartment, and to Dan. He had wanted to go with her to Paco's funeral, but she preferred to pay her last respects alone. Besides, someone had to take Bullet to his vet appointment, a follow-up before the trio headed back to the West Coast.

She made the drive across town to Sutton Way in a fog. At the apartment complex, she saw Della waiting on the sidewalk.

Darcy hugged her goodbye, promised to keep in touch, and then helped Dan load their bags into the 4Runner. After he lifted Bullet into the hatch, Darcy belted the dog into the cargo compartment and hugged him. She must have held on too long or too tight, for he tried to squirm free.

"You've had two rough weeks." Dan hugged her and then opened the passenger's door for Darcy. "I'll take the first shift."

She hopped in, eager to leave so much death behind, and ready for the drive home to California . . . and Charlene.

* * *

GENOCIDE
A Darcy McClain and Bullet Thriller

PAT KRAPF

Darcy McClain and Bullet Thriller #3

AVAILABLE ON AMAZON, NOOK, KOBO, AND iBOOKS

Sean Ireland, the first gay presidential candidate in US history, is guaranteed the election—until he's found dead at the Palace of Fine Arts in San Francisco.

Photo by The Dog Photographer, thedogphotographer.com

Pat Krapf was born in New Jersey but spent her formative years overseas and is still a globetrotter.

She worked in advertising and marketing for over thirteen years as a writer and product manager for the healthcare, aerospace, and architectural industries. She left the corporate world to write the Darcy McClain and Bullet Thriller Series.

She lives in Texas with her husband and giant schnauzer.

CONNECT ONLINE
patkrapf.com

Disclaimer

The author does not promote ownership of the giant schnauzer breed. Every prospective owner of any pet should thoroughly research that particular breed's characteristics before purchasing or adopting the animal. Caring for an animal is a lifelong commitment. Speak to reputable giant schnauzer breeders and educate yourself about this breed before choosing the giant schnauzer. Support Rescue—find groups here: giantschnauzerclubofamerica.com.